The BEWILDERED BRIDE

Advertisements
For Love Series

The BEWILDERED BRIDE

Advertisements
For Love Series

VANESSA RILEY

Entangled Publishing, LLC
2614 South Timberline Road
Suite 105, PMB 159
Fort Collins, CO 80525
rights@entangledpublishing.com

Amara is an imprint of Entangled Publishing, LLC.

Edited by Erin Molta
Cover model design by Teresa Spreckelmeyer with Midnight Muse
Cover art design by Bree Archer
Cover photography by Period Images
amoklv/Deposit Photos

Manufactured in the United States of America

First Edition August 2019

I dedicate this book to my friends, the ones who've walked a journey in which your steps were challenged, your truths questioned, and your hearts broken. Know that you are loved and heard. It is my hope that the fire in your spirits has burned away the dross and exposed the gold.

To Christine and Anita, you are heard.

Though Ruth's journey is told with sensitivity and respect, it may have emotional triggers.

Lastly, I dedicate this book to my beloved editor, Erin, and my inner matriarchal voice, Sarah M.

I admire you both so much.

Chapter One

The words between my Adam and the innkeeper left me shaking.

Get your bed wench out of here.

A chemise slipping from my shoulder exposed our so-called sin.

How dare you bring a whore to my good establishment!

The hate echoed in my head, rattling and shaking my conscience.

I was frozen.

Torn between fleeing and defending my love, I settled for hiding with blankets at my chin.

How could that horrible man reduce my vows said before God to something illicit and tawdry?

Plink. Plink. Scatter.

Coins dropped to the floor.

My hearing was sharp, sharper than my sight, and I could picture Adam throwing pence to prove a point.

Didn't he know points stabbed?

Even a rich man's son could be killed.

Adam came back inside our room and slammed the door. "My love, we must leave. Ruthy, we have to be on the road sooner than I wanted."

His voice was calm, like nothing had happened. He finished dressing, tied his perfect cravat, and leaned over the mattress, kissing my nose.

But I knew Adam.

He seethed.

He prayed and called for blessings but could curse like a hot-headed sailor.

My love's cheeks were red, flushed with anger, and he kept clenching and unfurling his fingers as if he'd fight the next person who crossed his path.

"I adore you, my Ruth."

My husband's voice—perfection. So sweet to my ears, if a masculine sound could be called sweet. I couldn't think when he whispered my name.

"Ruthy, my love, I'm going to the stables."

I pressed my hand to my middle and pushed hard on my stomach to squash the wiggles and tingles inside.

"Wait here for me."

"No, I must come with you," I begged to stay at his side.

"No, my Ruthy. Another time you'll get what you want. But this is for your safety. My wife must stay safe."

Mesmerized, I nodded. His power over me was complete. He took his gold cross from his neck and put it about mine. "So, you won't forget me while you dress."

The trance ended when he turned and reached for the door latch.

"Don't, Adam. Don't do anything rash." I wanted to say stupid, don't do anything stupid, but that would push him into trouble. His hot temper surpassed mine when he thought

I suffered.

"I won't, Ruthy. I won't be long."

Fingering the cross, I decided to try one more time to keep him. I feared that I'd never see him again if he left this room. My hands came together, palms flat and pointing up toward him. "Adam, please stay. Let me dress and come with you. I don't want us apart."

"I'll be back for you when our carriage is ready. My wife is not waiting in the cold." He came back and kissed my forehead like a reward for a good girl.

But I was his girl. And he was all mine.

Tossing me a wink, Adam slipped to the door again. "I'll be back soon, to help you lace up your corset and anything else I had a hand in removing."

My husband loved his jokes, but his jaw was stiff. His face remained beet red. Anger would eat him up.

The door closed with a *thud*. The lock *clicked*.

I was alone.

I climbed out of bed and found my shoes. Low boots with hard soles were better than bare feet when running for your life.

I paced around the smallish mattress of the rented room. The bedclothes he'd tossed off when the innkeeper had pounded on the door lay here and there. A pillow flopped half against the bedpost.

It looked like a struggle, where a volatile argument had occurred, not an abandoned lovers' nest.

The floorboards creaking under my shifting weight made my heart race.

I stopped, grabbed the pine footboard, and tried to breathe.

My ears perked to the footsteps outside my door.

I waited.

I suffered.

I kept watching the door that didn't open.

The pounding in my head grew so loud I saw stars and could almost envision Adam coming across the threshold. But I knew that was my fear twisting up my insides.

The vengeful innkeeper had given us an hour to leave. That time couldn't be up, not yet. Adam hadn't returned.

My only possessions—a balled-up dress, a nightgown, a silver brush—I tossed into my trunk. I should lock it up, close the metal clasps, but I wasn't done in this room and wanted to leave the way I came, on my husband's arm

I picked up my pearls from the bed table. The smooth beads felt cold in my sweating palm. Five days ago, I'd worn them for Adam as we'd married with the anvil priest.

Adam had beamed at me with a wide lazy smile as he had tonight, before the knock upon our door.

The pearls.

The pearls were now slippery in my hand. I tossed them into the trunk before they fell and burst apart. Papa had given them to me for my birthday, something to wear for my coming-out. Or for a wedding to a groom he'd choose.

My concerns for my parents pressed. I pictured Mama rocking, blank faced, in a chair, fearing her wild child was lost to the streets. Gone a fortnight, traveling from London to Scotland and only now heading back—I must be dead to them. Surely, they think me killed, even slaughtered like my uncle.

Adam had persuaded me to send no note. He'd said it was too risky then had smothered my complaints in a kiss. That silver-tongued devil could convince me the world was flat, that I was the Queen of England. One look at me with his deep-gray, almost black, eyes would send me spinning. He wove sweet words about me—I was better than Papa's silk— and I became boneless and agreeable and not myself.

I pounded the footboard with my palm. I was Mama's wild child, at nineteen, her oldest. I had caused such trouble—

breaking curfew, sneaking out, running from chaperones.

I sank onto the bed, trying to stop my sobs.

A full minute I sat before I couldn't bear it and leaped up.

Sitting on sheets that had lost the warmth of Adam's body but teased the scent of his Bay Rum cologne ripped everything wide open.

I didn't know who owned these tears—Mama, Adam, or me?

I had to get out of this room that now felt too big and empty.

Over my corset and chemise, I yanked on my favorite dress. I buttoned it fast and crazy, missing hooks and holes. There wasn't time to fix it, so I hid the uneven placard under my shawl.

This, my wedding gown, should be worn with care. Fragile, soft silk, colored in primrose yellow, I'd worn it with pride when I'd become Mrs. Adam Wilky.

Fussing and cussing sounded outside my door. Maybe the innkeeper had found another couple to evict.

I'd wait until the corridor cleared, and then I'd leave.

Quiet. No footsteps. No creaking floorboards.

Locking my heavy trunk, I then struggled with it, and walked out of the room.

I held my breath, tiptoeing with my head up.

Soon I was halfway to the stairwell, too far to turn back. My boldness and pride kept me from retreating. I shifted the trunk and mumbled that I was resilient. I was a Croome as much as a Wilky. That should mean I possessed strength like my papa and shrewdness like Mama.

But I was alone, and none of these notions seemed to stick, not when someone had cursed at me and wished me dead.

Resting for a moment, I brushed at the creases in my dress.

Mama's hot scolds about lazy bones admonished my soul. The spring muslin gown should've been folded, placed with its bodice lines straight on the chair, not tossed with lover's abandon, without thought or care.

I laughed, a gut-wrenching chuckle. Fleeing for my life had fashionable consequences.

Come on, Ruthy, I said to myself, modeling Adam's way of keeping me calm. We were only a half day's travel to London. A few more hours and we'd be at Nineteen Fournier to face my parents. The grief I'd caused shifted through my brainbox, raising questions I didn't want to think about.

Did we rush to elope?

Had we found love too fast?

Would this passion last?

Yes.

Moonlight streamed through an open window. I headed toward it like a moth, swinging my heavy trunk. I peeked out the glass to get a glimpse of Adam or the carriage.

Nothing.

The light of the stars made the silver band on my finger sparkle. Pride cut through the confusion in my bosom. *I am Mrs. Adam Wilky, the wife of a man who understands me better than any. He is worth it. I just need to find him.*

I forced my chin to lift, forced my limbs to move, forced myself to believe I'd soon be safe in my husband's arms.

Meow.

Glowing slit eyes crossed my path.

I ran. The heaviness of my trunk jerked my shoulders. Blinking, I turned the corner and saw nothingness, especially nothing soft or furry or as scared as me.

My sight wasn't normally bad, but thick-rimmed reading spectacles like Papa's would someday be mine.

Finally, finally, finally—I found the stairwell, dashed inside, and hid in its blackness.

Back flat against a wall, I filled my lungs and waited.

My breath caught in my throat, and I hugged my trunk as if it were Adam. He'd told me to wait, that he'd come back for me, but my heart was about to tear apart. I was afraid I'd never see him again.

Never.

Never ever were we to part.

Sweat dripped down my neck. My hastily done chignon fell. It was frizzy and damp on my neck. I couldn't fix it now. I needed Adam.

Counting my steps, I made it to the bottom of the stairs. Ten paces more and I was out the door. I held my breath again. No carriage.

I set the trunk down by my foot. Though small, the thing was heavy, very odd for a leather-skinned box holding so few items.

Cupping my hand to my face, I hunted for my love.

I saw nothing but road and fence.

Oh Lord, had he left?

I prayed with hands folded in front, fingers pressed high, eyes shut tight, like a good girl who hadn't broken a commandment, defying her parents, one who hadn't lied about going to Mrs. Carter's for tea. She was one of Mama's closest friends. Maybe they comforted each other.

"Where are you, Adam?"

He'd never leave me, not by choice.

Stories of his family's treachery slammed into my chest. All the air fled. I forced my breath in and out and tapped my foot to this rhythm then leaned out and looked from side to side.

Nothing.

No one.

No Adam.

Every cloak-and-dagger meeting by the dock, near my

father's warehouse, swept into my head, the motion roaring, swinging my balance like a fiddler's reel.

Whoosh. Whoosh. Whoosh. Every whispered conversation swirled.

Whoosh. Whoosh. Whoosh. Adam's walk, his smile, swam past my eyes.

He'd said his uncle was after him.

I'd thought it was a joke. Something that added to the mystery of him.

Had evil come and taken my husband?

Why did Adam have to be digging into his uncle's business, nosing about stuff that could get him killed? He could be slaughtered, like my uncle.

Papa's brother had been murdered for being too black and building his business in areas where my people weren't supposed to be. A bloodied jacket was all that had ever been discovered.

I'd found it balled up on the steps like he was nobody and nothing to this world.

That couldn't be Adam's fate, a bludgeoned cape that would haunt my mind forever. It would remind me of his walk, that swagger, draped in ebony velvet. The best time of my life had been loving him.

I looked down at my trembling hands.

My whole arm vibrated. I couldn't control it.

I was lost.

The panic that stalked my thoughts covered me, catching me in a fine fabric mesh. It was too wide. No seams to split. No way out.

Fear for the man I loved did me in.

I started sinking.

No way out.

No escape.

I tipped over.

Chapter Two

A Bride's Heaven

"I have you, Ruth. I have you."

Strong, bony arms caught me and pinned me to equally gaunt ribs.

"Breathe, Ruthy, breathe."

Adam's voice.

He'd found me, brought me from that gray place, not quite awake, not quite able to say anything. A place I'd visited more and more since finding Uncle's coat. When would my nerves surrender to my boldness? I wasn't this fragile, was I?

"It's fine, my Ruthy. I know the innkeeper scared you."

His voice touched my heart, cutting through my confusion.

I squinted and saw it was him. Tall, thin him.

He was a beanpole with arms—my beanpole.

Strong, pulse-racing tight, he held me. Who knew his embrace could offer the comfort of a warrior king like that hero in the *Iliad*…or was it the *Odyssey*—one of those poems he loved to read?

Peace settled upon me, and I let brave me return his

embrace, no shyness, not even in front of his driver.

Adam, my Adam, was here.

"Ruthy, I told you to wait. My queen doesn't lift her own trunk."

His voice sounded like a song saying my name. His pitch, a smidge lower than alto, sweet-talked the remaining shadows from my mind. He was good at convincing my fears and good sense to flee.

With my arm locked in his, Adam scooped up my trunk like it was paper and headed me around the corner.

One low star centered above my husband's carriage.

Husband.

I could breathe.

I could dance.

I could sing with gratitude for my husband. The innkeeper was horrid, the room terrible, but my Adam was wonderful. "Can't wait to introduce you to my parents."

Adam offered a small smile, his I'm-not-so-convinced smile, his let-me-change-your-mind smile, then moved to the yawning driver.

It was horrible this man didn't get sleep, either.

Adam came toward me. We'd literally been kicked out of this inn, and this man here, moved with the swagger of a prince.

His boots shined. A perfectly tailored coat hung beneath that cape. My prince.

I put a hand to his lapel and fingered the daisy he'd found and put in a buttonhole. "You took so long. Picking flowers?"

My nose wrinkled, though I loved the fresh scent of daisies almost as much as his tangy cologne.

"Well, they are your favorite."

Like the gentleman he was, he bowed and kissed my hand. "Why is my wife so nervous?"

How could I explain my fears for him, for us? I bit my lip

and closed my eyes for a moment. "You shared so much, last night."

"Yes, we did, my love." He brushed my mouth, handling me like a fine crystal goblet. The taste of him almost succeeded in distracting me, but this argument was too important.

"I wasn't talking about that. The conspiracy with your uncle. I'm scared. I couldn't wait. I had to see you. We've only been married five days."

"And four glorious nights. This fortnight of eloping from London was the best time in my life. I have you, my queen, at last."

He was back to kissing me again, smooth and gentle, each moment like a first, like a good last time.

His lips won. My fears disappeared. I stretched and wrapped my arms about his neck.

I'd never felt so much or so deeply. Every time he touched me, the more in love, the more in want, the more lost, I became.

"We haven't started living our happily-ever-after. Only death shall part us, nothing else. I'll always be yours, Ruth. Always."

He pulled a sliced document from his pocket and stuffed it in the lining of my trunk. "But you are right. We're not safe. The innkeeper's upset is the beginning. He may alert someone. My cousin Nickie warned me that Uncle won't be stopped this time."

Adam put my hands in his. His skin was warm but his palms damp. "If anything happens to me, you need this piece of the registry. Take it to my father, Wycliff. He'll take care of you."

"Who?"

"It's on the paper."

"Adam, what's this all about? Is that half our marriage registry?"

He stuffed my trunk into the carriage. "Yes. My half is already on the way to my father's."

"Something is wrong. Why would your cousin go against his own papa? That's nonsensical."

"I saved Nickie, Nicholas's life. He almost drowned. We have an amiable relationship. Hopefully that will be enough."

Adam examined me anew.

My wrinkled, misbuttoned dress made me tug at my shawl. I hid behind my folded arms.

"Ruth, my dearest, you didn't wear a coat. It's October. The slight wind has caused your shivers."

That wasn't it, but I'd already learned to lie. "Too much in a rush." I said. "I didn't bring one from home."

He unlaced his cape and placed it about me.

The velvet shrouded me, splashing down like ebony ink. "Papa would approve of your fabric."

He pulled the cape tighter about my shoulders. "The fabric king. Mr. Croome is one of the best in the trades."

Adam's sigh was hot on my cheek, the inch of my neck I offered.

"The night's chill will make you ill. And I've upset you with my crazed talk."

My fear of being found weak made me grasp tighter to his lapels. "You have to tell me everything. I'm not a wilting daisy."

"But you like daisies."

Adam pried my hands free and held them to his bony chest.

In my head, I stroked the birthmark, the strawberry shape below his throat. Such an intimate thought. It made me giggly to know so much of him.

"Up you go, my lady." He lifted me into the well-lit carriage.

He knew I liked the light, liked how it made things feel

safe and confined and cozy.

"Ruth, we are dusting our feet of this place."

Despite being so thin, thin like he had a worm, as Mama would say, Adam was strong and wonderful in every other way, so kind and handsome with his short-cropped wavy hair.

He climbed inside but kept his hands to his knees. He didn't tap the roof. "I wish there had been another way to marry. Something that would've garnered your parents' blessings. You may need them if things don't go well. But I must do what is right for my father. My uncle has embezzled from him and others. I made copies of the ledgers. Uncle Soulden and his business partner forged initials to the transactions to look as if my father is the thief. It's not right. Righteousness must win against the darkness."

I tried to ignore the scary words in his speech like *embezzled* and *forged* and *don't-go-well*. I needed to make a joke like Adam always did. "That vicar training in you is too strong, but maybe it blesses us."

"My father's fault. When he took me to St. George's, all those bright stained-glass panes never left me. But I am to be a gentleman running his estates, financing his business interests. You think you will enjoy being a gentlewoman, having parties?"

"My mama will appreciate that."

His face became more serious. The little lines around his dimples eroded to a frown. "What if you have to sit at the back of St. George's with the servants, because someone like the innkeeper can't imagine you are my wife?"

We were the same, but Adam's light skin gave him access to that different world, one where even Croome money couldn't buy entry.

I clasped his hand, my darker palm over his. "We'll figure everything out. I'm happy to be Mrs. Adam Wilky."

After patting my fingers like the patronizing fellow

he could be, he leaned back and folded his arms with the panache of a peer, far above a mere rich man's son. "Last chance, my Ruthy, my dearest darling. I know we are only a few hours from London, but we could turn around and head to Scotland. I'll spoil you rotten there. It'll be better until Nickie tells me the danger has passed. I can decipher the ledgers in peace."

"We must go to my parents, so they know I'm safe. I have to let them know what we've done."

"Not everything we've done, my dear. Some secrets should remain between husband and wife."

Oh, Adam. His wicked smile, his sing-song voice. "How can you get me so worked up fearing for our lives and then try to make me laugh?"

His soulful eyes, luscious and dark, beamed. "You need to be happy. You deserve it. I'm most fortunate to have your love. Any chance I could seduce you on a grassy knoll by some babbling Scottish brook? It would be safer, Ruth. So much safer."

"To London, sir."

He closed his eyes and became stiff. "What Ruthy wants, Ruthy gets. Then to London we go, and we shall hope for the best."

He bounced out, gave instructions to his driver, then slipped back inside. This time he sat next to me and looped his hands with mine.

I rested against him, leaning into his shoulder. His sweet scent, the Bay Rum, made breathing easier. Oh, how I loved it, loved him.

As the Croomes' wild child, I had my wildest dream in Adam Wilky.

A glance at Adam's perspiring brow sent a chill down my spine, one that didn't stop until it froze my toes.

Adam wasn't convinced that London was the right

decision, but he'd given in to me.

Maybe once we were settled and living a quiet married life, he could finally be comfortable.

"We may struggle a bit." His voice was low, each word perfectly formed as if he'd thought and thought again about what to say.

"You don't have to be so careful with me. I married you for you."

"Ruth, there are so many things I've yet to say." He stretched and again threaded his fingers with mine. "My father wasn't happy at me demanding to marry you. He'd picked out an heiress, a Mayfair neighbor's daughter."

I reared back, smiling big and proud. "I'm an heiress. When my papa calms down, you could discuss a dowry."

"No, Ruth. I don't want his money. My father begrudges me nothing, but he wants me to have a safe life. He wants me to assimilate into the *Ton*, to pass for something I'm not. He'd hate me having to sneak you into inns or seeing you sit in the rear of St. George's."

The passion, the angst in his voice barely masked his pain, feelings he'd never expressed. He'd always had jokes and punny phrases.

"Adam, you're working yourself up. What is it that you are trying to say? You're unhappy with me? You already have regrets?"

"Never think that. I could die a thousand times and will awaken in glory always loving you. I think I've outwitted Uncle Soulden. We just need to be undetected a little longer so my father can dismantle the dangerous man's business."

My husband was trying again to dissuade me, but this tactic wouldn't work. I'd offer him a compromise. "Once we see my parents, we can leave. You can take me anywhere. I'll go anywhere with you."

"No one can see us but your parents. My sister Cicely

has been sent away to school to keep her safe while my father seeks legal redress against Uncle Soulden."

There he was using those big words, biting that wonderfully soft lip which he should save for kissing. My husband, thoughtful, educated, and in love with me. That was all that mattered. "Our love is enough. We can do anything."

I smoothed my hands against his waistcoat. "Always so serious, always checking corners, watching for evil that never comes. You'll fret yourself into a head of gray hair, or worse, it will all fall out."

His tell-tale full lips drooped into a deeper frown. "You wouldn't adore me if I were bald?"

"Of course I would."

He smiled for a moment, then peeked out the window.
Were we being followed?

"Adam, when will joy hit you? I've spent five days as Mrs. Adam Wilky. I'm happy."

He retook my palm and played with my thumb.

My heart beat like a drummer boy.

"Sorry. I'm going to be like this until we get to London, see your parents, then disappear. Then you'll promise to listen to my cautions."

"Yes."

"No more making me rethink my plans?"

"Why would I agree to that? You need someone to keep you from brooding."

A hiss siphoned through his lips and fluttered one of my drooping curls.

"Brooding but lovable." Adam embraced me, wrapping his rail-thin arms about my waist. "I love you. I'll love you forever."

"When we settle, sir, point me to a kitchen. I'm going to fatten you up, make you overflow with happiness and tender beefsteak. You'll never regret choosing me, to live like me.

And I'm going to do my best to keep you distracted from nonsense."

"You will, aye?" He kissed my nose. "Ruth Elizabeth, my *loosey-goosey* Ruthy, my queen. You're my heaven. How can I fear anything when you finally promised to be mine?"

His head dipped. I sniffed more of his savory cologne and the daisies I so loved.

Then he took my lips.

His kiss made everything right.

Our happy forever had begun.

Chapter Three

A Groom's Hell

An hour of travel.

So close to London.

The man who moved under the discreet name of Adam Wilky, Chatsworth Adoniram Wilkinson, had entered hell.

His carriage careened off the road after being chased by bandits. His driver ran off at the sound of flintlocks belching, *boom, boom, boom.*

The assassins dragged Adam from his carriage, separating him from his wife, his poor, hysterical Ruth.

The terror in her voice was so heavy, and awful, and gutting.

How could someone not help her?

How could they do this?

"Let us go!" He said the words even as they bound him with more ropes, even as Ruth sobbed and shrieked louder.

He needed to break free and hold her one last time, to lie to her sweetly that they would be freed, unharmed, anything to stop those tears.

But Adam knew he would die.

He just wanted Ruth to live. "Let her go. She's nothing to this."

His answer—a club cracked across his face. *Wham.*

Dizzy, falling to the ground, he saw four men, two fast ones and two lumbering, slow ones, strike him again and again.

The lumbering ones.

A sense of knowing them punched through him, but it was hard to tell with his eye swelling.

Fists and sticks continued pummeling his flesh. The scent of his sweat and blood stung his nostrils, but he stayed close to the lead man. He'd know the name of his killers. Then he'd pray for them to rot in hell.

Blam. A blow to his jaw.

The world grew black for a moment, then snapped back. Uncle's ring. These were no bandits looking for gold.

Uncle Soulden.

A dying man should think of salvation, but all Adam could muster was the hope for vengeance, vengeance now, or in eternity, or both.

Holy righteous anger coursed through him.

The desire to be a flame to burn them up made him lunge at them. These evil men needed to be consumed with the hellfire flooding in his veins.

He punched back and dragged off the sack covering Uncle's face. "Uncle, how dare you?"

A few henchmen stopped kicking Adam.

Maybe they could be swayed. "I'm the son of a peer. Let us go, and he'll pay your ransom."

"Adam, help!" Ruth screamed and kept crying out his name. "Don't kill Adam. Stop beating him."

He squinted and saw men holding her back. His Ruth!

"Let her go, then do your worst."

Adam shouted the words again, tossing them over his

swollen lips. "She's just a woman. Nothing to this."

"Nothin' but a witness."

The voice was a confirmation. Nacknel, a ship captain, Uncle's fixer. *Was the lumberer in the back Johnson, Uncle's partner in his firm?*

Adam seized a breath. Emboldened like his father, he jerked up. "How dare you? I'm the son of a peer. The wages of sin is your death. Don't add to your judgment by killing innocents."

Someone shoved him, but the laughter had stopped.

There were at least one or two men who might fear judgment.

Soulden wiped his hands of Adam's blood. "Finish him."

"What's the matter, Uncle? Not man enough to do it yourself?"

"The ledgers, boy. We know you copied them. Where are they?"

"Don't know what you mean, Uncle. Beating me or her won't make me remember."

Dark hair and eyes, the man shouldn't look anything like Adam's father, but he did.

Uncle spit on him.

Adam couldn't wipe his face. The ropes to his neck kept him from even brushing against his jacket. The high-collared knot of his cravat was probably the only thing keeping him from suffocating. "Your fellow embezzler. Show your face. Let me know who's to blame."

Soulden picked up a stick and cracked it across Adam's back. "Tie him good, Nacknel. I don't want to hear his voice again."

"Lord Wycliff!" Adam shouted the name three times. "He'll pay a ransom if you let us live. The truth will out."

Adam lunged again. He was thin, but strong like a lion. He headbutted one of them. The man fell to the ground.

Curses and orders ensued.

Wrenching an arm free, Adam scrambled. *Pow.* He punched one man in the nose then rammed closer to Ruth, almost near enough to wrench her away.

His effort was for naught.

A henchman seized him again, the ropes growing tighter and tighter about his neck, dragging him back.

The distance between Adam and Ruth was like a river, wide and flowing with his blood.

Another punch landed on his gut, doubling him over.

That poor organ, that wise organ. He should've listened.

Lord, he knew better.

Ruth's happiness had been his weakness. Now it would be his death.

Blam. A knock upside his head spun him to the left.

Adam coughed then vomited.

Swoop.

He wouldn't beg.

He refused to scream. "To hell with you all."

He didn't recognize what was left of his voice, harsh and guttural. The ropes burned and cut more into his flesh.

"Adam!"

His Ruth sounded so frightened, so lost and hurting.

For her—he'd steal, he'd wither, he'd beg. "Let her go." He reared up. "I could get you money."

Another blow was his answer. He sank again to one knee.

Then the fiends mocked him. They'd sell him like an enslaved man.

Adam was enslaved to none but Ruth's love. She was all he needed. If he'd not given in to what she'd wanted, this one time...

No. No, this was his fault.

She screamed, and he dragged his captors to reach her.

Adam was wild, clawing and scratching and flinging his

fists.

But the ropes about his neck dug in deeper. He could barely breathe.

She yelled his name and begged for his life.

He tried to tell her he loved her, but words and air couldn't both exist in his throat.

Then some fool hit her across the skull with her trunk.

She sank to her knees then sprawled headlong into the dirt.

Her curly hair was matted in blood.

Her beautiful body convulsed then stopped moving.

Adam stretched, linking his fingers with hers, and touched a lock of her curly hair for a last time.

A shadow covered him.

A gun butt cracked his skull.

Stars and blackness draped him.

Better to die than to live without Ruth's love.

Chapter Four

No baby, no whoring, no, none of these things for me.

I wasn't pregnant, nor any of the horrid remarks my mother's knitting circle had insinuated for the past two hours.

My special punishment, my personal reminder of hell for loving Adam Wilky.

Tuesdays.

Tuesdays were when the dragons gathered.

Mama's gossipy friends visited in her parlor at our family's townhouse at Nineteen Fournier Street. They were the dragon council, gossips who breathed fire with their snide comments, especially when Mama left the room. Thank goodness she was here.

"Mrs. Croome," Mrs. Carter said. She was Mama's oldest, dearest, and meanest friend. "You putting t'ings together the menu for Ruth's upcoming wedding breakfast? Her second wedding should be nice, like a first."

"Ruth and her barrister are still getting to know one

another," Mama said. "We shall have to see."

Chuckles ensued, but I held my tongue and savored the sweet citrus scent of my chamomile tea.

I had to remain calm in front of the council to make it to my appointment, to get the proof I've needed for four years.

The clicking of bone china cups on brilliant white saucers was loud enough to cover the laughs, all the jokes made at my expense.

Things had to change.

"Ruth," Mama said, sitting in her favorite high-backed chair near the fireplace. She sat directly across from me, a blurry vision of seafoam blue.

As always, Mama wore a freshly starched mobcap, a splash of creamy lace atop her silky dark tresses. Hints of gray wove about her chignon like a delicate basket. Reserved and powerful. A tigress in disguise.

"Your knitting is much improved, daughter, but don't you think you need your lenses?"

Lenses. Spectacles. Horrible, heavy headache-inducing things that brought everyone's scorn or pity-filled faces perfectly into focus.

Knit one, purl one.

"No. I don't need them for knitting."

I made a show of looping the scarlet yarn about my needle. I'd become an expert at knitting in the solitude of the country cottage where my parents had exiled me until the gossip had died down. Such awful gossip.

Ruth Croome, the whore, found in a brothel.

Ruth Croome, the liar, ran off with a man but was abandoned.

Ruth Croome, the jilted lover, lying about a man who never existed.

But the worst gossip—Ruth Croome Wilky, the fake widow.

All my pain, every bit of my life was a joke in our tight-knit community here in London.

"Ruth, I can ring Mrs. Fitterwall to get your spectacles. It would be no trouble."

"No, Mama. They give me headaches for this close work."

I felt my mother glaring at me, wishing I'd take the hint and obey.

Didn't she know that there was a point when embarrassment lost its power?

My heart had died with Adam. I was a shell, nothing but nightmares and shame had been poured inside me for four years. It had burned up all my dreams, all the things a young woman should want. But it had birthed light onto the only thing that mattered, simple gratitude.

Food on my plate. A plate. Clothes for my baby and me.

Receiving my trunk, the one stolen from Adam and me four years ago, had resurrected something new. The dream of being a respectable lady, like Mama, lived again. Finding proof of my truth made me want to leave the house, something I'd rarely done these past two years in London.

Chatter continued amongst the four women, these friends—Mama, Mrs. Daly, Mrs. Johnson, and Mrs. Carter.

Mrs. Johnson, a new addition to the knitting circle, stayed quict. Shc'd pick up thc othcr ladics' bad habits of poking at me soon enough.

The mantel clock gonged three times.

Each hollow brassy noise that echoed in my chest rattled in that empty spot near those lungs that had proven easy to fill with fear.

My nerves.

They were bad. I didn't blame them. They'd been bad since Adam's murder.

Mama set down her latest project, an emerald-green baby's blanket, on her lap. "Dear, are you feeling well?

Perhaps you should stay in and miss this evening meeting. You set it quite late."

That was the only time Papa's groom, Jonesy, could go with me. He was a sweet, ruddy boy whose weakness, a cleft in his lip, was on the outside. He saw my hidden weakness, my nerves, and helped me in those hard times I had to leave the house. "It's not too, too late, Mama."

Knit one. Purl one.

"Ruth, it will be dark by the time you get back. You don't see so well in the dark."

Shots fired.

Mama shot a cannon ball at me. I must be reminded that I became frightened stepping out of the house. It had been at least seven months since I'd last tried.

"Ruth, you do look pale. I think you should miss this meeting."

Mama's voice sounded calm, but the tigress fooled no one. She sought to control her reformed wild child. This meeting was for my boy. When it came to Chris, I would be steel—strong and unbreakable.

Knit one, purl one.

Chin lifting, I smiled big. "No, Mama. I won't miss my appointment. I'm looking forward to it."

That was said with the appropriate amount of bravado. Bravado. Adam's word. I laughed this time, maybe out loud.

In my head, I pictured Mama frowning, a full one, as if she'd bitten into the tartest lemon.

Didn't she know? Mother and daughter were the same—stubborn, determined, fast knitters.

"Then wear your glasses, dear. You'll need them."

"Yes, Mama."

A headache was worth not being barred from leaving. I had a theory that a blurry world would keep my nerves away. Now I was going to have to be completely brave.

Knit one, purl one.

Fingering the watch on the simple silver chain I'd pinned to my shoulder, I felt the limbs had moved, but not by much. The glass had been taken off so I could guess the time without looking. Leaving by carriage was still twenty, twenty-five minutes away. That's when Jonesy would be back with Papa.

A watched pot was slow to boil.

The same could be said of me.

Every decision, every word out of my mouth was scrutinized. This critical light made me slow and deliberate. For the past six months, I had stewed upon offers of marriage I'd received from a newspaper advertisement. A silly gambit my sister and her friends had convinced me to do. It had given the knitters something new to discuss. That was a blessing.

Yet, I didn't want a husband or anyone to tend to in bed. I'd rather have cold sheets and accidentally spill Bay Rum on them.

But I had a son, and his needs outweighed everything, even my nightmares. I had answered Barrister John Marks, a busy, humble man who had taken a liking to my son.

And Chris liked him. Another reason to accept Marks's offer in the upcoming week. He had made his intentions known at Mama's dinner party two weeks ago. A proposal was in the offing.

"Did you read about the strange suicide? The boat captain, near the docks?"

That squeaky voice had to be Mrs. Daly's. A small, fashionable woman close in age to Mama. Mrs. Daly loved the newsprint gossip as much as my mother.

"Nacknel was his name," Mrs. Daly continued. "Did he do business with your husband, Mrs. Johnson?"

Mrs. Millicent Johnson was the blue-eyed wife of the head of a shipping company. Her husband serviced Papa's business partners upon occasion. She was of Spanish descent with striking olive-shaped eyes. The new-mother-to-be sat close to me and was always helpful, almost acting as if we knew each other.

"I'm not sure," Mrs. Johnson said and sipped her tea, "but the suicide is the talk at my husband's offices."

Mrs. Daly clicked her tongue. "Seems odd for the magistrate and coroner to call it a suicide when the man was found beaten as he was."

My pulse raced.

In a blink, I watched Adam be struck. I blinked three times, saying to myself, *be calm, don't lose your wits*. I couldn't miss this meeting.

I put down my needles and wet my drying tongue with a swallow of tea. "Beaten to death? That's tragic."

Mrs. Carter snorted. Her cup runneth over with malice. "My husband tells me his gambling caught up to him. *Whack*, *whack* over a jack." Her thick island accent gave a smooth rhythm to her hateful words.

"Ladies, let me go check on our cake. My guests need scrumptious cake."

No, no, no.

The door shut. My eyes closed and I counted.

One.

Two.

Three.

"Is this appointment with a new doctor, Ruthy?" Mrs. Carter asked. "Or has our girly been doing somet'ing with that would-be-fiancé that requires doctoring?"

I gulped air and waited for the rest of the twisted counseling to begin anew.

Shaped like a squash, small on top, big on the bottom, Mrs. Carter leaned near. The peppermint scent of her hand lotion could smother a cow. "You've been naughty again, Ruthy, haven't you? We told you to save your desires for the wedding night. Be frigid."

Frigid wouldn't be a problem.

The barrister and I had had a delicate conversation when he'd mentioned the topic of marriage. Very delicate to talk about taking time and separate bedchambers. "Thank you, ma'am, but shouldn't you save your advice for your girls?"

Mrs. Carter's nose wrinkled. Her own daughters hadn't wed yet. They had the sense to be picky and the ideals to know they deserved to be treasured. But harpies like their own mother would call them spinsters.

The nasty woman tugged at her lacy cuffs. "Do the barrister a favor. Make the man think you enjoy him like it was a first time."

Why would Mrs. Carter offer such advice to me, a widow with a child? I knew what desire was, what it felt like to be sought after by a man. I knew too much of it and didn't want any part of desire now.

Lips clamped shut, I tried to sculpt a proper ladylike response but failed.

Nothing but improper comments centered on my tongue: *Hell no, huns. Go away, goosecaps. Shut your lips, sauceboxes.*

Adam used to tell me those low-class insults and mix up his own. The young man had been from a well-to-do background but had spent far too much time at the docks rather than the ballrooms, because his family was in finance for shipping and such.

I pressed on my temples. Adam had been in my mind since exchanging letters with the barrister. Even more since my trunk had arrived. That lost thing, four years gone, had shown up two weeks ago.

"What say you, Ruthy? Your Mama's not here to quiet you. Tell me you're respectable, girly. Lie to me."

No baiting. No loss of my dignity. "Mrs. Carter, I will

speak my mind. I'm a respectable widow. Please remember that."

Mrs. Carter batted her eyes as if she'd heard my voice.

Maybe I'd forgotten how to use it.

No more. "My time with my husband was short," I said, controlling my tone, smothering my anger. "But Mr. Wilky had my firsts—a first kiss, a first confession of love, a first surrender in his bed. The barrister, or whomever I marry, will gain an older, wiser woman, one that knows what true love is."

Though I couldn't see their expressions, the silence told me all I needed. They'd heard me and could not discount my truth. I desired to live for me and my son. If I chose, I'd have an honorable marriage of convenience. I'd keep the gentleman's house, keep his name in esteem, and keep his trust.

Then maybe we'd find something more, but I would be grateful for a clean, safe house that was mine to manage, and a good man for my son to model. In time, he would be grateful for me—a good woman, a woman to be an asset, maybe even his queen.

Mrs. Carter's big blur, her thick arms like coconuts, began to clap. "Nice say, Ruthy. Mr. John Marks will believe you. But you can tell us...or should we be watchin' your waistline?"

All the women snickered, but I shuddered. I wasn't wanton. I desired to be respected, and it hurt to be deprived of it for my one crime—having no legal proof of my marriage to Adam.

Mrs. Johnson put her hand on mine. She shook her head, dangling her sleek blue-black curls. "You do look pale, Mrs. Wilky. I know pale."

Thinking of Adam, of losing Adam, shredded my insides anew. Hating my weak eyes, I wiped at the moisture pooling in my lashes. "I didn't sleep too good last night. Nothing more is wrong."

"Didn't sleep too *well*?" Mrs. Daly's possession of language skills was perfect and as stiff as a piece of fine furniture. "You do look sickly, Mrs. Wilky."

Two weeks and little to no sleep had taken a toll. Fourteen days since my lost trunk landed on the steps of the Croome house.

Since its arrival, everything had come back and not just at night. I was a walking nightmare, and I kept seeing Adam's death—in the shadows, down the stairs, outside of Nineteen Fournier.

The creases under my eyes must have creases. "I'm fine, ladies," I said. "Thank you for your concern."

The door to Mama's parlor creaked, and the patter of little feet came to me.

My beautiful three-year-old son, Christopher, tugged on the dull salmon-pink print of my gown.

I scooped him up and prayed the women wouldn't make any jokes. My boy was perfect and was smart enough to understand. He already asked questions about his *papa*.

"Mama," he said, "I want outside."

I tweaked his nose. "No, Chris, you're just getting over a cold."

He poked out his thin lips. Brown eyes looking dull, the boy was just a day from the sniffles, but even healthy, I hesitated to let him outside in the open.

My nerves couldn't be put on my baby.

That couldn't happen.

He couldn't suffer because of me. Never.

I kissed his forehead. "Grandpa will be home soon. Maybe he'll go with you for a little fresh air."

Chris tossed his chubby arms about my neck, giving me one of his best hugs. He smiled as if I'd given him a new toy. He scooted down to the floor, fighting his light-blue pinafore and running to the hall.

"A little wild boy, aye, Ruthy. Definitely in need of a true father."

"Mrs. Carter, I'm not up to your teases."

"Ruth, I could get a physician to come." Mama came close to my chair, inspecting, fretting. "It wouldn't take too long."

She would return to hear me speak of weakness. "No. I'm…I'm fine."

"It would be no trouble."

"No, Mama."

Her offer was a trap. To admit to being sick and weak would mean I'd miss going to Adam's family because I'd have to wait for the physician. There was proof at Blaren House, the address Adam had written on the back of my half of the marriage registry…the half that remained in the lining of my missing trunk.

Adam Wilky's half was at Blaren House, I was sure of it.

Having both pieces would prove my truth, that I'd been a *wife*, who had married too young, to a man who wasn't prepared for the dangers of this world, a man whose secrets had destroyed us.

Knit one. Purl one.

I fingered my watch. Still didn't hear Papa's carriage.

Knit one. Purl one.

"Ruth," Mama said, her voice steady and calm, readying to criticize. "Your stockinette stitches are much better but try doing something more decorative for the barrister."

I pulled the scarf to within a few inches of my face. Horror. I saw the uneven stitches. Mama was being kind. This was awful.

I undid the last row. "I think Mr. Marks likes things uncomplicated."

That wasn't the right word for the man who had accepted

my son and my predicament like it was a normal thing to be perceived a fake widow.

Mrs. Johnson leaned in and turned up her face, smiling her *I-have-a-secret* smile. "Your new friend is up and coming. Popular, too."

He was.

Barrister Marks was a nice man and a fierce advocate for change, one who'd attracted many female spectators to the Old Bailey with his spirited defenses. "I'm lucky."

That shut everyone up.

Luck and *me* in the same sentence were earth shattering, a volcano's explosion in the offing. Forget the curse of Ham. My problems were Job's. No one had such bad luck, not like me. But going to Mayfair today would end this.

"Daughter?"

My mother's tight tone sliced through my jumbled thoughts.

"Yes, ma'am?"

"I asked you to offer Mrs. Carter more tea. Her cup looks empty."

The softly spoken command called to the little girl still hidden in my bosom. I snapped to attention and lifted the pot and served the serpent to my right.

This side was the weakest of my vision, but I took pride in my aim, not spilling a drop.

The heavyset island woman, whose monied connections were rumored to involve the unscrupulous sugar plantations of the Caribbean, picked up the full cup and slurped. "You look flustered, Ruth. That will serve you well with your *second* marriage. I'm sure your barrister will appreciate the pretense in bed. Girly, a man might take used goods, but definitely doesn't want to be reminded of the bargain."

Mrs. Carter's indictment hung in the air like the rosewater scent Mama used to freshen the curtains. A little sniff didn't annoy, but a full whiff was overpowering, suffocating.

"I'll remember that, ma'am,"

She leaned near. I couldn't miss her sneer. "You must smile more when he's around. It will ensure that banns are read…this time."

Giggles. Full belly laughs.

Old, wild me might grab her or shake her or say some truth she wouldn't want uttered about her family, but I was new me, the me who wouldn't disrespect Mama or dragons. "Say your insults direct. Don't hide behind half jokes. Come for me head on."

The chuckles stopped, but Mrs. Carter sang the gossip refrain, the melody that had followed me these four years. "Runaway Ruth, Wanton Ruth, Bad-luck Ruth. Be easy. It's just jokes."

Fine. I wasn't new long-suffering me, but old volcano Ruth. I exploded and swatted the cup in front of me. It flew across the tray spinning toward Mrs. Carter. It clicked against a saucer.

The way the big woman jumped, some of the brown liquid must have landed on her. "Clumsy!"

Clumsy tigress Ruth. "Sorry," I said in a practiced easy voice. "Be aware, ma'am. All this talk has me jittery. It makes me very unpredictable, maybe a dragon, like you."

Warning delivered. I stood. "I should go get a towel for you before I leave."

Mama rang a bell, and Clancy, the Croomes' faithful butler, came into the room. He appeared too fast, like he'd been on the other side of the door, staring through the keyhole.

The doting man with big, bushy silver locks and big arms like Papa possessed a gleaming ebony mantle. He sopped up the tea with a cloth. "Mrs. Wilky, your carriage has been sent for. It'll be here in a few minutes. Your father's still out. You won't be able to use his."

I kept my face from falling. Jonesy wouldn't be able to go with me. I'd have to do this alone.

"Very determined to leave." Mrs. Carter's voice was loud, but her Jamaica rhythm was uneven, maybe a little flustered. "Be careful, indulging your friends. You already had one *late husband*. Marks, for one, looks too healthy to meet the same fake fate."

More snickers.

Even Clancy chortled.

"Stop, Mrs. Carter," Mama said. "Let things be. He who is without sin gets to cast stones."

The laughs stopped, but the ladies would continue to convict me.

Always the butt of jokes, I was sick of it, but this was the push I needed. Nothing would stop me from getting my proof. Nothing.

The other half of the marriage registry would show that I was married, in a ceremony filled with promises of forever.

No one believed me, not without undeniable proof. That's what it took for the world to believe a woman, whether she be damaged or whole.

I balled up my yarn and jabbed my bone needles into the pile. "Ladies, it's always a special time to sit with you. Pity this will end when I marry."

Wool bundles in my hand, I turned and walked the ten paces to the door. With my head held high, I left the room but pushed the door a little too hard. It slammed.

Mrs. Carter's laugh filtered past the threshold.

I sank against the wall and wrapped my arms about my yarn and the poking needles.

One step closer to proof, Ruthy. I could do this. One step at a time all the way to Blaren House. I wouldn't stop until I had both halves of the registry in my hand.

Chapter Five

The Widow's Sister

Waiting for Clancy to announce my carriage, I paced outside Mama's parlor and tugged my long sleeves, as if showing my wrists were scandalous. This was my nerves wanting me to hide. Leaving the house was always so hard.

My sister, Ester, came out of Papa's study and stood close to me in the small hall.

She held her baby son, Josiah, in her arms. "I see you made it out of the dragons' den."

"You can join me in the dragons' den any Tuesday."

"No thanks." My sister's voice sounded soothing, even sympathetic. "I don't knit well enough, and I don't know how you survived Mama's friends all these years."

"Part of my punishment. Until I'm married, in a ceremony in front of God and the gossips, I have to pay. Part of my testing. How will I be made gold without a few trials?"

My words sounded cheery, but my fingers rattled my bone needles. I peeked at my baby nephew and cooed at the innocent boy, so like Chris. Golden-colored skin. Good grips with his tiny palms.

"Having you here, you and Christopher, feels right." Ester stepped close, close enough for me to see clearly her olive face. It beamed bright but her lip twitched.

Oh no. The girl wanted something.

I moved my watch chain away from the boy's fingers. "Out with it, sister."

"Nineteen Fournier is so big. Must you and the barrister leave when you are married? Do you have to live somewhere else?"

"Yes! As soon as possible," I said the words without hesitation.

Ester's head dipped as if she'd been struck. The perfect daughter would never understand.

Josiah's mouth felt wet, so I wiped spittle from his puckered lips. "He hasn't proposed. And when I do marry, I'll still be in town, not far away. You can come to me on Tuesdays to escape Mama's knitters."

"I don't want to lose you again."

Lose what?

The shell of the person I once was.

A wild child forced to live so carefully.

A target made to endure wounds from dragons like Mrs. Carter.

I shook my head with some violence. That was despair. That wasn't me. I lived. I knew my truth. I was grateful that I wasn't what the gossips said. But every day was a battle. If I made it out the door, Fournier's front door, I was a winner, today's lucky winner.

"You, my lovely sister, will visit often. You will stay late and drink tea in my very own parlor. You will read me and Chris Shakespeare."

The smile on Ester's cherub face blossomed. "That will be wonderful. We could do that here. Tonight? I know I haven't been as supportive as I should, with the baby and my husband running for Parliament, but—"

"Please stop." Shrugging my shoulders, I rubbed my thumb along my nephew's smooth cheek. "Your priorities are good. Josiah is looking stronger. He'll be crawling soon."

"Please, Ruth. You're my sister. I want us to be close again. I love you and my nephew. I don't want you two to go."

"Little Chris is everything, so full of curiosity, so sweet. I need him settled in a new situation, something less crowded. Something of my own where I can count my steps and know things won't change. My slippers won't move from the spot I put them. And clocks, my clocks will sound as loud as possible."

"Marriage to Barrister Marks does that? My Bex says he's a good man, honorable, a fighter for abolition, but he works a lot."

"Yes. Yes, that's perfect for me."

"Mr. Marks will stay away long hours, and your sight isn't better. Chris is so active."

That was Ester's polite way of saying I'd be blind, that darkness was coming for me. Another judgement for the sins I didn't commit. Eloping could never equal Adam's brutal death and all the things done to me.

I am dwelling again. This is my personal trap to keep me here, not venturing outside and gaining my proof.

"Ester, sweet Ester. Nothing has stopped the shrinking of my sight, but I've made an amiable truce with my faltering vision. I'm learning how to manage. Adam used to count…I will be fine, and Chris will be great. You and yours will be my honored guests."

I reached and smoothed the wrinkles forming on Ester's brow. "I get fewer headaches without the lenses, and I don't have to see sadness on cute faces like yours. There are benefits."

Ester didn't say anything, she just cooed at Josiah.

There wasn't much to say.

I loved my sister, but this was my truth. My pile of

spectacles on my bed table attested to it. And Croomes needed proof, undeniable proof to believe anything. That was another of my truths.

My wool fell when Ester pulled me and Josiah tight against her.

"Sorry, Ruth."

I kissed her cheek. "Once I'm married and secure, we'll have those Tuesday teas like Mama. I won't make you knit."

Mrs. Fitterwall came down the steps from the upper rooms. "Time for Josiah's nap. Your heavy shawl is on the table at the front, Mrs. Bexeley. Your coat, too, Mrs. Wilky. Here are your spectacles."

The woman shoved her open palm close to my face.

I was livid. I knew her hand was near. I knew how the red-haired housekeeper moved, like there was a crook in her neck from not stretching.

I didn't complain. Maybe she thought she was helping, holding my crystal spectacles three inches from my face. "Thank you."

I put the heavy lenses on my nose. Spotting my yarn, I scooped it up. I knew the answer already, but I asked anyway. "Where are you going, Ester?"

"Yes, where, Mrs. Fitterwall?" Ester's prim mouth was open wide.

"With your sister, silly goose. That's what Mrs. Croome said."

My mama didn't trust me and had appointed a guardian, the perfect daughter, to accompany me. I nodded and didn't let my disappointment show.

I shut up and took it.

Mama tigress was still in control. Her words had been said from on high. Mrs. Fitterwall should've had the commandment etched on stone tablets. Trust must be earned.

"Yes, come along, sister."

Bewilderment settled in Ester's topaz eyes. She tugged at the bodice on her simple beige gown. "Ummm. I should change."

"There's no time. Give your son to the housekeeper and let's go."

She did, and Mrs. Fitterwall hummed a lullaby and took the wee lad up the stairs—with that crook-necked movement of hers.

"Ruth? You never go anywhere."

Her voice held such surprise.

Just what I needed to bolster me, a doubting Ester. I chuckled inside.

"I'm glad you are getting out of the house for a bit, but Ruth, I don't have to go with you, if you need privacy."

Ester's soft eyes whimpered. In another moment, she'd repeat platitudes about waiting on change, prayers for patience, or some comforting Job-like concession on long suffering.

There was no time. My strength would wane if I didn't go now. Ester could be helpful when I took that first step out the door.

I put a finger to Ester's mouth. "You look like a suitable chaperone. You'll keep the wayward daughter from a new disaster."

My sister didn't move.

I sighed and tried again. "Come with me, Ester. I want you with me. I need you."

"I don't have to go, Ruth. I trust you."

I looked at the door. She'd help going down those steps. "You shall come. Wear my coat. That will fix you up. I'll wear your shawl. We'll both match in pink. And that's your favorite color. We're in fine Croome fabric as we visit my husband's family."

Ester moved with me to the door.

With my spectacles, I study it.

The smoothness of the ebony-painted wood.

The glass sidelights that let in the sun.

The strength of it, a barrier to keep out the world.

"Your husband's family. The barrister's family? That's an odd way to put it when you haven't married him."

"Not him. Adam Wilky, my late husband."

She tugged my arm and pursed her lips as if she were going to share a secret. "But Adam's made up. There's no family to visit."

I took all the lies told about me and pushed the anger to my hands. The volcano swirling in me blew open the door.

The carriage sat close to the house, like Jonesy would do for me.

My chest shuddered. I gripped Ester's arm tightly. "Come see how fake Adam Wilky's life was. Let his father attest to his existence."

Ester started forward. I matched her strides to make myself go over the threshold.

We made it.

The air was different, so different out of the house. It whipped at my face.

My panic stirred, but I'd learned to ignore the frenzied feeling that made my lungs burn.

Closing my eyes, I leaned on Ester and soon we were on the pavement. I blinked, and I saw the carriage standing in front of me.

I jumped in so fast Ester must've thought I'd lost my mind. Well, I had years ago, but a survivor did what she had to do.

The carriage moved.

Ester stared at me. She must have thought I was crazed. Part of me was. I'd put hope in Adam again. I prayed his family, his wealthy Mayfair family, didn't see my face and turn us away.

Chapter Six

THE WIDOW'S COLD FEET

The carriage moved down Fournier Street fast.

"We'll be on Gracechurch soon," Ester said, in a way meant to both inform and let me know we could turn back.

I put on my spectacles and looked out the window.

Shops. Houses. People.

I didn't know the streets anymore.

That saddened me.

I thought of when I had. I thought of the docks and Adam walking me to Papa's warehouse near the Thames. We'd done that every week for six months.

For just a moment, I let bitterness sweep over me. It blasted through the knitted weave of the shawl, rattling the spaces betwixt my ribs. Adam's loss became fresh in my mind again, and I hated how I'd let the size of my world shrink.

My fault. My fears. My fleeting fire—my hands couldn't hold on to it. With proof, I'd shut up the naysayers. I'd be able to be bold me for more than a few moments.

I sat back on the seat and adjusted my spectacles, but the heavy things gave me a clear view of my sister's frown. "Say your peace, Ester."

My sister took off her straw bonnet. Her chin lowered as if she couldn't hold my gaze. "I don't know where to begin."

"Ask your questions or repeat the lies I've heard for four years. Lord knows they are numerous."

Ester raised her head at my chuckles. Her topaz eyes were fiery. "Going to find an old beau, the man who deserted you, is not worth your time. It's a scandal that should never be mentioned."

She grabbed my hand. "You are worth so much more than a dandy who lied and lacked faith."

"Adam was fashionable but no dandy."

My sister pounded the seat as if she had become frustrated. "He didn't know the jewel that you are. How can you debase yourself and crawl back to him? Great, you found where the scoundrel lives. Slap his face and leave him be. I'll help you. If I'd known, I'd have brought a poker."

Part of me was quite proud of my sister's outlandish streak. Part was touched by her love for me. But a big part of me needed her to believe my truth.

I folded my arms about the plain shawl, no fringes, no special collar, plain, plain peach in hue. "You finished? My Adam was no bounder. Before you think of striking an innocent, know that Adam did not trick me. He did not bed and dump me. He was none of the lies you've been told."

Ester's angelic face scrunched with her lips poking out. She flattened her palm against the ebony cloth of the tufted seat. "Then tell me what happened."

"Adam Wilky was an actual man. We did marry at Gretna Green. He was killed by a bunch of evil, horrible men who robbed us on our way back to London."

"That's not what Papa and Mama said. Papa found you in a brothel."

I had been so sick when Papa had come for me. I may

have been confused in what I said, but I'll never forget the disgust in his eyes carrying me out of Madame Talease's bawdy house.

A headache started.

I rubbed my temples. "I married Adam. I had no proof when Papa located me. I'd been beaten, brutalized to the point of death. I doubt if anything I said made sense to Papa. But Adam and I went through a ceremony. I know Adam loved me, and I watched him die, protecting me."

Ester gasped, she paled, looking like an ashy angel. "But it was fake. Adam Wilky was invented. Mama said it was a lie. Papa's lawyers found no proof that a man by that name existed."

"A lie is what they call the truth when no one believes it."

I dug into the reticule and pulled out the halved page of the blacksmith's registry. "See, this section says C. A. Wilkinso... and Ruth Eliz... The rest is cut off. My half had been in the trunk I received two weeks ago. Adam's half, he sent by post to his family's residence, Blaren House. That's where we are going."

"That makes no sense. The registry has to be available for everyone to view to maintain its validity. Why would you do something like cutting up the record that could validate your union?"

"Adam did it. He knew his life was in danger and that our marriage made me vulnerable to those hunting him. He took the registry, cut it in half, and sent his piece to his father. If his father has Adam's last letter, then maybe he will give it to me."

Ester held the torn parchment paper to the window. "This says Wilkinso. You've gone by the name Wilky?"

Was it wrong to be mad at a dead man?

I hated Adam for his secrets, as much as I hated that he was gone. I was conflicted and hurting, but these should be old wounds. For the past two weeks I'd told myself so many times it didn't matter, that he'd had reason for this deception. Just more of his cloak-and-dagger ways. Truthfully, it made everything hurt all over again.

I took back the old document and smoothed it against my knee. "Wilky, Wilkinson. None of it matters. You don't believe me."

"Ruth, is it possible he took the document to get rid of the proof? That he'd changed his mind and thought it more convenient to have no evidence?"

It was possible, but I'd never let Ester know that.

The wrong last name was why Papa had found no evidence of Adam.

Time and hurt had a way of shifting things. Adam, hero or villain? Who was he? Why had he had so many secrets?

Ester put a hand on my shoulder. "Is it worth confirming that this man you risked everything for was a scoundrel?"

Scoundrel. Liar. Those were words I'd have never thought about Adam, until two weeks ago.

He could be all those things and still tragically dead.

For a moment, I wanted to make the carriage turn back. I should keep the lies I'd lived rather than find the truth and know how stupid I'd been.

I'd loved Adam with everything. I'd given him everything, and he couldn't even give me his true name.

I felt weak, for I was weak.

Sinking against the seat, I wished to fall into the tuft of the fabric and never come out. I wanted to be a hairpin that slid into a crack and was lost.

Then I remembered my son.

He'd look for me like he did butterflies and birds and frogs. I wasn't doing this for me. Chris needed to have a name, even if it was the wrong one.

Turning the plain gold band Papa had bought to replace

the one taken, ripped from me like the cross Adam had given me, I stopped hiding. This was my truth. "I married Adam. It was a legal ceremony. The name is cut off, but it's Wilkinson. Adam's father, Algernon Nathaniel Wilkinson, that is who we are to meet. He lives at the address Adam scribbled on the back. I need both parts. That's my proof."

A sad sigh left Ester. She folded her arms and tucked a palm under her chin. "If he wrote the wrong name, the marriage is invalid. His family can claim it wasn't legal. Christopher is as pale as Josiah. The white Wilkinson family will not claim you."

I knew this.

I didn't think Adam would be so cruel, but I never thought he'd lie to me, either. I closed my eyes. "I have to believe the good in him. He did not take me to Gretna Green just to have at me. We married. I was a bride. I was loved."

My voice sounded strong. I saw my sister nod and back down. But she didn't see my confusion, my growing doubts.

My stomach quaked and turned. The panic I thought I'd beaten started to return, creeping at my feet, making my toes ice-cold. I moved my hands to keep them from freezing.

"Ruth? Ruth?"

"Yes." I sat up and told myself I was strong. "Yes, Ester."

"Where are we going? Where does the Wilkinson family live?"

"Mayfair. The address Jonesy says is in Mayfair."

"You told Papa's groom, but not me?"

"Yes. I didn't want to be a bother." I didn't want to hurt my sister, but she'd never support me, not on this.

Ester took off her glove and rubbed the back of her hand as if it were Aladdin's lamp. The motion, no doubt, was to highlight the brown pigment of her skin. "Mayfair means peers, the richest in London. There's no reason a rich family will give us anything. Acknowledging that one of their sons married a Blackamoor will not be done, not with him dead."

"I have to try. Adam was mulatto like Mama. Even if the Wilkinsons toss me out, I have to try. For Chris, I have to."

"Marry and get your son a father. What if the Wilkinsons want some sort of custody of your boy? They could set up a guardianship who could make sure you lose your son. My friend, Theodosia Fitzwilliam-Cecil, she suffered greatly from a horrid guardian."

I hadn't thought of that. The lack of truth had harmed Chris, but would gaining the Wilkinson's acquaintance also bring harm?

I put the document into my purple reticule and set it on my knees. "I won't lose Chris seeking the truth. That can't happen. What will he think when biddies like Mrs. Carter tell my son he's a bastard? He's not. I was married when I conceived. That I know."

The sparkle in Ester's eyes died, replaced with questions I didn't want to answer about Chris.

I tossed my head back against the seat bolster. "We'll see if the Wilkinson family will acknowledge the existence of Adam and if they kept his last correspondence. We won't mention my son unless I have to."

"If these people don't acknowledge or know this Adam, will you be fine?"

I didn't know. I couldn't think of that possibility and not fall to pieces. I hadn't realized how much hurt I'd buried inside until that stupid trunk had arrived.

I gritted my teeth and cinched my velvet reticule. "I've survived the worst. What's a slammed door?"

Ester picked up her bonnet and rotated it round and round in her palms. "Let's hope that is the worst."

I said nothing and allowed the *click-clop* of the horses to eclipse the awkward silence. I grasped my watch, my palm absorbing the trembling of its ticking. Then my knees mimicked the rhythm, followed by both hands.

I shook all over.

The panic, the rage in me began to win.

Ester reached for me, linking her thin fingers with my shorter ones, almost as Adam had used to do.

Adam. Don't let me hate you more than I remember loving you.

Then I thought of my luck, my bad luck, and I shook more. "I should've brought my knitting needles. It gives my hands something to do."

"You actually like knitting, Ruth?"

"It's something I've trained my fingers to do. As long as I concentrate, I don't have to see the yarn to get it right. I don't need these horrid headachy lenses. I think that's an important trick. A skill to show off at parties."

I chuckled long enough for my sister to join in, but it wasn't a jest, just the acknowledgment of my final truth. Someday, blindness would stop teasing and would swallow me whole. I wasn't afraid of losing my sight. I feared never being able to prove I wasn't a liar.

No more thinking about things I couldn't change. I was grateful to have a piece of the registry. Grateful to know I wasn't crazy or that my injuries hadn't made Adam up. "I'm grateful you came, Ester."

"Me, too."

My sister's slight grin would be the last thing I focused upon until Mayfair.

Head pounding, I took off my spectacles and sank into the cushions of the seat, sans wanting to slip into a crack.

I watched the blurs passing the window. The shapes— blobs of gray, swaths of burgundy—had to be the limestone and fired-brick buildings.

A long, throaty hoot. That was probably a barge floating down the Thames. That would make these next blobs warehouses.

The world wasn't so scary in a closed, moving carriage with everything blurry.

In another twenty minutes, the carriage stopped at Blaren House.

I was thankful, so much closer to the truth.

I hadn't fallen apart being away from the house.

Ester moved to the door first. "Put your spectacles on, Ruth. I'm not letting you out of the carriage if you don't."

"You are taking your duties as chaperone a little too much like Mama Croome."

"I'm serious, Ruth."

I flipped on my spectacles and followed Ester out of the carriage.

Blaren House.

Big. Wide green lawn. Huge chiseled stones. Stately. Elegant.

As we moved forward, something ran toward us.

Chest thumping faster, I stopped and pulled Ester behind me. I wouldn't let my sister get hurt.

A woman ran past, clothes barely on her back. "He's crazy!"

Other people ran past us as if Blaren House was on fire.

My sister tugged on my arm. "Ruth. It's an upset. Let's go. Let's get back into the carriage."

A *snap*, a *crackle*, a *pop*. These new noises rose over the screams.

More men, even a woman in black and white, fled down the limestone steps.

I planted my heels against the pavement. "It's only an eviction, Ester. You've heard of them. Some of Papa's workers have gambled away their wages. They lose everything."

"Yes, my husband has stopped a few of those procedures for widows of Papa's workers."

This manicured lawn erupted like a brawl in a bawdy house. Incredible.

Another *snap.*

That sounded like a whip. It sounded as if it sliced the air into shreds.

My chest beat as if it had gone crazy.

If the Wilkinsons were evicted, I'd never find them.

A woman bumped into me. Scantily clad, perhaps draped in a sheet. "That man is crazed. Run for your lives."

Cold sweat slipped down my neck, chilling my spine.

The openness hit me where I stood.

I needed to run back to the carriage or to the wide-open entry of Blaren House.

Something kept pulling me, but I wasn't moving.

That open door was all I could see. I hoped that one of the Wilkinsons remained. Someone who knew Adam.

"This isn't a good time to visit, Ruth. Can't you see that?"

I heard my sister. I heard her fear, but all I could focus on was a door and the truth.

Volcano me, dragon me, wild child me, ran. I moved faster and faster to Blaren House's entry.

I heard my name but kept heading to that doorway.

On the first step, someone bumped me and sent me spinning.

But I had to get inside. I pushed up the next step. Getting inside was all I wanted.

Another man knocked me. My glasses flew as I went down.

My neck hit first then my head bounced on the limestone.

The impact knifed through me.

Sharp sensations shredded every muscle.

In my eyes, colors and darkness struggled for control.

The panic had me. It was winning. I prayed not to faint, for the pain to stop, for darkness to leave me alone.

"Ruth!"

Ester? I should fight for her, but I couldn't move.

A big blur stood over me.

Did he whisper something?

Did he say my name?

A roughened palm scooped beneath my neck. He cradled it then caressed my jaw.

The blur hoisted me onto his shoulder. "Ah! The bed wench I ordered is here!"

The boast gutted.

My temples exploded as I flailed down his back. My face slammed into a hardened backside.

I couldn't yell. Couldn't beat on his big legs. Darkness had me.

"Put my sister down!"

Headstrong volcano me had brought trouble onto my sister.

Aching, I succumbed to the inky blackness. It swallowed me whole.

Chapter Seven

THIS WOMAN

Good God.

This woman…

She made time stand still. His boots weren't on the steps of Blaren House but planted in front of the forge of Gretna Green's blacksmith. He'd committed his life to a very young bride, to love and protect her. Then it was all taken away. Chatsworth Adoniram Wilkinson, the Baron of Wycliff, had vowed never to surrender and never to lose again.

But this woman…

One gaze at her face and a sense of knowing swept over him, then a fierce wave of protection.

His stone heart awakened. Joy, then abject fear, seized the useless organ.

In a blink, he was young, a fool so in love he couldn't eat or breathe or think. His every action centered on her—having her, knowing her, pleasing her.

This woman, his woman…

She was everything: a sun, the moon, the stars, all the firmaments of the universe.

People ran around him. Everyone screaming.

But he went back deeper in time to the docks near the Thames. A strong breeze had kicked up sand, making him turn to shield his eyes. That's when he'd seen her standing near the warehouses. So beautiful with honey-brown skin. By the time he'd made an introduction, he was in love, worshiping her chocolate eyes flecked with indigo and gold. And those lashes, curly and long, he couldn't wait to touch them, to touch her.

"Let me through." A little woman, a pretty negress, hit at Lawden.

"Wycliff," his man-of-all-work called out, "we must finish this, sir."

"Yes. Finish. Keep all away."

Yet, Wycliff didn't move. He couldn't crack his sjambok. This woman…she'd died.

He'd seen her take her last breath, witnessed the convulsion that had stolen her life. At that moment, his heart had turned cold and black.

He'd wanted to die and take everyone who'd hurt her with him.

Now he had a different plan for vengeance and the means and the power to complete it.

"Wycliff, are you done?"

The trance broke. He lifted his head, snapped his sjambok whip. "Be gone and tell everyone. Blaren House has been restored to its true owner."

"Don't hurt Ruth! Let my sister alone."

Oh, the sweetness of the name, *Ruth*.

His Ruth, His Ruthy. His miracle.

One man stopped running. He stood half in the bushes leading to the street. This one might run and report directly to Uncle Soulden or Wycliff's cousin, Nicholas.

With everything at stake, Wycliff made his antics large,

swinging his sjambok over his head. "A mighty bed wench delivered on time. A lovely celebration."

Lord. If Ruth heard that slur, she'd never forgive him.

He sounded as awful as that innkeeper had their last day together, the last day they'd lived as man and wife.

Her little sister, the screaming thing, slipped around Lawden and ran at him. "Let her go, you beast!"

Oh, this was a bad time for a family reunion.

One slovenly soul, one whom Wycliff was sure he'd frightened into thinking his life was going to end, stopped and gawked.

What type of message would these henchmen take?

Wycliff snapped his sjambok twice. The leather whip crackled, stealing the casual smiles of those still looking toward Blaren House.

Ruth's sister made it up the steps. "Ruth, hit him. I won't let him hurt you."

Keeping Ruth on his shoulder, he backed up to the threshold. The sister followed as he suspected. "Two bed wenches for the price of one. Madame Talease is most generous and knows my healthy appetite."

His laugh sounded lusty to his own ears. Repugnant, but it worked.

The goons started leaving again.

The short woman leaped at him and beat at his chest. "Put my sister down."

He laughed, even snapped his whip to make things look as bad as possible—not like a man who'd just found the wife he'd thought dead. "Inside, you. I'll have to complain to Madame. She knows I want my wenches compliant."

The sister hit him again. Lucky for Wycliff, Ruth was tall and draped over all things vital.

The insistent thing punched him again, hitting his arm. "We are not—"

He spun the sister, clasped a hand over her mouth. "As far as I'm concerned, you're sisters of the flesh. Well, I am of the brethren that needs great entertainment. We can negotiate a bigger payment inside. That is, if you please me."

She struck him hard, bit his finger.

He whispered *forgive me* and shoved the fiery sprite inside.

Wycliff marched into Blaren House and barred the door. "What's your name?"

"It's not bed wench. Put my sister down. Let us go."

He moved toward her and the little lady scrambled deeper into the wide hall. She picked up one of his uncle's gaudy porcelain statues. The cheap imitation of Giambologna's *Abduction of the Sabine Women* was hideous. A brutish sculpture of Roman soldiers stealing brides, hauling them away, sort of like Wycliff was doing. He'd have to get rid of the trash later.

The sister held it up as if she'd toss it. "Ruth, I'm here. I won't leave you. Ruth, wake up."

"You're a feisty one, ma'am. But you're more likely to hit your sister than me if you hurl that odious thing."

"Listen you, you let us go."

He chuckled at the passion in the sister's voice, as if he'd ever let Ruth, his Ruthy go. "I need to make sure she's unharmed. She took a hard fall. Come with me Miss…"

"Mrs. Bexeley."

"Come, Mrs. Bexeley. Bring your ugly statue. Consider it a gift for my rude reception. Your sister may have a concuss of the skull."

The little woman lowered her weapon. For the moment, she might trust Wycliff. Well, she had no choice, since her sister was upon his shoulder.

He curled Ruth into the fullness of his arms, carrying her as he had when he'd been a scrawny young bridegroom taking her across their wedded threshold.

A week of living and loving. The best time in his miserable thirty-year life. Ruth had been his everything, his best dream. Her death had been the nightmare he could never outrun. How could she be alive?

Her head bobbled, and he tucked it under his chin. Still beautiful, from a crown of curly tresses to the scar above her right eye.

Beautiful and alive.

How was this true?

Had he finally given in to madness?

Did madness smell like citrus and roses?

Did madness have a sister-in-law poking him in the back with the porcelain statue's breasts?

Lawden met him at the door to his study. "Lord Wycliff, I came in through the rear. I have the grooms securing the rest of the house."

"Good. Give the lady's driver a guinea and send them away. I'll see to their transport."

Mrs. Bexeley pressed close and touched Ruth's cheek. "Wait a minute. You can't—"

"It's done. There's no time to argue. We must see to your sister. Come into my study. We'll revive her there."

He started into the big room, his father's wonderful study, and paused.

Freed from impressment, newly back to London, he'd slipped into this room four months ago. Blaren House had become a secret gaming hell. Gambling and debauchery had filled the rooms. No one had noticed Wycliff easing into the study and taking the ledger book he'd hidden on the tall bookshelf behind the big desk four years earlier. The information inside had enabled his current plan to destroy his enemies.

Mrs. Bexeley shoved him in his back again. "You stopped

in the doorway. Put her down or put us in a carriage. You can't keep us."

"You can leave." His tone was harsh but true. Ruth was all he cared about, all he'd ever cared about. "I'll take care of her."

Stepping fully into the room, he tangled his fingers in Ruth's hair. A thick healthy curl. His wife was alive.

Another shove to his back hurt and would probably leave a bruise. "I take it you wish to remain, Mrs. Bexeley?"

"This is not funny. Put her down."

It was funny and tragic and humbling. He debated putting Ruth on the gaudy fur rug, the desk, or the settee by the bookcase. From what he'd witnessed during the eviction, particularly the indelicate situation on the desk, every bit of Blaren House would need to be washed with lye soap.

"I...I think the settee is best." Supporting Ruth in one hand, he moved to the striped satin bench and covered it with his cape then laid his love upon it. Tall, gorgeous Ruth's feet dangled over the settee's padded arm.

Wanting to hold her hand, touch the satin of her lips— lips he still dreamed of when he allowed his mind to be undisciplined—he forced himself away. Ruth must awaken and recognize him before there could be any celebration.

"Go to the sideboard, to the right of the desk, Mrs. Bexeley. There looks to be something like brandy there."

She ran to it, picked up the crystal decanter, and shook it. "Will this help Ruth?"

"No, but I could use a drink. Pour me a glass. Get yourself one, too."

She hefted the bottle, one hand had the statue, the other the liquor. "I don't want jokes. Just let us go."

He undid his cravat very carefully and left his collar buttoned. "I told you, you may go. This woman won't, not until she has awakened and can leave on her own power."

His sister-in-law bit her lip. She put the bottle down and then put the statue on the desk with a *thud*. "If you hadn't sent my driver away, I'd go get him, but I'd never leave you alone with my sister."

"Then I would have dealt with your driver as I have the thieves I evicted from Blaren House. This woman will go nowhere, not until I know she's well. An injury to the head is very serious. Catch, Mrs. Bexeley." He tossed her his cravat.

"Soak it in the brandy. We'll use it as a restorative."

Mrs. Bexeley's head shook, but she did as he requested. "Did I hear your name to be Wycliff? I need to tell my husband and my father who to go after."

He could tell the sister loved Ruth, but he didn't care. Wycliff's world was shifting. Part of the revenge he sought had been for Ruth's death.

Now what?

Could he half destroy his enemies?

"The name's Wycliff, the Baron of Wycliff. Make sure they go after the right man. Vengeance should be earned. Hurry with the cravat. I don't like how she's breathing."

If he was assured the scum he evicted wouldn't return, he'd send his man for a physician. *Ruth, be all right.* He stroked her hair, lifting a strand from her face, then studied the rise and fall of her chest. His mind again went to four years ago—the night before she had *died*, their last night at that foul inn.

They'd loved one another, and she'd slept close, right at his side. The scent of lush roses had anointed her skin, and like now, he'd watched her breathe, thinking how perfect the moment had been. It had been the beginning of forever.

Oh, was he stupid, as Ruth had often called his actions when she'd teased him about being overcautious.

He should've known heaven and hell were separated by hours. They should've gone north and not returned to

London to face her father. Then they wouldn't have been attacked. Perhaps they'd be here at Blaren House now with arms and arms of children.

Happy-ever-after was rubbish.

Well. It had been until a few minutes ago, when he'd learned Ruth was alive.

Wycliff dropped to his knees and carefully traced the wide scar on her temple. How much pain had she endured for their love?

Mrs. Bexeley stood over him. "Here."

He took the brandy-soaked cloth and mopped at Ruth's nose.

Nothing.

No wrinkling of her nostrils.

No lines crinkling at her lips when she smiled.

Nothing.

He'd felt nothing for four years. Now she was here, and he felt too much.

How was he still enslaved to this love?

And how had she lived?

Was she still ticklish about her ribs? Did she miss him?

When she opened her eyes, would she love him still?

"It's not working, Mr. Wycliff."

"It's Lord Wycliff. She took a hard fall."

"Do something. Call for a physician."

He seized the opportunity to put both hands to Ruth's face. He massaged her neck, savoring the feel of her blood coursing, her pulse strong beneath his fingertips.

His stone heart became mush ladened with memories. If she didn't awaken… He couldn't lose her again.

That loss wrapped about him, heavy like iron chains, dragging him low, his horrible throat closing up as he drowned.

Mrs. Bexeley knelt beside him. "Are you a physician?"

A cough forced air into his chest. "Some training. Patched up a few men on my frigate." He soured at how empty his raspy voice sounded. He tapped the brandy to Ruth's nose again. "Awaken *la belle au bois dormant*, my sleeping beauty."

Ruth choked. Her eyes opened.

He held his breath and waited for hints of her wits returning. Hints of recognition.

She started flailing her arms. "Ester? Ester, are you here?

"Ruth." Mrs. Bexeley pushed Wycliff out of the way. "I'm here. Focus. Let your eyes warm to the room. You took a hard fall."

Her breathing remained uneven, as if Ruth had run up and down a long flight of stairs.

Fear for her health battled his impatience. *Recognize me.* He waved a hand over her face. Her pupils didn't move, not until he was inches from her face. "How do you feel?"

She swatted his fingers. "Who are you?"

His mouth became dry, drier than a desert. "Wycliff, dearest."

"Lord Wycliff is full of jokes, Ruth. I'm here. Are you much hurt?"

Grasping her sister's arm, she sat up an inch before flopping back down. "A headache. A bad one, but I'm fine. I'm fine. Did they move things around again? The lamplight—it's wrong, the glow is in the wrong place. I hate when they move my things."

"What?" Mrs. Bexeley smoothed Ruth's palm. "We're not at home. We're at that Blaren House. You went to see Wilkinson, your Adam's father."

"Oh." She rubbed at her neck. "For a moment, I thought Mama or Mrs. Fitterwall moved my things again."

She put both hands to her temples. "Never mind. What happened? Did I panic?"

Ruth hadn't looked his way. She hadn't looked about the

room. Something was very wrong. And why did she come for his father, especially since the good man was only here in spirit? "It's irritating, dear, to have your things shifted," he said. "I know it to be irksome, like having something stolen."

"Hush you." Mrs. Bexeley helped Ruth lean against the settee back. "Can you stand?"

His poor Ruth looked so pale, so fragile.

She'd had a bad fall, but would that alone confuse her?

He tried to push away the memories of the blow she'd taken to her head. During their attack, the trunk where he'd hidden the other copied ledger had smashed against her skull.

Wycliff shook himself. He was never this timid. "Ma'am, you lost your balance. The uproar at Blaren House did that. Sorry, my dear."

He gripped his sjambok, his favorite whip made of the toughest leather of rhinoceros skin. Curling the end of the long shaft about his palm, he readied to snap it. Then he thought better of it. The noise of it might upset Ruth. "Why did you ladies come tonight? As you can see, I have just taken control of this place. I'm not ready for guests."

Ruth took her sister's arm and stood. "Take me to Wycliff."

Her sister led her as if she were a blind woman.

Wobbling, she approached and stood in front of him.

This was the moment.

He dropped his sjambok and opened his arms.

She raised her hand to his face.

The sweetness of this reunion flooded through him, like a dam breaking. He dipped his head to kiss her fingers, but she reared her hand back.

Smack.

She'd slapped him, hard. "You frightened me nearly to death, Lord Wycliff. That wasn't right."

Still feisty.

He rubbed his stinging face. The gold band on her finger surely left a mark upon his cheek.

Gold.

The one he'd given Ruth had been silver.

He stepped back a safer distance and stood against his desk. "I suppose I deserve that, but I have a one-hit rule."

Ruth broke free of the sister and stepped closer. "That was for calling me a bed wench. And this is for tossing me over your shoulder." She reared back again.

He caught her palm and held it. "One shot, madam. Even if you are rightly offended."

"I'm a respectable woman. So is my sister. Do not forget this."

"What are respectable women doing at my residence without a proper invitation?"

She drew her hand away, and he loathed letting it go.

"I came to see Mr. Wilkinson."

"Which Mr. Wilkinson?"

"Algernon Nathaniel Wilkinson."

At least she didn't say Soulden or even his changeable cousin, Nicholas. "Oh, A. N. Wilkinson, the late Lord Wycliff."

"Oh." Ruth looked down. "Oh."

"He's dead, Ruth. Let's go," Mrs. Bexeley said. "We need to go. Please send for a carriage."

"No. Wait. He might know." Ruth's voice sounded softer than before. "I came to ask about his son."

A fire lit in Wycliff. Ruth came to look for him but couldn't tell he stood before her. His throat burned white hot. "The late Baron of Wycliff died two months ago."

He stared down at this woman whose lips were close enough to kiss. "I'm now the head of the Wilkinson family. I am Lord Wycliff. I can help."

"Then did you know Adam Wilky? Did Adam live here?"

"Yes, Adam lived here."

A sigh left Ruth as if he'd answered some sort of prayer.

Mrs. Bexeley tugged on Ruth's wrinkled skirt, a pale thing of pink and lace. Sweet and pale, not a choice he remembered his wife liking.

"Let's go, Ruth."

"Ester, did you not hear him? He knew Adam Wilky, and he said he lived here."

Were those tears in her blank eyes?

Ruth turned and hugged her stiff sister.

Mrs. Bexeley patted her back. "But Ruth, that doesn't prove the rest of your story. Whip man just said he knew him."

The color that had birthed in Ruth's cheeks drained. She looked as if she'd faint as she put distance between Mrs. Bexeley and herself. "Yes, why would you just hearing someone say I was telling the truth be enough? I need proof of Adam Wilky being a true person and undeniable proof of our marriage."

"Proof?" he said, barely masking his curiosity, his hope. "Proof concerning Adam? You think he's alive?"

"No. He's dead." Ruth folded her arms. "You know he's dead."

Her confident rebuke would be perfectly done if she had not swayed. She wobbled, then tipped forward.

He caught her before she fell. "You're not…steady."

Pressed in his arms, she smelled of sweet brandy and roses. Her heart drummed against his chest, and his pulse gave chase. It hadn't forgotten the rush, the joy of holding her, the heady feeling of finding the one woman who gave him purpose beyond the rage.

Yet, Ruth knew him not.

Well, he'd never been a man who had it all. "You'll stay, until you are less dizzy. I insist."

"I'm fine. You're the one that sounds out of breath.

Making fun of women too taxing? Release me."

Forcing himself to move, he lifted her atop the desk. "Sit, until I am convinced you won't tumble down the stairs. Since I am to put you in one of my carriages, I think it necessary you comply."

Mrs. Bexeley came close and tried to catch Ruth's hand. "Let's take a moment. I can't watch you fall again."

Ruth folded her arms, leaving Mrs. Bexeley's palm in the air. "I'm sorry to be such a bother."

"It's not your fault. It's this crazy man."

"I'm not crazy. I'm handling business, but the wee one is right. You could tumble again. Now explain to me what your proof business is with Adam. As I said, I am Lord Wycliff, Adoniram Wilkinson. I know, such a horrid, pretentious name. I never use it."

That was true. It was why he'd gone by Adam and had given everyone that name so the gossips could never tie him to the fights he'd found himself embroiled in. He'd never wanted to distress his father.

Wycliff walked around to the other side of the desk and glanced toward the mirror framed above the sideboard.

Did he look so different?

He wasn't gaunt anymore. His hair was cropped low to not show the kink of his curls. Passing was the root of his power, the only reason he was alive, but his Ruth knew that.

"I'm waiting, ladies. Which one of you shall go first? Should I toss a coin?"

If Wycliff were a bigger man, he'd let things be. Ruth couldn't find Adam. His world was no safer. His uncle and his ilk were still dangerous.

But a man who loved as deeply as Wycliff wasn't capable of giving up. He'd never relinquish an opportunity to win Ruth back. Never. Not even if she wore another man's ring.

Chapter Eight

Remembering Adam

My sister could fuss, make eyes at me all day, not that I could see her doing it. I was not leaving Blaren House, not yet.

I heard a chair move behind me. I assumed it was Lord Wycliff sitting at his desk.

Ester was a small pacing blur and could hold her breath and turn blue as she did when we were younger, but nothing would make me go. I wouldn't budge, not without the truth.

Dizzy, head pounding, I could only see blurs and shadows. Yet, I knew this Lord Wycliff stared at me.

I felt his gaze upon me, hot and heavy, making me wonder if I was properly dressed or how dirty I'd become after falling.

No shrinking from this light. Wycliff was the key to the proof I needed.

"Ruth, the man we came to see is gone. Let's do the same." Ester's blurry pink dress moved in front of me again, back and forth—frown in focus, frown out of focus.

"Please, Ester. Stop."

Lord Wycliff put his boots on the desk next to me, close to my hip. Hessians, I imagined, with something that swung when his feet shifted. A tassel dangling mid shaft. Fashionable, expensive boots.

A tang of polish hit my nose. The man might be crazy with a whip, but he did possess some fastidious habits...like Adam.

"What is it you'd like to know of the Wilkinsons or Adam?"

The graveled voice, low, hoarse sounding—grated. I didn't know why. It just did.

I rolled the shiny gold band my father had bought to perfect my widowhood. "Did you know Adam was attacked on his way to London from Scotland four years ago?"

It was the longest sigh I'd ever heard, but then he said, "Yes. I know. Adam was coming from Gretna Green."

"Then you are aware he married?"

Another long sigh, this one punctuated with something sounding like a grumbled curse. "Yes."

My sister stopped pacing. "How do you know for sure? You weren't there, were you?'

A third long, guttural groan sounded.

But I was taken aback by Ester's tone.

The haughtiness. She didn't believe any of this. She could jab me with knitting needles or knives, but nothing would hurt worse.

I stared at the blur of boots by my hip because I couldn't look at Ester. "He knows because he saw the other half of the registry."

"Yes. I saw it."

"Oh," Ester said.

That was it. Four years of living with everyone calling me a liar and that just summed up my life in five words.

I became speechless, barely able to release my own sigh.

"Ruth really did marry Adam Wilky or C. A. Wilkinso as it says on her half."

"C. A. Wilkinson. Yes."

"Then it is also true, the story about them being attacked. That Adam died?"

Ester's tone, so full of disbelief, began to scrape my hollow insides. I felt nauseous and promised to never again be laid bare like this. There was no one to trust but Chris.

Noise shifted behind me, then something moved in front. A man's hand, rough, smelling of leather, lifted my chin. "Follow my finger with your eyes. This will tell me if there is a concuss of your skull."

It took a few moments before his index finger was within my field of view, as the doctors called it.

His sigh was warm on my cheek, and the way he touched my neck, so gentle yet strong—it brought a little relief to my headache.

"I take it no one can believe in a love like yours and Adam's. Both so young."

"Not so young. I was nineteen. I'm a wiser twenty-three now."

"It was young to be swept away so completely." He made a loud swallow like it hurt to talk. "Adam said he felt oneness with his love, like no other."

A chill went through me. The voice was dark and twisted, but his words, those were Adam's.

I moved his hand from my face but held his fingers for a moment. "It sounds as if you knew Adam well. He took the registry from the blacksmith's shop. No one believes we wed. They think he is a liar or a blackguard who used me."

"But you know you wed, Ruth."

He said my name as if we were friends. We were not. He was some high-handed lord who believed he had a right to such intimacy. I dropped his palm. "Call me Mrs. Wilky."

"Do you think Adam a blackguard, Mrs. Wilky?"

"I don't know anymore. Time hasn't been kind to his

memory. And everyone talking ill of me for trusting him...
I don't know."

Another long sigh uttered.

"Adam was no liar. He married Ruth Elizabeth Croome."

He said my full name. Even in this raw voice I heard
sweetness. I let him take my hand again.

He rolled it in his big, rough palms. "This is not his ring.
Have you remarried?"

"No. Not yet. You sound angry." I balled my fist and
shook it at the tall blur. "Are you disappointed that Adam
wed a Blackamoor?"

Lord Wycliff chuckled. "No. Adam had fine tastes. Who
would be disappointed in you?"

"Plenty."

"You're beautiful, well-mannered, a bit of a hot temper
underneath. But you are to remarry?"

I lowered my hands to the desk and tried to pretend I
didn't hear the disappointment in his voice.

"An offer will come soon, so no getting ideas." Ester's
voice was sharp.

"Then I'm on time to give my approval. You're a
Wilkinson. I'm the head of the family."

"Lord Wycliff, I want nothing from you or your family.
No money. Just answers."

He was in front of me again, hovering.

"Mrs. Wilky." His finger traced the scar on my temple, the
mark I'd tried to hide with curls. "You suffered greatly from
the attack. Yours and Adam's enemies will suffer threefold."

Ester tried again to take my arm, to elbow her way into
the privacy of my and Wycliff's conversation. "What? What
did he say?"

I bit my lip for a moment. I did want those men to be
brought to justice, but I didn't have Job's patience to suffer
more losses or to see the wrong people hurt before vengeance

came. "No talk of revenge. No more bloodshed. No nothing."

My sister, I pictured her standing at a distance, wanting to hear Lord Wycliff's whispers, my replies, but it had been so long since anyone had believed me, I wanted this moment to last. I wanted this moment for me.

"Ruth, ask him your questions so he can send us home. No, I'll do it. Do you have the other half of the registry?"

"Mrs. Wilky, you need spectacles. The lenses, they are thick?"

The man ignoring Ester made me want to chuckle, but had he ignored my distress about revenge? I gave up and nodded. "Yes. Lord Wycliff. Ester, did you get them?"

"No." My sister said, her tone simmering in frustration, the way she did when Papa teased. "There was too much happening."

"Ladies, I apologize again for how I received you. I used an awful jest to make my enemies think nothing of you."

That sounded sincere, even reasonable, given this was Adam's relative.

"But you were seen. Until I'm assured you're safe, I'm obligated to see to your protection, to our family's protection."

This time, I sighed and bit my tongue. "Ouch."

His hands went to my face. "Are you well, ma'am?" There was more gravel and husk to his voice. "Where does it hurt? Let me make it better."

The flirt was examining me like those physicians Mama paid to come to Fournier Street. But this touch was different. I was a treasure, not the negress specimen some were loath to be near. "My head aches."

"Oh, we can't have that, my dear. May I touch your neck again?"

"You're already touching me."

"I suppose I am, but I want to make sure it's allowed. I'm still on shaky ground with my poor greeting."

"Yes, you are, but do what you can. The tension won't relent sometimes."

"I accept the challenge."

Gnarled and slow was his speech, but I felt him grinning at me. I didn't care, not the way his hands eased the pain.

His fingers made faster motions, big circles at the nape of my neck.

The pressure, the urge to vomit eased. "To bring such relief. Grin away."

He laughed, the rumble low and throaty.

"Ruth, make him let you alone. We can't trust him."

Was he taking liberties?

Perhaps, but it seemed his fingertips knew where the pain was, and he'd chosen to rid me of it. "Hush, Ester."

"Ruth, Wycliff's staring at you like a dog hungry for a bone."

"Are you staring…like that?"

"*Hmm.* Yes. Yes, I am. You are lovely. One doesn't see such works of art at the mercantile ports. I've been a seaman for a while. Only London has such beauties. Here, you can wear your hair uncovered, something not done often in the Indies."

One of his gifted fingers again traced the scar at my temple.

That was the only lasting reminder of the truth about me and Adam.

Shame filled me.

My cheeks heated. I caught his hands. "I'm feeling better. You can stop."

"Sister, why are you giving comfort to this cretin? Bed wenches, he called us."

Ester was at my side, maybe looking around Wycliff's shoulder. That image brought me a chuckle. "I'm not a bed wench, and neither are you. You say all the time it doesn't matter what others say. How different is this?"

"We are here to learn about Adam Wilky, not to let a blowhard touch my sister's face."

Wycliff sat with a *thud* on the desk. "I know everything of Adam, Mrs. Wilky. I'm sorry for your loss, for everything."

Done with everyone's pity, I clenched the edge of the desk. "I only want the truth."

"Of course, ma'am. Ask anything."

That was one of those open-for-interpretation responses. The man was flirting, but I was immune to such passions. My reticule remained looped on my wrist. I risked Wycliff's ripping my proof, but I needed to hear his reaction. "This is my half of our marriage registry."

"Our marriage registry?"

"You know what I mean. Mine and Adam's."

He put his hand on it and mine. "May I?"

For a second, maybe more, this was Adam in front of me—same height, same way of hovering, and asking permission. But my Adam was dead, and this was a mere relative, a copy.

"Lord Wycliff, it's all I have of Adam, but you can see that this is valid. Do you have the other half?"

"I've seen it. It was sent here four years ago. I don't know where it is now."

So close.

So close, and I'd lost again.

My Job's luck won. Well, no boils or falling roofs with this judgment. I'd walk out of here the way I came, without that smidgeon of hope the registry had offered.

In my head, I recited my gifts, my blessings—*Chris, a home, clothes, food, the kind barrister, knitting.*

Still, my face felt wet. This loss undid me.

"Why are you crying, Mrs. Wilky?"

"I've come. I came out of the house. And you don't have it."

"I see. I wish I had everything that you needed."

Could a raspy masculine voice hold such melancholy? Lord Wycliff's did, and it tugged on me.

With my thumbs, I smeared the tears on my cheeks then wiped them on my shawl. My poor Christopher. Nothing will change the gossip about him now.

Digging into my reticule, I tried to finger a handkerchief, but Lord Wycliff put one in my hand. "I haven't been believed for four years. No...no friends or family. No one. And you saw Adam's half. You said it so soft and easy, like I'd asked about the weather. But you don't have it."

"Sister, I'm sorry." Ester's voice was heavy, and she clasped my shoulder.

"Ma'am, there is nothing soft or easy about me. I've been away for a long time. The letter could be anywhere. You've kept the registry all these years. You still love Adam?"

"What? What kind of question is that? Hand it back." I flailed my arms. I must've looked wild.

"Here." He slipped the paper against my palm.

I took my time and folded the registry like a precious pinafore, then slid it into my reticule. "I didn't have this until two weeks ago. It was sent to me."

"Two weeks? Mrs. Wilky, someone had the registry for four years and just sent it two weeks ago?"

"Yes. That's what I'm saying. Your belief turns to disbelief quickly, too?"

"No. I'll believe anything you say. I can tell you are a woman of honor. You're guided by your heart. That's what Adam believed."

That used to be me, but I couldn't be guided by what I didn't have. "What's with your voice? The remains of a dry cough? An injury?"

"An injury. All wars have costs."

England's wars had injured and maimed so many.

"Sorry." I laid both hands flat upon the desk and turned toward the direction I heard his voice. "What relation are you to Adam?"

"We were close…like brothers. He told me everything about the woman he loved, Ruth Croome. You love daisies. You think your middle name, Elizabeth, makes you feel like a queen."

Adam's words. At least Adam couldn't tell Lord Wycliff that he was dead because we'd returned to see my parents. My fault. I pushed the guilt into the back of my mind. It needed to stay there.

"You have one beloved sister. I believe Adam said you described her as perfect and sheltered."

I wanted to laugh at the memory, but now this felt like another violation. Adam had given away their privacy. "Adam had no brother. Who are you?"

Ester grabbed my hand. "This is parlor games, Ruth. He's speaking in riddles. It's obvious he's a cousin."

"I share Adam's bloodline. I'm related to you by marriage. The concern you hear in my terrible voice is for you and all my new relations, the Croome family. The men responsible for harming you and Adam were never brought to justice."

"Harm? Adam was murdered. He was horribly killed, and I watched him die."

"Then you understand why I must protect you. I'm honor bound to do so."

"Ruth, how can we trust him? He's crazed. He threw you over his shoulder."

Ester was right in a lot of ways. Logical in her assessment. But the rebel inside me didn't want logic. I wanted vindication. "You say you were close to Adam. He never spoke of you."

"I suspect he didn't say enough about a great many subjects."

That truth stung, hitting hard at my empty chest. "Well,

I didn't come for a reunion. I'm aware that Adam's family did not approve of him marrying me. He said that it was him choosing his mother's heritage over his father's."

I heard the clink of a decanter and the spilling of a liquid.

"You are right. Many in my family did not approve. For me, knowing how he loved you, I think you perfect."

"Ruth, he's flattering you for some nefarious purpose. He doesn't have the registry. We can stop this and leave."

Ester was right again, and I hated that. "You don't have the other half of the document. Please get us a carriage so we can leave you in peace. Peace is the most important thing."

"Is that all you want? When did you ever give up so easily?" His voice sounded accusatory, but it was better than disbelief.

"I want nothing more."

The screech of a chair being pulled out sounded behind me. If I had to see him beyond today, his silent footfalls would make me crazed.

"Mrs. Wilky, I know what to do to fix this and give you my protection."

"But you don't have the registry." I pivoted upon the desk to see the big blur of Lord Wycliff sink into a chair. Then I waited for him, this new Wilkinson, to destroy my world again.

Chapter Nine

RUTH'S PROOF

Wycliff leaned back in his father's chair, in the hallowed study of Blaren House where his father had conducted his finance dealings. His wife and his sister-in-law, the disgruntled duo, were in front of him, readying to leave. He needed an offer for them, not a monied transaction, but something that would be agreeable and keep all sides close until Ruth remembered him and their love.

He picked up his glass of brandy and downed it. The liquid scorched his terrible throat and made him growl in his chest. This wasn't how reunions should go. He'd read Homer's *Odyssey*. It was his favorite. Odysseus had been missing for ten years, but he came home to a faithful Penelope. It was four years for him and Ruth, and she was being courted by other men.

It wasn't fair to hold a vibrant Ruth to vows when she thought him dead, especially how she'd suffered.

But Wycliff had never, ever stopped loving her.

In his head, he'd imagined a reunion beyond some pearly gate. More than once when his frigate had come under attack, he'd thought he'd see her in the morn. He'd welcomed it and had wanted to be locked in her arms again.

Yet, each time he'd lived.

Then his father had secured his release. Wycliff had returned in time to spend the man's last two months on this earth with him. Together, they'd righted the stolen monies from the recovered ledger, but he hated that his father wouldn't see Uncle Soulden and Johnson's downfall.

Ruth receiving her trunk after it had been missing for four years was not a coincidence.

"Shall you keep us in suspense?" She waved her hand at him. The glint shining from the gold band hit him in the eye.

"No, my lord," Ruth said, "No. Finish your glass. Keep us waiting."

Feisty.

He spun the crystal glass on the desk. "The country house may have Adam's personal effects. I will send someone once I've settled into Blaren House, but until then, I'm your proof."

"You're my proof?"

She bowed her head. Her shoulders slumped, showing every inch of a defeated soul. "Then I've lost."

"You never gave up this easily. I mean, not from all that Adam shared."

He stared at Ruth. Well-dressed but in a muted color, not the bright hues of their youth. The woman wasn't in want for anything that he could see, not that she was the type to be enticed by money. How had she survived the attack? What was her life like now?

"This is purgatory," he said.

"Yes, it has been."

"No, Mrs. Wilky, that's what I'm feeling right now. If things had been different, Adam wouldn't have needed to take the registry in the first place."

"Ruth, Lord Wycliff is stalling, no doubt for some nefarious purpose."

"Can't I merely be reveling in the memories of Adam and the woman he loved? Mrs. Wilky, has your sister always been so cynical?"

"I'm not cynical," Mrs. Bexeley said. "I'm suspicious. Let's forget about the registry and him and go home. Home is safe."

"Your sister is right. I don't have the other half. In a few weeks, once I've settled my business affairs, I'll be dedicated to finding this paper. I will get it for you."

Her lips lifted then floundered. "I won't be able to stall the barrister much longer. He's asked me to marry him. I wanted proof before I accept his offer. I need to go into a new marriage with all the questions of Adam's honorable intentions resolved."

Her sister frowned, "Barrister Marks proposed? You didn't say."

"I told him I needed time to think it over, to see if it was right for me."

Sitting on a proposal and doubting my intentions?

No. No to marrying someone else and no to doubting my love.

No marriage. Not over my body, dead or alive.

Barely able to contain the fury sweeping over him, he tapped his desk again, his finger drawing *N*s for never, never going to give her up, never. It took all his strength to not leap up and confess. "Adam had a sister. She lived here. She would know exactly where his possessions were stored, but she's missing."

Ruth's soulless eyes gained a sparkle brighter than the crystal sconces lining the study. "He did have a sister. Cicely's missing?"

"You remember her? Yes, I'm hunting for her. She was

upset at their father's passing and went to stay with friends." Cicely was livid that their father had kept the fact that Wycliff was alive a secret. Their father hadn't wanted to get her hopes up, if release from the impressment could not be secured. "I'm her guardian. I received word of her disappearance from school two weeks ago."

Ruth put her hands to her scar. "Two weeks? My trunk appeared two weeks ago."

The look on Ruth's face matched his concern that the incidents were linked to the Wilkinson's unfinished war. "If you could wait until I find her, if you postpone things—"

"No. My plans are my plans."

What Ruth wanted, she always possessed. "Then I am your proof. I can attest to your marriage. I will convince everyone who doubted."

Ruth's brow creased. Her lips parted, and he was entranced.

"Yes, Mrs. Wilky. Think on it. I can attest to the great love Adam had for you."

"But you must be busy. And the search for Cicely—"

"Cicely, she's a sweet girl, such a gentle nature, but she can be thoughtless. I'm sure she'll turn up. And I might need your advice about being a guardian to a young girl. Adam said that you were clever on so many things."

"I know how Adam loved his sister. She was sent away for her protection. He'd be crazed if he thought her lost. If I had known how to contact her, I would've befriended her. I'll pray for her recovery."

The way Ruth's voice trembled made him feel horrible. He didn't think she'd be so moved, but Ruth was his other half, of course she'd fear for Cicely. "Adam would want your situation resolved and his sister located. I can do both. When can we meet again?"

"We?" Mrs. Bexeley started waving her hand, as if she

were directing birds in flight. "No. No. Her and you? My sister and wild whip man? No."

"It's a sjambok, Mrs. Bexeley. And I held it low, not intending to strike them, just to put fear in their hearts."

"Well, it worked on mine. Ruth, you can't be involved with him. This is dangerous. You can't do anything dangerous. Your eyesight is too poor. You have fits. This is the first time you've ventured from Nineteen Fournier for something other than church or a doctor in two years."

The grimace forming on Ruth's face made the sister jump back. "It's wild, something a willful spirit would do. Lord Wycliff, we live at Nineteen Fournier near Cheapside."

"Ruth, this crazy peer—"

"Baron, ma'am."

Mrs. Bexeley tiptoed back to Ruth. "Sorry. But this crazy baron shouldn't be around you. Your nerves are bad."

The door to the study opened. Lawden came inside and bowed. "My lord, you have an appointment."

Wycliff moved from his seat and stood between the sisters and his trusted aid. "Prepare the carriage and take these ladies to Cheapside. And look outside. Mrs. Wilky has lost a pair of spectacles."

Ruth nodded. "Nineteen Fournier is in the old Spitalfields part of Town. And thank you for looking for my spectacles."

"It shall be done." Lawden backed out the door.

"It will take a few minutes for my man to bring things around. While we wait, is there anything you'd like to know about Adam?"

Ruth looked down, never up or at him, not that she could see him. "Why was he so secretive of his name, even to me? I hate that he didn't trust me with the truth."

Wycliff hated that he'd done that, too, but that was how he'd navigated the world. Loving Ruth hadn't been part of his plans.

Sidestepping the sisters, Wycliff scooped up his ebony cape and put it about Ruth's shoulders. "He had his reasons. I'm sure if he'd lived, he would've told you all."

"At lease he completed the registry with his true name. I can take comfort that he didn't go to such lengths just to invalidate our union."

That was what she thought.

No. Never.

He opened his mouth to confess, but how would she react when she already had so many doubts of his character? He fixed the collar of the cape, taking a chance to finger her falling curls. "He had his reasons. Perhaps as we reminisce, we can discover what they were. When may I see you again?"

Mrs. Bexeley grabbed her sister's arm. "We need to be out of here, Ruth. This is not what you want. There's enough to fret about with my husband giving his abolition speeches or Papa's business. Must you fret over ghosts, too? Do you, Lord Wycliff, want that for her? Would Adam?"

He didn't want Ruth in danger, but she was. The person who sent the trunk knew of her existence. That already put her in danger. He helped Ruth down from the desk but couldn't resist leaving his hands about her waist.

Firm, probably still ticklish. "I owe Mrs. Wilky the opportunity to clear up confusion about her late husband. I can only imagine what you endured mourning a man who died too early. You're too young to be a widow. You and Adam, you two should've grown old together."

She poked him in his chest. "While you may have read it in the paper or a coroner's notice, I saw his murder with my own eyes. And in your voice, I hear fear again. The conspiracy Adam talked of was true. They may have his sister."

"No, I don't think so, but you remember Adam's ramblings?"

"I remember too many things, mostly how he suffered.

And my regret of how things could've been different if things hadn't been left unsaid."

He should have let her slap him again.

That would hurt less than knowing her memories of Adam weren't good.

Her love had waned. His hadn't. That was unfair.

Mrs. Bexeley shook her fists. "Remember Chris. You can't have this man around him. If we leave now, we can put Chris to bed. He needs you safe."

Ruth backed away from Wycliff, her shoulders slouching. "Yes, Ester. You are right."

The way Ruth crumbled.

It was the first time she'd acted afraid, and it was over this *Chris*. Her child? Her sister's?

Anger again simmered in his gut.

A child, a potential marriage—Ruth had kept living, even though he hadn't. Four years ago, he'd been a man who'd lost everything, just when he'd found all he'd needed in Ruth.

Now he was poised to win, but he'd lost Ruth.

Stepping in front of her, he adjusted the drape of the cape. It dragged on the ground. "Loving Adam was a choice. Having me about you to remind you of him, that's your choice, too."

"Thursday. My mother's throwing a garden party for friends and family. I need you there to tell my parents about Adam."

"Thursday. Excellent. Adam said you were a woman who knew her own mind."

Horses brayed. The carriage Lawden ordered had arrived.

"Uninvite him, sister."

Ruth's glorious lips parted. "Thursday at two. As part of my Wilky family, you should be there. I need you there."

If she could see his smile, she'd know he'd be there. "Yes,

I cannot wait to meet your family and friends." And this Chris.

"Good." Ruth turned and walked straight into the doorframe. "Clumsy. Well. At least it wasn't moved."

"No. It wasn't, my dear, you are still unsteady from the fall." He slipped his arms about her waist again and held her close. "Use me to feel grounded. Let me know when you are ready to move forward."

"Release her, Lord Wycliff," Mrs. Bexeley said. "I can help her."

"And let my cousin fall? Never." Before either woman could object, he had Ruth up in his arms.

Hands placed in respectful places—looped about her long legs, a palm under her arms nearly cradling her ample bosom—he carried her, all the way to the carriage.

"This was not necessary, my lord," she said. Her tone was low and crisp, not husky as when passion claimed her.

Memories of her smile, her laugh, her joy at small things like daisies—would haunt him tonight. "Carrying you, Mrs. Wilky, was very necessary. I'll never let you be hurt again."

Lawden assisted Mrs. Bexeley inside and tossed him a pair of broken brass spectacles.

Wycliff held on to Ruth's door and handed her the frames. There was just enough glass left in the brass that maybe she could see him.

Ruth put the spectacles to her face and eyed him, but her expression remained unchanged.

His man coughed and pointed his head toward the second carriage.

Shutting the door, he stepped away and waved to the driver.

Soon, the carriage moved down the street at a pace far too fast for Ruth to remember, and leap out, and run back to him.

Lawden came beside him. He was a red-haired Irish man who'd apprenticed in Blaren House as a steward. The fellow literally had grown up with Adam and had taken care of his father while Adam had been lost to the Navy.

A spiritual man of good character and height to boot, Lawden was the only person Wycliff trusted. "The third step of your plan, reclaiming Blaren House, is finished. Well done."

"We have an addition to my plans, Lawden."

His man's bushy brows lifted. "You never change your plans. All the steps are in place. We have steps four and five to go."

Yes. The defrauded money had been restored to his control. Yes, everyone who cheated his father had begun to pay. Yes, he had Blaren House. Four: Blaren House had to be restored to its former glory for his sister's enjoyment. Five: all the men who had *killed* Adam and Ruth had to lose their livelihood and freedom.

But this woman—threats to her safety could ruin it all.

Wycliff kicked at a rock, surely scuffing his meticulously polished boot. "We have an addendum to four."

Lawden pulled out his blunderbuss. "We get to kill them? Now that's—"

"No. I promised my father I wouldn't. He knew I'd be the prime suspect and with prejudices as they are, I'd be lynched again. No, they all will have their downfall."

"Oh." Lawden lowered the gun. "Sorry, my lord."

"Blaren House should be remade for its mistress, too. That requires gaining a wife. Lawden, I need to know everything about the Croomes. Everything, every relation, every business associate, every scandal. I especially want to know what Ruth Croome Wilky has been up to."

There were questions in Lawden's green eyes. "That was your wife?" He snapped to attention as if his question had stepped over a line. "It shall be done, my lord."

"She was, and she needs to be again."

Wycliff patted Lawden on the shoulder then climbed into his carriage. They'd visit another of the Blackamoor brothels tonight. Word in the underground of London had spread of the reward Wycliff offered for Cicely's safe return.

A tip about a girl matching her description had surfaced this morning. His gut said it wasn't her, that this could be a trap, but Wycliff couldn't leave anything to chance. He was determined to save his sister, determined to have his revenge, and now, determined to have Ruth back in his arms again.

Wycliff wouldn't rest until he'd won in every way.

Chapter Ten

To Be Believed

Arriving at Nineteen Fournier, I clutched my sister's arm as we headed out of the carriage. With my broken glasses settled upon my nose, I could see about three feet in front of me. It was good to have my sister guiding me.

I didn't want to work so hard, trying to see things, or fretting about the things I couldn't. Not now. I needed the security of being in the house. Then I'd dwell on my proof, my new cousin.

Bunching up his rich jet cloak to keep it from dragging, I loved the feel of it and the smell caught in the fabric, Bay Rum cologne. The fragrance—tangy, savory, Adam. This was his scent. Tonight, because of Lord Wycliff, I missed him.

I was truly sad for him, the first time in a long time. My lost love wasn't a blackguard as my papa had tried to convince me.

Hearing the baron say Adam had truly loved me, that the false name and the torn registry wasn't for fraud but for fear of my safety—made all the difference.

I passed over the threshold. The light of the entry was

bright. It held me. It welcomed me, and I breathed.

"Are we going to talk about this, Ruth?"

"No." My tone was flat. I didn't want to explain what was going on inside me, how I doubted my memories, my Adam's motives—not tonight.

"That was a hard fall, Ruth. I should send for a physician. Lord Wycliff is not one."

"No."

The sighing sound of Ester muttering to herself didn't sway me. I needed to see my son then fall into bed with this Bay Rum cloak. "Goodnight."

I clasped the stair rails and readied to flee. The second floor looked dark. The fingering of my watch revealed ten. That was the latest I'd been out since eloping.

"Hand me that man's coat, Ruth. Clancy has retired to bed by now."

To give it away, Adam's scent, was giving away the little bit of truth we'd found. "No. I'll keep it for now." I slipped my hands against the fine satin lining. "I'll press it and return it to him on Thursday."

My sister unbuttoned the coat she'd borrowed and laid it in my arms. "We need to talk about your inviting that stranger to come to Mama's party."

"He'll need to come for his cape. I want him here, Ester. He needs to tell Mama the truth about Adam."

My sister frowned big, like she'd spent an evening with finicky Mrs. Carter, not the baron, the only one who could validate my story. Rather fitting for the Croome wild child, a wild witness.

With a hand on her hip, she leaned in close. "Ruth. He's dangerous."

"He's family. Isn't that what Mama's parties are all about? Estranged family and strange friends coming together."

"The man kept staring at you. It wasn't right."

"His eyes work. Is that a problem?"

Ester shook her head, but that was her way of not accepting things that went against what she wanted. "No, Ruth. Lord Wycliff was staring at you. It was too intense. This will lead to disaster."

"Would it be better if he had pity in his eyes, like you, Mama, or Papa look at me?"

"Ruth, that's not what I mean."

"Yes, it is. You want me to accept what you think is best. Listening to all of you, I've accepted everything, even giving in to the notion that my life was lies. Four years is long enough to be tragic, long-suffering Ruth. I want the baron to come, to tell the truth. In exchange, he can stare at me all he wants."

"Your friend, Barrister Marks who you've corresponding with, who asked you to marry him, will be here Thursday."

"Marks is just a friend. We have no formal agreements. Maybe he'll meet my new cousin." I flung my hand like a whip. I might've even chuckled, but I looked forward to seeing Wycliff. He was my proof until I found the other half of the registry.

The front door opened, and Mr. Bexeley, Ester's husband came in. Tall with dark hair and deep-blue eyes and a tan from healthy outdoor exercise, he put his papers on the table and swept my sister up in an embrace. "Good evening, Mrs. Wilky, my dear…Ester."

He released his wife. "Is everything well? Have you two had a disagreement?"

I slipped my broken spectacles into my palm. "Not at all, Mr. Bexeley. Give your wife a big kiss. Thank you for going with me today, Ester."

"Mrs. Wilky, you left the house today? Good for you."

Bexeley was a gentle soul who loved my sister dearly. Ester was his greatest encourager. They were a perfect pair, the Shakespeare lovers. They'd overcome so much to be together.

"Good night." I held my breath and headed into the darkness of the upper level. A breath and a step. A breath and a step. All the way up, but I heard their whispers.

"Bex, we went to Blaren House and met a crazed Lord Wycliff."

"Blaren House. Wait. Mrs. Wilky, Ester, are you two all right? I heard there was a great upset that happened there. It's quite the talk of some of my colleagues."

"Good night, Ester, Bexeley." I gave up breathing and just marched up the steps. By the third floor, I exhaled. I was happy my sister had found love. I was. Every girl needed that feeling just once. May Bexeley and Ester always have that joy.

I tiptoed into the nursery. Josiah was asleep in his crib. My Chris snored in his.

With my free hand, I tucked covers onto his feet. He'd kicked the blanket loose. That was something Adam had done.

I put on my spectacles and looked again at my son.

My son. Chris was getting big. Soon he'd need a big-boy bed. "I love you so. I'm going to be smart for you. I'll secure your future."

I wasn't that young girl with a head filled with promises any longer. I was a woman, a mother. No sweet talk would fill my empty chest. A flamboyant, staring man was the means to restore my name, nothing more.

I kissed my fingertips and touched his sleep-warmed brow. I eased out of the nursery and walked the fifteen paces to my room.

Tossing my broken lenses to the bed table, I shed my coat on the footboard. Then I found matches and lit my lamp. Snuggled in Wycliff's cape, I fell on my bed and wanted to drift to sleep with Bay Rum cologne in my nostrils.

The door to my bedchamber opened. No knock. No

asking.

Ester rushed in. "We need to talk about him."

Shrugging my shoulders, I reached into my box on my table where I kept all my old pairs of spectacles. "I'm rather tired and your husband is home. Shouldn't you be with him?"

Ester shut the door with a *thud*. "He has to read something and make notes for his speech tomorrow."

"Please be quiet. Mama's a light sleeper. The last thing I need is for her to be up here, too."

"That baron was all over you. He looked hungry, like, like—"

"Your friend Lady Hartwell and her lust for chocolate biscuits?" I sat up and laughed a little. "He's Adam's cousin. What do you know? Adam was a real person. Oh, look at that, a living, breathing person. Shouldn't you focus on the truth you heard, not a man looking at me?"

"I'm sorry I didn't believe you. I am so sorry. And I will make it up to you. But Ruth, you didn't see how this Wycliff was looking at you. If I hadn't been there, who knows what he would have done?"

I had been alone with men, the worst kind of men. Wycliff didn't frighten me.

I pulled at the shawl that still wrapped my shoulders and held it out for Ester. "You're exaggerating." I waved my hands like the preacher whose message of damnation became too lively. "You think he will look at me the same when he hears his cousin's deception has labeled me a liar, a harlot, a long-suffering knitter?"

"I will apologize forever, but sister, he's dangerous…and that whip thingy."

"It's a weapon. Ask mama about what our grandfather used on his enslaved people in the Caribbean."

Ester came closer and grabbed my hands. "I'm saying this all wrong. And we've treated you badly."

"I was happier in my cottage in the country. Alone with just a servant and Chris. My eyesight was stronger, and the walls were smaller. No one came crashing into my room to tell me what they needed to say to absolve their guilt."

Ester's lip trembled.

I was being harsh, but years of living under a cloud were hard to shake.

"Ruth, why did you come back? I thought you *wanted* to be with us."

"Mr. McAllister said I'm not going to get better. My field of vision, as he put it, keeps growing smaller. It will become nonexistent. Chris needs more supervision. He needs people who can watch him as he grows. I thought my place was here. It's not."

"We're not ogres. Are we?"

I rose from the mattress, took my sister's arm, and pointed to an empty spot below the bedframe. "Tell me what you see here."

"Nothing. The room is cleaned and dusted."

"You should see bed slippers, Ester."

My sister's brow scrunched up. "Mrs. Fitterwall moved them? She probably put them away so you wouldn't trip."

"I know where I put them. It is specific and purposeful. Now I *will* fall, hunting for them."

"The housekeeper didn't mean anything."

"No one ever means anything. Everyone is trying to decide what is best for me. I need my independence before it's gone. I need my own now. Two years of this is enough."

"Ruth, I know we keep doing the wrong things, but we love you. How do we make things right?"

I sank back on my bed and covered my legs in Wycliff's cape. I recited my list of things I'm grateful for in my head. "I don't know."

Ester bent onto her knees and was soon out of the focus

of the weak lenses. Her blobby image was at the closet door. Then she returned with my puce satin bed slippers. My one frivolity.

She handed them to me and stood. "Everything you've mentioned is understandable, but why bring a man you just met here, near Chris? Why do you trust him?"

Why do I?

Was it a gut instinct?

Or something much simpler and coarse, like the feel of his hands on my face. The rich smell of his cologne.

I wasn't that shallow.

It was Adam. Some of the words this Wycliff used sounded like him. We'd courted for six months, always walking and talking together, his hand in mine, so many soft caresses. The blur of Wycliff could be Adam with a bad, bad cold. That wasn't a bad thing, not when he thought me truthful.

"This makes no sense, Ruth. You're not reckless, not anymore."

"Ester, he believed me at first sight, that I was Adam's wife. He didn't ask for proof."

"He's a man carrying a whip. You're not stupid."

I stayed silent on my bed. I pretended that I was alone and hoped Ester would go. I didn't want words with my sister. I loved her deeply, but my hurt would erupt and burn her like volcano's lava.

"I didn't mean that, Ruth. I want to protect you."

I took off my lenses. My limited sight had made her disappear.

She must've understood, for I heard footsteps moving away.

My door closed. It was a soft push.

I lay back and stared at the nothingness I saw of my ceiling. Ester was right, in a way. Wycliff was dangerous, probably had a bunch of secrets, just like Adam.

I prayed for Cicely to be returned, unharmed, in good spirits and far from any troubles men could bring, including Adam's cousins.

I wrapped myself fully in Wycliff's cape. The sweet scent of it eased the tension in my shoulders. He was my proof. All I needed was for him to come here and explain to Mama and Papa everything he knew of Adam. He needed to brag on Adam so much that I'd forget the dire straits my husband's murder had left me in.

Maybe the baron's testimony would be a good substitute for the complete registry.

No, I'd still be called a liar or a stupid woman.

I needed both halves of the registry.

Wycliff was the key to getting Adam's. I would be nice to him.

I'd convince him of the urgency of locating it. Thursday couldn't come fast enough.

Chapter Eleven

His Morning Blues

Wycliff wasn't a morning person.

Noises coming from downstairs forced one eye open and then the other.

God bless Lawden. Wycliff had left him orders to start the repairs on Blaren House.

That doggone-diligent man must've started.

Putting his hands to his face, he tried to block the sunlight sneaking into his bedchamber from curtains that had been parted an inch. Lawden.

Might as well get up, even if it was to close the curtains.

Lazy bones, as Ruth would say, but it should be Wycliff's reward for doing good. He'd freed a girl from a bawd last night.

It wasn't Cicely, but another young woman in a bad situation. Maybe his sister was indeed off with her friends, still upset that their father had kept silent about Wycliff's impressment into the Navy. He'd been serving a life sentence on the HMS *Liverpool*. Was thinking him dead better than the remote chance of her brother being freed?

Wycliff rubbed his burning eyes. Would that sliver of hope have meant something to Ruth or added to her misery?

Well, a sovereign had bought the fair-skinned prostitute's freedom, and four guineas had given her money to start over. One less exotic fantasy removed from the reach of peers.

The money didn't matter. Wycliff was glad to use his money and all the funds he'd drained from his uncle's accounts. The fool had never changed any of his banking or finance mechanisms. Soulden had been a brilliant, evil genius, creating dummy accounts in Wycliff's father's name. Yet, the duplicity had made it easy for Wycliff to move the money on the old baron's behalf.

Father had been a spy for the Crown during the war with America. Trying to recruit free blacks to side against the rebellion, he'd met and married Wycliff's mother. Working with his father to drain Uncle's fraudulent accounts had given the old spy one last mission. It had been a good two months they'd spent together before he died.

The noises coming from downstairs sounded strange. Now Wycliff had to get up.

He dropped one leg then the other over the side of the once-majestic bed. The solid walnut frame had been painted a ghastly red.

This would all have to be changed. This house needed to be set in a wash basin and scrubbed clean of Soulden's and his cousin Nicholas's awful taste.

Wycliff stretched. Yawns poured out of his weary soul.

Was that a curse coming from downstairs?

Now he hurriedly pulled on breeches, his boots, and a robe, a fine burgundy brocade cloth with gray piping—a final present from his father, welcoming him back to England, making him feel human again.

He picked up his sjambok, tucked it behind his back, then trotted to the massive curved stairs that ended in the center of the wide hall.

His cousin Nicholas Wilkinson and Captain Steward, one of the ship captains who worked for Uncle Soulden, stood in the midst of the marble tiles and piles of Blaren House's gaudy furniture ready to be sold. Lawden waved them toward the door.

His man didn't realize Wycliff had expected them today, just not this early.

"Gentlemen." His voice sounded hoarse and raw. He hated that, almost as much as the putrid yellow paint on the walls and the broken pieces of chair rail moldings of the abused house.

"Adam!" Nicholas waved at him. "I need to talk to you."

"Nickie, you've tracked mud into *my* Blaren House."

"Adam, we must have a word with you alone."

"I'm not in the mood. Come back in a month."

Nickie tapped his dirty boot on the floor. More muck came off. "I won't be in business next month."

Good. Wycliff folded his arms, trying to look as if he wanted to consider the request. "At such an hour, gentlemen? This had better be good. I was quite busy."

Nicholas laughed. "Yes, I heard. Madame Talease has the best girls."

Good. The horrid bed wench comment had worked. "What do you want?"

His cousin stuck out his hand, and Wycliff left it to hang in the air.

Older than Wycliff by three or four years, his cousin looked mostly the same. Same height, same beady, light-blue eyes, same bulbous mole above his lip. New—a swirl of gray strands in his blond hair and a gut not in want of a meal. Living off stolen money must taste sweet.

Situation assessment time. "Lawden, once we are done here, make sure we have a good breakfast this morning.

Something with fresh cream."

"Adam, we are not here for breakfast."

"But I am. It's the only reason to leave bed. Isn't that right, Lawden?"

"Yes, my lord. No oranges, my lord. Will that be a problem?"

That was code for the men had come alone.

"No. Not at all, Lawden. But what of bread? I want bread." This chatter asked if he was armed.

"Only the best bread for you, my lord."

Good. Lawden was armed. The fellow's short blunderbuss was loaded and ready, hidden in his coat.

"Beef steaks, my lord?"

Great. This meant beef steaks for breakfast. The delicious cuts of meat made every meal delicious. Wycliff hadn't gotten enough of them since being back to London.

"Adam," his cousin said. "I do hate interrupting you, but this is important."

"Well, you never cared if I ate before. Why start now, Nickie? What is it you want?"

Nicholas spun his hat, gripping it tightly with fingers that reddened more and more with each rotation. "For days, we've been trying to see you at your father's cottage. You disappeared until you secured a writ of eviction."

"My whereabouts are my own. If Blaren House becoming a gaming hell is an example of your stewardship, I dare not seek your advice."

"That was my income. I needed it to break free of my father. You know how I hate what he does."

"No, I don't. You know Uncle Soulden is horrible, a cheat, a liar, a murderer, but you stay. How many deaths is enough to be your own man?"

The captain nudged Nicholas in the back. "Get to asking him about the money, Wilkinson."

"Yes, right. Adam. Sorry again for the loss of your father."

"I am sure you grieved mightily. Call me Wycliff, Nickie. Respect my title. Captain, let me spare you the family banter. No money. Now both of you—out to the streets. It's breakfast time."

The polite smirk drained from his cousin's face, like corn dripping from a large hole in a sack. "Wycliff...we must seek a truce."

His cousin's hesitation in using the name Wycliff was amusing. Was it a dagger to the heart to say it, a title Nicholas had thought he'd inherit?

The man edged closer, within slugging range. "I'll call you anything you want, if you restore our credit. Seems our coffers have come up empty, and none of the bankers will lend any money. I need to get the captain paid so his ship can be underway.

Captain Steward grunted yes, but his gaze held steady in Wycliff's direction.

It was the confused look some gave him when his hair wasn't meticulously combed so the kinked curls looked straight. Did he need to parse out what he was—negro, white, or other?

The captain should just settle that Wycliff held the power. In the end, that's what mattered.

He eased his grip on his sjambok. "The answer is no. All my funds are for Blaren House. It is in need of so many repairs and better art, but that 'stolen bride' sculpture is growing on me."

"I need money for the pay," the captain said. "The Wilkinsons are bankrupt, a hair away from debtors' prison. They've left me in bad straits."

Dark hair, muscular build, the captain, from all accounts, was an honest man. His flaw, as Lawden had discovered, was excessive drink. Given enough brewed porter, he'd tell you all the secrets he knew. The captain knew a great deal, all the inner workings and business connections of the shippers to the East Indies and the Caribbean.

"You understand what a crew deserves, how they deserve their wages," Wilkinson said. "You served in the Navy."

The gall.

The unmitigated gall to make what was done to him sound noble. Wycliff clicked his tongue. "Wilkinson, Steward, you'll have to find another source to fund your businesses. Maybe you should sell something. Nickie, your son, he's four or five? That's not old enough to be impressed in the Navy. Pity, you miss out on gaining a few bits."

Now Nicholas's pale face was a mix of red and aubergine purple, like a bruised eggplant. Such was the way with very light skin. Wycliff's face could go very pink when warmed with raw rage.

"You know about my son?"

"I hear he's a fine lad. His mother is your longtime mistress, a very handsome woman. A delightful actress and expensive, too. Miss Smith wears some of my mother's jewelry. Do you and Mrs. Wilkinson get a chance to see the lady's performances or are they private, just for you?"

Nickie started sputtering.

Wycliff chuckled. "I suppose that type of family reunion would be odd. Worse than this one."

"How do you know this? You've only been back two months."

"Cousin, I've learned never to waste an evening or good gossip."

Nicholas grimaced, making the lumpy mole near his lip seem larger, like it would burst.

"Ad…Wycliff, I know you and my father have had differences…but this is me. Your cousin, your friend. Remember, I saved your life."

"You didn't. You didn't stop the press gang from selling me to the Navy. What was it you said? Same as dying or worse, serving each day knowing it was a life sentence. I suppose you could have told them to kill me instead. But I had frightened the men enough to forgo that. I could've been freed."

"It wasn't like that. And I couldn't go against my father."

"I remember Uncle and his friends being at the attack that killed my companion, but not at the docks. He left that for you."

His cousin didn't blink at anything except the phrase companion. Wycliff would have to look into that...later. "Golden boy. Go get new credit, sell things—possessions, not people. Just making that clear."

"Lord Wycliff," the captain said. "You're getting us wrong. You can't just leave us high and dry."

"Ad—cousin. This will ruin me. Help your family."

"Did you help my father whilst I was away? Your father helped all his fortune disappear. Uncle Soulden let the creditors have at him, and he had to sell much to keep out of debtors' prison."

Wycliff tapped his nose, the one Soulden had broken in that brutal attack on him and Ruth.

"Very odd for my father to be in that position. He wasn't poor. Makes one wonder who embezzled all his funds?"

"You know...that is terrible. My father should've helped, but you know how they warred. I wonder how you have money. Did you get part of a bounty?"

"Yes, you could say that. With the HMS *Liverpool* retired, everyone is enjoying freedom. Go tell Uncle to enjoy his freedom while he can. He'll get nothing from me."

Lawden moved toward the door and opened it wide. He even made hand motions, waving them to leave.

Nicholas started to go, but the sweating captain caught his arm.

"Just wait. My lord, is there any way to persuade you. Higher terms? I don't want to end up like Nacknel. I won't be stoned by my men."

"Stoned?" Wycliff forced his rough voice to sound surprised. "I heard Nacknel was beaten to death for his gambling. Shame that happened to Uncle Soulden's dearest friend."

His cousin's face turned redder and redder. That mole was destined to explode like gun powder.

Nicholas stepped closer. "Are you behind the rumors, Adam? How did his men know he was out of money?"

From his cousin's shifting stance, Wycliff knew the man was about to attack.

Wycliff wiggled his fingers, readying to wield his sjambok. "Were the rumors about Nacknel not being able to pay true? Sad."

Rubbing his chin, Nicholas looked at the captain then back toward Wycliff. "Everything could be made right if you restored our credit. The bankers say you have plenty of money. A good word from you to back the financing would do it."

"No, Nickie, my darling Nickie. No."

"Cousin. Nacknel was savagely beaten. All our shipping captains face the same fate."

"I remember savage. Nacknel was responsible for my voice." Wycliff pulled at the collar of his nightshirt and exposed the scars, the gnarled skin scabbed over the lacerations from his near lynching. "You think Nacknel's suffering was enough?"

The captain stepped back. His eyes glazed. Perhaps he now understood how bad the blood was between the camps.

Wycliff closed the distance. "Steward, tell all the captains of the shipping lanes to never gamble on payroll. Men protecting their families can be very dangerous. Men with reasons for revenge are deadly."

Eyes darting, as if he could measure the nets closing in upon him, Nicholas shook his fists. "Somehow, you're responsible for this. You were almost a vicar. How could you be so cruel?"

"Even vicars have to overturn tables every now and then. But me responsible? *Hmmm.* I don't think so. But I may have mentioned the rumor to someone. Can't remember who."

Whack. Nicholas punched him, his knuckles connecting to the bone under Wycliff's eye.

When he advanced again, Wycliff tripped him and dumped him onto the marble.

Then he drove his knee deep into the man's chest and lodged his sjambok against the fool's windpipe, crushing and choking.

Lawden blocked the captain from intervening.

"I think this is a fair fight, Nickie. The two of us, not a crowd of hired men. What do you say, Cousin? Can't speak?"

"Get...off." Nicholas kept struggling, swinging his arms.

"You want mercy, Nickie? You want me to think you're my friend? You laughed pretty well knowing I'd have a slow death as a barnacle on a frigate."

"I could've let them just kill you."

"They were too scared of God's wrath and the fear of killing a peer, from all the scriptures of judgement I coughed out. That's why Nacknel did what he did to my throat. To stop me from telling the truth."

Flailing, Nicholas tried to punch at Wycliff, but no one could stop a man who had every right to kill his enemy. Nonetheless, Wycliff promised his father to never use his hands to kill. This show of strength was to prove a point.

Nicholas dropped his palms to the tiles then went still. "Can't...breathe."

"I gave you one hit. Did you feel powerful doing it

yourself? I should let you die now for striking a peer."

Nicholas's motions—the wild swinging of his arms—stopped when Wycliff stiffened his sjambok.

When he felt the fool might pass out, he relented and stood. "Captain, take him out of here."

Gasping, Nicholas wobbled to his feet, wrenching at his neck, rubbing at the marks, ones that would go away. "I couldn't go against my father. Maybe you and I can make a deal. Maybe you and I can partner."

"My blessed mother, she was a poet, you know. Her words stay with me. *A son can slay, a fool can die, a stupid man, not am I.* Thieves have no partners, Nickie, just dupes they've yet to injure."

Pawing at his neck, Nicholas undid his cravat. "Maybe there's something we can give you."

Wycliff's thoughts tossed between Cicely and Ruth, but he kept his face blank. "There's nothing you have except Uncle meeting Nacknel's fate. No extension of credit from any bank until all your debts are paid."

"We'll be ruined. *I'll* be ruined."

"Send your father to jail. Have him rot for his debts. He needs to wake up every day with no hope. That's what you did to me. That was the pain you gave to my father." Wycliff cracked his sjambok. It made a thunderous echo in the bare hall. "Be gone."

"The money he and Johnson took—it's gone. There's nothing to return."

The captain dragged his cousin toward the door. "Let's go. Your father will find a way. He always does."

The fearful look on Nicholas's face, with that mole bulging, foretold that he didn't think Uncle Soulden could get out of the trap that had been sprung. Or that Soulden's way out would be bloody.

"Wycliff, I know of something you want."

Twiddling his fingers, Wycliff waited. "Make it good. I love a good rumor."

"I don't know if it's true—"

"Nickie, don't waste my time. You have nothing. I don't follow fools' leads. Use this opportunity to be your own man. Start over. Conduct your business ethically. You'll sleep better. You'll be an example for that son you keep in the shadows."

"You said you could reason with him." The captain slugged Nicholas's shoulder. "I'll not be beaten out on the docks, like Nacknel. You're on your own, Wilkinson."

His cousin chased after the captain but stopped at the entry. "Don't touch my son. He's a good boy. He needs to grow up and be better than us."

True.

Wycliff would never hurt an innocent person, especially a child, but he needed his cousin to think him dangerous and a match to their cruelty. "Then don't force my hand, Nickie. Send Uncle my greetings. Shut the door on him, Lawden."

Wycliff waited for the door to be barred then started toward his study. He touched his stinging face, right under the eye socket. "Well, that's a new way to start the day, Lawden, dispensing enemies."

"It's dispatching enemies, my lord. You've won. Wilkinson seems a broken man."

"Dispensing as in advice, Lawden. A wounded dog still has teeth."

"Did your mother really make that poem?"

"No. But it sounded bold, didn't it? She was a much better poet, but she did warn about dogs and teeth." Wycliff slipped his sjambok through his palm. It wasn't done striking out. He could feel it.

"The good news is they don't have Cicely, for Nickie would have said so for leverage. The bad news is that Nickie might be aware of Mrs. Wilky but isn't sure."

"You know that face of yours is going have a bruise when you go courting your wife."

Lawden was right. Wycliff had more to be concerned about. He had to make sure that Nickie never located Ruth. She must never be at risk. That meant Wycliff would have to ensure his Thursday visit with Ruth wasn't his last.

Chapter Twelve

A Garden Party Dilemma

I looked out Papa's office window at the courtyard behind Nineteen Fournier. The little stretch of clipped grasses and yellow aconite flowers waved in the breeze dancing in front of the thick hedges. A lovely spring garden. Mama surely knew how to make any place special.

My eyes hurt from straining. I tugged off my spectacles and put them upon the desk.

I jiggled open Papa's top drawer. That's where he kept his folding knives. He'd had many made after his brother's death. I liked the pearl-handled one the best. I slipped it into my pocket and closed the drawer. A little protection for outside couldn't hurt.

If I talked myself into being brave, surely I could walk outside, but the yard was different than the pavement out front. Most thought the garden safer, with its delicate twirling petals.

Not to me.

It seemed like a clearing in the woods, and I found myself looking for a way to escape. It was completely nonsensical, but that didn't stop my pulse from pounding.

Gripping my hands together, I felt my palms slipping against my thin satin gloves. Mama and Ester thought me so proper. They didn't understand how I needed the fabric to wick away my perspiration. The gloves hid my fears very well.

I fingered my watch on my chain. It was at least fifteen after two.

Where was Mr. Marks?

If he were here, I could walk with him into Mama's garden.

Putting on my spectacles, I peeked through the window. Nothing of the barrister or anything I imagined Adam's cousin to look like. No clear look at him, but I hoped he was like Adam. A small bit of me wanted him to share Adam's nose or his eyes.

Adam.

I'd dreamed of him last night.

He was alive, making me laugh, singing to me and Chris. In my dream, he liked my son. He loved him. Once my boy was in bed, Adam returned to me, walking with that swagger. With my eyes closed, I kissed him. It was everything, everything I wanted and missed. Then I awoke alone, lying on Wycliff's cape.

Ester poked her head into the room. "You can't hide in here. The party is in your honor."

"Mine?"

"Yes, Mama thought this might help nudge you along with Mr. Marks—an excuse to wear a pretty dress and have a suitor about. That's what I overheard her saying to Mrs. Fitterwall."

"A party for me. I suppose I can't watch from the window."

My sister came into the room. She looked like spring in her muslin dress of saffron yellow with India ink-printed jasmine flowers. A wide straw-brimmed bonnet, rimmed in matching grosgrain ribbon, shadowed her lovely olive face and the strand of pearls Mr. Bexeley had given her for her birthday. She looked so elegant and was so loved by her husband.

"Take my hand, Ruth. Come with me. You bolstered yourself and went to Blaren House. You can take a few paces outside into the garden."

I twiddled my spectacles and searched for reasons to delay. A headache, a coming storm. Nothing that would stop a pushy, well-meaning sister. "There are known dragons out there, Ester."

"There are people who will protect you, too. I'm here."

I smiled at Ester and prayed my expression mirrored hope and happiness, not the anxiety of waiting for Wycliff.

"Barrister Marks will be here soon," I said. "He's big and tall and can fight all the ghosts I let play in my imagination. With him, I'll venture out."

"Nothing is going to hurt you, sis." She extended her hands toward me. "I won't let them."

Clasping that open palm seemed too far to stretch. It required too much strength, strength I was saving for Mr. Marks, for our couple's walkabout. I didn't know if I could go into the garden twice. "Mr. Marks will be here soon."

Ester lowered her hand. It hit the desk with a bang. "I don't mean to push, but I don't know how to help. I want you to trust me again. I want to know how to fix us."

Didn't she mean fix me, her crazy sister?

No one could.

Not the physicians, not the crazy elixirs which made my eyes whirl.

Not Papa's brandy swirled in tea.

Not even the suggested dover pills—opium. Thank goodness, Mama had said no to that.

Nothing stopped the tremors once they started. The

terror rattled everything in my mind, my body. It curled an invisible hand about my mouth, dragging me backward as it squashed my screams. Even as I tried to resist, it raped my soul. It kept stealing me, those bits of my spirit that made me strong and funny and fearless.

I wiped my damp gloves along my cheeks. I was getting worked up. My composure was slipping, and I wasn't even out of the house.

"I'm here, Ruth. I won't let anything happen to you." She put her arms about me, and I held on to her.

I am grateful for her, for my family, for clothes, food, and my Chris.

Her strength filled me. I took Ester's hand. "A few minutes in the warm sun with my beautiful, pushy sister should happen. Let's go."

Good. I sounded normal, not confused or scared. Good.

Ester steadied me and led me out into the hall. "Will you introduce the baron to Mr. Marks? How do you think he'll like your cousin?"

Tightness clenched my stomach again. I couldn't tell if this was defensiveness or Wycliff or that back door coming at me. "He should like him just fine. You should, too."

"He's not my cousin."

I looped my arm tighter about Ester's. "Marks and Wycliff are both handsome men, are they not?"

Ester didn't respond. That meant Wycliff was good-looking. Nothing was wrong with having a handsome cousin, was it?

I lifted my head as we came to the threshold. I couldn't press my sister for her thoughts on Wycliff, not with the whitewashed doorframe beckoning me. I glared at the plaster-cast acanthus leaves on each side of the entry. They taunted me. *Safe inside, danger outside.*

"No need to answer, my fretting sister." I forced a laugh.

"I've my spectacles. I'll be able to fully examine Wycliff, head to toe."

"In front of your friend, Mr. Marks? Ruth, you can't do that."

"Can't do what in front of me?" John Marks, the tall barrister, tall like Papa, stood near. My suitor, an answer from a newspaper advertisement—rumpled chestnut hair matching a wrinkled coat and cravat, soulful brown eyes with crusts of sleep in each—had arrived. Had he slept in his office again? The man worked so hard.

He reached for my hand and took me away from Ester.

"You came directly from work, didn't you, sir?"

His steady eyes widened. "Yes. My latest trial is very taxing, but I said I'd be here this time. Perhaps showing you I'm a man of my word will induce you to accept my offer. I want to marry you, Mrs. Wilky."

"I need more time. My parents need to see you more."

"Then let's go to them." He had a strong hold on my hand, not threatening, but not slack.

The next I knew, he'd whisked me through the door.

The motion was fast.

The change in light from dim to blindingly bright made my head spin.

My chest pounded.

My bosom sounded hollow.

I hooked my arm tighter about his.

That made him smile down at me with his big blue eyes.

My practiced smile. Was it still there?

"Mrs. Wilky, I daresay you are getting more used to me." He slid my palm, my clutched palm, down and took my hand in his. "Your parents are about. We shouldn't look so forward."

I nodded. I might even have agreed out loud. We walked a little farther. Mr. Marks on one side. My terror on the right.

Ester was close behind us. Bonnet on, short ivory gloves, but she was there.

I smiled.

I breathed a little easier. Croome girls might have words, but we made sure we each were safe. I loved that frustrating bonbon.

Blinking, I forced my eyes to John Marks. He could be my future, Chris's and my future. The sooner I learned how to feel secure with him, the better things would go.

Marks took his time guiding me about the garden, chatting with this one and that, complimenting Mama on the food, Clancy on the manicure of the hedges.

Yet my terror stayed on my right side, the side with my scar, the worst part of my vision. The trees, the flowering hedges in the distance didn't seem so scary, but I did keep looking back to the house.

My barrister was personable and chatty, even with the knitting women.

Mrs. Daly could find no fault in his diction. She may have even smiled back at him.

I paid attention as much as I could, but I felt my gaze drifting, hunting through the crowd for the shortest path back to the house. My lenses weren't as strong as the ones I'd broken at Blaren House, but anything was better than seeing a few inches from my nose when I was out where things could get at me.

We crossed Mama's path again.

Her ice-blue gown with ruffs of Brabant lace about the hem made her seem beautiful and serene. She didn't smile as much at Marks as she did at Ester's husband. I didn't know why.

"Mr. Marks," she said, "you must have a slice of my cake. Did Ruth tell you that she loves baking? She's a good baker, too."

I looked up, and Mr. Marks had that pout on his face, the beg-off frown.

"Mrs. Croome, this is a lovely party, but I'll have to wait on the dessert. I have to leave. I have to meet with my solicitor. New evidence has been discovered for an upcoming trial."

Mama's prim expression stayed perfect, and sweet, not an ounce of disappointment exuded.

But I knew how she liked people eating her cake.

I was torn, because if Mr. Marks left, he would have to take me back to the house, but Mama worked hard for her parties.

"You're never able to stay." Mama's tone gave her away. "One wonders what kind of life my daughter will have if her husband works all the time."

The tone sounded delicate, but the words weren't.

A stranger would think it was just a mother offering a slight critique. This was Horatia Croome's shot over the bow. Croome women might fight, kick, and scream, but they had one another's best interest at heart.

For the first time in a long time, I was proud to be a Croome.

"Mr. Marks," Mama said, "at least go say your good-byes to Mr. Croome. He's over in the shade with my grandbabies, Josiah and Ruth's son, Christopher."

"Yes, Mrs. Croome." He released my hand and left me.

I focused on Mama, not the distance back to the house, which was now at least thirty paces.

I folded my arms, clutching my long sleeve, my elbows, and tried to breathe.

"Ruth, you hear me. You're fine. Don't embarrass yourself. You're good."

That was Mama's encouragement, raw and gutting like a slap.

But it was enough to make me hide deeper into myself.

My terror stayed with me. My skin felt clammy. My palms wet through my gloves. But my posture was perfect, and this Croome girl held her chin high.

Something touched my hand.

I looked up and saw Mr. Marks. He took my arm and escorted me back into the house.

Crossing the threshold made me happy. It didn't matter what he said. I giggled at being led inside.

"Ruth?" He cleared his throat. "I'm sorry. I have to head to the Lincoln's Inn. There's always so much work. You do understand?"

"Of course I do."

He kissed my forehead. "That's why we'll be great together. You feel my drive for justice. You know how much my clients need me."

My joy faded. Disappointment took its spot. It hit me that he was leaving. "I understand that you do what you must."

The look on his face didn't seem encouraged. His smile was a little lawyerly. Had he become like a judge who'd heard false testimony?

His lips thinned, and he leaned down close to my ear. "I know that you wanted me here longer. I came this time, but I've work to do. Work now, then my schedule should be clear next week for a drive in Hyde Park. I'll be fully available for any little outing or ritual you have in mind."

Rituals?

I'd been open about my fears, my panics in the letters we'd exchanged. Was all of this a ritual? Were gatherings with my family rituals? "Next week, Mr. Marks. If your schedule holds, that's something to look forward to."

"Mrs. Wilky…Ruth, don't be like this. I'll make it up to you." He fumbled with the silver pocket watch Mama had given him as a Christmas present when she'd thought my accepting his offer was imminent. "A drive in the park next week will be wonderful. You'll have my undivided attention."

A closed carriage would be wonderful. "Tea here would be nice, too."

"Ruth, I'll make this up to you."

I wouldn't beg him to stay. I'd begged enough for a lifetime. I was safe in the house, where I needed to be. Ours was an honorable arrangement, a platonic one.

No overthinking things.

No expecting more or giving more.

I pinned on that practiced smile again, one Mama would be proud of. "You go and prepare and win that trial for me. I'm inspired by your dedication."

He kissed my cheek. "Next week, Mrs. Wilky."

The man hummed and bounced his way to Clancy at the entry.

Should I follow and watch him don his hat and coat and wave as if I were pleased?

I didn't have it in me today. Instead, I turned and went to the threshold and looked out at the garden party.

A hand wrapped along my arm. "Ruth."

Ester's friend, Mrs. Fitzwilliam-Cecil hugged me. With her arm wrapped about my waist, I was ushered outside to where Ester and her other confidante, Lady Hartwell, stood.

Mrs. Fitzwilliam-Cecil was a vision in sage, the viscountess one in light burgundy. Ester slipped to the other side of me as if to block my escape.

Breathe, Ruth. Shut up. Take this. Smile.

"We are so excited for you." Lady Hartwell was gleeful, her bisque bonnet set like a tiara on her auburn curls. Her baby bump was starting to show.

"I'm glad you all could make it," I said. "You just missed Barrister Marks. He couldn't stay. A trial needed him."

Mrs. Fitzwilliam-Cecil beamed. "Men and their work. My husband is working on his latest play, and his brother,

Lord Hartwell, is helping him keep track of all the children."

"He's so happy with lots of children." Lady Hartwell held a plate of sweets, a pile of chocolate-dipped biscuits. "Mrs. Wilky, I saw Mr. Marks leave. He's been paying you a lot of attention. Will you be our fourth successful bride by newspaper advertisements?"

I shrugged. "It's still early in our courting."

"It's been since November," Mrs. Fitzwilliam-Cecil said.

Lady Hartwell wiped her mouth of bonbon crumbs. "She's taking her time. More time for your mother to help with my situation." She patted her tummy. "The Fitzwilliam family will probably have her move in with us the month of my lying-in. Someone will have to keep my husband calm."

Clancy offered a sparkling tray of lemonade to the ladies. I abstained but tried to pay attention to these kind women. Their friendships with my sister were long and deep, their lives perfect and settled. I just wanted to go back to the house.

The wind rustled in the distant bushes, louder than their easy chatter. I was alone, even with these women. Sometimes it felt as if I were on Gracechurch Street looking through the shop glass, knowing Croome fabric was sold inside but I wasn't welcome.

Stop it, Ruth. Let's turn over a table. Launch into a drinking song, one Adam and I had heard at the docks. Wild, unpredictable me had been silenced too long. "Ladies, I'm grateful my sister has such good friends, and you each make things better for others. Mrs. Fitzwilliam-Cecil and the flower-shop girls. Lady Hartwell with her women's hospital."

They clinked their glasses.

"Ester, will you return to reading Shakespeare at Lady Hartwell's charity in the summer?"

"Yes, Sis." *Tinkle. Tinkle. Tinkle.* They tapped their goblets again.

Air went in and out of my empty chest more easily. I felt

my confidence rise, sans a drunkard's tune. "Lady Hartwell, if a young mulatto woman was on the streets, would she be welcome at your charity?"

"She could be, if there's an opening at Magdalen House." Lady Hartwell stepped closer. "Mrs. Wilky, is there someone you're looking for?"

"Yes, my late husband's sister is missing."

A brow raised on the pretty woman's face. Doubt shadowed her hazel eyes. "A sister missing? How could that be?"

Confused at the response, I squinted at her, even tweaked my spectacles. "My late husband's sister, she's a young mulatto girl. She's missing."

Ester elbowed Lady Hartwell.

Then I realized that this council of friends was the same as Mama's. They'd been told the lies. All the things I'd endured, all the things I'd suffered, were fiction to them. These women needed actual proof, too.

This was worse than staring through heavy shop glass.

My sister had betrayed me.

These were nice women, but nice women believed I was a liar.

My chest felt hollow, more than empty. I searched for the house. I didn't even have it in me to fake a smile and beg off properly.

Ester stepped into my path. "Ruth, these are my friends. We share everything. I told them what Mama said."

I took off my spectacles, burying them in my palm. I couldn't look at her. "I surrender to your truth. I'm going to shut up and take what you think I deserve."

Lady Hartwell put a hand on my shoulder, and I startled.

"Mrs. Wilky," she said, "what does this missing girl look like? Please tell me. I'll look for her."

"I knew what she looked like four years ago—light-colored skin, about my height, thin, thin like Adam, but she may have changed. It's hard to shake, tapeworm thin, but don't do me any favors."

I tried to move away, but Lady Hartwell held my shoulder. "What's her name, Mrs. Wilky, so if I see her, I can let you know."

"Cicely Wilkinson," I said the name low, like a secret.

"I'll search for her," Lady Hartwell said. "The streets are dangerous for a lost girl."

"Thank you, ma'am. You almost sound as if you believe me."

I found the blur that had to be the house and ran. Impulsive, not cultured, I fled. *Slap, slap* went my slippers through the grass. When I slammed on my glasses, the house was ten or twelve paces.

Ester caught up to me. "Ruth. Ruth, please stop."

Clasping the doorframe, I took a deep breath. "Go back to your friends. You respect them."

Plunging deeper into the house, I went to Papa's study. Collapsing into his chair, I flopped my head on the desk blotter.

I stayed there, like that, until a handkerchief mopped at my face.

It smelled of wild bay leaves. That was Bay Rum cologne.

Sitting upright, I took the cloth and dabbed at my tears.

"A farthing for your thoughts."

The gruff voice sent tingles to my skin. I should be afraid to be secluded in my father's tiny office with a stranger, but somehow the baron didn't seem that strange. Not today.

I took a good look at him. Lord Wycliff was tall, tall like Adam. Well-built with low, dark-brown, almost black hair. And a beard. No, he wasn't like Adam at all.

Under his right eye, the space of exposed skin not covered in manicured fur were bruises, big black marks that made his eyes seem blacker.

They weren't alike. Adam wasn't stupid enough to be hit.

I sighed and wiped my face. "My thoughts cost more than that. Struggling for funds?"

He sat on the desk beside me. His low chuckle vibrated upon my neck. "Why are you in the house and not enjoying your party? My absence driving you to tears?"

He was very close, too close, but comfort exuded in the shadow he cast. I remembered that I didn't have to convince him of anything. He'd believed in Adam and me, even before I'd showed my half of the registry. "Tears of joy, perhaps?"

The baron put a hand on my shoulder. "You, Ruth Wilky, are certainly worth more than a farthing. I always start negotiations on the cheap, then escalate. My father taught me finances."

Hadn't Adam said things like that? I stiffened and moved out of the chair. "You're late."

His hands dropped to the desk. "But I haven't been crying. Who wants to explain first?"

I sniffled. "Why do you care?"

"Do you expect me not to? Am I not to wonder why a beautiful woman has no joy at her party?"

"It's my party. Can't I cry if I want? Don't I get to choose?"

"Mrs. Wilky, you're on the brink of a nasty sob. Do you miss me that much?"

"Stop making fun because I have emotions."

"Never. Your feelings, your tears, all are an expression of your passion." His voice was softer, if a guttural baritone could be soft.

"Then I am the most passionate woman you've ever met."

"I hope so. Adam would say, except for his mother, you're the strongest woman he knew. She expressed her feelings in poems."

My chest rattled. Tears threatened again, because I knew

how Adam loved his mother and her lovely poems, her *death* poems. "You don't even know me, and you believe everything Adam said about me."

Lord Wycliff came near. "Adam and I were of one mind. He had great taste in women."

I was cornered, with bookcases at my back and a baron with bear fur coming closer. My spirit was not to be caged, not by him or any. I was inside the house. I was strong. I pointed my finger at him. "You are too forward. You flirt too much. Stop. I said no. Back away."

With a half step back, he bowed in place. "Mrs. Wilky. You're a queen, a queen that should be honored and admired. What is it that you want?"

I looked into his eyes, eyes that could almost be Adam's. "A friend, not a suitor, no lusty anything. I need a friend."

His gaze was intense. His mouth pressed to a line, then a grin, then a brilliant smile. Who knew bears could smile like that?

"Then you shall have a friend, Mrs. Wilky."

The baron retreated and sat on my father's desk.

I didn't believe him. I said *no* and a man listened? I crossed my arms. "It's that simple? I ask one thing and you behave?"

"Yes, Mrs. Wilky. It's that simple."

I adjusted my spectacles and studied this unpredictable man, bear fur and all. "I should go get your cape. I have it upstairs."

"Keep it for now. Show me this house, instead. It's an unexpected jewel."

"Yes, people in Mayfair don't think people like us can have such nice residences."

"Well, this isn't Mayfair. It's not even Cheapside, but it's quite nice."

I felt my brow creasing, not sure if this was condescension

of a peer or the poor expectation that some Blackamoors lived this well. "My parents worked very hard."

Wycliff moved to Papa's other bookcase, poking about. "A few books by Shakespeare. You should have a few more classics. The old poets. Homer is a treasure."

He turned around. High collar, crisply pressed cravat, indigo waistcoat with gold threading on the buttonholes with an ebony tailcoat to finish his polished look. Very nice, very formal.

I looked at him inspecting the bookcase, and I decided he was handsome, despite the bruises, despite the fur. A closer glance and I saw what I didn't want to. Wycliff could be Adam's twin. "Adam should have told me he had a cousin that looked so much like him."

"Do we favor? Lucky me. Do you mind my looking so much like your husband, handsome and strong?"

My mouth might've dropped open. If I didn't need the baron to convince everyone of Adam's existence, I'd have sent him away. It wasn't good having a reminder of the joy I'd once possessed.

"Mrs. Wilky, from what I've seen, this is quite grand. The pond with the birdbath has my interest."

To know of Mama's pond, he must've been here for a while. "How long have you been at Nineteen Fournier?"

"Longer than a few minutes. Long enough to watch your barrister leave and hear women make snide remarks. Maybe too long."

A little stunned at his honesty, I rubbed my temples. "Sounds long enough to me."

"I've waited patiently for a moment of your time, but if my enthusiasm and admiration make you upset, I'll leave right now. You have power over me, Mrs. Wilky. What will you do with me?"

I should have told him to leave, to allow me a moment to

regain my composure, but something inside was too afraid I'd never see him again, the one person in the world who believed me. "Don't go."

He came to me. I watched his swagger with his silent steps. He held out his arm. "Show me this world of yours, Mrs. Wilky. Your friend wants to meet your parents and see where you live."

His thick arm, well-muscled, pinned my arm to his side. We fell in step, a perfect rhythm, with him guiding me until we reached the doorway to the garden.

I couldn't go out there again. I'd had enough the last time.

"Take off your glasses, Mrs. Wilky. Maybe people won't upset you if you don't see them."

"That would mean trusting you completely. I don't know about that."

"Trust me, Mrs. Wilky. I'm a good fellow. I'm your friend. I won't let anything happen to you."

Slipping my spectacles from my ears, I handed them to him.

I heard the rustle of his jacket as he slid them into his pocket, then felt the gentle tug as he led me into the warm sun. We walked into the garden. I wondered how people would react to Adam's cousin, but a part of me didn't care.

I had a friend, someone who believed me.

Chapter Thirteen

THE OBSERVANT COUSIN

Wycliff walked with Ruth into the Croomes' garden.

He thought better of heading straight to the crowded center of the party, but staying close to the house on the stone patio or sitting at the small tables didn't offer the privacy he wanted. Instead, he steered Ruth to the cobblestone path that edged the garden.

With each step, her nails sank deeper into his jacket. If she became more agitated, she'd push her fingers through his sleeve. That would be a waste of good tailoring.

He stopped as a guest crossed in front of them. Ruth was poised as she introduced him to one person after the other. She could tell who they were without her glasses.

Then why doesn't she recognize me?

Perhaps he wasn't giving the observant woman enough clues to his identity. He'd have to do better. Ruth needed to figure out who he was. Wycliff couldn't risk triggering one of the fits her physicians had described. Lawden's report on Ruth was heartbreaking and as shocking as the information on the rest of the Croome family and friends.

He tapped his boot and swayed to the enticing rhythm of the fiddler playing near the refreshment table. Wycliff made note of what Lawden had described in his briefing. The Croomes had a controlled lawn that could be observed only by the townhome to the right. The only entrance to the garden was through the Croome house. This place was safe.

Nodding to another guest, he and Ruth started moving. The cobblestone path that circled the grass like a border to an imported silk rug seemed smooth enough for her slippers.

He'd heard of the hidden gardens of Spitalfields but had never seen one. This unexpected oasis of manicured hedges, a sweet stone bench overlooking a glass mosaic birdbath, and a fishpond delighted him.

But did this delight Ruth?

Were these her tastes or her parents'? If it was hers, he'd match it at Blaren House.

He patted her arm and stopped thinking of the future he wanted—her with him in Mayfair, them loving each other again. He'd enjoy this garden today and pay attention to his friend, and protect her from everything fretting that brow.

"This is lovely, Mrs. Wilky."

Her eyes were shut tight. Her deep-honey complexion had drops of dew along her forehead. It wasn't raining, but was his love caught in a storm?

He sensed her fear, could hear the rapid changes in her breathing. The echo of throaty hitches stuttered through him.

The panicked fits—was this one?

"You're suffering in silence, Mrs. Wilky. Not good."

"Habit." She brushed at the curls falling to her face. "Ignore me and keep walking."

"Can't ignore you. Impossible."

Ruth wasn't the same, not the woman he'd married four years ago. He should blacken his other eye for thinking she would be.

Physically, she was the same beauty. Her eyesight was terrible. He'd been close to her face, close enough to kiss that fetching nose—a little wide, a little pointed at the peak, perfect nose.

She no longer had a sense of peace. Wycliff saw glimpses of her spirit and quick wit, but he suspected those moments were few.

Tease her.

He'd tease her to set her at ease. "I'm not a fan of ignoring a beautiful woman. Instead, convince me to be at your beck and call."

"Make nice with my parents, and then you need not see me again."

"That was harsh, Mrs. Wilky. Can't you show your cousin some care?"

"I'm not used to my cousin showing up and having a bruised eye like a ruffian."

"We make sacrifices."

Good, feisty girl. His Ruth was in there, trapped behind those long lashes and far too many clothes. "I apologize for being late."

"Business or personal? Something about Cicely?"

Her voice sounded rushed. *Let it be concern for me. See me, Ruth.*

But her blank countenance disclosed nothing.

"Both," he said, "but nothing of Cicely, not yet."

She nodded and stepped closer. It was intimate, her being next to him. And she smelled like fresh roses.

Being a good cousin was going to be hard. Remembering that she didn't love him or even care for him as he did her would probably kill him, again. "I was late, and I try never to be such, but I made a stop to John McAllister & Son. I have new spectacles being made for you."

"Nosy." Her steps slowed to nothing. "What did he tell

you?"

Those nails of hers dug deeper into his arm.

People buzzed all about. This didn't feel like the place to say anything that could be overheard. "Walk a little more. Let's go to the end of your wilderness. Then abuse me."

"No. No. I don't want to be near the trees."

"Then we'll make another circle. I like walking with you."

"Just like Adam. Fine. Then tell me what you discovered."

He remained silent until they moved farther from the sea of prying ears—fashionable men and women in sleek top hats and waves of bonnets hosting every color of ribbon.

"The chatter has lessened, Wycliff. Tell me your nosy news."

She didn't ask how he'd found the doctor—Lawden. Or how he'd found time to visit the busy establishment—Lawden. Merely what Wycliff knew of her condition—interesting.

"McAllister's assistant said your sight—"

"Field of vision." Ruth glanced up, wide blank eyes, tension set in her jaw. "That is the new fancy term they use."

Feisty.

That was a smidgeon of old Ruth, and she'd always hated him being nosy. He cleared his throat. "Yes, your field of vision has steadily diminished these past three years."

"Did he use words like blindness or fits? If you are going to mind my business, get all the details."

"Yes. He talked of panics and being disoriented."

Her head moved from side to side, as if she were looking at their peaceful surroundings, but he knew she saw nothing but sunlight and blurs. "Never disoriented. I know where I am when I pay attention. Take me back to the house, Lord Wycliff."

"As you wish, but I'd rather stare at you in the sunlight."

"You can do that in the house. I'll be more comfortable."

He glanced at her. Pretty, upturned button nose, heart-shaped face. So lovely. "But I like the way you look in the sun."

A hint of a blush warmed her cheeks. "You are a flirt, my lord, but I'm not. I'm a mother. My head is not easily changed."

"I don't want you to change."

He couldn't help himself and pushed back that errant tendril that fell upon her scar. The long dark mark made by that foul trunk was vicious, so deep. "I like you as you are."

Her lip trembled. "Let's walk some more."

He led her past the refreshment table. On the other side was a big, tall, solid-looking man. His skin was polished jet. He balanced a young boy on his lap and a babe in his arms.

That was Mr. Croome and both children, his grandchildren—either could be Christopher. But only the older boy could possibly be Wycliff's son. A newborn couldn't be the seed of a man dead four years.

He wanted to stare at the older lad, to look for hints of his mother or father in the young scamp's gold complexion, but he couldn't. He wasn't ready to meet Mr. Croome or Christopher, not until he made Ruth comfortable.

She clutched at his arm. Again, her nails pinched through his jacket. "Are you done staring at the food? Do you need a plate? Mama's party fare is quite nice."

Ruth knew where they walked. Good she was aware of her location. He pried at her thumb. "The biscuits and cakes look quite good, but your grip has me thinking I'll forego eating for now."

"Tell me what else the McAllister's tattlers said? What have they hidden from me?"

"Hidden? Mrs. Wilky, your fingernails are sharp. That's not a sculpture beneath the wool. It's a true arm, flesh and blood."

She let go. "What did they say? How long did they give me

before I'm blind? They may have given you a direct answer. They don't say everything sometimes to Blackamoors."

It was humorous and tragic how she didn't know him and how she assumed his race. *Ruth, we are the same.*

He pressed her palm flat on his arm, pumping his forearm to prepare for more abuse. "The physician was unclear. He said it could degenerate in a year or remain as it is forever."

"Oh. That's the same as what they told me."

There was an air of disappointment in her voice. It reminded him of waiting for word from his father on the HMS *Liverpool*, waiting every day for Captain Collier to come to him and say Wycliff was freed.

"Take me back to the house, my lord. I'm done out here."

"We have quite an audience watching us. Going back now will seem as if we've had words. That's not a good cousin or the makings of a character witness. I'm your proof, remember."

She bit her lip.

Her mouth was still the same, a magnificent wonder of taupey-pink flesh in desperate need of exploration.

Soon. Very soon. Then he'd know if he had a chance of winning her from the barrister.

He steadied Ruth, weaving his fingers with hers. "Just a little longer, Mrs. Wilky. I haven't visited with your parents. Trust me."

"Then take me closer to the house. I want to feel its shadow. Then we'll get you to my parents."

"As you wish, Mrs. Wilky."

"See, my lord. You are good at being at my beck and call."

He couldn't stop his laughter, nor could he miss the number of people watching them.

He bent his head close to her ear but became distracted by the scent of roses clinging to her long neck. "There is a group of women looking this way."

"Old or young?"

"Young. They're smiling. Must like what they see. I do."

"You're a bad flirt with terrible *sight* jokes."

"I'm a terrible flirt, and I've been known to be punny. It covers my discomfort. My voice is grating, but I'd never joke about your sight. I'm like you. I don't trust easily, either. My guard is a thick shield."

She pivoted and crashed into him.

He held her for a moment, nothing more than a few seconds to keep her from falling. Heaven was in that blink of time. "Cousin, we have to stop these unplanned caresses… while people are watching."

Ruth shook her head. They walked on.

He steered her to the little area within a square of hedges, close to the house but private. He stopped at the stone bench he'd spied earlier. "How about we sit? Perhaps, if we are still, a dove might land on your birdbath."

"Yes, to sitting, but I fear the party is too noisy for birds. You didn't say why you trust me."

He waited for her to sit, tucking her slippers beneath the hem of her beige gown. This dress was billowy and beige. The sleeves were long, almost balloons. So not Ruth, the color part or the style. She had been stylish, bold with gowns that had shown her fine figure.

It was almost as if she tried to hide. How do you hide a sun?

Smoothing his waistcoat, he plopped down beside her. "It's quite simple. Adam trusted you with his life. He was a great judge of character. Thus, I trust you."

Her cheeks warmed. A bronzy tint kissed her deeply honeyed skin. "It's that simple for you?"

"Yes, that simple. Adam was a great reference."

She relaxed more, but her posture remained straight and composed. Good baroness stock.

But he wasn't composed, not on the inside.

His arms wanted to be about Ruth again. The feel of her, the scent of her—all was a torture for a man who was desperate for her. He forced his gaze to the birdbath and the deep pond in which it stood. The water was a little cloudy with slick water lilies floating on top. White dead nettles plants rimmed the pond with large shells, seashells. A few of the white heart-shaped petals stirred into the emerald broth. In the middle was a fragile-looking pedestal that supported a large bowl. The birdbath was formed from small indigo blue tiles.

"This is lovely, Mrs. Wilky. It's peaceful here."

"What peace? The party is quite loud. I still want to be in the house." She lifted her palm. "May I have my lenses."

"Only if you promise to hand them back if things overwhelm you."

"What?"

"You were at Blaren House in the company of a stranger. You were poised and calm, especially after my lousy greeting."

"I'm an expert at adapting. Ask my family."

He reached in his pocket and produced her spectacles. "You've learned to survive. There's strength in that."

She slid them on and looked over her shoulder. "I do like it here. This is close to the house. I watch my son gather rocks. We skip them across the pond."

"How will you handle new places when I escort you out?"

She scooted away from him. "I'm not going anywhere with you."

"I need my cousin's help. Blaren House will be completely redone, rejuvenated from top to bottom. I'd like your opinion on everything. Adam said you had great style and a way with color."

"Stop. I only need you here to convince everyone of Adam's existence. I'm not looking for anything more. I don't need you gaining ideas."

This courtship was becoming trickier by the second. She'd talked of wanting a friend, but now she retreated. Women and consistency, was this a fleeting notion?

Go slow, Wycliff, he told himself. He was in love with Ruth. She tolerated him for her own goals. Such were the inequities of his life, but rather shrewd on her part. "Fine. But may I ask your opinion on things upon occasion? Would you help me out a little, dear cousin?"

Ruth nodded but her focus was upon the pond. Perhaps she loved the stone birdbath. He could install one at Blaren House for her.

Rubbing her temples, she removed her spectacles, laying them between them on the bench. She stretched and picked up a rock from a small pile by the foot of the bench. A smooth, black basalt stone was in her palm. She skipped it across to the other side.

Her aim was perfect, a straight line close to the birdbath. She didn't strike the pedestal.

"Nice aim or beginner's luck?"

"Shall I do it again?"

"Yes, but on the other side of the birdbath."

Her smile became a little bigger. She picked up another rock. This was a round piece of gray slate. She flung it and again it skipped the surface of the water, like a gull. The trajectory matched the last but on the left of the birdbath like he'd asked.

He clapped his hands. "Wonderful. This is your pile of rocks and you practice often?"

"Must have party tricks. My son likes it here the best. Doing something with my hands helps when I have to be out here."

Son. The baby or the little boy? Time to find out. He leaped up. "While you are smiling, let's find your parents."

"No. Wait. Just stay and watch the ripples in the small pond. Sometimes, you'll hear a frog's moan."

Her mood had changed again. What a puzzle she was. Well, that hadn't changed. She had intrigued him before, and he'd fallen for her before he'd even known it.

"I can't decide if you want me to leave, Mrs. Wilky, or if you want me to stay. I have rather large shoulders to comfort you in this turmoil."

"That you do."

Was that a smidgeon of appreciation for him? Ruth used to tease him for being tall and lanky. He picked up her lenses, thin brass like the ones broken at Blaren House but made with slimmer glass. "Tell me why we're procrastinating."

A small grin bloomed then disappeared.

A check of their surroundings—Mrs. Bexeley and a few other women edged closer. "Talk to me Mrs. Wilky, before we have an audience."

"They know. You're the only one who doesn't."

Crossing her arms, she held on to her elbows as if she were cold, but even her vacant eyes brimmed with fire, something akin to defiance. "For four years everyone wanted me to forget Adam. They wanted to take my memories away. They wanted Adam to be a lie. He wasn't."

"I know."

"You can't know. He was a flesh and blood man who loved me more than he loved himself. You're here at my parents'. You will tell them the truth. Perhaps they will believe you. Why not? You're a man. A peer. Why wouldn't they?"

"Use me for your advantage."

Her hand popped up, palm wide, fingers stretched.

"Four years of branding me a liar are ready to magically disappear. You think the pain goes away, too?"

Wycliff put his hand to her wrist and lowered it. "You know Adam was a person. You're no liar. You're a truth teller."

"But I want to forget everything. I wish I was a liar. I'm disappointed in how my life has gone. Then I feel guilty, for that means denying Adam, a man who died for me."

She pressed at her temples. "I want to feel justified, but what if you're not believed? What if we never find the other half of the document? What if I never have a legal, valid way to show I was loved and honorable? These are my fears. Please, sit with me, not moving. I need another minute before this sliver of hope is put at risk and destroyed."

Wycliff wanted to confess right now, to honor what she'd suffered. This was his fault, thinking that taking the registry would keep her safe.

Yet, his admission now would make her seem more of a liar or foolish for having him here at her party. She needed him to be Wycliff, the eccentric peer, not Adam the fool.

It was good she still thought him dead. A dead man couldn't be a live friend.

Wycliff pulled her hand to his chest. "If Adam had known how you would suffer, he would've done things differently. He should never have headed to London. He'd been warned. He knew better, but he still went. It's his fault."

"See, you weren't even there, and you know the fault is mine. He wanted to head to Scotland. I should've let him. He made the choice to please me."

"You weren't responsible. Adam made up his own mind. Even if he valued your opinion, he still made the decision."

Ruth picked another stone. This time, when she tossed it, she hit the birdbath dead center. A piece of tile chipped. The bowl moved. The rock fell with a big splash into the pond.

"My fault. He listened to me. He died doing what I asked. I've suffered every day since. Maybe that is my punishment for causing his death."

No.

The attack was his enemy's fault and his.

Yes, he'd headed toward London to make her happy and to protect her from her fears for her parents and their disappointments, but the decision had been his.

Wycliff was a wiser man. Security outweighed everything. He'd do anything to keep her safe.

"I'm your friend, Mrs. Wilky. What happened was the fault of the evil men."

She held out her hand. "My spectacles. I wish to see you change my mind."

He put them in her hand.

After balancing them on that button nose, she squinted and leaned into him. "Well friend, what happened to your face? I don't think my physician punched you. Or did he? Is that what you warrant for being nosy?"

"No. I typically get people to tell me what I want without these consequences."

"I don't have your special powers, my lord. I don't need them. People whisper just loud enough to ensure I hear their horrible thoughts."

"Hear mine. You deserve better."

She shrugged. "Who hurt you, Wycliff?"

"Someone who vented his anger because his crimes have caught up to him. He's angry because I won't help him. He'll not do it again."

"Well, Lord Wycliff, I won't punch you in the eye for being nosy."

"There's that."

She reached to the ground again, but her pile was empty. "Chris will have to get me more. I like flat stones.

Chris…Christopher. An older child who could gather stones. Possibly his son.

"Mrs. Wilky, let us get on with the introductions."

He stood and helped her up, slipping her hand firmly into

his. "I'm with you, my dear, like a knight to his queen. I'll make sure that you are believed. I won't rest until everyone knows that Ruth Wilky is a truth teller."

"Queen, *hmm*." She wiped at her long lashes, then took his hand and kissed it. "Stop letting people hit you."

That was unexpected, such an open expression of affection. She still had that power to confuse him. "Let's find your parents so I can tell them of the goodness of Adam Wilky."

"No, let's walk a little more."

More time to prepare was good. He needed to be convincing. There'd be no chance to win Ruth if he failed.

Chapter Fourteen

A Widow's Friend

Wycliff had my hand and he guided me away from the still pond waters, but my soul was anxious. I was not restored.

The baron was smooth, not taking my baiting comments, allowing me to be honest about how I felt about Adam. He took all my hurt and sorrow about his cousin and remained sweet.

I couldn't share all my truths—that Adam was the hole in my chest, the space where a heart should be. I'll never feel toward anyone the way I felt for him.

This was for the best. That deep kind of love had too many risks. I'd never gamble like that again. My son needed his mother to be reasonable and smart, not a dreamer.

Wycliff tugged hair away from my face. He thought himself clever, trailing his thumb along my cheek.

It was sweet, a more romantic gesture than the barrister's.

But I was immune.

Wycliff's touch would never be a caress that vibrated through me, all the way to my spine. It would never send those tingles and sparks, like embers dancing in a flame.

I'd have to be vulnerable for that. I'd have to trust someone with the intricacies of my thoughts and the intimacy of my body. Never again.

He smiled at me, but I wasn't stupid. His motives were obvious, despite his patient words. He wanted what Adam had had. He wanted me.

Wycliff cleaned my glasses and returned them to my face. "See. Good as new."

"You noticed I was broken?"

He frowned but didn't answer and started us moving again.

He didn't take the bait of that barb. I was grateful for that. I needed to be me again, a less sarcastic woman who spoke her mind and danced on hot coals because she wanted to. That was me.

"Mrs. Wilky, do you think your mother will approve of me? I left the sjambok in my carriage."

"A little." Well, that wasn't true. Mother would love him, a baron at her house.

If I had to be on a man's arm, it surely didn't hurt that Wycliff was big like my father, tall and brawny like him, too.

"Take your time examining me, my Mrs. Wilky, my Ruthy. See what you think of me. I don't mind the scrutiny."

With a nod, I did just that and took another glorious look at the handsome man. The beard made him more mysterious. I liked that.

His nose was thin and unremarkable, but his lips, they were smooth and full, something I hadn't seen on anyone but Blackamoors. "Only Adam called me Ruthy. It's Mrs. Wilky to you. That will change if I accept the barrister's offer."

"Now that is a problem. How did you meet the busy barrister?"

I lowered my head to the baron's wide chest and couldn't help but notice how everything fit snuggly to his form.

When I looked up, he smirked. He knew I admired him. "A newspaper advertisement. There's nothing safe to look at when it comes to you, Lord Wycliff. You are handsome. Maybe I should leave off these spectacles."

His hands were on mine again. "Is that such a bad thing to be handsome?"

"Yes. Because you do remind me of your cousin."

"When you speak of Adam, I don't hear much love."

"Is it possible to love someone so much and hate him, too?"

The cough, the pause, the next cough said everything I needed to know. No one understood. "Sorry, I shouldn't be so honest."

"I needed to know this. As you said, I'm nosy."

"Let's keep moving, Lord Wycliff. Someone will talk."

He started guiding me, but I saw questions bubbling.

"Why did you risk everything to come to Blaren House? I know how much of a toll it took to come. I'm a survivor of a war, my personal struggles nearly killed me. What made the difference for you, Mrs. Wilky? What drove you up those steps to Blaren House?"

"Christopher. The chance at getting the other part of that registry is for him."

A smile came to the baron's face. One that was unexpected. One that reached for a possibility that I couldn't confirm. Chris was Adam's by marriage. I wasn't sure by blood.

Wycliff put his hands to his back. "I'm glad you came. When you are ready to talk of Adam, the good and the bad, I'm here for it."

"Find the registry for me. That's what I need. Nothing else." I folded my arms about my middle, but this was my truth. "I deserve to be made whole. The proof does that."

"You are a truth teller, Mrs. Wilky. Never doubt that."

I had doubted me. Then the trunk had arrived. I would work harder at being me. That hot-coals-walker, the dragon-slayer-in-training. "All this sweetness from an hour of association, half of which I spent unconscious on your steps. I must have mystical powers."

"I didn't leave you. I couldn't. I feel I know you. Call me one of those sentimental fools who becomes entranced by a woman at first sight."

His dark-gray, almost black, eyes fell upon me like a shadow, a good shadow like the house. "I want your friendship, exactly what you asked of me in the house."

Why didn't Barrister Marks look at me like this? We'd corresponded for six months. We'd met on a couple of occasions, but never once had there been anything more than a respectful glance.

Nothing this warm, nothing like this.

I blinked and pushed against the baron's hard stomach—one that wasn't scrawny like Adam's. "If you mention anything about destiny, I'll leave you and find my way back to the house."

"The truth gets me sentenced to solitude?"

I stilled my hands on his waistcoat and stopped smoothing the lines of the silken weave. I realized that I kept touching him. I'd crossed that boundary. I jerked my hands away. "Truth is what I need more than anything."

"Yes. Truth. I see."

I backed up to put distance between us, to move from the warmth that swirled between him and me. It was too much, too soon, and I was too wary. Turning to run to the house, I rammed into Mrs. Carter.

"Ruth," the awful thing said, "still clumsy, girl. Never you mind. You look lovely today. So pretty in innocent peach."

She grinned, but not at me. Her face had lifted toward the baron. "Introduce me to more of your mama's people.

You come fresh off the boat for a visit?"

What?

Why did she mention Mama? What was the dragon talking about? "Mrs. Carter, this is my Mr. Wilky's cousin, Lord Wycliff."

"Cousin? Ruth, it's one t'ing to have a fake husband. It's an entirely another t'ing to invent fake relatives."

Lord Wycliff chuckled. "I assure you, madam, I'm not fake. True flesh and blood."

He took the woman's hand and kissed it.

Hopefully, the poor man wouldn't turn into a frog.

"He's a cousin to my late husband, ma'am. He's just arrived in London."

"Odd, we're hearing of him now. Ruth, your sister's husband, the actor turned politician, he could've picked someone more convincing. All mulattoes are not related."

Used to jeers, I shook my head and started to the house, but Lord Wycliff didn't move. "I assure you, I'm Mr. Wilky's relation, and I've been in the Navy a good while. From your accent, I take it you are from Demerara. Ah, Demerara women are so feisty."

"I'm from Jamaica, my lord, not Demerara."

He folded his arms and clicked his tongue. "But your pitch. It's not right for Jamaica. Are you embarrassed about being from Demerara? Such a lovely island. And so friendly. My frigate mates tell some lovely stories about arriving at the hotels for the mulatto balls."

He winked at her. "You probably were very friendly, Mrs. Carter, a beauty like you."

I'd never seen such.

The woman turned ruby red. "I am not Demeraran. I didn't go to the balls."

"Oh. I'm so sorry. I hinted at you peddling flesh at the main hotel—oh, there I said it. Sorry."

Mrs. Carter took a step back. Was that a hand on her hip? "I don't know what you mean. I've never peddled anyt'ing. I'm from Villa de la Vega, a town central to Jamaica, not the balls."

"If you say so, ma'am." Lord Wycliff winked again. "Perhaps I am confused, your tones… I'll keep this to myself."

I wasn't slow, but the sputtering I heard coming from Mrs. Carter made me laugh out loud. "Cousin, it's not right to tease."

Neck shifting, head spinning, the dragon backed up. "I see Mrs. Croome by the refreshment tables. Good day, my lord. Ruth, tell your cousin not to joke so much."

I'd never known the lumbering woman to move fast, but there she was, tottering away as if the plague had broken out.

Wycliff had defended me. I hadn't asked him to do that to anyone but my parents.

I was grateful.

Grateful for food and shelter and family and now Wycliff, my new family.

"Shall we continue our walk, Mrs. Wilky?"

He said my name with pride. Today was the first time since my wedding that I'd felt this proud.

I was happy to retake the baron's arm. "Thank you. You didn't have to do that, but thank you. I did lie once about going to her house when I eloped with Adam. She kept my mother encouraged when I disappeared."

"One mistake doesn't equal years of abuse. Besides, I couldn't resist tweaking her Jamaican nose. They are very prideful of their homeland. Unfortunately, the HMS *Liverpool* was in the East Indies, not the west. My research says Mrs. Carter's people indeed owned a series of island bawdy houses. Her mother is rumored to be a result of such an encounter."

"How do you know this?"

"I'm a nosy man. Knowing things is my business, and I was here in enough time to hear Mrs. Carter disparage you."

"Oh." It was all I could say. My shock and my gratitude made my head a little dizzy.

"That woman drinks your parents' raffia, eats their teacakes, and talks ill of you, even with the lovely lady I assume is your mother. Mrs. Carter is a shameful saucebox, a hellish hun."

The blood stilled in my veins. Then jolted forward and flooded my eardrums. Adam used to make up insults like that. I looked up at Wycliff again, studying his mouth. "When the hun said you were like my mother's people, does that mean that those lips are inherited from a different free people, like Adam?"

"Noticing my mouth? Is this a new interest? Would you like to examine how it works?"

He was funny, but I sensed his humor was a way to hide.

"If I'm white or mulatto, does it matter? Your sister's taste in men, and that of her friends, seems to indicate that race does not matter. Your choice of Mr. Marks seems a preference of young Croome women."

"No. We loved first, then thought about things like that later. For me, I want an honorable and kind man. Someone to be a father to my son and to protect me. That's my only requirement. Papa has his own ideas. Mama wants to throw a wedding breakfast. If you don't want to say or if it's wrong to ask… I want truth in everything. You'll never know what it's like to fight to hold on to truth."

"I know what it's like to fight to hold on to my dignity and my rights. I know the pressure to give up on hope. Yet, something burned in my chest that didn't let me give up. I'm thankful for this strength, for my faith. I look at you, standing here in this garden, in your right mind and beautiful and strong. I think we are both blessed."

The raspy strain in his voice, harsher and hoarser than before, made me sigh. I wondered what horrors he'd lived. What regrets plagued him now?

My hands shook with shame. I'd assumed that since Wycliff looked good on the outside, that he didn't have pain. I abandoned my resolve not to touch him again and placed a pinkie upon his wrist, where his sleeve exposed his skin.

His arm was rough, bearing evidence of scars. "Sorry."

"Nothing for you to be sorry about. You are a truth teller, and you know I'm not saying everything. For that, I am sorry."

We took another silent lap about the party. This had to be the longest I'd been outside.

The world didn't look so scary in Wycliff's shadow. I understood he knew pain, probably horror. I found an odd camaraderie in that.

"Honor and kindness are your only preferences for a husband, Mrs. Wilky?"

"Well that, and not a sack of bones. You know how skinny your cousin was." I sighed. I was more sad than mad about Adam, another first in a long time. "But his kindness won me over. He was very clever."

The baron looked over my head and then maybe to the sky. "Since I'm not a sack of bones, reasonably intelligent, and wish to lavish attention on you like a queen, do I have a chance to deepen our friendship?"

"No more jokes, Lord Wycliff. Let's find my mother."

He bit upon the lip I'd begun to admire. "Or let's find a truly private place to answer your questions. What Mrs. Wilky wants to know, she should know."

I threaded my hand more tightly about his arm. He headed us toward the house. A wave of happiness skipped through me like my rocks skimming the surface of the fishpond.

We halted, a dead stop in front of my mother.

"Ruth, Mrs. Carter says you have a guest. I've been so busy with the party I assumed him a friend of Mr. Marks."

"No, Mama. This is my friend. This is Lord Wycliff, my late husband's cousin."

I tweaked my spectacles and observed the surprise in her countenance. It was small then broke over her face in an unexpected smile. Then I saw the glint in the baron's eyes as he kissed her hand.

I hadn't lied.

I hadn't lied, and now she believed, at least a little. "This was my Tuesday appointment, to meet him."

"It's a pleasure finally to greet you, ma'am, and on such a joyous occasion, a lovely garden party. My beautiful cousin was so gracious to invite me."

I stared at him. Such earnest words. His tone sounded sincere.

"Yes. Yes, Ruth is." My mama's small voice was low, barely a whisper.

But I knew her.

Her calm words masked her shock. I reveled in that moment. I wanted to strut in lacy puce slippers and dance with Wycliff spinning me in a crazy waltz. But I stood still and smiled.

"You must come to dinner, Lord Wycliff, sometime next week. My husband has gone inside to rest. He's still gathering his strength."

"Yes, from the warehouse fire. I used to love that warehouse. I saw it often from the docks."

Mama's face looked different. Something worse than shock, maybe conviction bloomed in that quivering lip. Maybe she was sorry for not believing me. Maybe she could be proud of me for surviving.

"It would be my honor, Mrs. Croome. I intend to see a great deal of Mrs. Wilky these next few weeks. I intend to get to know this part of my family and seek my fair cousin's advice on decorating my Mayfair townhouse."

"Mayfair? Yes, if Ruth is up to helping."

"Mrs. Wilky was going to show me more of your house. I do love the Huguenot architecture."

"Show him, Ruth." Mama kissed my cheek and went back to the party.

My joy at her shock disappeared. This couldn't be this easy.

One word from a man couldn't be all it took.

I was shaking when Wycliff placed my hand on his arm, livid when he guided my slow steps toward the house, ready to erupt when I saw the dark hall floor under my slippers.

People came inside, stepping around us, but I could go no farther.

Wycliff put his hand to my waist and moved me to the side, into the hall near Papa's study.

This wasn't proper, but it felt natural, his hands on me.

His countenance was close. His breathing was as labored as mine. "Let's let you rest, then go outside onto the street. Privacy for us."

"The front of the house? No. I've had enough of being outside of these walls."

"I see, Mrs. Wilky. You still don't trust me?"

"I just met you this week, Lord Wycliff. You've studied me and my family. I know nothing of you."

"It's enough. It's more than enough when you just know we are to be friends. I need you to—Lawden's at the door."

He lowered his head as if he were pained. "It seems I have to go. I'd like to come for a walk tomorrow."

My pulse raced. "No. There's something planned."

"The next day."

"Saturday, no, and Sunday's church."

"Then Tuesday, it is, cousin. Please, no refusing

me, Tuesday, Mrs. Wilky. I haven't met my little cousin, Christopher."

I remembered how I dreaded Tuesdays. I thought of how the knitters would act when they saw the baron. And Chris, Chris needed to meet him. "Yes, Tuesday."

"Look at me, Mrs. Wilky. I cannot wait to be here again. I'll do what it takes to win your trust fully."

Against my better judgement, I leaned in, on tiptoes to kiss his cheek, but I missed. I brushed his lips, then his furry dimple stroked my nose. It didn't feel bad. The opposite of bad.

Mistake.

His Bay Rum scent clung to me as his strong hands returned to my waist.

Bigger Mistake.

I let him.

Part of me wanted to linger like this. I was lucky he had to go.

"I'm loath to leave, Mrs. Wilky."

"A walk on Tuesday with my son, Lord Wycliff. You're smart, smart like Adam, but he'd never trick me. He'd never hurt my boy. I'm taking a risk to introduce you to my greatest treasure, my Chris."

"You've always taken risks." Wycliff's gray-black eyes bored down upon me. "I'm worth it. I'm sensitive to your predicament. You can trust your friend to protect you."

He pressed his mouth to my open palm. The heat of his breath burned through my glove down to my damp skin. The softness of his lips on my wrist whispered trouble. "Tuesday, noon, Mrs. Wilky, we begin with another walk."

Beginnings.

They brought fortunes and dangers. Was knowing Wycliff—mysterious, nosy, sensual Wycliff—worth the bargain?

Everything screamed *yes*. I clenched the hand he'd kissed to my bosom. "Tuesday. No being late. No new bruises."

With a larger, wicked smile, he turned, tugged on his hat, and then he and his manservant left.

There was no reason to venture back into the garden party.

My friend was gone. The only person who truly believed in me and Adam had left. Little Christopher didn't count. He believed in Father Christmas, too.

I unfurled my palm.

And thought of Wycliff returning Tuesday. It couldn't come fast enough.

Chapter Fifteen

A WALK WITH COUSIN WYCLIFF

Knit one. Purl one.

My fingers worked fast. This poor scarf had started to take shape. My concentration seemed perfect, but it had to be. This knitting Tuesday in Mama's parlor was different.

Wycliff's appearance at last week's garden party had spread like fire. My past was in question, but in good ways.

Knit one. Purl one.

No sneers.

Knit one. Purl one.

No taunting advice.

Knit one. Purl one.

No Mrs. Carter. Her chair sat empty.

I should rally and gloat, but my nerves were in a full-speed hurly-burly, thinking of Wycliff, wondering about him.

By accident or by choice—some hidden desire had stirred deep in me. I'd allowed him the liberty to hold me. And I'd almost taken the liberty to kiss him.

Well, actually I had kissed him, if that barest lip to lip counted. Did it count if I thought of Adam when we touched?

The watch on my chain read thirty after eleven. He was to be here at noon. I had to be calm. I had to be smart. I had to undo this last purled row. It was uneven.

Mrs. Daly leaned over and sipped from her tea. "It's a shame Mrs. Carter's gout is bothering her, the poor dear."

"Yes. It is a shame," Mama said. She reached for my chain and straightened it. "She will miss the baron's visit today."

Mama seemed nonchalant, talking about her friend, but I caught her looking toward the window and the something extra in her voice when she mentioned Mrs. Carter.

When I squinted, I saw Mama's purled row was uneven, too.

That was odd for her.

Mrs. Johnson kept looking at me. Her creamy brow looked moist. She fidgeted in her chocolate-colored carriage gown. The lady was nice enough when she wasn't joining in on the teasing.

"Are you well, Mrs. Johnson?" The words were out of my mouth before I'd thought better of it.

The woman shrugged. Her complexion seemed flustered with ruddy-red cheeks. "Yes, Mrs. Wilky. I'm fine. Just a little unsettled. My husband's business is in trouble. He is seeing a lot of unrest on the docks."

"More repercussion from Nacknel's suicide?" Mrs. Daly brushed her hands of the crumbs from the lavender teacakes she'd devoured. "I'm hearing that many of the shippers are experiencing delays. It's chaos."

"All will pass, ladies. It always does." Mama's voice was soothing, but her stitches on the canary yellow blanket she knitted became worse.

Was Papa's business in jeopardy, too?

He used the shipping lanes to transport goods. I glanced at Mama, tweaking my spectacles to see what she wasn't saying.

Crisp white mobcap, pressed and pinned in place covered her stately graying locks. The azure-blue silk gown with shiny brass buttons on her long sleeves seemed a little fancy but highlighted her pale-gold skin. Were more guests coming or was this pomp for my baron?

"Ruth, do you need to change? Your cousin will be here soon."

I was comfortable in my light-gray silk. Long sleeves, not much trim. It was a simple gown, one that said walking, not courting.

Mrs. Daly smiled at Mama, like they'd forged a conspiracy. "Yes, Lord Wycliff. I hear he just inherited his barony."

"Yes. He's in financing," Mrs. Johnson said, then sipped her tea. "Shipping finance."

Mrs. Johnson seemed agitated and too concerned with the baron's business, but I'd not inquire. Adam's number crunching had been deadly. I'd have no part of Wycliff's situation.

I purled another row, right spacing, even. "Lord Wycliff, my late *husband*'s cousin, will be here soon. Let's not let him catch us gossiping."

I loved saying husband, loved the reaction they all wore— frozen smiles, eyes lowering. Penance, perhaps? If I glared at each of these awful counselors long enough, I might see respect.

So, I did.

Pow. I caught Mrs. Daly—she smiled back.

Wham. Mrs. Johnson peered at me. Boy, she looked guilty.

Snap. Mama. Glorious Mama, nodded and beamed, beamed at me.

It was silly and childish and freeing. I loved it.

The sound of the outer door opening and shutting made me shiver with pleasure. I turned to the window. A big blur, a carriage-sized blob was outside.

Wycliff had arrived early. And there went my courage.

I held my breath, listening for footsteps, but all I heard was Clancy's heavy footfalls.

The parlor door opened with a bang.

"Lord Wycliff has come calling, Mrs. Croome. He's here to see Mrs. Wilky."

I lifted my head and caught his gaze. I sensed his confident smile, his swagger as he advanced. "Ladies."

In the baron's arms were two bouquets, one fine set of hothouse roses, the other a bunch of daisies, each wrapped in crisp white paper.

"For you, Mrs. Croome." He gave the roses to Mama. Then he spun and presented himself to me.

Glad for once to wear my spectacles, I savored the sight of him. Dark bottle-green waistcoat cut over snug beech breaches, finely polished boots. I didn't mind his freshly trimmed beard or how it framed his handsome face. Sort of made him mysterious, like a pirate with a sjambok. The dormant adventurer inside me perked up.

I took the daisies and sniffed the sweet petals. Daisies were happy flowers, so free and easy.

"Leave your knitting, Ruth," Mama said. "I'll put it away for you. Clancy, find vases for these lovely flowers. Thank you, Lord Wycliff."

The butler took the bouquets and began to leave, but not before Wycliff pinched off a daisy and put it in his buttonhole.

Adam used to do that.

I ducked my eyes to the scarf I was knitting for Mr. Marks's upcoming birthday, but my head was filled with Wycliff. How could such a simple thing like a daisy in a buttonhole make me happy?

"Mrs. Wilky?"

The baron's raspy voice centered me, led me back to the

truth of where things were. Though he looked like Adam, Adam was gone, and wasn't returning.

Wycliff extended his hand to me.

I took it. Rising from my chair, I noted again how good the creamy-white petals and happy brown button of the daisy looked against his ebony tailcoat.

The baron was tall and handsome and endearing with the flower, but was I admiring a memory or my husband's cousin?

"Mrs. Wilky, I've thought of nothing else but our walk."

Mama picked up my yarn and jabbed the needles into the bundle. "You're going outside, Ruth? Mrs. Fitterwall has made tea and a light nuncheon upstairs in the dining room."

He glanced at me, then turned to Mama. "Ma'am, I thank you for your generous hospitality, but I'm partial to walking. I've come with the expectation of walking. I don't want to disappoint my lovely cousin."

I took his arm and stared at Lord Wycliff, the man who'd just defied Horatio Croome…and lived. "Mama, the baron is very busy. A walk will suffice."

"Very well," she said. "Do take care of my girl. Her eyesight sometimes makes her nervous."

"I'll protect her, ma'am. She's all I have left of my dear cousin, her poor husband." His face sobered, ridding his countenance of the smile he'd borne when he'd entered the room. "I'll keep her safe."

"Good. She's a good girl. She's had too many troubles." Mama put down my yarn. "Mr. Wilky's son, my grandson, is upstairs. He had a fever last night. Too much outdoor play. You will have to meet him later this week."

"Yes, Adam's son. Soon. I cannot wait to meet the lad."

His face remained blank, but his raspy voice sounded confident.

I tugged on the baron's sleeve to quicken our exodus from

the room. I didn't want anyone imposing upon Wycliff or having him make promises without having met Christopher. He hadn't seen my boy's beautiful spirit. I didn't want my baby rejected.

I tried not to push my cousin out of the parlor, but I did.

He started laughing.

The low chuckles prickled my skin. "Filled with mirth, Cousin? But do you think you were a little heavy in your praise of Adam?"

He wove his fingers with mine, blocking me from slipping on gloves. "I take nothing for granted. Nothing."

I enjoyed the respect Wycliff's appearance had brought to my life and the thoughtfulness of a man who brought me daisies. But I wondered what other things he had on his mind.

• • •

Wycliff tugged on his cape and waited for Ruth to slip on her bonnet.

Her graceful fingers made a slipknot of the shiny celestial-blue ribbon and tightened it under her chin. Elegant, but her gown was so simple, so plain, a washed-out gray that did nothing to draw out the spirited woman he remembered.

He'd have to fix that when she was his again. Was it bigamy to marry one's wife twice?

Swiping at his brow, pushing foolish thoughts from his head, he focused on the first steps. He was very far from winning Ruth. The barrister might be a contender for her heart. His life was less complicated and had none of the baggage of the Wilkinsons.

Ruth had to want Wycliff, had to marry him again. The squeaky-clean barrister needed to go away. Pity, Lawden had found no vice or scandal on Marks.

Unfortunately or fortunately, the barrister was a good

man.

"Wycliff, are you well? You look as if your thoughts are heavy. Are you plotting something? Something nosy?"

"Nothing nosy or deadly today, I can assure you."

Her head tilted to the side, but she took his extended arm. "A simple no would suffice. If you are busy, we could postpone this outing. I'm in no rush to be out of the house."

"There's no other place I wish to be."

A slight smile graced her mouth. It still needed exploration, deep exploration. To merely gain a light touch of her kiss at the party and then have to wait five days to be near those lips again—torture.

"So how was your morning, Mrs. Wilky?"

Ruth didn't look at him. She seemed very focused on the brass door latch.

No peep from her when Clancy opened the door.

A loud breath swept through her lips when they took the first step onto the high stone entry.

Together, they took one more, then Ruth stopped.

He tried to nudge her to take one more, but she was frozen.

He fingered her chin, where soft curls fell. "The day has a gorgeous sun, cousin. The only thing I liked about being on a ship was the noon sun. It was so warm and broke through the endless skies."

Her breaths remained loud, lingering like she choked. "You don't say."

This was harder than he'd thought. Ruth used to love walks. They'd chatted endlessly as he'd escorted her from the docks to the warehouse. Her face had brightened when he'd described architecture or talked of poetry. That was what they had done, the first six months of their acquaintance—long strolls, all by themselves, no one staring, nothing stopping them or their dreams.

He rubbed his stomach. "Let's go back inside and enjoy those treats your mother talked about. The dining room will be more private. We'll talk low."

She shook her head and tightened her already-tight grip along his arm. "That's not a problem for you, is it?"

"My voice is terrible. I take it you don't like it."

"Very terrible, my lord. But what choice do you have? It's not like you could sing a wondrous melody. Or whisper my name as if it sounded like a church hymn. Adam sang quite well."

He freed his arm from her nails and put a hand to her shoulder. "No, you don't want me to sing. My voice is gruff, quite rough. More suited to bar brawls than a vicar's homily."

"Adam wanted to be a vicar. Did you know that? Of course you did."

He hesitated, then he decided to be bold and place his arm about her, along her middle. "Don't be scared, Ruth. Let's go back into the house."

She put her hands on his, anchoring him in place. "Your hands are rough, too. And it's Mrs. Wilky."

So formal even though she let him hold her. "My hands? Too much sea salt. Too many decks needed swabbing. Am I not refined enough for you? It seems I'm losing your tally."

"What tally, Wycliff?"

"The one for your admiration. I suppose Adam and now the barrister are smooth in comparison to old, grizzled me."

"You're not old."

"But I am losing."

She lifted her chin high. "You were going to answer questions for me."

"I was, but we have an audience by the window."

Ruth squinted and peered around his shoulder. Could she see the ladies staring at them from the large picture frame window of the parlor?

"Mrs. Johnson and Mrs. Daly are looking at us. Mrs. Wilky, that dining room sounds as if it could make for a perfect retreat."

"Mama will get them away. I think you are becoming a favorite relative."

The curtains closed.

Ruth was right. But someone could still peek. The question was, did he care to hide his admiration of his cousin?

"I think no walk today, my dear, or anything that looks like kissing cousins. We seem rather cozy on this step."

He tried to turn and lead her inside, but she held fast to his arm.

"Not yet. The roar in my ears hasn't settled. Please don't move. Hold me. Be a holding cousin."

"No begging anything of me." He pulled her tight against him. "Perhaps this does meet my criteria for privacy."

"Your standards are low, Wycliff."

Oh, her sense of cutting humor had stirred. It warmed him to his bones, like the sun on the deck, like a body pressed against his—warm, curvy. All of her hidden in drab, dowdy gray.

"Not so low, my dear. I'm standing in the entry with the right cousin. Not Adam's cousin Nickie. He's definitely not one to stand beside."

"Awful, Nicholas." She shivered.

"You remember him? Did you meet him with Adam on the docks?"

"I want to forget him, all who hurt us."

How many stories had he told Ruth of unreliable Nickie, his sometime-friend, sometime-enemy cousin? He hadn't realized the depth of the treachery between them.

"I should do something for privacy, Mrs. Wilky."

He moved and shared the step with her. He put his back to the window and spun her to face him. "See, my cape comes in handy."

"I still have your other one. I like it. I like the smell of it, of you."

"Bay Rum? You like? Doesn't seem like your fragrance."

"Yes, I love that cologne. It was Adam's."

"The man had great taste."

She held his gaze and that feeling of the two of them against the world wrapped about him.

"I think we need to walk, Mrs. Wilky. If we stand like this much longer, I won't be a good cousin. I'll be a man who's fallen for a good woman."

She took off her spectacles. Then those wicked, teasing fingers slipped across his chest and put her lenses into his tailcoat. "I'm ready. Escort me."

"I'm sorry. I'm confused on your orders. Do you want to walk or are you asking me to have at you now?"

"Walk, my lord."

"An order from a woman is an interesting thing. Yes, ma'am, my spirited minx."

She shook her head. She was easy again, more relaxed, more old Ruth, his Ruth. Good.

Yet he was hot and bothered, falling more in want of her.

Ruth looked as if she could arrange flowers.

"Do you have anything else for my pocket—a necklace, a handkerchief? Feel free to use me."

"What?"

"Never mind." Wycliff started down the steps, taking her with him. They made it to the last one, but he did not stop. He kept going, leading her with fingers entwined.

Like a boat in still waters, she floated alongside him. In silence, they walked a block and then another.

They were in step. It was like old times, except it wasn't. Her face was pinned to his chest, her knuckles had become white within his palm.

"Tell me how to make this better, Mrs. Wilky."

"Do you truly wish to meet my son?"

Wycliff loved a turn of phrase, the punniest puns. Something stung when she said her son, not theirs, not hers and Adam's.

Was this her way of admitting the truth, that Christopher Wilky wasn't…

He pushed questions of the boy's paternity to the back of his mind. Ruth thought him dead. Whatever had happened, what choices she'd made, even if she'd found comfort in her grief—none of it mattered.

Wycliff was here now, and he'd take on any responsibility that made Ruth happy. He owed her that. "I do wish to know Christopher Wilky. It will be my pleasure to meet him, to be a part of his life, Ruth."

She started to free her finger, flicking at his knuckles. "It's Mrs. Wilky."

Wait. That was now the concern, familiarity? He let go and stopped.

She crossed her arms but stayed close to him. "Truth is what I want. Things that no one can say are lies. You were going to tell me the truth about you."

"I did say that."

"Well, Lord Wycliff?"

He felt his legs bracing, preparing for exactly what she wanted to know. Maybe she'd caught his clues—the daisies, the walks, the cologne. *Let her ask now if he was Adam.* "Yes, ask anything."

"Are you a mulatto like Adam? Or just blessed with fascinating lips."

The tension in his limbs fled and a good laugh came out. But Ruth wasn't chuckling.

"You like my mouth? Perhaps you need a better tasting to be sure?"

"Are you passing like Adam? He believed passing was part of his power."

"Yes. It's kept me alive on more than one occasion."

"Your world, even as a peer, is just as dangerous as Adam's?"

His world wasn't Adam's. Wycliff understood how things worked and how things turned on charisma and charm, finesse and finance. "Were you considering my world, being more a part of it than a walk-mate?"

"I don't know what to think when I'm with you."

"Then that's good. You shouldn't have to think or fret when you're with me. I'm in control of my life, more than Adam ever was. I allow people to assume what they want. If they want to do business with a white man, that's fine if their gold is true. Your father uses solicitors to conduct his dealings. I like a direct hand."

He smoothed her fingers within his palm. "A direct hand with everything."

"You know so much about my family. You've studied us. That's very nosy of you."

"It's part of the effort I put into things I want. The Croome family is mine now."

"We're not possessions or pawns."

"Aren't we all playing games? Pretending when necessary. Ignoring things that don't suit our purposes. Going full-bore at what we've determined is good."

"What a pretty way to put being manipulative, my lord."

A chuckle fell from his lips.

He didn't want it to drop, but Ruth had that way about her, sticking pins in his arguments when he took on airs. "Fine. I'm nosy. I need to make up for lost time in knowing the Croomes. I'll use my means and any charm this raspy soul can muster."

"I'm at such a disadvantage, Lord Wycliff. I'm not traipsing about to find secrets. How can I trust you, implicitly?"

He looked down the street and saw his carriage and Lawden's watchful eye. It was very open, very attention-seeking to stand here. "You trusted me to take you on a walk. You can trust me with more."

"Adam never trusted so easily. Not even me. Look at the things he kept from the woman he married."

"Mrs. Wilky... Oh, horse feathers, Ruth. Adam was stupid, as you often said. He didn't realize that you were all he needed, more than power, more than the respect he craved. I trust you, and I'm willing to tell you anything, if I can call you by the name my tongue wishes to possess."

Her lip trembled, and a smile perched upon her lips like a delicate dove. "That's a pretty sentiment. A fine begging, even with your voice. Yes. Call me Ruth, but only when we are alone."

"Then we shall have to be alone often."

Her laughter was easier. She took a step, leading him down the pavement, bold like old times. Yet, Ruth couldn't see that far in front of her. Then it hit him. She trusted that he'd keep them safe.

He put a hand to her waist to guide her, to keep her from cracks or uneven places. "We'll go to the end of the street and back. If you feel nervous at any point, claw my arm. Demand I take you back. I'll do so immediately."

Her steps became shorter, the closer they came to the end of the street. "A hundred and fifty steps. Wow. That's far."

Distract her.

That was what he used to do walking her from the docks to her father's warehouse. "So many because you have delicate feet. What about we get you larger boots?"

"No gifts. Your flowers are enough."

"Do you feel better earning things?" He stopped and put his hands to her cheek, brushing lightly until her eyes opened.

"See, there can be a benefit to my coarse hands. You'll be more aware of me."

"That could be a benefit, but your footfalls are too silent."

Ruth peered up. No hiding. No coy fluttering of lashes. No labored breaths. It was how she'd looked at him that moment at the blacksmith's when she'd promised to be his. The world had been just theirs. It must be theirs again.

"Lord Wycliff, what do you see when you look at me?

"The answer to my prayers. Dreams I didn't know I wanted. We are nicely matched, surely you see this?"

She dug into his pocket. Touching him, stirring up all manner of things in his chest. She might as well have reached in and given his dark, bruised heart a shine.

"I want my spectacles to see you, Wycliff, as you look at me."

He caressed her chin. "You could just kiss me and gain the rest of the answers you seek. If it's a good one, you could get account numbers, invoices, anything. I can be easy like that."

Her eyes, soulful, dark orbs with swirling hints of henna and questions, focused behind her lenses.

"Say it, Ruth. Say what's on your mind."

"I met Adam on the docks, close to my father's warehouse. He stopped some men from bothering me, then walked me back to the warehouse. He stayed with me until I was safe. I asked him if he wanted something to eat. He said my friendship, if he could earn it. The way you just said this, you could be easy like that, the way you tilted your head, I hear him saying it in his sweet voice. Why do you have to remind me of the good of him?"

The good?

That meant there was bad, more than what she'd already said.

How had Adam become the villain?

Those beastly women in the Croome household were the ones persecuting her.

He started them walking again, remaining quiet until they'd made it to the corner.

Fournier was vacant. No carriages, no children playing, no lovers walking about.

Just them, a man escorting his wife, a woman that didn't know him, who didn't want to because he'd failed her. His throat tightened, but he forced his words to be said. "Adam was good, a good person. He loved you with all his heart."

"You say that like it's a consolation, Wycliff. If I'd truly known the danger, I wouldn't have eloped. Five days of marital bliss do not equal four years of pain. Maybe he'd have lived. He'd still be that sweet young man in want of a meal by the docks, and still alive."

"Not being able to prove the validity of your marriage to Adam has wrought this much suffering? How can you forgo the love that he said was so strong?"

"I have a son, Lord Wycliff. He bears a false surname. His name should be Wilkinson."

That would only be Adam's fault if the boy was indeed his or born within a year of his death. He clasped her arm about her waist and left no distance for evasion. "Is the boy Adam's?"

"Adam's dead. Christopher's mine, all mine."

That wasn't an answer.

But the calm she'd had before disappeared. She was shaking. He put his arms about her and kissed the scar on her temple. "Christopher is my concern now, too. He's mine, Ruth. I claim him like I've claimed the Croomes.

"You claim my boy?"

"Yes. I'm going to take you back to the house. Trust me. I'll get you there safely and swiftly."

"No. Not yet. Prying eyes can't see us. Neighbors are

working. We are sort of alone."

They weren't. His grooms had patrolled earlier and would again in an hour. Lawden sat in Wycliff's carriage out front of the Croomes', trying not to look their way, but failing.

Her pinkie touched his mouth. "They are smooth."

"They can be, Ruth. Here's a quick answer."

He leaned in.

She did not move.

Wycliff dipped closer and blew a breath onto her lips. "May I?"

One, two, three, three and a half.

He gave her a small peck. Then a bigger one. And a bigger one.

Then she kissed him back.

Four years, two continents, two seas, and death, this feeling had never left him, like he was falling and being caught in the softest net.

She had a delicious mouth, one that curved perfectly to his. Her sensitive lips trembled when he whispered her name, vibrated when she moaned his.

Had a kiss done it?

Had that broken the spell? Had this moment returned his wife to him?

He sought to draw her closer. To trace and embrace what was his, what was meant to be his.

He took her hand and put it to his chest, drawing her fingers beneath his waistcoat, snaking her palm to his heart. "Warm it, Ruth. Reach in and own it. Make it shine bright for you."

Her hand tightened on his, and she allowed a deeper kiss.

Heaven was in his arms. But that always meant hell was next.

Ruth pulled away but wiped her thumb along his mouth. "Those lips are nice, but no more, no more, *Wycliff*."

She said his name like she had to remember it.

It was time.

She craved truth. He needed to give his, theirs. "Ruth, I need to tell you something."

"No, you don't. I know you're not Adam. You're too thoughtful, and I feel safe with you, so much more with you."

His chest hurt. She'd kicked him in the teeth and complimented him in the same breath. "I've a secret that I can keep no longer from you. I need to confess."

"No. Don't force your secrets upon me. I don't want to know. I don't want my world changed or ripped asunder. Be silent on it."

What?

He rubbed his face, searched for a joke, but his throat was dry, knowing his wife wanted no part of Adam. But he was Adam.

"I don't know how to respond."

"Don't. I'm not looking for a confession of love or a kissing cousin, Wycliff. Promise me that this will not happen again."

"That's hard to do when this kiss has so much promise."

"I was curious. It was wrong to use you."

"Ruth, use me up. Burn me with your fire."

"My son's fake name has been made true. I can't compromise you and ruin things again."

"Maybe you should reconsider. I'm very willing to be compromised, and I have time for it. Seems Mr. Marks does not. He didn't even attend you at church."

She pulled at the strings of her bonnet. "He's…he's been busy, but you've been watching me."

"I can't help watching you. I was in the vestibule, making sure you were well, that you didn't fidget too much. Your sister talks too much. Bexeley fell asleep. How, I'm not sure."

"You've been very nosy."

"I said you are under my protection."

She gripped his cape as if she needed to hold on to him to stay upright. "Is my family in danger because of you?"

There was no danger, for he had the situation under control and he had taken every precaution. He flexed the muscles in his hand. "Have no concerns. I have everything secure."

"Then they're coming again, the men who killed Adam?"

The trembles in her limbs became more and more pronounced. "I need them gone for good."

Ruth crumbled at his feet, a ball of gray silk. She swatted at his arms, fighting him like she did not know him.

"It's me, Ruth. Let me take care of you. Let me protect you."

Her hands slowed, and she nodded. "I'm grateful for food, for shelter, for family, for my son, for you, Wycliff."

Her voice was low, but he heard her, her words. It patched up at least one hole that her honest disappointment in Adam had wrought.

Wycliff scooped her up into his arms. "I have you. I'll never let go."

He rushed, running at top speed down Fournier Street, cradling her to his bosom, speaking words of strength to her. He might have even said he loved her. Flying up the steps, he shouldered open the heavy door.

Then he held her in the empty hall. Waiting for her to strengthen, he kissed her brow. "You're safe Ruth. You're safe, back in the house."

Clancy came. "Do we need to get the doctor to fix her?"

"No," she said. "The fixing is for me to do. Put me down, Lord Wycliff."

Her voice sounded stronger than she looked, but he complied.

Setting her feet to the ground, he kept her palm,

bolstering her from swaying. Soon she patted away his arms. "I'm better. Thank you."

With his fingers to her throat, he undid her bonnet strings, taking the same care he had with the ribbon of her stays, all those years ago. She needed to know how he longed to care for her. This time, he could be trusted with her love.

He kept her palm. "Adam failed to protect you from his enemies. I will never fail you."

She pulled off her coat and gave it to Clancy.

"Mrs. Wilky," Wycliff said, "I'm going to leave you now. I must see you tomorrow. Let's take another walk."

She wobbled to the stairwell. "Don't you think we've had enough? I need to lie down."

"I'll never have enough of you. We'll just stay in your garden."

Her back was to him. Her foot dangled, but she did not take the next step. "Why? Nothing more can come from this."

"I need to meet Christopher. I need to see Adam's son."

He made the bold proclamation and waited. Ruth couldn't deny him that.

She turned and adjusted her spectacles. "Yes. You need to see Christopher. I think he'd like to meet his big cousin."

Wycliff bowed. He knew better than to press her on anything more. He knew she'd never be his unless she felt completely safe.

The end of his uncle's business needed to hasten. Soulden Wilkinson walking free, not in debtors' prison, was dangerous. He could strike at Ruth or the Croomes. Wycliff trotted down the stone steps of the entry, thinking about how to finish off the evil man. It needed to be done before Ruth decided Wycliff couldn't keep her and her son from harm.

Chapter Sixteen

Her Morning Blues

I didn't want to get up this morning.

Rainy mornings should be spent in bed, hiding beneath the covers of my pine bed.

I'd left the window open last night, so the early dawn shower sent nippy air into my room. My arm ached as it often did when the weather turned cool. The knitted bones in my forearm were stronger, but I still hated the questions the lump drew when my sleeves were short. I detested explaining.

It didn't matter. I was grateful I could write and hold my son.

The fresh air filled my chest. Rain or shine, a soft mattress was the best remedy for being spent.

Tired beyond measure, I turned on my side and curled deeper into my favorite fuzzy blanket, a knitted piece of mint-green wool. Something Mama had made for me when I was eight. It reminded me of my old life, the simpler one above the warehouse. The softness of the well-loved wool—it felt like it knew my body. I could hide in it.

This blanket was safe and smelled of lavender. I liked

lavender, but I loved Bay Rum. I slept on the baron's cape again and let his fragrance surround me.

My new cousin, my kissing cousin. He'd been sweet to me yesterday. He was coming to see Chris today. I knew I smiled thinking of Wycliff.

He acted as if he loved me.

Adam had said he'd fallen for me fast like that. That scared me, a little.

I'd let Wycliff kiss me, and I'd kissed him.

I'd told him he did not remind me of Adam. That wasn't quite true. He kissed like him, the way I remembered he had—passionate, toe curling, like the world would end if he couldn't touch me.

If I closed my eyes, it was like I'd kissed my husband. I kissed Adam sometimes in my happy dreams, in those blissful half-awake, half-asleep moments.

But his arms had never felt this safe, not like the baron's.

Wild me, kissing a boy on my street. I'd wanted Wycliff's lips because I'd craved all the good pieces of Adam. I'd become me, that brave girl who'd talked to a boy she'd met on the docks.

Noises sounded outside my room. The day at Nineteen Fournier was well underway. Little Chris would be up soon. He didn't understand when I grew quiet. Last night, my boy had kept asking, *Mama ill? Mama ill?*

Yes, I was—on cold nights, on rainy mornings, and sometimes outside.

But I was a good mother, one who didn't want her son to be afraid.

I needed to repeat that I was wonderful as I was. I was alive. I was grateful to have Chris. I was grateful these topsy-turvy moments did not spin me so far that I couldn't come back. I had seen girls at Madame Talease who had gone mad, crazed from their troubles.

I wasn't mad or witless. I was good, good enough, better than good.

With a few blinks and a rub to my eyes, I started my day. The familiar blurs and shadows of my room offered comfort. Nothing in my vision had changed. That made me sigh.

My door opened.

This time the knock was Mama's.

"Ruth, wake up, dear. You have a guest coming. This time he'll meet your father."

If there were ever a more dangerous statement to begin a day, that was it. My guest…meeting Papa. The shock of it drove me to shoot straight up.

I dangled my feet over the side of the bed. Stepping down, my cold toes found no slippers. The puce, deeply pink things had been moved again.

Fingers tapping on the bed table, I found my spectacles.

Mama was in the closet. The sound of her fumbling through tissue paper separating my gowns annoyed me. She was doing this for the baron. Had she forgotten that it was up to me to choose?

And she'd never done this for Mr. Marks, but the barrister had never visited two days in a row.

"Ah, Ruth look at this. It has details at the bosom and on the sleeve. It's lively."

The rust color was rich, made for a woman who didn't mind being seen. *Is that me? Do I want the baron's attention?*

She held the dress to my chin, then laid the heavy silk over my stiff arm. The damask silk felt cool to my sleep-warmed skin. "Yes, Mama. Thank you."

She kissed my forehead. "Christopher is already downstairs. He's looking forward to spending time with Lord Wycliff."

Mama moved to the door, even clasped the knob, but turned. "I hope you are looking forward to seeing him, too.

He's quite attentive."

I lifted my gaze from the silk to Mama.

She stood still, with her hands fidgeting at the door.

Was she lingering, to hear me agree?

Was she checking to see if my fit had passed?

Or was she hoping for something else—that smiling at a pretty dress erased four years of not being believed. No silk, no matter how bold or fancy, would hide that proof came in the form of a man and not her daughter's words.

Stoic Mama stared back. The silence between us grew.

I waited for her to say, or even hint at, her *sorries* out loud. Didn't she know the wild child was a stubborn tigress? I was quick to love, fast to offer sass, and slow to forgive. That was me.

"I'll send up a maid. Do you need help with your hair, Ruth?"

When we were little, Mama had always done our hair. Ester was tender headed. She'd hollered something awful.

But not me. I was strong, and I welcomed the finish, the perfect braid, the hoity-toity chignon and our two faces, Mama's and mine, smiling and shining in the mirror.

They'd survived another hairdo-ing together.

I was still her stubborn wild child, and I'd survived four years by myself. "I can manage."

My mother nodded, then left.

The door closed. Very easy was the sound, not a slam, nothing showing finality or disapproval. Perhaps that meant she'd return and try again.

I fingered the lace on the gown's bodice, the long sleeves. Maybe I'd welcome another try. Maybe.

But I was grateful that she'd reminded me of who I was. I needed to stop forgetting.

With Wycliff coming, I prepared myself to comfort my child if the baron looked at Chris and saw nothing of Adam.

My baby couldn't be hurt. If he wasn't Adam's, Chris's paternity would be the one lie I'd accept.

My baby dreamed of a father. I'd give him one that Wycliff talked of when he described Adam—brave, loyal, loving to me till he died.

Not the Adam I knew—seductive, secretive, steeped in danger.

• • •

Wycliff arrived outside the Croome house. It should be a good morning for him. His uncle's business partner, Mr. Johnson, had put out word of more cancelled shipments.

Soon the skeleton crews that ran his cargo would run out of bones. Men didn't work without pay. Whether a farmer, a sailor, or a henchman, money made things happen.

With Wycliff cutting off their access to financing, the business of his enemies had begun to falter. Their debts were mounting. One by one, Johnson's and Uncle Soulden's empires would erupt like match sticks. Those debts would be called. They'd be inmates in debtors' prison soon.

The deal he'd struck last night with Captain Steward would make the explosion happen faster. It was only a matter of time before bankruptcy. The men who had destroyed his life would spend the rest of theirs in one of the rat-infested jails—Fleet or musty King's Bench. Perhaps they'd go to the one they'd almost sent Wycliff's father to, Marshalsea. That one was the worst of the worst, where they charged broke prisoners for leg irons.

Wiping a hand through his hair, he stepped out of the carriage. When he donned his hat, Lawden handed him the basket.

"You don't look happy, my lord. Every step in your plan is working. And you've been invited to see your lady."

"A wounded animal is never more dangerous. Johnson and Uncle will grow desperate. If I could convince my lady to marry me today, I'd have her better protected, her and the boy."

Lawden tweaked his cravat. "Then get in there and be convincing, my lord."

"If I was as convincing as I was yesterday, she'd banish me for sure."

"Faith accomplishes much."

Faith was all Wycliff was holding on to when it came to Ruth. He didn't have much else. Adam was the villain to her. She craved truth, and he, Wycliff, still kept his identity from her.

In the past, he'd thought his secrets had protected his father or Ruth. In the end, he hadn't even been able to save himself.

She'd erased the Adam she'd loved from her mind. Maybe that was what he deserved. "Do you know what happened to my wife after the attack? Any new information?"

Lawden brushed lint from Wycliff's onyx cape. "No, my lord. I can find nothing."

"No signs of Cicely, either. I hate this. I hate not having all the information—not controlling things."

"That would be where you turn to your faith. Believe in Mrs. Wilky. Believe in your love. Believe that all will work for your good."

Adjusting his grip on the basket handle, Wycliff started for the entry. "Wish me luck."

Lawden fixed Wycliff's high collar. "You have more than luck. You have right on your side."

"Are you sure?"

"Yes, my lord, I am. Go convince her that things have changed, except your care."

That was what he needed to remember. Everything he

did now was to fix the past. Making Ruth happy and secure, that was the greatest wrong to right.

He stopped on the top step. Perhaps he was looking at things wrong. She did willingly kiss him. A woman like her didn't allow such liberties. Just a little more finesse, an inch of yielding, then she'd realize they were meant to be. He could taste her, she was so much a part of him.

The idea of tasting Ruth was a good one.

The door opened.

Clancy took his hat and cape. "I'll let Mrs. Wilky know you are here."

"I know." Ruth's voice floated from above. "I'll come down for my cousin."

Wycliff followed the echo like a happy puppy.

At the base of the stairs, he watched her descend. She wore a warm rust-colored gown with delicate silver lace banding below her bosom. The color brought out the jewel tones of her warm honeyed skin and enhanced his appreciation of her fine figure.

This was his Ruth. Bold, vibrant colors.

He almost stopped breathing.

That wasn't difficult given the damage to his throat. Everything awakened inside when she took his hand.

No giving up. Never.

No way he could live without her in his life.

"Christopher is in the garden," she said. "I could get him. I hope I don't have to clean him up to present him to you. It's muddy outside." She poked at the basket lid. "Are we going somewhere?"

Could eyes frown? Ruth's had. Spending time with Wycliff should not be a drudgery.

He tucked her hand into the crook of his arm. "I thought we'd go into the lovely gown…garden again."

Behind her spectacles, a mischievous glint sparked in her

gaze. "What did you have in mind?"

"Many things, but we'll start with sitting outside in the sun, close to the house."

He led her to the doors to the garden and swept her through them before anything changed her mind.

He helped her sit at the small table on the short stone patio. "See, we can feel the warm sun, watch your son, and still be close to the house."

Her tentative smile turned into a conclusive one. "What's in the basket?"

"Wickedness."

"Wickedness. You would be a Wicked Wycliff? That's an insult to someone who keeps surprising me."

"All depends upon how you say it, my dear. Could be an invitation."

She smiled, and it eased his spirits.

He slid the basket to her. Ruth had always liked surprises. "Open, says me."

"Quick with a quip, Lord Wycliff?"

"Sometimes." He inched the basket closer. "Open it, Ruth."

She flicked open the woven lid and giggled.

Her hands sank into the rectangular-shaped box and pulled out a crisp baguette and her favorite Cheshire cheese and dates. Sugared and pitted dates. Ruth loved those treats.

"Adam told you everything, didn't he? Tangy, creamy, beigey cheese?"

"Maybe. But some things I shall have to discover for myself." He put his hand upon hers. "Some things I'll enjoy learning and relearning."

"You sound like a suitor, not long-lost family."

"Ruth, I have thought of nothing but our kiss. There's more to say, but you aren't ready for that truth."

She broke a sliver of the bread, the crusty end, her favorite, and popped it into her generous mouth. "No, I think it might be too much. Thank you for taking care of me yesterday."

"I'll always take care of you."

A little boy hopped in front of their table. He had a barrel hoop in his hand, rolling it and running. Ruth's sister, Mrs. Bexeley, had a bundle wrapped in a dark-blue blanket. She was all smiles, chasing behind the small boy.

The young fellow turned in their direction. He ran and popped up into Ruth's awaiting arms. "Mama, Mama. We saw a frog."

"Yes," Mrs. Bexeley said. Her tone was low. She did not share the fellow's enthusiasm. "A big one by the birdbath."

This was Christopher. Gold skin. Black, curly hair, dark eyes like Ruth. Could be his.

She swaddled him for a moment and set the lad down with a kiss to his forehead. "Chris, I want you to meet—"

The boy promptly wiped his forehead then hopped and bopped and started running.

"Don't play in the pond." She called after him. Chris was long gone.

"He's quite energetic, Ruth."

"Yes, he is. If you spend time with him, you will learn that."

"Is that permission to spend time with Adam's son?"

"Yes. You are his cousin."

"As Adam's son, he's my heir."

Her eyes darted. "Does that mean you're laying claim to Chris?"

How did he get showing an interest in the boy wrong? Wycliff shoved a date into his mouth. "I want to know your son. I meant no offense."

"Sorry, Lord Wycliff. My sister has me on edge about my son's custody. She thinks you're a crazed lord who can appoint yourself a guardian or something."

"I hadn't thought of that." He put his hand on hers. "But I'll do nothing to hurt you. You have to know that."

She rolled her palm and clasped his hand. "Good, because Christopher is all mine. Adam didn't live to see him birthed, to wipe his bottom, or mop his fevered brow. He's mine."

"Well, there's a way to fix all of this. I can get to know my heir. You can be secure learning to love me. Marry me, Ruth. Come to Blaren House and make it in your image, make it a secure and wonderful place for you and Christopher."

Ruth choked a little and put down the date she'd bitten. Sugar granules powdered her lips. She looked like a dessert.

Delicious.

"Those are some bold intentions. I suppose you only go slowly or fast. Nothing in between."

"There's more I could say, but I'll save that for when you've had a chance to think about my offer. You should know how I wish to be good to you."

"No."

He put his hand to his throat, making sure his jaw was in place. "Such a quick dismissal, ma'am?"

Ruth looked down. "You haven't spent time with my son. I know the barrister will tolerate him. I don't know what you will do."

"I'll be a father to him, a good one. Say you'll marry me and let me take care of everything."

"You say you want to marry me. Why? Today is the first time you've mentioned my son in your plans. I don't know what to think."

"I was trying to win you first, before I ingratiate myself upon the son. What heartache will the boy have if he were to become used to me and then you decided you don't want me?"

"He's your heir, regardless of what I do. He's Adam's son,

isn't he?"

Why does it seem as if she's asking me who the boy's father is?

He took her hand. "Are you ready to dismiss this barrister in favor of me?"

"I know what I'm getting with Mr. Marks. He knows what he's getting with me. He's honest. He works hard, and I've been honest to him."

"And he's not here, but I am."

"You don't mind my weaknesses? My sight and my faltering moments? Or the fact that I might be frigid?"

There was no way that could be, not his warm, passionate Ruth. He put his hand upon hers. "I don't think it possible. If you are trying to run me off, try something else."

"What if I said I only wanted a marriage of convenience, nothing more? Would that be enough for you?"

Was she serious?

Did she not sense the passion burning in her? That kiss on Fournier Street had been a fire to his soul, a lamp brightening his bruised heart.

"Is that the only thing available? Did the barrister agree to this?"

"I'm asking what you would accept. Would you settle for a platonic marriage of convenience?"

He should've put brandy in the basket. He needed to be cold drunk to agree to worship her at a distance.

But what if that was what she wanted?

"Ruth, I'll take what you are willing to give. As much or as little of your heart as you offer, I want it."

"My heart is gone. Gone four years. Can you understand that?"

I'm Adam. I am Adam. I'm Adam. The confession was on his tongue. Would his truth make a difference? Would she hate him more?

He tugged at his collar but made sure it did not slip. "I'll do anything you want, but I'll try every day to make you so much in love with me, you can't help but kiss me like you did on Fournier Street. I won't resist you, Ruth. I won't even try."

Her tense smile turned into an easy laugh.

"I'll try hard to be irresistible."

She laughed more.

The knot in his throat eased. He wanted Ruth in every way, but he'd be patient. She was everything.

"I'm torn. You are sweet to me in your own manipulative way."

"Slightly manipulative. Maybe a smidgeon overconfident, but I believe in us."

His little heir hopped and waved. As he made another lap, she signaled to him.

"Christopher, come. This is your cousin, Lord Wycliff. Lord Wycliff, this is Christopher Wilky."

He stuck out his hand to the boy.

"How tall are you, Wicky?"

"It's Wycliff and tall."

The little fellow bounced, then pointed to Mrs. Bexeley. "You're big, but my aunt is not tall."

Wycliff picked him up and looked at the squirming boy eye-to-eye. "I think you will grow big, big like your father."

"Big? How big is that?"

"*Hmmm.* Let me think." Wycliff glanced at the boy again. The skin coloring was right. He could easily be a blend of Ruth's and his. The wavy bob of hair on the boy's head could be Wycliff's mother's or Ruth's father's.

Chris put his chubby hands on Wycliff's cheeks. "Do you know?"

Wycliff jumped and held him high. "This big?"

"Bigger, bigger."

Leaping into the chair, he lifted the boy higher. "This

size, like a giant?"

"Yes. Yes." Christopher clapped and laughed. "You talk funny."

"He is funny." Mrs. Bexeley came near and tapped her short boots on the patio stone. "Put my nephew down."

"He's playing with his cousin, Ester."

Ruth's tone was lyrical.

Wycliff had done something right. He jumped down, and Christopher whooped.

"Just like a frog's hop," the boy said. "I saw a big one at the pond. Wanna see?"

"Come, Christopher, let's let your mother talk. We'll take one more turn before nap time."

He stuck out his lip. "But I don't like nap time."

Ruth gave her son a hug and patted his shoulder to get him moving. "Go on with your aunt. You can show your big cousin the frog another time."

He smiled and hopped all the way until he caught up to Mrs. Bexeley holding her baby.

Wycliff sat back down to a smiling Ruth.

"You could be good with him, my lord. I see that."

"Who is he named after? Not your father or Adam?"

"It was the name closest to the African Chipo."

"Christopher is not an African name."

"No, it's a good English name for Chipo, a gift of God. Christopher is a gift. No matter who his father is or the lack of having one."

Ruth said the words clearly. Did she have doubts of the boy's paternity, or was this a test of Wycliff's commitment?

He liked tests, even if this cut a little close. "He's a gift. He's your son. He is a gift to me."

"After the attack, my father found me in a brothel. Did you know that?"

Fine. This isn't a test, is it?

He glanced at her before picking at a piece of the rich, savory cheese. "The boy's my heir because you were married to Adam. It doesn't much matter whose seed he is, does it? Have I passed your wicked traps?"

"I'm very tired, Lord Wycliff. I think you should leave."

"What did I say? I did not mean to offend you."

"You act as if you'll care for me like Adam always promised, but you're judging me. Your raspy words are meant to go down smoothly, lovely and sweet. But there's control in all you do. There are secrets in your eyes, even the way you look at Chris."

"You can see all that? Even when you avoid my gaze?"

She stood up, pushed at her chair. "I'm losing my sight. I'm not stupid. You'll say anything to win. I'm not a possession. Please leave."

"You'd rather I hide my desire for you or go about ignoring you like the barrister? A husband for the sunny days, never for the rain?"

He stomped to the doorway but stopped. *This is not how this should go.*

Clever Ruth had baited him. "I'm a passionate man, Ruth, but you are everything. I'll do or be what you say: friend or lover. I'm not innocent. I have secrets—big ones that eat at me, but it's all to keep you safe. I think you need safety more than anything. I can give that to you."

A crash and then a scream sailed through the garden.

"Chris!" Ruth ran but stopped halfway.

Wycliff dashed past her, faster than a sjambok's snap head, straight to Mrs. Bexeley.

The fish pond. The birdbath had fallen from its pedestal.

Christopher's aunt had set her own baby down in the grass and was drenched, standing in the pond trying to keep Chris's chin above water.

"Frog," the boy said, taking in another mouth full of the

soup, then his sobs matched Mrs. Bexeley.

Wycliff pushed into the pond. Holding his breath, he stuck his face into the water and moved leaves and flowers. The boy's pinafore and his foot were wedged under the fallen birdbath bowl.

He reared up. "Keep his head above the water, Mrs. Bexeley."

Gulping another breath, he knelt in the pond. Crouching down, he lifted the bowl and then the pedestal shaft and unhooked the caught pinafore. He tossed pieces of the broken bowl off the boy's foot and pulled the sopping wet boy to his chest. "I have him, Mrs. Bexeley."

Then he looked to Ruth. "Christopher is safe. I have him."

He stood up straight and helped the soaked Mrs. Bexeley out of the pond.

The boy put his wet arms about Wycliff's neck.

Mrs. Bexeley picked up her screaming baby. "I took my eyes off him for a minute."

"Boys know how to get into trouble." He came over and poked his wet finger at the little one. "Watch this one, too. Boys know how to scare their mothers. Christopher, let's take you to yours."

Wycliff looked up and started running again. Ruth was on the path to the pond but in the same spot he'd sped past her.

He put his arm about her waist. His arms were wet. He'd made her beautiful gown wet. But like a sailor paralyzed by the aftermath of a battle, she needed to move. She needed to awaken from this fog. "Your son is well, Ruth. Christopher, tell your mother you are sorry."

"I wanted the frog, Mama. I jumped. He jumped."

Tears streamed down her face.

Get her below, pull her to the hull, the entry of the

Croomes' house. "Come on, Christopher. Let's get your mother back to the house."

He towed Ruth all the way until they stood in the hall.

"I knew you'd get to him." Her voice was muffled against his lapel. "I knew you would."

He drew her closer and put the lad into his mother's arms.

She sank to the floor, holding on to Chris like he'd slip away.

This moment felt private, with Ruth repeating her words of gratitude.

Could he belong to it? He truly wanted to. He had to.

Kneeling, he put his arms about them both. When he looked into the boy's brown eyes and swooped his hand through Christopher's fine, wet hair, he was grateful, too.

"Ruth, you need to get him out of these damp clothes. He can't get the sniffles again."

He lifted her to her feet and led them to the stairwell to the upper levels. "Take care of your mother, Christopher."

He watched them go up the stairs before he headed to the door.

"Thank you for saving my son."

Her voice was loud, bouncing off the chandelier and the neat plastered wall.

He swallowed hard, forced his throat to work. "Adam's son. You two are my family, Mrs. Wilky."

Tugging at his collar, he hoped she didn't see his scars. "I need to get out of these wet clothes. I'll visit with your father tomorrow, if he's available."

"Lord Wycliff, please come tomorrow. We could have tea. I'd like to have tea with you."

With a hand to his collar to keep it from falling, he nodded. "I'll be here."

Ruth smiled then took her son up the stairs.

Wycliff knew battle shock. He also trusted his gut. Ruth

was still suffering from their brutal attack, but did she have another villain?

Found in a brothel.

He picked up his hat and cape and stepped out of the entry. She'd said her father had retrieved her from a brothel. Could that be her aversion to a passionate marriage?

He grew sick to his stomach.

No wonder she hated Adam. Ruth had been left unprotected. Had she been forced to work at a brothel? Lawden must find out what had happened to her. Some of the bawdy houses he'd been searching for his sister, they needed to be questioned about Ruth.

His heart thundered.

Anger overtook him.

Some bawds treated their women as slaves. Could that have happened to Ruth? Is that why she didn't know if Christopher was his?

Did he care for Ruth enough to agree to a platonic marriage?

This all had to be a test.

Tomorrow, he'd clear up everything. There was no way he could have a platonic marriage with a woman he desperately loved.

Chapter Seventeen

THE PATRIARCH NEEDS A WORD

I sat in front of my mirror, balancing my spectacles by pushing them up and down my nose, as I tried to get the focus right.

Wycliff was coming for tea. I had an urge to take a little more care.

Ester popped inside, whipping through the door I'd purposely left open. "Here, use these pearl pins. They will make your curls so pretty."

"Thank you but no, Ester."

I grabbed my brush but saw my sister's reflection in the mirrored glass.

Why did she frown? Why were her lips trembling?

"Out with it, Ester."

"I didn't mean for Christopher to be in trouble. I didn't look…for just a moment. He could've been hurt."

I turned and grabbed my sister and pulled her into a hug. "Chris is fine. He's fine. I'm his mother, and I couldn't even get to him. If not for Lord Wycliff… Let's not talk of this anymore."

My sister wiped at her eyes. "He did us a great service.

I'm indebted to him for saving my nephew. I know this is wrong to say, but I still don't trust him, Ruth. He's hiding something."

Everyone has secrets.

I did. I'd hinted at being found at a brothel, and the man hadn't even blinked. Too smooth. Or because of his nosiness did he already know?

"Ruth, Bex thinks he's involved with unrest at the docks. The Wilkinson family is deep into shipping. There are strikes and strange occurrences. People have died."

"One man. A mulatto man is responsible? Ester, do be serious."

Pacing, Ester crossed her arms about her sand-colored shawl. She was a desert priestess and oracle of bad news. "How do I help you see what I see?"

"Sight puns are beneath you. Maybe you can try something from your favorite Shakespeare."

Tugging at an errant lock, I pinned it high on my head. I took one of the daisies that had bloomed from Wycliff's bouquet and slid it right into my braid before forming my chignon. "I do trust him. And I owe him my son's life. That has to mean something. Why should I question his business dealings? Maybe he is as good as Papa at keeping family safe from his dealings."

"That could be, but Papa's been at this a long time. This Lord Wycliff has come from nowhere. Bex can find nothing on him other than his father retired to the country four years ago."

I put down my brush, then swung my legs and turned on the stool. The hem of my mulberry gown flapped as I faced Ester. "You had your husband look into him?"

Cornered, my sister folded her arms. "Yes. I had him look into the barrister, too. You remember Mr. Marks, the man with whom you've been exchanging letters."

"Perhaps he's forgotten." I picked up the parchment wrapped with a scarlet ribbon. "Another regret. He'll not be able to take me on a drive this week. Next week, he will."

"He is very busy. He saved a widow from being convicted of coining. That could be a capital offense, forging false coins."

I pushed at my brow and remembered how differently my sister and I thought. "I respect the work Mr. Marks does, but he has forgotten this widow, the one here on Fournier Street. What would be my Christopher's fate if Lord Wycliff hadn't been here?"

"What are you saying?"

"I don't think Mr. Marks is for me. I chose him from the men responding to my newspaper advertisement for his respectability, but I need to think about Christopher. He's an active boy. He needs a father who is around. He's lived long enough without one."

"You need to be loved, Ruth, and cherished and safe. Maybe none of these men are it."

"If Lord Wycliff was Lady Hartwell's or Mrs. Fitzwilliam-Cecil's choice would you be saying this? Or is it because you still think my judgement is not sound? You don't trust that I might know my own mind."

"It's not the same. My friends—"

"Yes, your friends. Women who you respect."

"Their husbands are all safe. And Bex and I. I almost let him go because of the danger he faces as he fights for good. Our uncle, Papa's brother was killed. Remember how his bloodied coat was laid in front of Papa's warehouse?"

"I remember. I found the jacket. I had come from a walk and found it on the steps."

"I forgot that."

"And I witnessed my husband die a brutal death. I saw it. I bear the scars of the attack. Don't you think I know danger?"

"I fret too much." Ester's lips went to my crown and she put a big sloppy kiss along my scar. "I want you to be happy, Ruth, but I won't be silent."

"You never are, Ester."

"Papa could hire another servant to keep watch on Chris. Then you can refuse Marks and Wycliff."

"I still want my own. I want my slippers untouched. My own knitting parlor."

"It's Mr. Whip-thingy. He wants you, and you've always liked danger. I remember you sneaking out to the docks."

Yes, I used to be much braver. Somehow, I felt like that girl again, with Wycliff. "The whip is a sjambok. If you hadn't gone with me to Blaren House, you wouldn't know about it at all."

"But he still wants you. It doesn't seem decent, and if you get carried away, he'll leave you a fallen woman. Then a respectable man like Mr. Marks won't come near you."

I raised my head, anger blooming and filling my empty chest. "You don't think I am smart enough to avoid a compromise? You think I don't know how to handle Wycliff?"

"Honestly, no. If one part of your story is true, then the rest is true. I know why you chose Mr. Marks. He is the safer, passionless choice. Wycliff is fire. I don't want you to be burned."

What if I want to be burned a little? What if I, the dormant tigress, want to be a little singed? Maybe Wycliff could take away all the horrible memories and I could lie in his arms unafraid. Maybe he could make me forget the bad. He reminded me so much of Adam, the good parts— kissed soft like him, so attentive like him. But the man had to be smarter to keep me and Chris safe.

Was I folding Wycliff into Adam or Adam into Wycliff?

That was wrong, yet I couldn't help it. I wanted the best of both of them.

Ester held on to me. "Ruth, do take care."

"I need more time to sort things through. And I want the baron to be a part of Chris's life. Chris is a Wilkinson. He should never lose that connection."

"Ruth, I'm saying what's on my mind, like we used to do. I have to look out for you."

She started taking down one of my braids. "I will make this even. And don't worry. Papa and Bex are talking to Wycliff as soon as he arrives. They'll figure out his game. We're not letting anyone take advantage of you."

I closed my eyes so Ester couldn't see the fear those words wrought: Papa and Bex talking to Wycliff.

This couldn't be good.

Wycliff had better not be dishonest. The ramifications would hurt not only me but my beautiful son. The tigress in me would come out and rid my life of anything that could hurt my Chris.

$$\cdots$$

Wycliff sat in his carriage outside of Nineteen Fournier.

He didn't know what to say. His throat felt so dry, almost stripped of words. "Lawden, are you sure?"

His man, his trusted advocate, nodded his head. "Yes, my lord. I'm sorry."

Folding the flexible end of his sjambok betwixt his fingers, Wycliff cleared his throat. "She was one of Madame Talease's girls."

It made sense. The madam who specialized in exotics, as they called Blackamoor and mulatto women, would have had his Ruth. He'd checked with Talease to see if Cicely had been intercepted but had never received word.

"We've been checking for my sister at the bawdy houses in town. I should've been asking more questions. I made a joke about Ruth and her sister being Talease's bed wenches. How awful I am."

He punched at the low tufted ceiling, a jet-colored silk roof that matched the onyx seating. This was a crisp, orderly place for the madness in his head.

No one could begrudge Ruth for doing what she had to survive, work for Madame Talease. Living, eating, a roof over one's head was everything. Talease didn't force her girls. She was known for that.

"My lord, you need to get in there."

"In a moment. You rarely shock me, Lawden."

This bit of news explained Ruth's alleged frigid nature, her aversion to a full marriage. Talease's girls were highly sought after, well cared for, often kept as courtesans for rich men.

"My lord, your toy for the child." Lawden handed him the frog puppet.

Christopher. The sweet boy.

Wycliff shook the toy and watched its limbs move. "Nice."

He'd thought he'd be able to look at the boy and know his flesh and blood. With Ruth as one of Talease's girls, he'd never know.

He wiped at his face and started out of the carriage.

"Wait, my lord."

Wycliff turned back.

Lawden again handed him the toy. "Your cousin Nicholas Wilkinson has been to Blaren House twice today. He knows you made a deal with the Captain. He's talking about old times and friendships, my lord."

"I can't think of him or any Wilkinson now." He passed the toy back. "Tomorrow, with this gift. Tonight, it will look too calculated."

"Maybe it is time for you to wrap up this intricate courtship. Get the girl and go on a long wedding trip. The things you set in motion will follow through even without you being in London."

"I won't run. That gives Uncle Soulden and Johnson a chance to strike. I ran before. Not again. My enemies stole the life and care Ruth should have had. Not again."

Lawden adjusted Wycliff's collar. "Good, my lord. Then go in and win the woman and the boy."

His man made it sound so simple. Perhaps it was.

"Thank you, my friend."

Wycliff exited the carriage and pounded up the steps.

As he entered, a young woman came toward Clancy, cradling her pregnant middle.

"Mrs. Johnson, I'll see about your carriage." The butler stepped out the door.

She stared in Wycliff's direction.

"Do I know you, ma'am?"

"No, but I've heard of you, Lord Wycliff. I'm Mrs. Loftus Johnson. My husband is in shipping."

Mr. Croome's business dealings were as tangled as Wycliff's. He was a perfect match to this family. He nodded and moved toward the stairs. Family of enemies were off-limits. They weren't responsible for their husband's dealings.

"You know the name, Lord Wycliff. He's in a bit of bad straights."

Of course, he knew the name. Loftus Johnson's wealth came from his dealings with Uncle Soulden. The men were thieves. They were tightly knit. They were dirty. Because of Wycliff's plans, they were both facing debtors' prison.

"I'm sorry you are distressed, ma'am."

She played with a shiny black tendril curling about her milky face. "He's mighty desperate. I don't know what he'll do. What if I knew where a ledger was? Would that buy help?"

Wycliff had copied two of Uncle's ledgers. One he'd hidden in his father's study, the other in Ruth's trunk. This second book had more of the men's dirty dealings and the false entries that had placed blame on Wycliff's father.

But dead men served no prison time. Wycliff didn't need the second copy for his plans to succeed.

"What are you asking, Mrs. Johnson?"

"I know Ruth from a long time ago. I have the book now."

His gut was a dangerous thing—so was a woman bent on proving something. Lawden's earlier information on Croome's business associates should prove handy.

"I congratulate you. You were one of Madame Talease's girls? Old Milly, done come up."

Her cheery face froze.

She must not be used to people identifying her from her former life at the brothel. Ruth's trunk must have ended up at Madame Talease's. Miss Milly must have stolen it from her at the bawdy house.

The attractive woman blinked her luminous blue eyes a dozen times before any words came to her lips. "I have. I'd appreciate it if you keep that to yourself."

"I hear discretion is the better part of valor."

"Yes." She moved back toward the exit.

Clancy returned. "Our fellow, Jonesy, he brought a carriage around."

"Thank you." Mrs. Johnson pulled on her chestnut coat and fled.

Chuckling to himself, Wycliff pulled out his pocket watch. It was late. Christopher was probably in bed. He'd like to check in on the little fellow.

"Might I see you for a moment?"

A deep baritone voice caught Wycliff's attention. He turned and saw a very big man, an easy six-four and two hundred pounds, coming toward him. The patriarch of the Croomes, Josiah Croome.

The man wore a slate-colored jacket against his deeply-bronzed skin.

"Now, Lord Wycliff."

"Mr. Croome, I presume? Yes, we were to meet yesterday, but for the frog incident."

"Thank you for that. I hear you had some quick thinking. Right, Bexeley?"

A younger fellow stood beside Ruth's father. He was tall, athletic, and as pale as Wycliff, paler.

"This must be the legislator, Mr. Bexeley, the husband to Mrs. Wilky's sister."

Bexeley's deep-blue eyes slid away, but his confident smile remained. "Let's go to Mr. Croome's study. It will be an easy chat."

He wasn't concerned about the politician, they were about the same height, but Wycliff was more muscled. Working the depths of the frigate had given him the ability to hold his own, added power to delivering his blows.

The older man, though crippled in his leg and using a cane, probably threw a vicious punch.

What a time to be without his sjambok. Wycliff put his hands behind his back. "After you, gentlemen."

They led him down the hall to the room opposite the parlor, the book-lined study where he'd found Ruth during the garden party.

Bexeley shut the door. It closed with a solid slam.

"Gentlemen, is this the Croome welcoming committee?"

The politician's smile widened, but the old man's face remained stone.

"You are related to Wilky," he said, as Bexeley eased him into his chair. "Adam's cousin? He was a real person. Horatio was telling me Adam was true. Not a lie."

"Yes, Adam Wilky was a flesh-and-blood person, and he loved Ruth Croome desperately. They married in Gretna Green."

"So why are you here now?" Croome pounded the top of his desk. "Though I am grateful for what you did for my grandson, four years is a little late to come for a visit."

"Yes. I'm very late, but I've only been back to London since December, four months ago. Made it back in time to spend two months with my father before his passing."

"You are new to the barony." Croome sat back in his chair, as if it hurt his back to do so. "So is Wilky dead or run off?"

What a way to put things. "Ruth and Adam were attacked en route from their wedding, five days after marrying. It was believed that both died, but you know how hard it is to find a body when some murders are committed."

Croome sat up a little straighter. He surely caught the reference to his own brother's death.

The man nodded "Yes, Wycliff. That's true. You do your work, finding things out."

"Sorry for your loss, Wycliff," Bexeley said. With folded arms he leaned against a bookcase. "But my wife tells me you're up to no good. She described a horrible scene at your Blaren House."

"Your wife didn't lie. It was very chaotic when the ladies came. But you and Mr. Croome understand what it takes to clean house. Again, if I had known the ladies were coming—"

"You wouldn't have called them bed wenches." The politician sounded as if he were in Parliament, chin lifted, velvet voice echoing.

Wycliff clapped. "Good performance. You're missed on the stage. Yes, if I'd known they were coming, I would have cleaned house earlier, then broken out the good china, if the thieves hadn't already stolen it."

The politician looked perplexed, but Old Croome belly laughed. "Bexeley, leave us. I want to talk to Wycliff alone." The man's words were slurred, his face and hands bore signs of flames, but he was still as Wycliff remembered from the docks, an all-powerful ebony Zeus.

"You're sure, sir?"

"Yes, son," Croome said. "Go on. Find that young daughter of mine and let her enjoy an early evening without you running off for law-making."

Bexeley's smile broadened. The man headed out of the study.

Mr. Croome sat back. "What do you want, Wycliff?"

"Mrs. Wilky has been dealt an injustice. I intend to make all of that up to her."

"That's mighty nice sounding. I watched you with her at the garden party. My wife told me of how close you two have become. I might be slow, but not slow in the head, boy. Tell me, now."

The simplest truth was best. Wycliff put his hands flat on the desk and leaned. "I want her. I intend to woo her and beat the barrister at gaining Ruth's acceptance of an offer of marriage."

The man started to laugh again, harder and heavier than before. "You don't mince words, do you?"

"No. I have Blaren House that needs to be made a home. I want to integrate Ruth into my world, so I will require her time, lots of her time. I'll use everything in my power to sway her."

Croome pointed his finger at him, the index finger that could shoot lightning to strike down mortals. "Now, you're a little too direct. I don't know if I want her swayed. She's had a hard time. And if she wasn't lying about Adam, then there's a lot of other things she was telling the truth about. I found her, after Wilky died, at a brothel, Madame Talease's. You know what that means."

Yes. Yes, he did. Ruth sold herself to men who had a taste for Blackamoor women. The bawdy house was outside of

London. It might not even be that far from where they were attacked.

He nodded to Croome. "Everyone has a past, and whatever she felt she had to do to live, was because of Adam. He left her unprotected. I'll make everything up to her."

"Sounds as if you love her. You just met her, right?"

"Adam shared everything about Ruth, her strong opinions, her caring heart. I've seen her every day this week. I make up my mind very fast. I want her. I need her. I must have her…in my life."

Mr. Croome banged his cane on the floor. "Well that sounds convincing. Mrs. Croome says you are mulatto. If I squint, maybe. Are you?"

"My mother was once enslaved, but she was freed by her owners when they discovered her love of language. My father met her, this wonderful negress poet, in his travels in the Americas. He convinced her to return with him to England. They married here on these shores. It's why I inherited my title, from their legitimate union. Does it matter?"

"No. I just want to know what I'm dealing with and what type of troubles my girl should expect. White or light, many folks are going to be upset. What type of dowry do you want?"

"Nothing. I'll take her with the clothes on her back or without."

"Boy, you talk smart, but you sound crazy, just like Mrs. Croome. Is that what happens when the races mix? Lord, help my grandchildren."

"Do I have your approval, sir?"

"To marry, Ruth? Sure, I'll even root for you. Save me twenty thousand pounds. Yes. I'll bet on you, blackjack. But if you hurt her, boy, I'll come for you, Bexley will come for you. Hell, Mrs. Croome and Ester will, too. They all are a touch crazy."

"I'll never hurt Ruth, and I'll take great pleasure in

convincing her of my plans."

Mr. Croome powered to his feet, and Wycliff extended his arm to steady him.

"Sir, I intend to have her as my wife as soon as possible. I intend to tempt her any way I can. I'm determined. I'll not fail. She may be returning late or not at all."

"Wycliff if you just implied what I think, I need to punch you."

The door flung open and Ruth stormed in. "I heard what he said, Papa. I'll do it, then send him on his way."

Laughing so hard he might fall over, Mr. Croome headed to the door. "Wait till I leave. You don't want a witness to you beating a peer. Good luck, Wycliff."

The older man moved from the room and closed the door with a thud.

"How dare you? I trusted you. I defended you against everything negative, and you tell my father you plan to seduce me." Ruth swung at him, palm flat heading toward his face but he caught her arm.

"You already had your one hit, my love, on the day we met. You really need to stop this. That's not the habit I want for us."

"I heard you. I've never been more disappointed."

"And I have never been more enthralled." He pulled her into his arms but just kissed her nose. "Never mind the man-talk with your father. The question is, what are we going to do? You have a suitor who completely adores you and your son."

Fury was in her eyes. Her breaths were fast and fleeting.

"Yes, I want you. I think we should marry. Chatsworth Adoniram Wilkinson needs to wed Ruth Croome Wilky. I love you. What are you going to do with me?"

• • •

I readied to explode. I stood in my father's study with Wycliff. I was in his arms, and he grinned as if I hadn't heard his plans for seduction. He was smug, so assured that he could win and have at me.

"You are awful, Wycliff. No grinning at me, telling me what to do."

"My given name is awful." He kissed my palm. "Am I grinning at the most beautiful woman in the world? Don't be mad that I desire you and act like a man that wants you. Would you prefer me to lie and feign indifference?"

He wasn't indifferent, nor was I, especially not in his arms with my pulse pounding, punching the drums of my ears. Something would break, but the passion in me was broken.

With my hands on his shoulders, I struck him. My palms began to hurt from the repetition, the rhythm of me beating this immoveable mountain.

His hands slipped to my waist, strong, secure, yet easy. I could pull away from him if I wanted, but I needed to be in his face so he could see how disappointed I was.

"Wycliff, you go from caring and kind to Chris and then you joke with my father about seducing me. How could you? I had them trusting my judgement again. Now you've ruined it."

"I've done nothing of the sort. What I've told your father wasn't a lie. I was truthful. I intend to marry you. I want you as my own."

I ramped up the speed of my hands drumming upon his shoulders. I couldn't stop. I was too angry, too hurt. "All this time, defending me, making me think I could trust you. It was just to lower my defenses. You're a blackguard."

"This is beginning to hurt, Ruth. You'll leave bruises. You've seen how easy I get marks."

I groaned and kept working him. "You just told my father I'm a doxy. You want a harlot. You're Adam's cousin. All his cousins are evil."

"Ruth, I said nothing of the kind about you being anything but a wife. Always a wife, my honored partner."

"You already called me a bed wench. That's your plan."

"My plan is to marry you, to love you. You're a woman of fire. What's better to tell a man like your father, that I will ignore you or that my soul won't rest until we are one? I ache for you. I'll be as patient as you need me to be, but I intend to have a full marriage, one of respect and one of passion."

My head screamed—*lies, pain, never-ending pain.* "You think you're so clever."

"No, Ruth."

I said no. I said no a lot. I remembered saying no and being hurt worse. The memories that I kept beating back were present, replaying in my head, stealing from me, taking what I no longer had to give.

"Ruth, talk to me. Tell me."

Was I crying? I'd cried then. I'd shouted until an arm, a coarse arm, had crushed my throat and ripped Adam's necklace away.

"Ruthy, let me help. I'm here, Ruthy."

My face was a flood. Big, fat tears robbed me of the little sight I had. I couldn't scream anymore, they'd taken my husband, and they'd taken what was his.

Shut up and take it.

Someone tried to clasp my hands, but I wouldn't let him. I whacked him again.

"You're fighting something that's not me. Tell me what you see. Ruth, where are you?"

I blinked and I was half in the woods, half in Papa's study.

Adam was trying to calm me, trying to make me think this was not my fault.

But it was.

I made this happen. I claimed to want truth, but I only

wanted a sliver of *my* truth.

The piece that said honorable wife, aggrieved widow, desperate mother—that's what I wanted known. The other piece, the one that proclaimed me a victim, a victim of the worst kind—I wanted it buried in an empty bottomless hole.

"Ruth, it's me. Whatever is going on, let me help."

Wycliff was better than the rest. He forced me to own all the labels.

"Talk to me."

His raspy voice wasn't loud enough to cover the mocking laughter, the slurs, the taunts. The sounds of me dying and hurting.

Then I shut up and took it.

Volcano me erupted. The speed at which I slapped at the shadows increased. "Jokes, jokes. Jokes."

I knew Wycliff didn't deserve this, but lava rushed my veins. I couldn't stop.

I hit at him for failing Chris, for the shop glass I'd walled around me.

I punched at being stuck at every step.

Harder. Faster. Heavier.

I beat at the bottle glass that had become my lenses, the headaches that descended daily—the darkness that would come.

I knocked. I pushed. My hands were red, but I kept fighting.

No more shutting this up in me. No more taking it.

No more.

No more.

"Let it out, Ruth. I'm not going away. Fight with everything that you can."

The raspy voice resonated. It filled up the hollowness in my chest. It might just make up for the heart that had died four years ago. I looked up and Wycliff's eyes were closed.

He mumbled a blessing, then other things I couldn't discern.

I didn't want to.

The shame of striking him, of punishing him for things he hadn't done was too much.

Now I had to be rid of him. He was nosy. He'd figure things out, if he hadn't already.

My hand pressed at his throat to stop his sweet words. He winced and caught my fingers. Holding them at his side, he took a step back. "I'll be the proxy for this fight but tell me what we fight."

His voice was worse. It was as if by touching his neck I'd hurt him and made him hoarser.

Shame covered me more, like double-wrapping a present, but this was no gift. This was my nightmare.

I looked down at my reddened hands. They were scarlet, not much different than the mulberry color of my gown.

I thought of the worst thing to say to make Wycliff leave. "There's no *we*. Here's the truth. I've made you into Adam in my mind."

"I am Adam to you?"

"Yes, you are similar, you're just bigger. And your voice is horrible. You can't sing."

"But I am Adam to you?"

"Yes. I'm horrible, trying to make you into him. I'm mad at myself for doing that."

I stepped away, and he let my fingers go. My guise must be working. "I'm horrible."

"No, you're not. Do you remember loving Adam?"

"No, I remember none of that. I was a silly girl who cared for him and ran away for the excitement. It was wild. I was wild."

"You don't mean that. You loved each other."

I rubbed my head. I wasn't good at lying. Everything in me centered on truth, but I couldn't go on like this. "I'm spent, Wycliff. I need to be alone. Please go."

"May I see you tomorrow?"

"No."

"Next week."

"No more."

"This is it for us?"

"Yes."

Wrenching at his neck and the jacket that I'd wrinkled, he walked to the door. Those footfalls were still silent, still horrible. "I'll respect your wishes. Send for me, day or night. I will come."

"I won't. You've done what I needed. You've been my proof. If you find the other half of the registry send it, but your presence is no longer required."

"I'm not sure I can walk away. Fight me tonight, but don't give up on us."

"There's no us, just a memory of a man who's dead."

"There's more, Ruth, and what you won't tell me, I'll have to find out. I'm a nosy man. I should put my talent to use, to save you."

"The Ruth that needed saving died with Adam. Please go."

"I still owe you and Christopher protection. I'll see to that."

"Must you be as determined as Adam?" I put my arms about me, trying to stop my limbs from shaking, to keep from turning and running to Wycliff and saying, *I'm scared, and I need you.*

He put his hand on the door molding. "I don't mind being Adam. I know you loved him. You are my Eve, the beginning of everything for me. I've the strength to fight whatever harmed you, but don't lump me into those things that make you cry."

Then he blew through the door.

He was gone.

I fell into my father's chair, trembling, trying to think of things I was grateful for, but that list ended with the man I'd just made leave.

My headache and my memories had to go. I tossed my glasses to the desk then put my thumbs to my temples.

Pushing Wycliff away was for the best. I wasn't sorry. I didn't want to be manipulated. I didn't need a man with secrets when I had my own.

Tonight, I'd save me, put me first, but Wycliff wasn't done digging. My secrets needed to remain like my Adam, buried in an unmarked grave, lost in the woods.

Chapter Eighteen

Moving Forward Without You

The sun glaring through Wycliff's bedchamber window was a sight to behold, bright and burning through the wretched curtains. He still hated mornings, even more so after a night like last night.

A bar fight wasn't good, but he'd had to punch someone.

Wycliff's old, dark heart had started to polish up, to shine like it was healed.

Rubbish.

Losing the same woman twice gutted him. Life had been better when all he'd focused on was revenge.

Coughing, he sat up. The stench of the freshly-whitewashed walls irritated his sore throat.

Man. Ruth had a good punch, but she should strike at villains, not a man desperate to love her. A week had passed, and his throat still hurt.

Wycliff staggered out of bed and pulled the curtains shut, letting his sleep-deprived eyes rest. "Lawden, no sunlight. You'll not make me into a man who likes the morning!"

His shout went unanswered.

That was probably for the best.

His foul mood had surely tested his man's patience.

Rubbing at his rumpled hair, Wycliff thought of his mission. He yanked the linen panels open again.

Grooms circled the lawn below. Others protected Nineteen Fournier. Mrs. Johnson recognizing him had complicated matters.

Being on the outs with Ruth, Wycliff couldn't oversee their safety or make eyes at her or try to make her laugh again.

That galled.

Wycliff unclenched the curtain, his hands had twisted it miserably. The linen was badly wrinkled. No amount of smoothing and patting fixed it. He didn't need to add another task for Lawden or the limited housekeeping Blaren House employed. All this was a job for the mistress of his house. Ruth should be with him, hiring and instructing the domestic staff.

His wife.

She hated Adam, and now she hated him.

How could the truth go so wrong?

Ruth was angry, hurt, lost. She was stretched to a breaking point, like this mangled curtain.

He'd seen men break on the HMS *Liverpool*, seen that glassy look before they'd fallen to pieces. Wycliff was smart enough to know her reaction wasn't from his direct words with Mr. Croome. It was from something deeper. It had torn up his innards, seeing the pain on her face.

Was this reaction from the violence of their ambush or the violence of being one of Talease's girls? Or both? Though the madam was decent enough, her patrons could be any dreg of inhumanity with a coin.

A knock.

"Come in," Wycliff said and prepared for more problems.

Lawden entered with a mug of steaming coffee in his hand. "Good, my lord, you are up."

Wycliff took the warm cup. The roasted nuttiness of the steam wasn't enough to lift his fouled mood. "Nothing good about it but coffee."

"There is good, my lord. Captain Steward has kept his word. He's refused all of Johnson's and your uncle's shipments."

That was good. Wycliff's plan was moving along. "Yes, their mercantile stock will rot on the docks. Let's start calling notes. That will lead to others doing the same."

"My lord, your uncle does have other shippers. Smaller firms who are not in the same dire straits as the captain."

"True. But Steward is the largest and the other fish will demand full payment before any goods are loaded. Their remaining money will be eaten up, trying to stay out of debtors' prison."

Wycliff slurped the coffee. It was hot and stung his raw throat. "I need Uncle Soulden and Johnson to crumble before the month ends." He took off his robe and wandered to his closet and picked through his waistcoats. Dark, darker, dark with green. This damask print was surely Croome fabric.

"Send a few grooms to my father's…to my country estate. Bring his trunks, the oldest ones from the attics. One of them may have my half of the marriage registry. I should gift it to Mrs. Wilky as a wedding present from me for when she accepts the good barrister."

"She hasn't accepted yet."

"She will. The registry is the perfect gift. Something she can burn to be free of Adam and me."

"You are one and the same, my lord. Have you forgotten this?"

He glared at Lawden.

"Sorry, my lord."

"And I need answers from Madame Talease. She's not been at her in-town bawds. Perhaps, I can pay her to visit Blaren House. She likes gold."

Lawden kicked at the blankets that Wycliff had fought and tossed to the floor. "That's a mighty change in your mood and moral fidelity. Is burning the registry document to free you, too?"

"I wasn't an angel, Lawden. But no. Not that kind of visit from Talease. My profile is too visible to be gallivanting on isolated roads. Mrs. Johnson has seen me several times at the Croomes. That's dangerous enough, but I have control in the crowded city."

"Will do, my lord." Lawden picked up the sheet and threw it on the mattress. "Have you thought about trying to see Mrs. Wilky again?"

"No. She kicked me out. Perhaps I should burn the registry. It would remove proof of her impending bigamy."

"You're accepting this? That's unlike you, my lord, especially when you have something in your head."

Lawden was right. Wycliff was a goal-driven man, but what could he do if Ruth had decided against him? "I've already died to her. Only one man has been successfully resurrected."

"Two, if you count Lazarus, my lord. If you're going to wallow in the scriptures, be more precise."

"Precision, truthfulness. They both seem problematic."

Lawden went to the bed table and picked up the book of poems written by Wycliff's mother. "I see you've been reading the loss poems."

"Well, she had a way of describing death and endings. 'She feels the iron hand of pain no more.' Something good about that."

His man sighed aloud. "No one is good with endings, my lord. Your pappy was not. Neither are you. What's that gut telling you, Wycliff?"

"End my pursuit. Focus on finding Cicely. Send Mrs. Wilky that porcelain statue on my desk as a present, for she's the bride that escaped. Send the frog puppet for Christopher."

"Your gut says all that? It's mighty talkative to be a liar. You are a man of war, not a prince of peace."

"What?"

"You don't give up. You made a mistake. You miscalculated. What man in love doesn't?"

"But she hates me."

"She hates Adam Wilkinson, the boy she eloped with. I watched you two. I saw how she leaned into you when she was weak. She may dislike Adam, but Lord Wycliff has a chance."

"But aren't I both, Adam and Wycliff?" He started pacing. "She tossed me, Wycliff, out."

Lawden opened the curtains wide. The sunlight roared inside, filled the room, and made the ghastly red-painted bed shine.

He rubbed his throat. "I've been trying to get her to remember our great love of the past. Maybe that was my mistake, trying to remind her of Adam. Maybe she needs to see me, the not-Adam version."

"Yes. Show her what there is to love in Wycliff. Amplify what she loves."

"You are writing poems, too, Lawden?" He slurped his coffee and paced in circles from the closet to the bed table. "Don't be Adam?" He thought of Ruth and what made her smile. "I think I should be Wycliff, the big cousin."

"Yes, my lord. You have a responsibility to the young boy."

"Christopher. He's a good boy. He's my heir. He's a sweet child who thinks well of Adam. He will continue to think well of me."

He downed the rest of his mug, then handed it to Lawden.

"Christopher needs someone to teach him how to hunt frogs. I can keep a more careful hand in observing and protecting the Croomes if I'm welcome at Nineteen Fournier."

"Frog hunting is a fine pursuit. A lot nicer than roughhousing on the docks. You might find it a better thing to dwell upon than beatings."

"I didn't do anything too bad." Lawden must've heard about the barroom brawl. "Like I said, I wasn't always good."

Lawden shook his head. "My lord, you have too many things in motion to be reckless. You haven't won, yet. Your uncle is a dangerous man."

He was right.

It was dangerous to walk the docks with Uncle Soulden growing more desperate. And good old duplicitous Nickie could still cause trouble, too.

"No more Wicked Wycliff. I'll be more careful. I just needed to smell the water, look at the good souls working the lanes. It grounded me. The punching did help. Find the best place in London to hunt frogs. I think I and my little cousin need to do just that."

"Good, my lord." Lawden tossed him his mother's book and bowed, juggled the mug in his hands, then left.

Wycliff's thoughts turned to his mother. He went to the window.

Her morning sun, which rose divinely bright,
Was quickly mantled with the gloom of night;

Mother's words of sorrow mirrored the gloom in his spirit. Now the morning had made things bright again. He could make sure the Croomes were safe and get to know better the boy who should be his son.

That's what Wycliff should do, care for his heir.

His faith, that all would work out for the better, was still inside. His hope was deeply rooted, just like his need for revenge.

Both halves of Wycliff had to win.

• • •

I kept my lips firmly positioned in a frozen smile and hoped it wouldn't melt and expose me in Mama's parlor. In my hands, I held a beautiful piece of parchment wrapped with a ruby-red tie.

Clancy removed his silver tray on which he'd carried Mr. Marks's note. Perhaps the butler thought that the parchment bound in ribbon deserved an honorable way to be delivered.

But this note was from Mr. Marks.

It meant no visit, no tea with him today.

It saddened me, but I only half-expected him to show. The first time I'd received a letter with fancy ribbon, I'd felt so special. This prestigious man I'd been corresponding with through the *London Morning Post* had taken the time to bind his letters to me. I didn't realize that all his legal briefs were sealed in this manner. It was convenient for him to do so.

Mr. Marks's letters talked of his passions for the law and his need of a marital partnership to support it. Having spent the past week with Lord Wycliff, I realized the difference between attentiveness and tolerance.

How had I set my hopes so low?

When had I decided I didn't need attentiveness?

Mama set down her knitting. The pale-blue booties she was making for Mrs. Johnson's baby-to-come were almost complete. "How's Mr. Marks today? Will he be running a little late?"

"He's fine." The words left my throat, easy and sweet. I hid the disappointment stewing in my stomach. "He apologized for missing church Sunday."

"He's a hard-working man." Mama unrolled her knitting

wool. Her voice was very even. She should be disappointed from all the work she and Mrs. Fitterwall had done to prepare teacakes and biscuits for my tea.

I tweaked my spectacles and took a closer look at Mama. The woman didn't have on a mobcap. In fact, her typical walking gown was replaced with a resplendent burgundy carriage gown. "Mama, are you going to visit Mrs. Carter? Is her gout still bothering her?"

"Not today. But I may later in the week."

That was too succinct of an answer. Mama wasn't one to run on, but she seemed to be turning and looking at the clock on the mantle. "You look very pretty today, Ruth. Emerald green suits you."

I had dressed with a little flair. I wanted Mr. Marks to notice me. I liked the color, liked the way the gown nipped at my waist, the fullness at my hips. Yes, I'd dressed for him and for me.

Well, this would be the perfect clothing for knitting. "Thank you, Mama."

"Will Mr. Marks be here soon?"

My gaze dropped to the note in my lap. Having to say *no* thawed my frozen smile. "No tea today."

"You were going to be in the formal dining room with him?"

The surprise in my mother's voice shook the confidence I had, my resolve in accepting Marks's absence. "I'll make great progress on my knitting."

"If you accept him, how much of your life will be spent waiting?"

"I don't know." I held my breath for a moment. "I think that this is not going to work."

One. Two. Three. I waited, counting the seconds before she admonished me for being foolish, of losing this respectable man.

But she said nothing.

She looked over her shoulder toward the clock.

"Mama, do you have anything to say?"

Head down, her tidy gray locks looking shiny and satiny, Mama looped woolen yarn about her needles. "Read your letter. You must know where you stand."

I made up fanciful reasons in my head—A burning building, a lost orphan, ten other widows in dire straits. I pulled at the ribbon and unfolded the letter. "Books. He has to study case law. He thinks he may show next week, definitely next week."

"Will he show up for his own wedding day?"

Ah, the tigress did have an opinion. She'd approved of the barrister at Yuletide, but was she like Papa, rooting for the baron now?

Ester barreled into the parlor, her hands full of charcoals. "Did I leave my sketchbook in here? Ruth, I thought you'd be upstairs having tea with the handsome barrister."

"No. Not today. Something has come up for him." Again.

My sister offered me a small smile and patted me on the shoulder. "He's a busy man. You see how long Bex's days are."

But her man always came home to her and acted as if he hated to be parted from her. I was happy for my sister, truly happy. I merely wondered if I'd ever be as fortunate. When would my Job's luck turn good?

Maybe it had started to change, but I'd let my fears chase Wycliff away. He'd said to write to him. Maybe I should.

"Why don't you and Ruth enjoy the tea upstairs?" Mama said. "I can—

"What is he doing here?" Ester bolted to the window. "Why?"

"He who?" My heart beat hard. Mr. Marks had changed his mind. "My barrister? What a lovely surprise."

"No, it's Wycliff, and he's carrying a bouquet of daisies. Did you invite him, Ruth? I thought you banished him."

Chucking Marks's note on the table, I craned my neck to see what Ester saw, but these old lenses showed nothing but blurs. "I didn't invite him."

Mama rose from her chair and balled up her project. She jabbed her needles deep inside the wool. "I accepted his invitation. He's here for me and Christopher."

Ester and I weren't twins. A few years separated us, as did our differences in height and Shakespeare and knitting, but we looked at each other with identical mouths, wide-open *O*s.

Clancy announced the baron and led him into the parlor.

I fiddled with my spectacles to get a good look at him.

He made a slight nod in my direction but went straight to Mama.

She held her hand out to the exquisite man.

Buff breeches, a chocolate-brown coat, and ebony-colored waistcoat embroidered with indigo stars—why did he have to look so well and be here, when all I had was a note?

"Mrs. Bexeley, Mrs. Wilky." He bowed to us but then turned again to my mother. "These are for you, Mrs. Croome. Are you and my little cousin ready?"

"Yes, Mrs. Fitterwall is getting Christopher dressed. He's been jumping up and down all morning since I told him."

"Come, Ester, help me catch our little frog."

Ester's head swiveled between Mama's and mine. The girl lifted her hands to send me some sort of signal, but everyone did as Mama wanted. Ester followed Mama, almost dragging from the room.

The baron and I were alone.

I counted to three, pinned a smile to my lips. "I thought we had an understanding, Lord Wycliff."

He flopped into Mama's chair. "Yes. You made it clear

that you want nothing romantic between us."

I tucked away a confession of thinking of sending for Wycliff. "Then why are you here?"

"I promised the boy to teach him the proper way to chase frogs. I keep my promises."

"You said that to cheer him up from his fright."

"No. I said it because I meant it. That boy bears Adam's name. He's my heir until I marry and am fortunate to be blessed with a son."

A son? I hadn't thought of that.

"I've publicly declared that you are Adam's widow. There are expectations that come with that responsibility. I'm not ignorant of this. Nor do I take the responsibility lightly."

I hadn't thought of that, either. "Oh."

"And until the other half of the registry is found, I should act in a manner that supports our claims. I am tending to my heir, Adam's son."

I rubbed my temples. I'd completely missed these notions. My cheeks flushed with shame. I should not have discounted Wycliff's commitment to my son.

Mama returned with Christopher dressed in a hat and green pinafore that almost matched my dress.

Lord Wycliff bowed to the boy. "Are you ready to go, young man?"

"Gama says you and my daddy were friends."

Big tall Wycliff bent down to the child's level. "Yes. The best of friends. It's a pleasure to know his son."

He picked up the boy and set him on his shoulder, then stood.

Christopher whooped and held on to the man's ears.

"Hold on, little fellow." He held out his arm. "Mrs. Croome, are you ready?"

"Lord Wycliff, I'm afraid I must cancel. Mrs. Carter's in a bad way. Her gout is acting up. I suppose we must delay. I'm so sorry to have gotten you all the way out here for nothing."

He frowned for a moment, even biting that maddening lip. "Christopher and I could go on our own, ma'am. Right, young fellow?"

"No. You can't." My voice was loud and showed all my fears. "You can't take Chris."

"Ahh, Ma, no." Christopher kicked his legs out. "I want to go."

My mother looked my way, but she needn't have had that pleading look.

I launched from the sofa. "My plans have been cancelled for the day. I can go, if you must go today."

The look on Wycliff's face wasn't one of a man triumphant in accomplishing a goal. His eyes were penitent, the dark-gray, almost-black irises. They searched for answers I couldn't offer. "I suppose it best for Christopher to accompany me with a chaperone. I'm but a stranger to him. Master Wilky, is it fine for your mother to take Mrs. Croome's place?"

"Mama. Mama. Yes. She should go."

"You are right, Master Christopher. Your mother does needs to come." He held out his arm to me. "Mrs. Croome, I won't have these two out too late."

"I'm sure you'll take good care of them. Ruth, I'll give your best to Mrs. Carter."

Wycliff may not have been up to something, but the catbird look on Mama meant she surely was. She seemed happy that I was going with him.

We strolled into the hall, and I picked up the wide-brimmed bonnet that I'd set on the entry table.

"Mama, you going to chase frogs, too?"

I looked at my son and the man bent on entertaining him. "No, girls don't chase frogs. They kiss them and make them into princes."

"That's disgusting." Chris covered his cheeks.

Wycliff laughed, a good hearty one with his raspy throat. "I suppose it is, son. I suppose it is."

I stopped on the steps as they kept moving. I had to catch my breath. My head echoed the word, *son*. It was louder than the usual roaring in my ears.

Son.

It was just a label often tossed about to young men, but hearing Wycliff say it to Chris touched something deep inside.

The baron marched back up the steps. He put Chris in my arms, then as he'd done before, he put his arm about me and led me down the steps. The pace was slow. We took them together, one by one.

I closed my eyes and leaned into him. I peeked every few steps and was strengthened by the joy on my boy's face.

Wycliff settled me into the carriage. He sat me on one side while he and Chris shared the other. He took a frog puppet and put it in my son's hands.

My sweet boy jumped up and down. He leaped at Wycliff and hugged his neck like the man was a horse.

I saw Wycliff wince even as he hugged my baby. I wanted to know what was wrong, but I was so happy to see my boy being loved that I buttoned my lips. I didn't want to say anything wrong and ruin the moment.

I closed my eyes. I thought hard about breaking off with the barrister. Was a cousin spending time with my son a balance for an absent stepfather? I'd have to figure things out soon before Chris became too attached, for I had an offer from a man not here but had turned down marriage from the gentleman holding my hand.

Chapter Nineteen

FROG-HUNTING FRIENDS

Wycliff didn't know what to make of his fortune. Ruth and Christopher were spending the day with him. As much as he loved a plan that ensured things worked in his favor, this was unexpected.

And dangerous.

An active young boy who could run off and a woman who could become unsettled in open spaces were a great deal of work. He'd have to be sharp and lucky.

He gulped deep and hard when he saw Lawden drive off with the carriage.

What could go wrong? His brainbox pictured disaster, like fishing Christopher out of the Thames, frightening the little boy's panicked mother to death.

With Christopher in one arm, he shrouded Ruth with his other and kept her moving to the pavement leading to the dory boats.

She stopped at the steps. At the water's current height, Ruth only needed to come down two steps to enter into the dory.

"Wycliff, I've never done this before."

The low voice didn't sound frightened, but she wasn't moving, either.

Over her shoulder, he studied the scene. Placid waters. A tiny flat-bottom dory bobbing in the ripples of the breeze. The man he'd hired was at the helm. Another couple, a young man and his sweetheart, were seated on the far bench.

"Ready, Mrs. Wilky? My little cousin is very ready."

Christopher squirmed and wiggled like he'd jump into the boat.

Ruth seemed composed, staring straight ahead. "Settle down, Chris."

"He's just excited. I am, too. This isn't a frigate or my father's fishing boat. It's a first for me."

That drew a hint of a smile.

It was unexpected to see her happy at such a small truth.

The wonderful lift of her lips made his pulse tick up, becoming expectant.

Goodness.

He shouldn't be so aware of her—her breathing, the slight turn of her chin, the rub of her sleeve against his chest when she straightened Christopher's pinafore.

With a shake of his head, he moved around her and hefted Chris then flopped an elbow in front of her. "Mrs. Wilky, you will love sailing or hate it, but I am prepared to sacrifice my arm for you."

"Even after what I said to you in Papa's study?"

"Especially after that." He offered her a wink then moved into the dory and set Christopher on an empty seat. "Don't move or we'll never have adventures. Never, ever."

The squirming boy grabbed the seat, his fingers fisting and clutching the wood.

Wycliff kept switching his gaze from Christopher to Ruth to their surroundings. He reached out to her. "Come on, Mrs.

Wilky. Your son needs you."

She half reached for his hand, but he stretched, caught her fingers, and drew her forward. She only had one step to go.

He made himself dizzy, looking back at the boy, forward to Ruth, and everywhere else in general. "Come a little more. Then I'll have you."

She leaned a little, and he seized her about the waist. Drawing her near, he stepped back to Chris's seat.

The woman was still, but not shaking, then she put an arm about his neck.

Pleasure and pain.

The feel of her was sweet, but his neck was always raw.

"You smell good, Ruth."

"Mama always good. More adventures, cousin?"

"Master Wilky, you did a good job. Now we must keep your mother warm. Sit on the floor and hold her legs."

"No. No one holds me down. Sit on my lap."

Her son climbed up, and she buried her face in his hair.

Everyone was in place and safe. Relieved, Wycliff may have slumped against her. He definitely sighed and breathed in a mouthful of rose-scented air and creamy neck. Too cozy, he straightened. "Thank you for being a good sport, Ruth."

"I didn't expect adventure, Wycliff."

"I didn't expect you."

Her brown eyes sparkled, giving light to his soul, hope to his black heart.

"You seem flustered, my lord."

"I am. I thought Mrs. Croome and Christopher were to be my guests."

"Maybe the master planner needs spontaneity."

"Perhaps. Was Mrs. Johnson at Nineteen Fournier?"

"No, she wasn't. Why do you ask? You're moving on to married women?"

There was only one married woman he was interested in. "No. She made some interesting statements last time we met."

"Did she gossip about me? Did you set her right? She needs to hear the truth."

"She's concerned about her husband's business. My dealings are intricate. I will protect the Croomes, but no one else. I don't talk about my business with anyone, but I wanted you to know. Let her not press you because of me."

"Why? You don't think I can withstand?"

"The diamonds found about the Silk Road in India are hard and shiny, but men find ways to break them. You're a diamond of the first water. You need never to be bothered by anyone or any circumstance. I'll see to that."

She put Chris into his arms and leaned into Wycliff.

His attention shifted to the lad. He was so curious, pointing at everything. How much of his world had been limited because he had no father to love on him as Wycliff had?

"Why couldn't we simply take your carriage to Vauxhall, Lord Wycliff? I don't think I understand why you chose to be out on the water. It's so open, so vast."

Her voice was light, a mere whisper.

"You need to be distracted." He took her hand and threaded his fingers with hers. "Lawden will take the carriage by the Vauxhall bridge. I assumed with the sun so pretty and bright, Christopher would enjoy sailing. I heard that your mother used to enjoy taking to the waters. This was a treat for them."

"People are staring, my lord. So many rumors can be started about us."

"Our boat mates, those people behind us? They are looking at me, dearest, wondering how I could be so fortunate."

"That's not it. They want to know who we are, and why we are so intimate."

He looked over his shoulder again, then smoothed her back. "They think we should be intimate? It's a bit much to take orders from strangers, but it's advice I'll consider."

"Oh, you."

"Yes, me. Just because you are done with me doesn't mean I feel the same. Why else would I bring you daisies?"

"You gave them to my mother."

"Well, she was the only one talking to me. Your sister's still miffed."

"Why are you being so sweet? I tossed you out. I was hysterical."

His hand slipped again to her back. "A dignified sort of hysterical. I'm being sweet because I can be, because you make me want to be sweet to you. If you are still fretting about onlookers, a simple kiss will put all their questions to rest. We're just a family out for a day of pleasure."

The word family repeated on her lips. She looked confused and a little fragile.

He made a hearty laugh. "That's a joke, Mrs. Wilky. I suppose I do too much of that."

"I think I need to laugh more."

"Ruth, that's why we are a good match, but I am your friend. I intend to be one to Christopher. He's a good boy, an active boy."

He set the lad down again.

Christopher sat between Wycliff's legs, swatting the tassel on his boot.

"You don't have to say, but I want to know. Why did you come back to London? I had heard you were living in the country."

"I can't keep up with Chris, not with my poor sight. I needed to be with people. Chris needs a family, a big one."

Wycliff tightened his hold about her. "Glad to be of service. It's fine to need people. I need and respect you."

He looked down at Christopher and put his hand on the lad's head.

This could be Adam's son.

This was his son.

This would be his son. "My boy, how is the boat?"

"Good. But no frogs."

"Christopher, watch how the water bobbles. You, Ruth, close your eyes."

Her nose wrinkled, but her arm had circled Wycliff's waist. "Not doing it, sir. I have to watch my Chris frog, even though I know you are observing."

The dory floated to the center of the Thames. The craft swayed and rocked and made Christopher giggly. Ruth clung so tight to Wycliff, he felt the boning of her corset and loved the heat of her breath on his chin.

"I did not plan this, Ruth. I wish I could take credit for being the manipulative mastermind you think I am, but I'm glad you're here."

"Yes, Mama. Water and then frogs."

"Don't go hopping, son, until we are on solid ground," he said. "Agree, Christopher, or no more adventures."

"*Hmmm*. What? Water, my lord?"

"Chris," she said in a stern voice that made the boy stop wiggling, "listen to Lord Wycliff. You mind him, you hear."

"Yes, Mama."

The boy frowned, but with the next big wave, he smiled and slobbered.

"I'm not unhappy, either, Lord Wycliff."

She reached up, knocking at his cravat.

He cocked his head as if to ensure his collar stayed in place. This might be the only day they had together. He didn't want something like inconvenient truths ruining it.

Again, she stretched, and he jerked a little.

"See, Wycliff, you're jumpy, too."

"I suppose." He checked his collar. It still covered his scars. Returning his arm about her, he eased her against him.

"Are they still looking at us?"

He swiveled his head. "Yes. But they'll say nothing. They've made up in their minds that we are a family. Good strangers."

"You look very natural with Chris."

"I had an excellent father. I'll be a good one to him, my son."

She stopped looking up at Wycliff.

Maybe he'd said too much. But this was his truth. The truthteller needed to hear it.

"Hold to my leg, young man. I think your mother needs a bigger hug."

"Wycliff, I'm fine."

"Maybe I'm not. It's been several months since I've been on a vessel. My time wasn't happy. I was angry and grieving. It was hard."

Her hand closed about his.

With an arm about her waist, he dipped his chin, resting upon her bonnet. "I suppose we need each other right now. Listen to the waves, Ruth. They are lapping against the boat. Take deep breaths. Smell how fresh the air is. So different than London."

Ruth curled more into him. "Yes, different. Not like the docks."

Wycliff was at peace being a friend to Ruth and Christopher. It was the first time he'd felt that way since returning.

Wasn't this how things were supposed to be, them against the world?

Christopher climbed up on the bench and forced his way

onto Wycliff's lap. "Tell me now about my daddy. Gama says you knew him."

"Chris, this isn't the place."

Her tone sounded panicked, but she had nothing to fear. Wycliff would make himself sound great.

"Your father loved boats. All kinds of boats: big ones, small ones, blue ones."

"I like blue," Christopher said.

"And he was brave, little Wilky. One time he and his papa, they sailed on a river. And Ad… and your father caught a big fish, bigger than him. It was a big, stinky fish."

"I like big fish. Not stinky ones. What else? Was he nice?"

"He was and brave, too. The bravest. And he loved your mother more than anything. He didn't do everything right, but he did what was in his heart."

Ruth blinked her heavy lashes.

From the smile on her face, Wycliff knew he did good.

Chris yanked on his cravat. "But why did he have to die? I want to play with him."

Wycliff closed his eyes. This question was trouble. There was no easy answer to this, especially since he was not dead.

He touched the boy's face. "That's like asking why I'm tall and why you're short. Why your mother is beautiful and that woman over there is still gawking. Sometimes things happen. Sometimes bad men win. Then sometimes, sometimes, judgement comes, and everything is made good again."

"Oh." Chris frowned and then turned back toward the approaching island.

The attention of a child.

"Look at the foam cresting on the water. Mrs. Wilky, Master Wilky, this is why we have to have days like this. We are made to enjoy the water and the sun, all these creations. We live to remember this joy, not the bad."

Chris reached back and grabbed Wycliff's jaw and leaned

his forehead to Wycliff's. "You talk smart. That's what Grampa says."

"Yes, I've been told that."

"Grown-folk things. That's what Gama says."

Ruth's smile possessed a smile.

It hit him. The elusive peace Wycliff had been chasing was here in his arms. He needed to protect it at all cost.

The bad men that threatened this peace had to be finished sooner.

Adam—his memories and his faults—also needed to die.

Then Wycliff would be resurrected as a friend, Ruth and Christopher's friend.

He could be that and be content.

But Ruth was a truthteller.

Truthtellers needed truth.

Why did the truth and peace have to be diametrically opposed?

Why did grown-up things have to be so hard?

• • •

I truly needed opera glasses, something on a chain that I could slip on and off my nose with ease to avoid a headache and enjoy wonderful Vauxhall Gardens. The colors, the sights and sounds of the island, were brilliant.

This place was big, loud, and bright. It was wonderful. I purposed to be me, the me before all the bad, before Gretna Green, before everything. I'd be the me who'd talked to a cute boy on the docks.

"Twirl me, Wycliff."

"What, Ruth?"

"Twirl me, my lord."

"What? Now?"

Gripping Wycliff's hand so tight, I spun myself, then he

caught on and whirled me past the musical hexagonal stand.

A horn sounded. The notes vibrated through me.

Chris jumped up and down as I fluttered about Wycliff. I moved so close to him that I could be a part of his waistcoat. I definitely wore his fragrant Bay Rum cologne.

The baron smiled, a full one with his kissable lips.

He didn't say anything, didn't seem to mind.

I felt nonsensical having told him to leave and never come back. He was kind, and I was blessed.

"Christopher," Wycliff said, "let's see what the vendors have. Maybe we'll see a frog there?"

My son squealed with delight and hopped around and around us.

The baron was gentle with my boy and had called him son a few times. On the last one, I knew he meant it. I wondered why I was still fighting the draw to this man, especially when I knew how good he would be to Chris.

Faces whipped about me, coming in and out of focus.

But music surrounded me, keeping me here, grounding me in sweetness. It felt good. I leaned into this feeling. I was strong, my boy was gleeful, and I had a friend who adored me.

Huff in. Huff out. I puffed air into my mouth and kept my wits. The silk flags of orange and blue twirled in the wind. Was that a hot-air balloon in the distance?

Rough hands, worn and calloused, soothed my cheeks.

"Why did you stop leading me, Ruth?"

Had I?

I guessed I had stopped to admire the big silk ball, the enormous flames keeping it up. I tugged his palms down but held on to them. "It's so colorful here. I'm good. I'm wonderful. You're with me."

"Yes, I am. And you keep surprising me. I like your surprises."

I glanced at him, again absorbing the beauty of a man with luscious dark eyes. But Wycliff looked nervous, biting his glorious bottom lip. What would he think if I kissed him right here in this crowd?

The notion shocked me.

Bold me would do it, but what would come next? I wasn't ready for next.

"Mama. Mama. Game."

"Mrs. Wilky," the baron said as he wrapped my palm about his. "Master Wilky is intrigued by a game of chance. A barrel toss."

When I settled my spectacles, I saw my Chris on his tiptoes, stretching against the wood stand. His little lungs burst with giggles as he jumped up. "Game."

Hmm. Wine barrels stood on end, each missing a lid. "What is it? How does it work?"

"Toss the sack in the barrel—like that man, Mama."

My boy didn't know it was impolite to point, but I'd been remiss in bringing him outside around people.

Wycliff lifted my chin, his eyes claiming mine. "Not up to a game of chance? Is there another risk you wish to take?"

Chris tugged on the baron's jacket. "Mama has good aim."

The man chortled. It was a return to his condescending laugh.

I welcomed it.

Things were feeling too put together and seamless between us. I needed a reminder of why we couldn't be.

"I saw your mother's tricks in the garden, but this is not a parlor or a birdbath."

Wycliff's raspy voice sounded sweet poking fun at me. It was a wonder how an awful thing could be appealing.

I stopped him from moving on, holding on to his lapel, even fingering his cravat, like a saucy temptress. "Let me try."

"Uhm. Yes. I know you can do anything you set your lovely mind to, but these games of chance are set against patrons. I refuse to allow you to be cheated."

His words sounded gallant and almost delicate in a way, but I'd let my fear take away too much of the good. No more. That girl on the docks would try. So, I would do so.

"I can win with your help. Make the vendor go to the farthest ring, say 'here' and tap the barrel. Make him do that a few times with each one."

His brow lifted. Wycliff surely wasn't convinced, but he tipped his hat. "It shall be done."

A headache threatened, but nothing would stop me. Sliding my spectacles into my reticule, I squinted and saw a thin blur taking a shiny coin from my blurry Wycliff.

The baron put a sack into my palm. "Let's see you what you can do."

I heard Chris giggle. In my head, I saw his wide grin stretched between his chubby cheeks.

"Go, Mama."

My son, my happiness, cheered me on.

My friend hovered. I felt secure, but I had to show him my confidence. It wasn't lost in me.

I rolled my fingers over the burlap. The smoothness of the shifting beans inside was very different than my rocks.

The vendor shouted and tapped the barrels.

I made a map in my mind—noises, distances. I took aim.

With a flick of my wrist, I sent the burlap flying.

Thwack.

Boom. I knew the sack hit a barrel, but it fell to the ground.

Wycliff chuckled. He put his big hands on my shoulders and offered a massage. The feel of it made me tense, then I grew used to his touch. I craved it.

"Ah, so close, Ruth."

"A first try, my lord." Loving the feel of his thumbs caressing my neck, I pinched my lids tighter. The image in my head was of him and Chris, pure happiness, but I still had to prove myself. "Announce yourself again, shopkeeper. Strike the one I hit again."

The blur slapped the barrel, and it made a drumming thud. "It's here, lady, here."

I measured the echo, the vendor's yelp. In my head, I adjusted the angle of my elbow, the force at which the sack should leave my fingers, then let it fly.

Thwack. Swoosh.

I knew it hit the barrel, then the sack dropped inside.

Chris's screams of glee confirmed my accuracy. "You did it, Mama!"

Then clapping. "Well done, ma'am. A few weekly outings with Wilky and me, you'll have your shot cleanly made."

"Don't sass Mama."

"Chris." I tried to hush him but inside I felt proud.

"Yes, your mother has already taught me to watch what I say."

His laugh sounded tentative. I knew I wanted his friendship, again. I liked being with him without feeling trapped. I liked him. "Another go."

Wycliff put the sack in my hands, but I wasn't talking about the game. I wanted us to have another go.

Holding onto his fingers, I leaned into him. "When we have a moment, we should discuss things."

It was bold of me, to tell a man what I wanted, but I felt powerful. I was outside in the sun with my boy and this baron who respected me. I felt like me again.

His furry dimples showed. "You have my attention."

Sliding next to him, I positioned myself to throw, made a final adjustment to my wrist to how much power I would offer, then I let go and launched. The sack flew.

Swoosh.

Dead in the barrel, no rim.

Chris jumped, pulling on my skirts. I heard Wycliff clapping. "Well done, Ruth."

I gave them each a curtsy.

Wycliff took my hand, and I had Chris's.

"Impressive, my dear," the baron's whisper tickled my ear. "I suppose, persevering after a few failures is the correct course."

"It is." Confident from my win, I led them out of the crowd. Half up a grassy knoll, I stopped in place. "I don't know where to go next."

Yawning, my baby wobbled onto my emerald slippers.

"Wilky, I think our champion should take a rest in the shade."

Wycliff's arm wrapped about my waist, and I came to him. The embrace was gentle and reassuring. "You ready for a rest, Ruth?"

No, but I was ready for things to be different.

"What is it, Ruthy?"

"Lead me."

His hand found mine, our fingers entwined. We walked in step like we'd done this for years. He headed us toward the trees.

I didn't want to be near the woods, or Dark Walk, as it was called, but Wycliff and Chris stood with me.

Trust filled my chest, until I heard buttons being undone.

A gasp stuck in my throat, but it was Wycliff's coat.

"Ruth, I'm laying down my cloak for you."

He eased me to sit.

I couldn't stand not seeing anymore. I tore into my reticule and found my spectacles. With them on, I glanced at Wycliff and Chris.

The baron spun my boy around and around then set him

to the ground.

"Chris, stay put. Take care of your mother. I'll get us refreshments."

My baby was so happy, grinning and giggling. He'd had the best day ever.

With another yawn, he laid his head on my thigh. I stroked his short curls. "Love you, baby. You are my world. You are perfect."

I saw his toothy smile as his eyes closed. In my soul, I promised to give him more memories like this.

Soon, Wycliff walked toward us. His hands were full of things, but it was Adam's swagger that choked me up.

He moved the way my love had when he'd come to me on the docks, or that last night at the inn when we'd been turned out.

I couldn't speak or breathe.

The baron probably thought me silent because Chris had fallen asleep, but I was confused.

Who did I want? Moments ago, it was Wycliff.

Why did I see Adam when I'd started to let myself like his cousin? How dare Adam be in my head, when things were finally clear?

Wycliff carried a loaf with thin slices of mutton piled atop.

He eased beside me. "I suppose I overdid it with the boy. Being a good cousin is a little new for me."

I was nervous, struggling for what to say, and decided to joke. "Well, not everyone has an uncle like you and Adam. Doesn't promote strong families."

Wycliff groaned. His arm stiffened. "I don't want to talk about him."

"Adam?"

"Huh... No, my uncle. The man has wrought such evil."

"Sorry. Your relationship with him is as bad as Adam's?

I won't mention him."

"Good. I don't want this day ruined."

I'd said the wrong thing. His face had become so tense.

"I'm sorry."

"No, Ruth. I am. Adam made a mistake drawing you into his fight."

"What?"

"You eloped in the middle of a violent disagreement between Adam and Uncle Soulden."

I almost clasped Wycliff's hand, but I clutched the bread. "I chose to go. We thought we had to be together."

Wycliff shook his head. "Adam should've been strong enough to wait. He put a copied ledger in your trunk and dragged you off into the night like thieves."

"Copied ledger? He didn't. The returned trunk was empty except for the half registry. No jewelry, no books, just an old dress I can no longer wear."

Wycliff rubbed his forehead. "Empty save the half a piece of paper and an old dress? It doesn't matter. As your protector, I'll always keep my business from you, from you and Chris."

"That's where you are wrong. I didn't mind Adam including me in some of his doings. It was the secrets, the things he didn't share that made me question everything."

"That made you hate Adam. Will you hate me? I have secrets."

"Time does no justice when you are hurting, when you need someone to blame. What happened to Adam and me wasn't his fault."

"Ruth, I thought about what you said to me in your father's office. You're right about me. I'm no different than Adam."

"There was good in Adam. He died reaching for me."

Wycliff looked down at Chris and picked grass from his

frizzy locks. "I am sorry, Ruth."

His raspy voice sounded broken and distant.

I put a hand to his shoulder.

There was tightness in his muscles. I forgot myself and put my whole palm to it.

He didn't move, and he didn't stop my fingers probing the tension in his arm.

"Do you like?" His heavy graveled voice sent tingles down my skin worse than a feather's tickle.

"It's not very ladylike to admit that."

"Ruth, it's honest."

"Then yes, very much so."

If smiles could be lazy and unbothered and beautiful, his was.

When I squinted at him again, he frowned. "What, my lord?"

"Your head is hurting again."

"Any time I wear these spectacles long."

"Then take them off."

"Lord Wycliff, there's too much to see."

"This shouldn't be your only outing here. Your barrister should take you and Christopher often. That little boy loves it here."

"I'll mention it." If I saw him again.

"You're so beautiful today. You dressed for him?"

"Yes, but he had to work."

"That's a recurring theme. Something that ends with my gaining, then I do something to upset you."

"You've done nothing today. You've been perfect."

His smile returned, brilliant, even toothy. He reached over, took my spectacles, and put them in his pocket. "Close your eyes."

I did as he requested.

I trusted him.

His hands were at the back of my skull. His palms were rough against my cheeks, and I smelled food: the baked bread and mustardy shaved meat.

"The eye is a muscle. It can hurt when overworked."

"There's a lot to see."

"You have a nose, two ears, a mouth, skin, lovely skin. They should work more."

"How does one enjoy Vauxhall without seeing it?"

Wycliff knelt behind me, his fingers dancing along the nape of my neck. "You have a beautiful set of shoulders."

"Thank you, my lord."

His hands stayed on me, stroking circles. "Now listen to the music. Remember the band up in the stand. Can't you hear their music?"

"You're going to sing?"

"I'm trying to get rid of your headache, not make it worse. Just listen."

The rumble in his laugh was dark and delicious. I leaned back against him and felt his chest vibrating from his hoarse hum. The heavy ticking of his heart sounded better than my favorite clock. "Yes, this is good."

That dangerous feeling stirred, the one that wanted his kiss to follow where his hands had touched— weak temples, a lonely arched neck.

His beard skimmed the top of my brow, furry and soft. Such a sweet bear.

My pulse raced like it was in a marathon, but my headache eased.

He sat again beside me, shoulder to shoulder. "Now open wide. Let me put some of the good bread to your mouth. Open for me."

Hesitation wouldn't do, not for Wycliff. I lowered my lip and stuck out my tongue.

His chuckles trembled through me as his fingers went

to my mouth. Then I tasted a piece of fresh bread that had absorbed the gravy of the sliced meat. The tang of the mustard seemed to head straight to my nostrils.

"The bread is so good, but the mustard is so strong."

"Do I stop feeding you, Ruth?"

"No. Less mustard."

He laughed again and things were good, almost perfect.

Perfect would be Wycliff asking again to be more than a good cousin. This time I'd let him.

Chapter Twenty

WHEN WORLDS COLLIDE

The sun had begun to lower when Wycliff carried the sleeping Christopher out of his carriage. The boy snored like a mill saw but had a tight grip about Wycliff's neck.

Between this pressure and all the yelling and laughing he'd done, his throat was sore. His voice would be very hoarse if he was lucky enough to still have one.

Freeing his neck, he shifted the boy. Christopher was good and pure. He must take after his mother completely.

Wycliff stuck his free hand inside his carriage and clasped Ruth's. "Let me help you."

"Yes. I wonder if we have an audience looking out of Mama's parlor."

He half turned and saw lights burning in the front room of the Croome townhouse. "Well, they'll be pleased. I have returned you two at a respectable hour."

Ruth nodded and came close to his side.

She'd been silent in the carriage, but it wasn't an uncomfortable quiet. It felt like the peace of old comfortable friends.

The little boy yawned, his cap falling. Wycliff stooped, and he felt Ruth jerk a little.

"Just getting this." He handed her the knit bonnet then put his hand on her waist and headed to the entry. "You think he had fun?"

"Yes. You've been so good to him and me."

Christopher fit with them. Wycliff had thought it would make a difference, not knowing if the boy was his flesh. It didn't. All the feelings—the protectiveness, the wariness, and the pride he associated with his own father, bubbled. It grew more and more for Christopher.

Her fingers tangled in the strings of her bonnet. A few curls dropped about her darkening cheeks. "Did you say something?"

"Maybe. My thoughts might be too loud, unlike what's left of my voice."

"Your voice is not so bad. Not when you get used to it."

He adjusted the boy and then took the first step of the entry. "Christopher is amazing. If I can teach him to fish, he will make a fine Baron of Wycliff."

"That's my son, but he's only your heir until you marry, my lord, and have a son. We know you shall marry. Peers must."

He stopped on the third step and waited for her to join him. "I'll not comment, Ruth. I remember being tossed out the last time I shared my direct opinion."

She smiled then her expression sharpened. "I'm surprised that every eligible daughter in Mayfair hasn't been paraded before you at Blaren House. The marriage-making-mamas must be slacking off in their duties."

How could she be serious? He offered a soft laugh, one that wouldn't startle Christopher. "Fortunately, the sjambok eviction has put them off."

The door to the house opened. The butler, Clancy, had a

frowning look. Every time he'd seen the man, he possessed a cheeky grin. Now he looked mournful.

"What's wrong, Clancy?" Ruth asked as she handed him her bonnet and gloves.

Mrs. Fitterwall came from the hall. "Clancy, don't be upsetting Mrs. Wilky. There's nothing *she* can do about it."

Ruth looked down as if this was some unspoken dig, but Wycliff had that sense, that sensation crawling up his spine, that this was about him. "Why not let Mrs. Wilky decide? She knows her own mind."

"Yes, I do. Mrs. Fitterwall, put Chris to bed first."

The woman blanched as if she'd just heard Ruth's voice for the first time.

The housekeeper complied without a complaint. "Yes, ma'am."

Clancy fumbled with the buttons on his livery. "Mrs. Johnson's in the parlor with your mother." His voice became lower and lower as if he spoke in secret. "She's in an awful state. She's been asking for you, ma'am."

Ruth ran to the parlor, and Wycliff chased behind her.

When she opened the door, Mrs. Johnson was red faced, prostrate and crying on the sofa.

Mrs. Croome was there in her lace mobcap, seemingly unbothered. She'd even knitted. What type of dire situation was this?

Mrs. Johnson wiped her eyes on a very wrinkled handkerchief, something that had been twisted up tight. His cynical spirit thought it purposeful for dramatic effect.

The woman lifted from the sofa and came to Ruth, taking both of her hands. "You are here with him. You have to help. Make him help me."

"Me…him?" Ruth's tone wasn't quite questioning. It sounded suspicious. That was his girl.

"Talk to my daughter, Mrs. Johnson. Lord Wycliff, why

don't I see you out and let these two have a conversation."

His sense about things like cheaters, scandalmongers, and bad tailors nudged him. "Ma'am, I want to stay. I need—"

"He's the one. Mrs. Wilky, use your influence. Make him help."

Ruth folded her arms. "Make Lord Wycliff help what? What are you talking about?"

"Look at me," the hysterical woman said. "You know me. Madame Talease's brothel. We shared a room. I tended to you when you came. You have to remember me."

Ruth's blinked a few times. "I don't know you. Why are you lying?" She looked toward Wycliff's direction and then back toward her mother. "I was at Madame Talease's, but I don't know you."

Mrs. Johnson wiped at her eyes. "Maybe not directly. Your face was bandaged, your fever was high. I thought maybe you would know me. I hoped you would recognize me. I was good to you."

Ruth balled her fingers.

The room felt on fire as if the rage coming from her fists heated the air. She stepped closer to Mrs. Johnson. "You've been to this house many times over the past six months. Why is it important to announce this today and in front of my company?"

"Because your cousin is ruining my husband. We'll lose everything."

Ruth tweaked her spectacles. "You are here to blackmail me. My mother, everyone here knows that I was at Madame Talease's, sold to the woman after the vicious attack that killed my husband."

"No, Mrs. Wilky, no blackmail, but a favor. The baron is ruining my husband. He's doing it. You can get him to stop."

Wycliff half leaned on the fireplace, not denying or confirming anything. His business would never involve Ruth.

His worlds, his finance dealings, and his personal affairs would never again mix.

Mrs. Croome, who surely understood from all of Mr. Croome's dealings, sat silent, sipping her tea.

Ruth gripped the couch's high back. "Mrs. Johnson, I don't know how to help. Lord Wycliff is here. Appeal to him yourself."

Mrs. Johnson balled the handkerchief into her palm. "I might have something that I can give you, my lord. I have a book."

He had a feeling this was the missing ledger, but he'd let this woman expose her duplicity. "I'm sure the Croomes have plenty of novels. Probably one or two editions of the Good Book for meditation. I have poems."

"But this belonged to your cousin, my lord, Adam Wilky, her late husband."

So, Milly from the bawdy house had the second set of ledgers, the ones that told of Mr. Johnson's dirty dealings. Was that how Milly done come up—extortion? "Where did you get these books you believe to be Adam Wilky's?"

"From Ruth's trunk." The woman laced her fingers together and bowed her head. "I took it from the brothel."

Ruth's face was unreadable for a second, but then her frown pinched tight. Something was about to burst.

"You were here when my trunk came. You said nothing."

"I didn't want to expose myself if you didn't remember, but when you were dumped at the brothel, I cared for you. I thought there would be jewels in your trunk. I'd never seen such an elegant negress. I found the ledger hidden in the lining. I read it. Your husband identified things that Mr. Johnson didn't want known."

Wycliff's insides churned. He started to loosen his cravat. "You used the information to force Mr. Johnson to marry you. Why give up a document that proved his guilt?"

"It helped him come up to snuff, but I'm good to Mr. Johnson. He's happy. I'll give you the pages that indict Soulden Wilkinson. He's horrible."

Ruth shook her fists. "I don't care for this nonsense about how you schemed for a criminal husband. Why are you here now?"

"That Wilkinson name or most of the name on that torn piece of registry. Those people keep Mr. Johnson up at night. He thinks Soulden Wilkinson will kill him. Your cousin, Lord Wycliff, is now the head of the family. He can help. He can get my husband's shipments moving. Mr. Johnson's talking bankruptcy."

"So, Milly done come down? Or was about to." Wycliff covered his mouth and took a step back when Ruth glared at him.

"No jokes, Wycliff." Her voice was stern, powerful, more than feisty.

She pointed a finger at him before turning back to Mrs. Johnson. "Why didn't you say something before? You know the jokes I've suffered. You laughed with the circle of knitters, women who didn't believe I had a husband. Couldn't you tell I needed a friend, a true friend?"

"I'm sorry. I didn't want to admit my past as one of Madame's girls, either."

"Or that you are a thief?" Ruth's tone was icy calm, too calm. "I think you need to leave."

Mrs. Johnson came to her. "I know I've done wrong. But you know what it's like to be desperate. And you are a mother. My baby needs to know his father as he is, not a shell of a man who's lost everything."

She put Ruth's palm on her stomach. "Feel my baby's kick. Help this child."

Rubbing her temples, Ruth turned to him. "I don't know how to ask you this."

"Don't." Wycliff kept his words low. It was all he could muster. "This is not your fight. Keep your big heart safe and nowhere near this disagreement."

Mrs. Johnson stepped to him. "Please, for my baby. I can't go back to where I came from, and I love Mr. Johnson. I have to save him. Please ease the credit on him, Lord Wycliff. Let his shipments sail."

Johnson was as guilty as Uncle Soulden, but maybe he'd try to live right for this child to come.

Wycliff groaned but decided to offer an olive branch. "Tell Johnson to use Captain Steward. He found the money to keep his ship moving. I'm financing him."

"The captain was killed today on the docks. Someone started gossip that he cheated the payroll. His men rose up against him. He's dead."

Wycliff held back the choice words he wished to utter, the language he'd use on the docks. This was injustice, so wrongful, the murder of Steward. Nothing on his tongue was appropriate for these women.

"The captain was a good man. He had the money for his crew. I eased credit to him. He should not have been killed."

"He was murdered." Ruth's words cut through his gut. She was right.

This was his uncle's hand. A message—anyone associated with Wycliff, left unprotected, would die. Soulden the blackguard was wounded, but the dog wasn't done.

Mrs. Johnson lifted her hands to Wycliff. "Ease the credit to Mr. Johnson. Only Wilkinson's ships can save my husband now."

Wycliff turned away, fingered the garniture vases above the fireplace, fragile porcelain, easily broken with a shove or a careless hand. "Your husband can't be saved, not by me. Captain Steward was the only way, and he's gone. I'll see to his wife and family."

The dark-haired beauty began to cry. "You'll not help? Lord Wycliff, please. Ruth?"

Uncle needed to be put down like a mangy animal before he touched anything else of Wycliff's. "Your husband knows who is responsible for Steward's death. I suggest you and Mr. Johnson be very careful."

The woman wept harder and sputtered words that didn't sound like a lady, but old Milly-from-the-bawdy house. "Please work on him, Ruth."

Mrs. Croome set down her empty cup and took Mrs. Johnson's hand. "You must go. Leave the men's business to them. It's the best way."

The sobbing woman took Mrs. Croome's arm and left the room.

When the door shut, Wycliff prepared himself to hear Ruth try to change his mind and her disappointment when he refused. There was no changing on this, even for her.

Yet, Ruth said nothing.

Her silence made it harder to breathe. "Say something."

She rubbed her temples. "It's true? And Mr. Johnson knows you are destroying his business?"

"Yes. And I'm destroying Soulden Wilkinson. He led the evil that hurt you and Adam."

"Adam's uncle? Why does everything come back to him?"

"Ruth, I've asked nothing of your business at the brothel. Don't ask of my business. It's the only way to protect you."

"What?"

"Adam failed by involving you. He should've finished bringing his uncle and Johnson to justice before taking you as his wife. He thought he could have everything, instead he made you a casualty in his war. You deserve peace, not a war."

"Does that mean I won't see you again until you've won? I definitely won't see you, if you lose."

"You want to see me again, Ruth?"

She sat on the back of the sofa. "Is that all you heard?"

"That's all I needed to hear. I've kept my business separate from you and will continue to do so. You won't see that side of me. You'll have Wycliff the man of peace, not the one enforcing judgement."

She took off her spectacles and set them in her palm. "But peace and war are both you?"

He moved to her, stroking her jaw. She wasn't fragile. She was strong like bone china and had been tested enough. "We're good together. I need to see you tomorrow."

"You want to pretend that Mrs. Johnson wasn't here. That one of your business associates isn't dead."

"Nothing changes by acknowledging this treachery. Captain Steward was a good man who became embroiled with men who don't play fair. These fiends thrive on weakness. I'm not weak, Ruth. I'm not going to stop living because of their threats. I'll enjoy every moment. I know everything can change in an hour."

"I'm to accept that there is one side of you I'll never see. Have I no choice in this matter?"

He bit at his lip. "I accept you, Ruth. Everything. Even your desire for a friend, a platonic friendship."

Firm in his decision, he moved to the door. "It was a good day. Send me a note if you want to go for a walk tomorrow."

Wycliff marched out the door, grabbed up his hat and dashed out the entry.

"Wait."

Ruth had chased after him. She was at the top step and then bounced down another two to join him. "Don't go."

Outside. She'd come outside for him. The lady wrapped her arms about his sore neck. "I accept you, too. Just as you are."

Then she grabbed him by the collar and pressed her

mouth to his.

Her hands were tight, pulling at his shirt, her fingers a mere inch above the scars burned into his throat.

Wild—with her hands tugging on his collar, his coat—her kisses deepened.

How is this a platonic friendship?

He should push away. He should think of what she wanted, what she'd said she needed. "Ruth, wait—"

She purred. Her nails sank into his shoulders.

Control. None. The puffer was stuck in the puddin'. Ruth, as the old saying went, *made the love thick*. It was rather easy for him to get stuck in it. Four years, and he burned the same.

And he needed her, more than ever.

Wycliff dropped his hat and took her into his arms. So warm, so passionate, so Ruth, his Ruth. She was the only person to have him on edge, make him think he'd lost all, then spin him like a drunken top. "Oh, woman."

This seaman drowned, drowned in her fire, tasting and teasing, until he could stand no more.

"Break with the barrister. I beg of you, Ruth. Don't torture my soul wondering if I have a chance."

"I can't go on with Mr. Marks and feel like this. But I'm not ready to be won. There's so much to discuss."

If her affection remained white hot, there wouldn't be much discussion. "So, you'll break with Marks?"

"Yes. You do have nice lips, better than his."

Wasn't quite what he wanted to hear, but he'd take anything that meant she wouldn't consider another man. "Well, there is that."

Caressing her back, he held her, hoping his heart would slow, but when did fire make anything slow? "Tomorrow, Ruth. A walk. Be ready for me."

"Yes."

He waited until she'd slipped back into the house.

But he stood there, hoping she'd come back or even look for him out the parlor window.

A quick gaze to the upper level and he saw Ruth waving at him.

Four years, so many days and hours apart, and he was still as much in love with her as ever.

Small steps, Wycliff. Ruth wasn't where he was…yet.

After picking up his things, he fanned his face and climbed into his carriage.

Time to finish his enemies and make Ruth love him so much that silly things like a name wouldn't matter and a big thing like trusting him completely wouldn't be so hard.

Chapter Twenty-One

DINNER WITH A BARON

My new spectacles made things very clear. Sitting in Wycliff's carriage with our fingers entwined, I couldn't help but notice how handsome he was.

I'd never thought I'd like a beard. It tickled my cheek when he pulled me close. I was glad of it. It made me laugh. I needed to laugh, because Wycliff looked too much like Adam, an older, wiser one.

"Thank you for my spectacles."

His eyes were shadowed by the darkness filling the carriage. The sun had begun to set. I wanted to know his thoughts. I wanted to believe he was happy with me now, as things were. Spending time together. A few stolen kisses. Though, nothing was stolen. I readily turned my face to the beautiful bear.

"You broke your lenses during the eviction, my dear. It's the least I could do."

"I need nothing more. You've been so sweet to Chris and me this week. Walks, teas. He's still talking about Hyde Park."

He lifted my hand to his mouth. I felt his furry jaw. I giggled a little.

"My pleasure, sweet Ruth. Thank you for allowing us to go. It would have been perfect if you'd come, too."

"Knitting Tuesday." I said the explanation fast, so he'd know I was well and not begging off from a fit. I needed him to know that I was good, better than ever. I felt like me again, the me before Adam's death. Was it bad, to think that way?

"You love your knitting and your knitting parlor. Will I ever see any of this work?"

"I took apart a scarf I was making. I don't believe in giving something that was promised to another."

I meant the barrister's scarf, but my mind twisted my words. Part of me feared I was still Adam's.

Wycliff lifted my chin. "Did Mrs. Carter show? Is she still miffed?"

My mind couldn't quite grasp the contrast of how rough his hands were to how gentle his touch was.

His business had violent enemies, and yet he was sweet and relaxed with me.

"Well, Ruth?"

I held on to his hands. My grip was tight. I wanted to enjoy Wycliff. "Mrs. Carter is still miffed at you and now at me."

"What did you do, Ruthy?"

I let his raspy *Ruthy* wash over me and absorbed the intimacy, the closeness. "I asked for proof that she was from Jamaica to show you."

"Wicked."

He brushed those wonderful lips against my nose. Almost like instinct, my head tilted, and he accepted the invitation.

So gentle the pressure of his mouth on mine.

I opened for him, wide, almost wanton.

He caressed my neck, and I let him.

No squirming or wishing for his affection to pass.

I was present and enjoyed this man's touch. I'd never thought it possible, but no one had kissed me this sweetly, not since Adam.

Adam.

The minute that name crossed my mind, I froze. I was heavy with guilt.

Wycliff stopped and swept me deeper into his arms.

And I felt warm and loved and guilty.

I didn't want to make him Adam, but I didn't mind Wycliff being so like him, the good parts. Was it possible for Adam to have a twin? A furry sweet twin? Why were they so similar? It often felt as if Adam were kissing me when it was Wycliff.

"I'm glad you are letting me take you to Blaren House. A proper tour."

"A tour, my lord?"

"Yes, and dinner. I need your opinion on a few things. I do hope you don't mind."

I didn't mind being on his arm, but I was tense.

He had me out of the carriage in a blink.

"You don't need to fidget, Ruth." Wycliff's steps were unhurried, almost lazy, like he had no care.

I was torn between wanting to be through Blaren House's entry and loving the feel of his hand heating my satin glove.

"Your ideas of color for my house are what I crave. Your thoughts and whims are for me. I'm yours to command."

This joke, sort of serious, sort of sweet, sent a shiver down my skin. His graveled voice wasn't a church hymn, but it meant seasoned and secure, even desire to my ears.

Security wasn't the thing I knew I needed. Coming from the closely knit Croome family, it was the thing I didn't know I'd missed.

Wycliff had his palms about my waist, tight and low, as

he helped me up the steps. "My staff has prepared a feast for you."

"I don't need such trouble, and it's getting late."

"You need someone to make a fuss over you."

The doors opened before he touched the knocker.

The vile scent of fresh paint hit my nostrils. I brought a hand to my nose. "Paint fumes don't smell like a roast. It's quite the opposite."

"No. They don't. This is terrible. We won't dine down here. But…" He drummed his boot. "The smell is indicative of the choice you must make."

I fanned my face. "The choice to be sickened by fumes or to leave?"

"No, the choice of color you want in this grand hall."

"Color is a personal thing, Lord Wycliff."

"Blaren House is personal. I want the hues of the walls to be something that inspires you. I want to induce you to consider a more permanent friendship. I'm getting a bit old to be a bachelor."

"You're not old. What are you? Thirty, thirty-two?"

"Twenty-eight."

The same age as Adam. I crossed my arms to block the memories. The hopes of what could've been paled to what Wycliff promised.

"At such an age, I should be married. What do you think, friend?"

"I don't want to talk of this tonight."

He bent and picked up a brush from a bucket. "What of this?" He slathered creamy beige paint onto the wall.

I held my nose. The stench was strong. "Rather dull."

He stopped again, creasing his elegant buff breaches, and stirred a second bucket.

"Dull. I hate being a bore, but when do we discuss things?"

I stepped back and realized he'd painted an R onto the wall. "I exchanged letters with Mr. Marks for months before we met in person. I wish to take things slowly."

Tugging at his jade-green waistcoat, he bent to the second of the three buckets. This one was dead-salmon pink. He slapped a heart underneath the R. "Six months is about the time you were secretly engaged to Adam. That's a long time to wait. This is our third week."

"You can't count any but this week. I was also being courted by Mr. Marks."

Stirring the third, he whipped up an olive green. "True."

"No to that color. Do not waste your time with it."

He smiled and eased the dripping brush back into the paint. "I believe you are right."

I whirled away from the mirth in his eyes. I tweaked my lenses and enjoyed how white and fresh the hall looked.

"So clean, Lord Wycliff. No overturned gaming tables, no broken furniture. Does this place need anything? It is so tidy and bright. No place for shadows to hide. Leave it fresh and white."

"Tidy is important. It's not the feeling I want to evoke. But Blaren House needs color. It needs you."

I wasn't ready.

Not for his hands to slip about my waist.

Not for the rasp of his beard along my throat.

Not for him to move away and stand so far from me.

My hand rose, and I almost clutched his arm. Instead, I wrapped my arms about me. "You had the sconces cleaned. I don't remember them being so clean."

"Doesn't look the same? I'm surprised you noticed. The last time you were here, you missed quite a lot being tossed over my shoulder. Maybe a reminder is needed."

"Being tossed over your shoulder? Never."

"No, a new tour with you on my arm, inspecting things as

Lady Wycliff should. It would be a very proper thing."

"Why do you tease me? I'm not Lady Wycliff."

"Ruth, this is no tease. I want you to love Blaren House. It's quite large. The upstairs is fine, with many bedrooms for you to choose from, a nursery and schoolroom for Christopher, and a lonely chamber where I lay my head."

He took my hand and led me to the stairs. "Everything is up this way."

It was a grand thing, the curved staircase before me. Painted white and glistening with wax polish, every tread had been lit with beeswax candles set in bronze holders.

"The upper rooms, a stairwell to heaven, Ruthy. I'm a bridegroom preparing Blaren House for its bride. That bride would be you."

"I'm not your bride."

"A fixable mistake."

When I frowned at him, he lifted his hands in the air. "I only mean a special license and a quickly summoned vicar solves all ills."

My stomach had butterflies, not the kind that floated in love but the ones that fled in terror of little children with nets.

"The paint fumes have gone to my head. I think we should lcavc. I'm not dining upstairs."

His loud sigh was humorous. He kissed my hand right above my knuckles. "Somehow I knew you wouldn't."

He twirled me a full rotation and then guided dizzy me down the hall.

"The front parlor is being painted, too. It was ghastly yellow and red. Dinner is next door in my study."

A table draped in a white cloth stood in the center of the room. A silver candelabra burned brightly with two branches and two candles on each. Daisies were strewn about the base and atop the napkins.

Right now, the spot where my heart had gone missing

didn't feel so empty. Gads, I couldn't stop the smile bursting upon my lips. "Your patience is a wonder."

"I can be patient if I think I might win."

I couldn't be mad at the smidgeon of condescension in his tone. Wycliff *was* winning. He continued to prove he'd be gentle in everything.

The truth. I should tell him of what had happened after Adam had died, about Madame Talease. I'd written to her for proof about what Mrs. Johnson had said, proof of what I did remember. Madame's words on paper were what I needed to tell Wycliff everything.

He helped me into a seat then clapped his hands. Servers in icy-gray mantles, bearing shiny silver trays, came into the room.

As if they were timed to a minuet, one unveiled a plate of roasted oysters in their shells. Another, a fish grilled in herbs. A final dish, a platter of beefsteaks with onions caramelized on top, scented the air.

Crispy rolls that smelled of creamy butter and rich yeast were set in front of me.

"Ruth, I heard you were an excellent cook with choice ingredients."

I smiled, but I stared at the bread. The crusty golden goodness called me.

A last silver dome lifted, uncovering sliced tomatoes and potatoes.

All hearty dishes with such flavor.

The anticipation made my mouth water, especially the rolls.

"Is this good, Ruth?"

His voice broke the trance of the heavenly fragrance of the fresh-baked bread. I lifted my gaze to him. "Yes, it is."

I allowed my eyes to fully notice Wycliff, to admire the sheer masculine beauty of the man.

Trimmed beard.

Well-muscled in his dark tailcoat, his crisp white shirt and cravat. His collar reached high on his neck, high like the dandies wore, but he wasn't enslaved to fashion. Everything seemed normal and in place.

I was glad that I'd worn long sleeves, an evening gown of indigo with ebony embroidery about my waist and hem. I looked a match to his style.

My hope was that I pleased him, for he pleased me.

"Your study looks no different."

"Is that a problem? It's very much how the last Baron of Wycliff kept it. The fool, Cousin Nickie, didn't tamper with it."

That name burned my insides, but I wouldn't let him steal this moment. "I like this room, the desk, the settee, the odd marble statue on the desk. Is that woman trying to get away from that marble soldier?"

"Yes. Not the most romantic image, but her shape is quite fine. Your shape is quite fine, too."

"You know your planned seduction is not winning. You're not upset?"

He sat across from me and twiddled his thumbs against his napkin. "Is it called seduction if you are legally my wife? I'm curious."

"I'm not your wife."

"But you are considering it?"

I dipped my chin and studied my empty plate. "Of course I am."

"I'm not the diligent barrister. I might fight injustice during the day, but I'll be home fighting for my family, you and Christopher."

"That still does not explain all of your teasing and romantic gestures."

"Can't a man be romantic?"

"I suppose. Adam used to sing to me."

"That's not a gift I possess. You'll have to make do with my ragged voice."

He took my hand and called for blessings on the food, upon me and Christopher. He wished me peace from the crown of my head to the soles of my feet.

The gravel and gravitas of his desires for us pimpled my arms with fright, delight, and even a sense of discovery. Then those blessings hit me in the pit of my stomach. They were Adam's words, the way he'd ended each day, that one week of our marriage. I looked down at the perfect snow-white tablecloth, then right in those dark eyes. "Adam."

He didn't say a word for at least a minute, long enough for me to hope and then dread my wish, that Adam and Wycliff were one and the same.

"Yes, Ruth. What did you want?"

I rose to my feet to look for an exit, but there was none, not without Wycliff's help. "You'd answer to a dead man's name? Are you trying to confuse me on purpose? Why do you want me to think about him and not you?"

He stood behind me and put his arms on mine. My thin sleeves ensured I'd feel the roughness of his palms on my skin.

"Isn't it Shakespeare that goes on about a name, about the irrelevancy of it?"

"Sounds like it, but that's something for my sister to answer."

"I have a long formal name that I hate, so if you use another name and look at me the way you just called for Adam, I'll answer. I know it's me you want."

"Wycliff, don't you know how awful I feel, knowing that you are everything he was and wasn't."

"I don't have the voice you loved."

Guilt spun a heavy web about me. I drifted against him.

"That doesn't matter."

"I'm me, Ruth. If that's a blend of Adam, I don't care. I know I can make you happy. You make me happy."

"How? I haven't done anything. I keep pushing you away."

"But we end up here, with you letting me hold you. We are meant to be."

"What if I disappoint you? What if you built up something in your head because of what Adam told you? I'm not that girl. Surely, you see that?"

"More faith, Ruth. That's what you need. You dazzle me. I cannot stay away."

I was glad of his persistence, but I still had a truth I hadn't told anyone, not in a long time. I needed to tell him.

His lips sought the arch of my neck.

The thought of food and a confession disappeared. I wanted to be bold and turn to him, but my feet didn't work.

My conscience weighed me down. I wouldn't be free until I told him everything.

"Ruth, I lost everything once. I spent years struggling to understand why. I know what I need. It's you. Since the first day I saw you, it's been you."

"So, you fell for a bed wench on your steps?"

"No, a friend that I needed and had missed for an eternity."

I rotated like the hands on my watch face, ticking closer and closer to being consumed.

He nipped at my nose.

My head tilted up in response.

A double knock at the door made the bear growl.

"You should eat. I'll be back in a moment."

He took me to my chair, gathered his sjambok from the desk, then disappeared beyond the doors.

The sight of his weapon forced my rapid pulse to jitter.

Shouting erupted outside the door.

That voice.

I knew it, the tone of evil. Fear latched me to my chair. It was a heavy, invisible hand that clapped my mouth and punched at my bosom until all the air came out. You can't scream when that happens. I needed to scream, to shout, and save my Wycliff.

One of the men who'd killed my Adam, who'd killed me, was in the house.

• • •

Sjambok in hand, Wycliff headed to the hall. Lawden's signal meant trouble and he would return with bullets.

There was no time for guns with danger in his hall.

His heart pounded like a gong.

These two showed up at Blaren House uninvited?

A groom would be dismissed.

No one was supposed to visit while Ruth was here.

He entered the hall and saw them, Loftus Johnson and Nicholas. "Gentlemen, I am quite busy."

Johnson wrinkled his nose. "You're decorating while you destroy us."

"Yes. Now leave."

The portly gray-haired man headed toward a bucket of paint as if to kick it.

Wycliff couldn't allow it. With his sjambok, he hit the man's leg, toppling him over like Christopher's frog toy. "It took forever to clean up after my cousin here. I don't need you making a disaster, too."

Johnson rolled around, grasping at his ankle.

"Are you much hurt?" Wycliff curled his whip for another strike.

"Yes, my ankle. My back."

"Good. Cousin, drag Johnson from here."

Nickie looked nervous and sweaty. His dark-blue eyes were beady, his sunny locks ruffled. The mole as hideous as ever. "Wycliff, things are out of hand. You've proved your point. You've outsmarted us all. Relent. Leave us something."

"Like you all did me?"

"I let you live, Adam. I could've let the mob kill you."

"Like you did to Steward?"

"That wasn't my doing. You saved me from drowning when we were children. Can't you have that kind of compassion upon me now? Please, Cousin. Tell me what to do."

Wycliff shouldn't be moved by this. He didn't give a whit about his uncle or Johnson, but Nicholas, at times, had been like a brother. He snapped the sjambok to turn back the empathy he'd begun to feel. Weakness meant death.

"Please. You know I have a son. If you had one, you'd know how I can't face not putting bread on his table. Johnson's wife is about to have a baby. We repent of what we've done. Have mercy."

A lightning bolt from the heavens should blow through Blaren House's roof and strike Wycliff for even considering the notion. They were trying to use his beliefs against him. "I'm not the one who grants forgiveness for trespasses. Leave. Go pay alms to Steward's widow."

Nickie tried to grab his arm, but he bucked away and readied the sjambok to strike. This time he'd hit for blood.

"If my father lets you know how sorry he is, will that change things?"

"Nickie, don't bring that man here or you all will be dead by morning. Go see to these children who've made you humane. But don't fret. I take care of widows."

Johnson stood but rubbed at his knee. "My wife says you are partial to a widow now. What if we make similar threats?"

"Then you die now." He struck Johnson in the face with his fist and knocked him into Nicholas. "Lawden, let's kill them and dump them in the woods."

His man came from the top of the stairs with his blunderbuss loaded.

Nicholas's eyes bulged. "This is too public. You won't do it."

"You don't know what a dead man is capable of. You're all being watched, and as much as I have enjoyed your squirming. This must end quicker."

Nicholas tried to reach for Wycliff's arm again, but a snap of the sjambok kept him away. "What do you mean?"

"Johnson, for mentioning my interests, your note shall be called in the morning. If you cannot pay, your bankers, who are my bankers, will send for the magistrate. You will be at Marshalsea before tomorrow nightfall."

"Debtors' prison. Wilkinson, you said you could reason with him."

"Johnson, leave and go be with your wife. Your last night as a free man should be hers."

The man shook his fists at Nickie and limped out the front door.

"Nicholas, you have something else for me? Shall I call for your father's debts tomorrow?"

"No. No, Wycliff, but Father does want to see you. Let him plead with you. I'm doing for my father like you did for yours."

"You? You're protecting him from being convicted of a crime he didn't commit?"

Nickie's eyes went wide like Wycliff had lied. Maybe he was surprised that Wycliff had discovered the depths of his nasty deeds. "Out of my house, vulture."

"Please give him this one chance. Just one."

These fools would keep showing up and growing more

desperate. "Fine. I feel like going to the theater. Come to Drury Lane Theater. We can meet ten minutes before intermission. But let Uncle Soulden know that this war is over. I've won. Ruin is coming."

"Spare me, Wycliff. Let us start anew."

"No."

"I'm not the man I was."

"But you're still doing Uncle's bidding. What good is it to cry for forgiveness if you haven't changed your ways?"

"Sometimes mercy is given to those who don't deserve it. You're a fair man. I've heard how you're taking care of Steward's widow. I think Johnson had Steward done in for a lesson. Protect everyone around you."

No, that was Uncle's hand. Nicholas was covering for him.

"Please, Adam."

Wycliff didn't move, didn't allow his eyes to drift. Nothing to indicate he cared for anything.

"Cousin, I know if you think about it, you'll understand my choices."

He'd had sympathy for Nickie…once. Uncle Soulden was a terrible man. He had to have been a terrible father, but there was a point when a son, a man, had to choose which path to follow. "When Uncle is in Marshalsea, I'll see."

Nicholas, fist bulging, mole bulging, slunk across the threshold.

Wycliff's gut had been right about finishing off Johnson early. Mrs. Johnson was too close to the Croomes. He predicted she'd disclosed Wycliff's attentions to Ruth.

He took deep breaths, stretched with his sjambok. He needed to be calm before seeing Ruth.

Would Uncle rotting in Marshalsea for the rest of his life be enough for Wycliff?

And what of Nicholas?

Could a man asking for a second chance with Ruth deny

Nickie a second chance at being a better man, a father to his son?

Rubbing at his aching neck, Wycliff headed back to his dinner companion and hoped after tomorrow's theater performance his business would never again come this close to Ruth.

Chapter Twenty-Two

SECRETS AND CONTROL

It was the middle of the afternoon, and I sat at my mirror, combing and pinning my curls for my evening with Wycliff. I'd given my tresses a good stiff brushing, trying to make them look smooth before I secured them with a ribbon.

I hated the theater, the noise, the busy people looking to be seen.

I hated pretending that I hadn't heard one of Adam's and my attackers come to Blaren House.

Putting my head down on my vanity, I lay next to my silver reticule. This beautiful beaded purse had been a birthday present years ago. It would be perfect this evening to go with my mazarine-blue gown. The sleeves were full and slimmed at my wrists. I was elegant, covered, and colorful.

The reticule held coins, a starched handkerchief, and Papa's knife. Papa had a few, but this one with a pearl handle I'd kept with me these past few weeks. I didn't know why, but I had.

It was palm sized with a blade that folded. Even if I never used it, it was with me.

The orange polish that anointed the vanity tickled my nose. I fingered the outside of the reticule, slipping my pinkie up and down the seed-pearl trim.

Now, I understood why Wycliff carried a sjambok. I needed something to feel a little more powerful when evil came calling.

Should I tell Wycliff?

What proof did I have other than recognizing a voice?

Though some things could never be forgotten, I needed proof, undeniable proof before I accused someone of something so vile.

Madame Talease would know. I would write her and ask those questions I had avoided.

I sat up and glanced at my reflection. My bodice was lower, with lace covering up my curves. I had curves. I hadn't shown myself, not truly, not until Wycliff.

My neck looked long. It was devoid of a necklace, those things a fiend could twist and rip off.

Why did my thoughts fall back upon that memory? I didn't want to dance with pity. It wasn't my chosen partner. I chose joy. I could be happy about spending time with Wycliff *and* watchful. The noise of the theater was nothing to his fingers entwined with mine.

The theater was Wycliff's world, and he needed me. I could protect him.

The door to my room opened.

No knock.

Some things never changed.

Soft footsteps sounded behind me. Ester's.

"Where is Lord Wycliff taking you today?"

"The theater."

My sister looked pretty in a high-lace salmon-pink gown. I thought of Wycliff's paint and I burst. I laughed and felt at ease doing so.

Ester frowned, seeming cross enough to hold her breath. "You hate the theater. You went once with me. You've never wanted to return."

I rubbed my temples, pushing away that lingering headache. "I get uncomfortable sometimes, but Wycliff will find a way to make me comfortable. He always does."

Ester paced from the closet to the bed and then back. "I don't understand. You haven't seen the barrister, not once since the garden party."

"I wrote Mr. Marks. I sent him a note wrapped in red ribbon, telling him we should no longer correspond. I've heard no response."

"Ruth, Papa vetted the barrister. We've learned nothing about Wycliff except that he's in finance."

"Haven't you heard, Papa's rooting for him? I think he's betting on the Black Prince or was it blackjack? He doesn't have to pay a dowry if I marry Wycliff."

"Let me get Bex to dig around and find out more, then maybe you could reconsider the well-respected barrister."

I tossed my brush onto the table. "His letters are very nice, but I've seen him four times in six months. He's always working. Wycliff is like Papa, and he's making a space for me and Chris in his world."

I was done, done with my hair, with justifying things to a beloved sister who didn't understand. I lifted from my stool, kissed Ester's cheek. "You can wait downstairs and fuss at Wycliff."

One look at her flustered olive face and I knew my sister was just beginning her argument. "I sound like a nag, Ruth."

"You are a nag, Ester."

The pacing began again. "I feel so strongly. He's dangerous. I feel it in my soul."

"You know what I feel. I feel respected and secure with Wycliff. I didn't think I could have both."

"How can you be so sure of him? You would risk your safety and Chris's for a man you just met? Three weeks ago, he was a whip-swinging loon."

"It's a sjambok. You heard your Bexeley's voice on stage, and you knew it to be love."

"I was in love with his voice for years, but I grew to love the man passionately. I know the difference between infatuation and the deepest love."

"I know, too. I had it once, Ester, and everything was perfect. Things are close to perfect with Wycliff, as close as I ever thought I could get to being loved again. That's the worst thing, to let the bad make you forget you're valuable."

"Ruth, you deserve to be happy."

"That's something we tell others, to help us sleep. How many actually mean it?"

I spun and looked at my reflection—my brave reflection—in the mirrored glass. "I'm happy. I choose him."

Ester came to me and draped her arms around me. "I love you."

"I have been tested, Ester. I've come through as gold. I stopped believing that for so long. But I believe in me again."

"Because of Lord Wycliff?"

"It started with him, but it's me. Once you remember you deserve better, you won't accept less."

I turned Ester so that we could have both our faces in the mirror. "We Croome women deserve to be loved."

"And you deserve a better chignon. Let me make you a beautiful braid and pin curls for your wild man."

Wycliff was wild and wicked and wonderful. I just needed him to be lucky, luckier than Adam, and wiser, too. But he'd invited me and a devil to the theater. That didn't seem wise at all.

• • •

Sitting at his father's desk, Wycliff waited for word of Johnson's arrest. The magistrate would work quickly on behest of the bankers now that all his notes had been called.

It was a little early to be dressed in his formal black trousers for the theater, but he didn't want anything left to chance. This day felt fluid, and he hadn't heard Johnson's fate. The man needed to be locked away, no longer a threat to the Croomes.

Uncle would be next to pay. It was a mistake to think these evil men would go quietly off to prison.

He heard motion at the front door. Then a knock upon his study.

"Enter."

Lawden announced Wilkinson.

Wycliff readied his sjambok, but it was his cousin, not Uncle Soulden.

A bit of relief swept over him, but a baby viper was still a viper.

"Cousin, this is not the theater. Did you get lost?"

"You weren't joking. They came and got him. Johnson is with the magistrate."

"Yes. Marshalsea by nightfall. Did you think I stuttered?"

"You're just a step ahead of us. You and I need a truce. Things have gone too far."

Now they'd gone too far? "Your father tried to kill me. Killed my wife and Captain Steward, and *now* things are too far?"

"Well, you're not dead. Traitors need to be dealt with, and wives are replaceable."

That was a sad commentary. The man hadn't loved a woman like Ruth. How terrible for Nickie's wife and mistress. He set the sjambok down and pulled out his blunderbuss. "I hear cousins are replaceable, too. Or is that shippable, to be banished to the Navy. Stop with the pleasantries. Did Uncle refuse to come out of his hole for this evening?"

"Uncle wants to meet, but it's too public."

"Then there's no meeting. Good-bye, Nickie. Do come back and describe Uncle's expression when they come for him."

"Adam, Father is prepared to deal."

"I'm prepared for him to fail." He tapped his nose. "Perhaps we should meet at Captain Steward's grave."

"I didn't kill him."

"I didn't ask. I know that your side did. The captain had friends. I wonder how they will respond when they figure it out. I highly doubt the lumbering man here last night could rouse sailors into killing their captain."

His cousin sputtered as Wycliff had expected. He didn't have evidence of their hand, but Nickie didn't know. He wanted them looking over their shoulders, fearing retribution every moment. That would keep the Croomes safe and poor Cicely, too, if he ever found her.

Their side definitely didn't have her. She or Ruth would be the ultimate leverage.

Nicholas shifted in his seat. "Why don't you come to him?"

"I don't walk into traps."

"Then let him come here. He doesn't want this any more public. He's worried that the same runners that took Johnson will come for him at the theater. The man was rousted out of his bed."

Oh, so the men who'd ruined his life and his father's were scared for theirs. Didn't people know that if they sowed death, they'd reap it?

This was the one time Wycliff didn't mind being thought of as a rake, a tool to make the ground fertile for judgement.

"Let my father come to you. Guarantee his safe passage."

Wycliff tapped his desk, again fingering *N* for *no*. "I said no. Uncle will be torn to pieces if he steps a foot over Blaren House's threshold. I don't stutter."

"I suppose Fournier Street is also off-limits."

"Fournier?"

"Johnson said you're seeing a woman there."

"I see a lot of people. I see you."

"But you don't take me to Vauxhall. Still have a thing for those people. I haven't found one of them worth anything but a good toss."

His cousin baited him, Wycliff knew that, but there was something extra. Nickie had always tried to best him.

Wycliff sat back and shrugged. "Maybe you haven't found the right one."

He delivered the line as Nickie would've expected, but then Wycliff saw it.

The glimmer in the man's eyes, then a subtle smirk. "I've some experience. Madame Talease and such. I found the act lacking. But you always had better luck."

Wycliff's mind shot to Mr. Croome's warning about finding Ruth in a brothel. Then to Mrs. Johnson. She'd said she and Ruth had roomed at Madame Talease's bawdy house.

Was his cousin insinuating that he'd been a patron of Ruth's?

"Wycliff, are you sure there's nothing I could tell you? I'm sure I have some information that might be of use."

"Like what?"

"What if your wife did not die? What if she was last seen at a bawdy house? Wouldn't you want to know that? Would you pay a huge reward to find her?"

"I've moved on, as you said. But bring the little woman if you have her. Four years in a bawdy house, I'm not sure I want to see what's become of her."

Nickie balled his fists, then eased them to his side. "I don't know where she is, but Madame Talease does. The shrewd woman's been reclusive lately, staying at her bawdy house outside of town. I'm sure she knows what happened to your wife."

"I'll have to fit in a visit in a week or two, after Uncle's business has collapsed and he's jailed. Maybe we can go together, if you are not with your father in Marshalsea."

His cousin ran a hand through his sad, dark hair. "Nothing disturbs you. I tell you your wife could be alive, and you do nothing."

"You come with a story that sounds like a fairy tale. I don't live in fantasies. I like facts and figures, like how much you are losing every day as Uncle's shipments rot on the docks.

Nickie wandered to the sideboard. "Wycliff, you are cold."

"I'm blackhearted and you, Uncle, Johnson, and Nacknel made me this way. Enjoy."

His cousin poured a glass. Hopefully, he believed Wycliff's act of indifference. "Tonight is Uncle's only opportunity. I'll see you at Drury Lane Theater."

"No, Wycliff, here or—"

"Or where, Nickie, some darkened road? Finish your drink and go. Leave two bits for the service."

"Madame's prices are higher, but this tastes better."

Wycliff was too practiced in keeping his emotions buried. His face didn't reflect the acid he wanted to spew. "When the appraiser comes to Uncle's, set aside a few pieces of Wedgwood for me. Tell them I'll pay top dollar."

Nickie downed the glass and slammed it on the desk. It wobbled a few times before stopping.

But Wycliff wasn't done. "Oh, don't fret. I won't buy anything of yours. You've never known the difference between fine art and trash." Wycliff tapped the ugly porcelain statue that he'd left on his desk. "Yet, I do like this bride thing.

Reminds me of not letting things slip through my fingers."

"Drury Lane is your only offer? Fine, we will meet you there."

The man started to leave.

"Nickie, I'm considering stopping the war when Uncle is jailed and can't harm anyone else, but if any of my ladybirds have a feather ruffled… You don't want to see me angry."

Eyes darting, his cousin lost his smirk. "Nacknel is dead, Johnson is jailed. What happens if you are angry?"

He smiled at his cousin. "The tribulation. Final judgement and everyone will go to their private reward. Yours will be hell. Don't tempt me to start early. See you tonight."

Wycliff tossed his cousin a few coins. "This should pay for your admission. Uncle's, too."

Nickie caught it, opened the door, and almost walked into Lawden's flintlock rifle. His hands went up. He looked green, as if he'd vomit.

"Let him go for now, Lawden. We'll have target practice later."

Lawden waved him through and kept his gun aimed and pointed at the fleeing man until the outer door slammed.

The control Wycliff had mastered on the HMS *Liverpool* broke. He picked up Nickie's glass and pitched it into the fireplace. It shattered with a crackle against the iron pit.

"My lord?"

"The fool hinted at having my wife when she was at Madame Talease's bawdy house."

Lawden's face looked as mournful as Wycliff felt. "What do we do?"

"Have someone armed and ready to protect every last one of the Croomes, even the politician. I'm not sure where they will strike. I just know that they will."

"My lord, your hands. You look as if you will break the desk."

Wycliff yanked out his sjambok and cracked it three times in the air. *Pow, pow, pow.* "They want me blinded with rage. Anything hurting Mrs. Wilky will do that."

Lawden moved to the fireplace and stooped. He picked up a large shard of broken glass. "You put plans into motion. The Croomes are safe. Don't give in to despair."

"I want to dispense mercy and judgement, but I may be out of mercy."

"If one works at a brothel—who are you mad at, the client or the woman? Talease doesn't force her employees."

Wycliff was glad his man was careful in his speech. He couldn't take Ruth being called a harlot for being one of Madame's girls. He rubbed his beard. "I'm mad at me, Lawden. All this goes back to me. I was rash to leave Gretna Green. I made Ruth vulnerable. Whatever happened at Talease's is my fault."

"It's an odd thing, my lord. Men want fidelity and purity in their women, but how often do we keep to the same standard?"

That was true, but that didn't stop the buzzing in his ears, the hate stewing in his gut thinking his cousin had had Ruth. She'd met him once. He knew her to be Adam's. Could he have intentionally selected her? Had he hurt Ruth? Was Nickie responsible for her struggles?

His head exploded, and he grabbed his sjambok and strangled it.

Whatever had upset Ruth in her father's study had not been consensual. That he knew.

"Pull the carriage round in an hour, Lawden. As I stew, I'll forget to tell you."

"My lord, we have a tip about Cicely."

"Then let's leave now. No time to waste."

Lawden nodded and left.

If it was Cicely, he'd impose her on Mrs. Croome. That

woman would get her into shape, but his gut told him it wouldn't be. Cousin Nickie would have found her by now if she were in London, but Wycliff would check and then head to Ruth.

He reached into his desk and pulled out the ring he had fashioned, a single diamond, perfect and resilient, impervious to ruin. The gold woven about the gem held it secure. It was new. It symbolized a fresh beginning.

The past didn't matter.

Ruth didn't need to tell him her secret, but she would have to forgive his, about his name.

She needed him to be her friend, her loving friend.

He adored Ruth.

Their secrets should never keep them apart.

Chapter Twenty-Three

To the Theater

Ester followed me down the stairs. I felt pretty, but I wondered how this night at the theater would go.

We walked arm and arm into Mama's parlor.

"Ruth, I still don't approve of him, but I approve of you."

I didn't need Ester's blessing to go with Wycliff, but I was grateful for it. I put my arms about her and gave her a hug before sitting on the windowsill to wait for Wycliff's carriage.

"You have a good time, Ruth."

I smiled, but my nerves raged. This should be an amusement, but I feared what tricks Adam's killer would do at the theater. I nodded at my sister. "I will, Ester. I deserve to enjoy myself with Lord Wycliff."

"That is very good to hear, my dear."

Ester groaned. "Your footfalls are too silent. And this is a private conversation."

Wycliff came fully into the room. "But how else will I hear all this wonderful chatter?"

I folded my arms. "Don't get a big head about it. I can change my mind."

"It's your prerogative. It's mine to enjoy you. Methinks you are growing more convinced of partnering with me? My lonely life needs you."

Frowning, Ester tugged on her shawl and walked close to the baron. "Please prove my suspicions wrong."

She left, slamming the door behind her.

"You deserve a good time with me. I like the sound of that, Ruth."

Mrs. Fitterwall poked her head in with Chris in her arms. "Ma'am, he was insistent in coming down."

I went to Chris and kissed my son's head.

He jumped up and knocked off my glasses, but Wycliff caught them.

"Sorry, Mama." His golden face was a little red. He went to Wycliff and hugged him about the knees. "I'm so glad you came. I saw a frog in my book. I put my puppet on it."

I watched him pick up my boy and swing him about. His new heeled jet slippers made no squeaks, but I imagined the soles knocking against the floor. I'd love to hear the rhythm to know when he was about, to learn it, to look for him.

"Son, have you been good to your mother?"

"Yes, my lord, but it's only been a few days."

"I've been thinking about you, and how we still didn't find any live frogs. I was sure we'd see one at Hyde Park. I hate disappointing people I love."

He lifted a package wrapped with a red ribbon.

My gut twisted. Those ribbons had come to mean rejection. My hands were out as if to block the gift from Chris. "You didn't have to do anything. You've been too generous."

"Not generous enough. I've missed at least three birthdays. Here, my boy."

"It's not my birthday." Chris turned away and ran to my leg.

Wycliff went on his knees, wrinkling his onyx-colored

trousers. He cast a confused squint to me.

"Baby, you're not shy. And Lord Wycliff is your friend, our friend."

"He's given me too much. I don't need more, like you, Mama. No need anything."

Wycliff rubbed at his chin. "I need things, Christopher, and I'm big. I like to give gifts."

Chris rotated a little toward the baron. "I help by taking this?"

"Most definitely, son."

He'd said *son* again. It was intentional to signal that his offer was for Chris and me. We were a pair, and he wanted the pair.

My boy didn't take the gift, instead he went and clamped onto the baron's neck.

Wycliff grunted a little, like Chris had hurt him. "Open it."

My Chris released him and took the gift. Wildly tossing white paper bits and the ruby ribbon, he unwrapped a wood-carved frog, shiny with emerald lacquered paint.

With a gleeful laugh, Chris grabbed the carving, then he tossed his arms about Wycliff's neck again. "Frog. He can be friends with the other one."

Wycliff scooped him up and twirled Chris around like a bird. "A fine young lad needs lots of frogs. I have a question for you. You are my friend?"

"Yep. *Rib-bet.*"

"Do you think you'd mind if I was more of a friend to you and your mother?"

"Chris can't answer that." My words were rushed, but Wycliff was rushing me.

"Yes, I can say. Don't make my mama cry. And listen when she says don't play in the pond."

Mrs. Fitterwall and Mama came into the parlor. "Chris,

let Lord Wycliff alone."

"Yes, Master Wilky. It's time for you to go to bed."

"Look, Gama, Mrs. Fit. Frog."

"More frogs," the housekeeper said, and she took the boy and his frog hopping out of the parlor.

"Ruth, you look lovely. Such a handsome pair. Going to the theater?"

"Yes, Mrs. Croome. It's a lovely diversion as I settle back in to London. I must continue to lean on Mrs. Wilky."

"Good, but don't you think Ruth should wear jewelry? She's so unassuming. I want her to borrow my pearls."

"Or she could wear these." He reached in his coat and tugged out a velvet box. "I was going to save this for later. Or if I said something stupid, I thought this could get me out of trouble."

Watching Mama release a seldom-seen full smile, I shook my head. "A proper bribe, my lord? That was unnecessary."

"I've missed your birthday, too. Open it."

The box felt smooth in my palm. I opened it. Diamonds. One hung on a gold chain. Two smaller ones dangled from eardrops. All lay against a smooth black satin lining.

Mama looked speechless, but I felt a little like Chris. "I don't need this. I will enjoy this evening without a bribe. I'm spending time with you. That's my reward."

The dimples showing in his beard went a little pink. "If you want it as a loan, perhaps we could arrange terms. You know me to be in finance."

Mama cut him a sharp look, and he lifted his hands. "That was a joke, Mrs. Croome." He stepped closer to Ruth. "I would like you to have these. Try them for the night. See if they fit. Diamonds for a diamond."

"Good night, Lord Wycliff, Ruth." Mama looked back one more time then left the parlor. I think she was grinning.

Wycliff held up the necklace and twirled it. "Your neck is

lovely, would you do me the honor of wearing these?"

"No. Not the necklace." The words spilled out fast, too fast, but the thought of having something about my throat was too much. "Sorry. I haven't worn any necklaces since Adam."

"I'm not good with things about my neck, either."

I poked at the eardrops, watching the shimmer of the gold, the fire of the jewels. "Are they an heirloom? Did they belong to yours or Adam's mother?"

"No." He was silent for a moment. "All she had has been looted, ransomed off to pawns."

He lowered the necklace onto the satin and helped me put on the eardrops.

"These are new. Something I had crafted after the garden party."

"Why? And why then?"

He fingered the arch of my throat. "I noted how lovely and lonely your neck looked."

"It's a bribe?"

"Yes, and I need something to pretend to look at as I stare at you tonight. Shall we leave?"

I put the box on the table. "It will be fine to stare at me. I'll stare at you. You'll be the only thing in focus."

He took my arm and led me to the door.

It seemed like a lifetime passed to get my shawl and gloves, his hat and cape, then we descended to his carriage. My hesitation lessened. I'd become better at going outside, but only with Wycliff.

It was dark, but the baron had a lantern lit. The minute the carriage moved and we were away from Nineteen Fournier, he jumped onto the seat next to me.

I bumped his arm.

The big man winced.

My fingers were on his shoulder before I could stop

myself. "What happened? Are you hurt?"

He stilled my hands then drew each palm to his lips. "Good to know you care."

"What happened? Don't spare me. I'm not fragile when it comes to your safety."

"You are a rosebud but made of the strongest metal. You are a survivor."

"Then tell me what happened. It wasn't the men from last night."

"No. I met a disgruntled patron at a brothel."

"You went to a brothel?" A sick feeling went to my throat. It burned, but what should I expect? Wycliff had accepted a platonic arrangement.

Logic didn't matter. I was ill.

Wycliff lifted my chin. "I see you care a lot more. Let me answer what you won't ask. Lawden received a tip about a girl matching Cicely's description. It wasn't. I interrupted a peer, an earl with particular tastes and a willing participant. I did not go for my own gratification."

"You didn't. I mean, it wasn't Cicely?"

He started to laugh. "It was actually stupid to go. It was an in-town brothel, but it could've been a trap by one of my disgruntled associates."

"You mean one of those men from last night?"

"Let's not talk of this, Ruth. It's not theater talk."

"My poor Wycliff, you don't need someone to tell you how stupid that was. You need care." I settled against him, looping my arm about his tense one.

"He took me off guard. That won't happen again."

"I can contact Madame Talease. She would know if Cicely has been taken in. She knows the underbelly of the city."

"No. No more thinking of brothels. That's part of that list of things we don't talk of. We have an appointment at the theater." He kissed my fingers. "Tell me how you missed me."

I had to try again. I could help, and I started rubbing his arm. "Lord Wycliff, I can be of help with a number of things. I know Madame Talease."

"That's not theater talk. The theater, my dear. We go and enjoy. Tonight, we pretend to be normal people out for entertainment."

"It's never a normal occasion for a Blackamoor to be out in Society on the arm of a peer."

"Well, we should change that. London will have to get used to my good taste in ladies."

I wanted to ask what had happened last night, the names of the voices, to see if my mind recalled things right, but I didn't. Nothing mattered about the past as long as no one threatened him anymore. We had to survive the theater.

Raising his arms to stretch, he kicked out his legs. "Are you a free woman yet, Ruth? I'd love to come out of the shadows with this affair we are having, especially since it seems other women and bawdy houses upset you."

He twiddled his sjambok and lay it across his lap. He'd had it last night when he'd gone out to meet the loud visitors. Now he had it in the carriage.

My reticule hung from my arm. I was ready, too.

I tweaked my spectacles and examined Wycliff. Handsome in an ivory damask waistcoat, a crisply-starched cravat and shirt, in a very fine dark tailcoat under his mysterious cape.

His sore arm flexed against me. A second glance at his face revealed a tight jaw.

This jovial manner was a disguise. "You can tell me. I know you are upset. This is more than a bawdy house."

"You were always perceptive. You always knew…when Adam was bothered."

For a moment, Wycliff was more Adam, more the high-strung boy in want of a brawl.

"I think that you needn't stare but rest those eyes. Please feel free to hand those spectacles over to me at any time."

"Is this how it will go? You always shielding me from darkness?"

"You are my lady of the light. Tonight, you shine—no frets, nothing to be concerned about. No need to look for trouble."

"What did you say?"

"That you must be mine."

"No, Wycliff, before that?"

"Lady of the light."

"Adam used to say that."

"Is that bad?"

I put my head carefully on Wycliff's shoulder. I didn't want him hurt. "No."

"No one should face what you two did. You should be loved again."

"Says the man who wants me to marry him but has not told me what he feels."

He threaded his fingers with mine. "My father used to say something about actions shouting and the cheapness of words. Or was that my mother, the poet?"

"Easily said for the man who likes danger and carries a whip."

"Tonight, I will show you more of the pleasures of the world that Adam was too stupid to appreciate. We can discuss my whip later."

"I don't need to be swayed by your wealth. My family has means."

"Yes, they do. That's why peers dip into the merchant class for brides like you, with dowries, like your barrister. Excuse me, your former barrister."

"Marriages of convenience are common, even among

peers."

"As I said in your father's study, our marriage shouldn't be of convenience but of passion, lots of passion."

"Passion can be scary. It can be violent. I don't want that."

Wycliff kissed me on the nose. "You are wearing me down, Ruth. You are going to make me a eunuch. I'm almost to the point of breaking and agreeing to a marriage of convenience. But I am going to stay strong for you. Strong and irresistible."

I touched my temples.

"What is wrong?"

"I've strained too much trying to stare at you. Why must you be so fascinating? What will you do when my vision finally fades?"

He put his hand about my back and drew me to him.

"Wycliff, I've never admitted that I'm frightened by it. I don't let myself wallow or be angry. I know that you are trying to bring justice to those who hurt Adam. I figured that out when I heard those voices last night, those familiar voices."

Wycliff turned away and stayed silent.

Had I upset him? I had crossed that invisible line about not talking about his business.

"Ruth, I will see them tonight before intermission. I will be safe in this public place. It's the only way to keep them from Blaren House or Fournier."

My chest pounded, but I held on to my composure. Wycliff had just shared his deepest concerns. He thought me strong enough to know.

I wrapped my arms about him and gently tucked him to my bosom. "Don't wrinkle my gown. I want to look well on Lord Wycliff's arm."

"This deep blue is so lively. So sweet on your figure."

He traced the long scar on my face. "This wound, blunt and jagged, was caused by a heavy blow. It almost killed you.

It's surely responsible for the decline of your vision. But that didn't stop you. There is such strength in you."

My nails dug into his shoulders. I stayed away from his neck. I'd seen him wince once too often when Chris hugged him there. "Nice of you to notice."

"What doesn't kill me, makes me stronger?"

"You keep sounding like Adam."

"Ruth, never doubt how strong you are. I desire your strength, but if I keep something from you, it's not because I don't trust you."

"I want to help. I want to be someone you can count on, Wycliff."

"Because you are falling in love with me, Ruth?"

I didn't know what I felt, but it was deep and strong, and it scared me. It was as if I'd known him forever, but we'd known each other barely three weeks. "Maybe."

"I have to keep working until you are desperately in love." He kissed my nose again. "I do understand you, Ruth. I think you understand me."

Listening to him breathe, that raspy, throaty noise, I closed my eyes and enjoyed this simple moment.

I purposed to be present right now and enjoy it. For no one could keep all the dangers away. Not even Wycliff.

Chapter Twenty-Four

A Dangerous Intermission

Wycliff's neck was wet with perspiration as he sat in the small darkened theater box with Ruth.

It was perfect. An intimate setting. They even sat in the rear so no one could see them—no flintlocks, no angry relatives to barge in upon them.

Ruth looked perfect. A dark-blue gown that fit her well. He'd grown used to her long sleeves. Not much opportunity to touch her skin, but that might be dangerous.

He glanced at her again. From the upsweep of her hair, the lovely long neck, she was his Ruthy, wearing his jewels on her luscious lobes. Soon, a matching ring would be on her finger…again.

Yes. He was hot and bothered. His thick collar, combined with the warm Drury Theater air, was abominable. The battle stewing inside was worse.

The war he'd been trying to keep from Ruth would soon be outside of his box.

At least this was a public place, but Spencer Perceval, the Prime Minister, had been shot in public, murdered. Should he tell Ruth the truth of Adam, in case… No. Then she'd hate two men.

He filled his lungs. Eased his shoulders. His sjambok was at his feet.

His men were observing. They were armed, too.

"Lord Wycliff. This meeting has you deeply concerned."

"Yes, but the soprano is not singing the part as well as she should. That's more concerning."

"The more you joke, the more you are hiding. Adam used to do the same thing. Very annoying."

"We are two of a kind. Maybe that's why I am dedicated to you. You are quite lovely in bold colors." He leaned over and fingered the lace trim edging the bodice. "Not an inch of your gown is wrinkled. I was good."

She rolled her eyes, but a blush stained her cheeks. He edged closer. "You are stunning. And a challenge. This is good for me, I like challenges."

Wait. Was that a Ruthy toothy grin?

It was, and it confirmed everything he knew to be true. Keep her laughing and happy. Then all would be fine.

The music grew louder. The first intermission would commence in half an hour. The corridor behind him would fill with witnesses. Nothing bad would happen in Drury Lane but the singing.

He relaxed, letting the music invade the tension in his muscles. The tendons of his hand stretched to the tempo. Even the battered cords in his throat, the ones that missed singing, vibrated.

This meeting would have no tricks. This wasn't four years ago. He and his Ruthy weren't running. She was safe. Wycliff wouldn't fail this time.

Ruth fidgeted in her chair. She rubbed her temples. That was a telltale sign of a headache. Her new glasses hadn't solved the problem. He hated that for her. "Ruth, can I help?"

"No."

She took off her spectacles and cupped her hand to her face. The woman was gorgeous and miserable.

He fingered her ear, then her neck. "Will you refuse every gift for this tempting throat?"

She squinted and shrugged. "I don't like things that can be ripped or stolen. I needn't draw attention to thieves."

Exasperated, lovely, and miserable. Then he remembered she'd been at the first battle of his war. He cringed at the costs to her.

"You like the theater, my lord? Adam used to talk of going with his father. I suppose you love it, too? My sister and her husband do. Your future baroness will need to love this."

"You're back to being against me, Ruth? All because I love the theater? I can make it better. Do you trust me?"

Her wide eyes blinked, then she offered him a lazy nod. "As much as you trust me."

Oh, the difficulties of wanting a clever woman. "You need to stop struggling with your sight and resisting my offers. Accepting both might solve your problems."

"Is it time for your meeting?"

"Not yet."

"Oh."

She struggled to sit still, to breathe. It was slight, just a stutter to her lungs, but it was there. He shouldn't have told her, but it was so hard not to tell her everything.

She reached for his hand, linking their fingers.

"You'll never know how this comforts me, Ruth." He kissed her wrist and slipped behind her seat and pressed his fingertips to her forehead.

A murmur eased from her lips as he massaged her temples.

A ribbon, an indigo ribbon, was woven into her hair. He pulled it free. Her thick curls fell, but he needed this wide ribbon.

"I worked very hard at getting everything perfect. My hair has come down. What are you doing?"

"I have a better plan for this ribbon. Keep your spectacles off for now."

She raised a hand as if to object, then she stopped and put her lenses into her lap.

Very loosely, he drooped the ribbon over her eyes. "Listen to the music, Ruth. No more fighting the rhythm. Let it lead."

"Just listen? I can't see."

"Yes, just listen. Your hearing is the sharpest. Tell me the instruments."

"Drums. Anyone can hear that."

"That's the beginning. Just listen. Do you hear cymbals and trumpets? Let those differences tease the story to you."

She nodded, and he increased the pressure of his fingers to her temples. With his thumbs, he made small, delicate circles at the nape of her neck, following the trail he'd numbered, of spots that radiated pain, that made her sigh.

It took another minute for her to relax. Her breathing sounded regular and rhythmic, such sweet music to his ears.

"Ruth, I'll be in the passageway that leads to this box. You, Christopher, and Ciccly are the most important things to me. Forgive me. I never wanted my business to be this close to you. Never."

Clasping his hand, she drew his fingers to her cheek. "Nothing to forgive. I know you care intensely for us. Do what you have to do to stop them and then come back to me."

"This will make my world safe for you. I need a little more time to win. I need your patience. I reward patience."

"I need no reward, but your consideration of me as a partner means so much. You didn't have to tell me."

"Enjoy this music." He kneaded her shoulders. She sighed beneath his fingertips. "I need you here, not out in the hall. My enemies can't see you."

She lowered the ribbon and put on her lenses. "I don't want you hurt."

"I won't be able to do this unless you are safe in here, Ruth."

The curtains parted and Lawden stuck his head in and waved him forward.

Wycliff picked up his sjambok from the floor, kissed her cheek, then followed his man. His future was with Ruth, but he had to defeat the past first.

• • •

I tried to listen to the music, but Wycliff, my Wycliff, was in danger.

If he thought I'd sit still and wait like some good little woman for him, he'd lost his head.

Volcanoes didn't wait, they exploded.

I slipped on my spectacles and bounced to the curtains. Maybe I could hear something. Maybe I could help.

My mind kept flashing to Adam. How he'd fought for me. If these were the men who had killed Adam, they wouldn't stop with a meeting in the theater.

If I heard their voices, I could warn Wycliff. I'd been there. I knew their evil.

I pulled Papa's knife out of my reticule. My fingers gripped the mother-of-pearl handle and tugged the blade out.

I touched the curtains then stopped. My stomach twisted in upon me. I didn't hear footfalls anymore. It was now or dwell upon what I should've done. I couldn't live like that again.

With a quick breath, a short prayer, and a raised weapon, I opened the curtain and froze.

Wycliff stood there, shaking his head. "Ruthy?"

He marched inside, and I backed up.

"You agreed too easily. You're never easy about anything like this." He slid the knife from my fingers. "I see you meant business."

"You're meeting with one of the men who killed Adam. I heard his voice. I was there. I don't want anything to happen to you."

Putting my knife in his pocket, he bit his lip. "Ruth, I can't do what has to be done and think you are going to be rash."

In my head, I argued, saying *I want to help, I'm not rash, I want to share his burdens*, but I knew none of that would change what he had to do. "What if I say I'll marry—"

He grabbed me by the shoulders and kissed me.

It wasn't soft or easy.

This was wild and hungry.

His hands were everywhere, pinning me to him, spinning me.

I tossed my arms about him, held on to him. He was big and bold and everything my younger heart had wanted.

But I wasn't young.

I backed away, but he followed, all the way to my chair, still holding me, still kissing me. Melting into the seat, I found my bones had disappeared.

He sank with me, to his knees.

The kiss never broke, never stopped, never let up with its consuming flames. I wanted this. I wanted to be scorched.

I wasn't afraid, yet I trembled. I was lost but found my way in his arms.

Music surrounded us.

The tempo became my pulse. The beating in my ears was one, almost two hearts.

Almost.

For a new heart to exist in me, it had to know it would

live. I had to know Wycliff would.

We both had to outrun our secrets. I didn't know if we could.

I was weak and strong, submissive and demanding. It was my hands in his hair, my mouth pushing to explore.

"Oh, Ruthy." He released me. "We'll discuss marriage later, when I have a special license, and these horrible men aren't a breath away."

"He murdered Adam. I heard his voice at Blaren House. I'm the proof of it."

"I know. Both men I'm meeting are responsible for everything, for leaving you no choice but to work for Madame Talease."

My ears stopped working.

I clutched the chair. It was the only thing keeping me upright.

"Ruth, I don't need any more proof, but I need you to stay here. I can't be strong, fearing you'll be reckless."

My chest crushed, caving in, smashing whatever was there, but I tried to hang on to Wycliff.

He winced, and I held on tighter. There had to be a tomorrow for us.

"Trust me. Know that I'm right this time. No changing my plans." He pressed his lips onto my cold hand. "This time, my way."

He said it like I'd changed his plans before, like Wycliff was Adam.

My chest shuddered. *Wycliff was Adam.*

Going to the curtain, he opened it and let a groom, one armed with a short blunderbuss pistol, inside. "If anything happens, you get Mrs. Wilky to Fournier Street."

He slipped through the curtains, and I was left to muster up my faith and listen to Adam greet his killers again.

• • •

Wycliff closed the curtains to his theater box.

He'd crossed the platonic boundary with that kiss. It was emotional and passionate.

And she'd kissed him back.

She'd bloomed at his touch, not like a delicate rose. Her lips could scald hot coals.

He had to finish this war, now. Then he and Ruth could live in peace.

His groom was loyal and would follow his instructions, but Ruth was a different matter.

Yes, his old gut was always right. He knew Ruthy would try to help, but he hadn't expected to act upon his passion. He wasn't sorry about this, but his double life had to end.

Scooting down the hall, he focused on the battle ahead.

Lawden was face-to-face with Wycliff's cousin, and in the shadows of a snuffed sconce was the devil himself, Uncle Soulden.

Big, tall, one eye larger than the other from an old military wound, his uncle had towered over Wycliff's father and had terrorized his poor mother. The fiend had aged, but he was still a cyclops.

Wycliff's favorite Homeric hero slew the cyclops Polyphemus. No, blast it. Odysseus merely blinded the beast. Time to do better than that. Since he kept sowing murder, Soulden needed to pay—pay with his life.

Uncle clapped his hands, timed with the audience's reaction, then stepped forward. "Nephew, it's—"

"It's Wycliff."

"I wanted to see you. To commend you on your disloyalty."

"Hard to get more disloyal, Uncle, than having me killed."

"You hadn't learned to mind your own business."

Wycliff laughed. "Stealing from my father made it my business. How are you—with no money, no barony for Nicholas, and jail impending to rot out your years? Terrible, I trust?"

"You weren't killed. That fool Johnson sold you off to the Navy. You lived. That should settle all debts."

So Nickie had lied to his father. He couldn't even own what he'd done. Wycliff slid his hands to the shaft of the sjambok. "You did succeed in killing my companion. I was rather partial to her."

His cousin blinked and looked down.

Uncle didn't. He thought Ruth dead. Nickie knew otherwise.

Soulden shrugged. "Things happen. Again, that's the past. You're a Wilkinson. You've proved it. It's time we work together. I have lots of connections that you can use."

The notion of a coming-together made Wycliff want to toss his uncle over the balcony and ensure he crashed through each of the floors below. "I work with no one but men of honor. That's not you or Nickie."

"Wycliff, you want me to beg?" Uncle came closer. Out of the shadows, he looked even older but still deadly. There was no doubt in Wycliff's mind that the man would exact revenge if he could. Good thing they'd visited the bankers, in addition to the bawdy house. Soulden would be jailed in days.

"I just need one more shipment, Wycliff. Then Nicholas and I can start over. He'll be left something. That's what matters now."

"Do you think Captain Steward's widow would agree that you two should be left something?"

Nickie was jumpy, nervous. "I told you there was no reasoning with him."

"Things happen, Wycliff. What will it take to convince you to let bygones be bygones?"

"Four years of my life back with my father."

"We didn't kill him."

"You made him suffer, even set him up for the fate you now have, debtors' prison."

"There's nothing more to be gained, Wycliff. You've made me suffer. Nacknel is gone. Johnson committed suicide in Marshalsea this evening."

"Yes, but you are still here, Uncle. You're too old to be impressed into the Navy."

The music started to ramp up. Intermission would soon happen.

"Nephew, your father would want peace. You know that."

Wycliff felt his smirk fade. "Yes, but he's dead. Your absconded fortune is now gone, too, restored to those you've defrauded."

Uncle shook his yellowed fists, ones that used to strike fear in Wycliff. "Those accounts had more money in them. They had my profits, too."

"You've paid interest. Well done, gentlemen."

His cousin charged.

Lawden stepped in his way, guns drawn. "Gentlemen, intermission will happen soon. Let's be speedy."

Uncle Soulden pulled Nickie back. "In spite of all, we are family. Wycliff, you were the one who wanted to be a vicar. I've not forgotten. You lived. Now have mercy for Nicholas's sake."

"Pray for relief, Uncle. My answer came in four years."

Nickie shook free of his father's grasp. "We don't have four years."

"Then you have your answer, gentlemen."

Uncle Soulden glared, his face turning redder and redder. "You think you've won, but it's not over. Every man has a weakness, one that will bring him to his knees. I will find it. You're not invincible."

Nickie stuck his hand in pocket. "Bluster, old man. We've found nothing he cares for. Everything takes too long." He raised a knife. "A Blackamoor dead in the theater…"

The world slowed. The audience claps masked the sound of the hunted becoming the hunter.

Wycliff pushed Lawden out of the way. Then snapped his sjambok and lashed at Nickie's hand. The knife fell to the floor.

"Nickie? Showing off for the old man? That's wasteful, since you, darling Nickie, are responsible for me 'living'. It wasn't Johnson that had me impressed, but golden boy."

Soulden's big-eyed-scowl at his son was priceless and cruel to a fool bent on proving himself.

The rest of Wycliff's grooms came from the stairwell and laid hands on his uncle and cousin. "Take these fellows back to their seats, the cheap ones. Make sure they watch the whole show. It's quite good except for the soprano. Theater before prison, gentlemen. Oh, I called your notes today. You're done for. My deck-swabbed hands need do no more. That should make my dearly-departed father proud."

Wycliff picked up the knife and lent a hand to Lawden, helping him up.

Intermission began.

The corridor filled with patrons. Wycliff watched his men escort the muttering fools past his box and then down the stairwell.

He waited until the last moment, until the heavy door slammed shut.

Lawden walked with him, and they cut through the crowd and headed to the theater box. "Nothing like poverty to make a man born to means crumble, but you shouldn't have told them about the notes. They may flee."

Wycliff handed Lawden Nickie's knife. He had Ruth's. "We should've tossed them down the stairwell. That would be more satisfying, but they've no money to go anywhere. I want them sweating so they can't be concerned about Ruth. It will be Marshalsea for Uncle before Friday. I can handle Nickie. His father's disappointment in him will destroy what's left of the fool."

"At least you didn't let them hit you, my lord."

"No, Lawden, they did enough of that four years ago."

Wycliff went into his box and allowed the groom to leave.

Ruth was sitting with her arms folded about her. He stood in front of her. "I'm fine. All is well."

Her countenance was shadowed and angry.

"It's not well. This is happening again."

He tried to touch her, but she wouldn't allow it.

"It's the same as four years ago. We're the same."

He put his hand to her cheek, and she jumped. It was as if she didn't recognize him.

Was this a fit?

Had his absence triggered it? "Ruth, everything is almost over. We are almost free."

"No, we aren't. They'll kill you. I heard them. I heard them as they passed by. I *heard* them."

Wycliff realized that she wasn't in shock.

She remembered their voices from the night of the attack.

He knelt beside her. "You heard them, not just him? Two voices?"

"Yes. Two."

His uncle had been at the attack, Wycliff knew that. But Nickie, too?

Music started below.

The play began again.

Wycliff clasped Ruth's hand. He had to know her secret, everything that had happened after he had "died."

Chapter Twenty-Five

The Boundaries, The Choices

In Adam's carriage, I couldn't get comfortable, not with the fact that this man had misled me, but that the same people who'd hurt us were still after us.

We'd left the theater, but I kept looking out the window to see if we were being followed.

I couldn't look at him, not while I decided how hard to slap him.

He nudged my hand and gave me Papa's knife. "This thing is too small to be effective." He sighed. "Ruth, I don't want to take you back to the Croomes, not like this."

"Go ahead and decide. It's not as if I need to know, when you decide things."

"Your opinion matters."

"Does it? I told you I heard the men that killed Adam at the theater. They said they are going to kill you."

"My uncle and cousin are upset. They want me dead, but I've outplayed them. They won't win." He brought his thumbs to his lips. "You're sure Nicholas was at the attack? You don't know his voice from Madame Talease's?"

"You are the worst."

"What?"

"So caring and kind. My champion. Lies."

"Ruth, I care so much I ache for you."

"Why not just call me a liar, Liar? Ruth can't be reliable because of her vision. Ruth can't be trusted because she suffers from fits."

"Your vision is poor, and you do have moments, but I believe what you are saying. Nickie is more involved than I thought."

"More involved? I was there, Wycliff. I know what happened, but everyone makes up an excuse as to why Ruthy *be lying*. The girly is *a lying*." I mocked him like I was Mrs. Carter with her condescending voice, daring him to admit the truth.

My tears wouldn't quit. Adam was alive, sitting across from me, lying to me, thinking me capable of falsehoods.

"I believe you. If you say my cousin was there, that he directly sought to kill me, then yes, he did."

"Kill *me*? That's what you said."

"Yes, Ruth that's what I said."

"Now you admit it, just so you won't lose an argument."

"Ruth, I am Chatsworth Adoniram Wilkinson. I hate that name. I shortened it to Adam, then shortened it again to Adam Wilky."

"Why? Why did you do this to me?"

He took my hands and put them to his face. My fingers sank into his silky beard. "It's me. We lay in bed that morning until the innkeeper kicked us out. I wanted to go back to Scotland, you wanted to go home to see your parents."

"I remember."

"I remember your birthmark to the right of your delicious bosom that looks like a date. We joked about it, and I promised to feed you a mound of sugared dates while we lay in my bed. I know you are ticklish—"

"You should have told right away. You are so cruel. So manipulative."

"Look at me." He knelt in front of me and picked up the lantern. Positioning it close to his face, he caught and held my gaze. "Look at me, Ruthy. Look past age and the changes that nearly dying caused. I know I aged centuries thinking you were killed by my enemies. My voice, Ruth, because of the ropes they bound me with, I'll never sing a melody to you, never as I once did. But my heart is the same, still stupidly yours. Does a name matter?"

"I saw you die. I watched those men wrap a rope about your neck. I saw them beat you to death. You should've told me this miracle. Or is this a last manipulation?"

He set down the lantern and ripped off his cravat. "Undo the buttons to my shirt. See the scars."

I poked at the top button as if it would bite, but then undid the rest with a hunger to know every inch of him.

There were the scars. Horrid scars ringing his neck.

A gasp left me.

The flesh at his neck looked so pained. I trailed a finger over the roughened skin that had scabbed over the burns. The rings seemed so dark against his light skin. "Adam?"

"Yes, Ruth."

I fingered his birthmark on the breastbone below the gullet of his neck.

"I've been wrestling with how to tell you. Agonizing every day. I've thrown so many clues into your path, I've lost count. Then it dawned on me. You didn't want to remember, and I couldn't blame you. I, as Adam, caused you so much pain."

My eyes stung. Tears flooded my face. "I'm another pawn for you to push about."

He took my hands from his throat. "No scheme. No pawn.

We're a miracle. When I regained consciousness, Uncle's men had me. I kept repeating I was a son of a peer and the verses of judgement over and over. The wages of sin are death… So many verses."

He swallowed, and I saw it pained him. "Those men didn't want to take any chances that they were indeed killing a white man, a peer's son, or maybe it was the thought of hell's fires. They kept me in a pen a week but were going to let me go when Nickie arrived. He gave me over to a ship captain and impressed me into the Royal Navy. I was there four years, thinking you were dead, plotting my revenge."

I wanted to lunge at him, fall from the seat into his arms, but I kept still. "You misled me."

"I wanted to tell you, Ruth. Then I just wanted to love you. I wanted you to love me without all the pain. To admit to being Adam would bring back all the memories, all the bad."

"You thought me too weak."

"Ruth, you hated Adam for what you suffered. I hated me, too."

Part of me wanted to wring his neck, part wanted to hold on to him, so I gripped him by the collar. "The men at Blaren House and at Drury Lane, all were involved with the attack. I know Nickie was at Blaren and the theater. I'll never forget his voice. I hear his voice sometimes."

"What are you not saying, Ruth?"

"I need proof. You won't believe me if I say." I released him and rubbed my temples. My headache was so strong. "Were you ever going to tell me?"

"I waited for you to recognize me, but you didn't want to see Adam. I wasn't going to force you. But you love me as Wycliff. I know that, Ruth, I know it—"

"Like you know your own name? Here is my plan. Take me to the door, Adam-Wycliff. We will not tell a soul of this. I'm tired of bringing lies home to the Croomes."

"Ruth, what happened after I died? They dragged me away. What happened to you? Did they sell you to Madame Talease?"

I was shaking with anger. Wycliff had lied and now wanted my truth. He wanted to make me guilty to justify him.

"We need to go to Madame Talease. We'll get proof of my story. You need proof, just like everyone else."

"You'll do nothing of the sort. No more danger for you, Ruth."

He helped me from the carriage and took me to the Croomes' front door.

"You want danger, Ruth. Marry me again, marry your husband and commit to building a life with me. Do it. It's wild and crazy. It's us."

His breath was on my neck, his arms about my waist. Adam, the only man I'd ever loved was alive and a liar.

But I still felt that draw, that craving for his embrace, for his furry beard on my face, for his love to surround me, consume me, and burn away the past. "This is too much, *Wycliff.*"

"You have two days. No more living without you. That's all I can do. You're my wife. I want you and Christopher to be with me. It takes two days to secure a signature from the archbishop. I'll come for you in two days."

"What of your revenge plot? Will that be done?"

"Uncle Soulden is destined for debtors' prison. My war will be done."

"What of Nicholas? Will he pay, too?"

"I'll figure something out."

"No, you won't. You can't give him what he deserves. Not until I have proof."

I needed to write to Madame Talease to get her testimony. I needed to give it to Wycliff.

He tried to kiss me, but I made myself stiff in his arms.

I couldn't pretend that his deception hadn't hurt me. I had thought Wycliff was truth.

"Ruth, send for me."

"I'll think on this." I couldn't use the name Adam. Adam was dead. He could not be the man who'd made me feel so alive these past weeks.

I ducked into the house and watched him storm away.

Only one person knew the truth. She was my proof. I'd write Madame Talease right away.

• • •

It rained two days straight. Mama had the windows open, and the perfume of dampness, mud, and rosewater surrounded me in her parlor.

I sat, knitting an ebony scarf. I wanted to give it to Wycliff to cover his horrid scars, but I also wanted to tie it around his throat and strangle him. Strangle him and his secrets.

He was Adam. He was Wycliff.

Mad at the two men who'd claimed to love me, I knitted. Stupid me. The first time in a long time I'd trusted myself, and I'd been cheated again.

And I ached.

Wycliff had heard how much I hated Adam, but I had never mentioned how much I'd loved him.

I had. Those feelings had been forgotten. I should've remembered them before Wycliff thought there was nothing good in my memories.

The parlor chairs were in place as if it was Knitting Tuesday, but it was Thursday. All the seats were empty, except Mama's.

The woman looked unbothered. I must look terrible, falling to pieces.

Clancy brought in the silver service, but only two cups

were on it.

"Mama, are Mrs. Carter and Mrs. Daly not coming? What about Mrs. Johnson?"

White mobcap in place, delicate lace shawl slipping down her active arms, my mother shook her head "I didn't invite them. Just us two."

Uh oh, that means she wants to talk.

An excuse, where's an excuse when I need one? Chris running down the stairs, the house is on fire. Ester wanting to hear theater nonsense. Nothing.

Resigned, I bent my head, my glasses slipping to my nose, "Yes, Mama."

"Ruth, tell me about Lord Wycliff."

That was one of those blanket statements—to allow me to inflict my own wounds.

I smoothed my poppy-pink gown. It was bright, no way to hide on the sofa or between its pillows. "Nice, Mama." I made my tone easy and light. "He's nice."

"Is that it? You've spent quite a lot of time with him. You should know more of him."

Know him?

Everything and nothing. He was my husband, the man I'd had my firsts with—the first kiss, the first time enjoying the comfort of a man who loved me.

Knit one. Purl one.

The man who'd held me tenderly, singing my name when the pain and pleasure of his love had overcome me. The man who'd caressed me when I'd had a nightmare about my uncle, when I'd cried for my parents' fears.

Adam had seen me bare, and bold, and now as Wycliff, broken then reborn, remembering the diamond that was me.

Knit one. Knit one. Purl one.

My palms were damp. My needles were slipping. "I know a lot of his character, some of his business."

"Ruth, what of his parents?"

"His father recently passed. He doesn't say much about his mother. Wait, he did tell me. She was a poet from America."

"Has he mentioned anything of his people?"

"He has an uncle who hates him. Why do you ask?"

"Ruth, he has a choice, as did I, to live one way or the other. But he's not mentioned that other family. He's told your father he wants to marry you. Will you be his wife in secret?"

"I don't think so. We've been very public at the parks, the theater." I poured two cups of tea and sipped mine dry. "He asked me last night. I've not accepted him."

"Ruth, I know why you considered the barrister. Many men answered your advertisement. You chose the busiest one. One who looks at you with nothing in his eyes."

"Marks was not disrespectful. He's a nice man."

"Yes, he is. He'll make a good public husband. You serve his political needs. Your father's money serves his monetary ones, but what of your needs? You deserve to be treasured, not just possessed."

"It was a marriage of convenience." I wanted to say everyone was entering into them, but that was juvenile.

"Wycliff wants a full marriage. He looks at you with everything in him."

"He's made no secret of wanting me."

"This has the makings of being right." Mama moved from her throne and sat beside me. "Ruth, are you ready to be married again?"

I was married and a widow and just confused. I couldn't down another cup of the burning hot tea. "Why talk of this now? Not with Mr. Marks."

"Marks, bless his soul, will let you be. You can wander about his house, run his staff, and sleep in your separate bedrooms. He may want to share upon occasion, but he'll let you alone and keep on with his mistresses."

I felt my eyes popping wide, maybe flying from my face. "You didn't mention this when I told you of Mr. Marks's intentions."

"I was very angry when you ran off with Mr. Wilky. I was furious that you were at a brothel and stayed there instead of coming home. Then you had a baby in that tummy. I was enraged, that you'd put yourself into that position."

I jumped up and moved away. "Must we talk about this? I forgave you. You forgave me."

"Ruth, I accused you of being a harlot. That was wrong. I didn't listen to you about what truly happened. I couldn't accept what had happened."

"Please. Don't say any more."

"Ruth, you told me many things when your papa brought you back from the brothel. Then you healed up and said nothing. I did think you lied. I sent you away to have the baby, but I'm guilty of so much wrong."

"Mama, please don't repeat what I said."

"For you to be married, then all the rest is true. All of it."

My eyes leaked. They were wet and sticky.

"Baby, it's one thing to give away your sugar in the throes of young love. It's another to sell it of your own free will. It's a horror, a terrible, terrible thing, for the sugar to be taken. That's what happened to you."

Mama wasn't talking about baking or sweets but soul ties and abuse.

She remembered what I'd said had happened when Adam had died. His killers had had at me.

I'd been told to sit back and take it. Then my family told me to forget.

My mother held me in her arms. She cried. We were both hot, sticky knitters.

"Ruth. Ruth, baby. You need to tell Wycliff. He needs to know."

"I need proof. I'll tell him when I have proof."

Mama held me tighter. "You need nothing, no proof when a man loves you. None, when you believe in yourself."

"How is that? You didn't believe me. Madame Talease can verify my truth."

"You've been tried, Ruth. You've kept living. You've raised a beautiful son. You didn't give over anything to despair, especially not your baby."

"Chris is all mine. He's none of them."

"Memories have power. I had to tell your father what happened to me, what happened in my home, by my own father."

I squinted and saw the heavy tears in Mama's eyes. I didn't want her to see me as weak. I didn't want that legacy.

But then I looked at Mama, really looked at her. I saw a survivor's face. I saw the beauty that had come through the fire. I wanted to be Mama—to have her strength, her grace.

"Ruth, I'm four years late in comforting you, of telling you it wasn't your fault, that you are lucky you lived."

Four years too late, but better late than never believed.

"Tell Wycliff. He wants all of you, the good and the bad. There's heat in the air about you two." She put my hand in hers. "Tell him, so he can be sweet to you. Then he'll be gentle. He'll understand. Your father understood. My attacker was my own father. At least you don't have to recover from that."

No, it was Adam's cousin. He'd led them in it. Someone who Adam had once trusted.

I was an all-or-nothing person. If I faced the truth, I needed all of it. I'd written to Madame Talease yesterday. I needed her to answer soon.

She was the proof I needed for Wycliff.

Mama and I poured new cups of tea. "What if he can't

look at me? What if I can't make myself please him? What if he can't please me because I see the others and not him?"

"Not every man or every mother can be strong. But you are gold, pure gold. You deserve gold. We're not soft when it comes to our worth. We're strong. Uncage your spirit. Be wild, my wild child. Be free. Then accept Wycliff's love, if he is for you. Or toss him away. Know your worth. You're gold."

I believed Mama, but my head was stuck on proving my truth. I sipped my tea, taking my time, enjoying the citrus taste of the chamomile. "I'm glad you didn't have the knitters here today."

"The ladies?" Mama laughed. "My friends, they are vipers. I set them on you these past two years to toughen you, for you to regain your fire. You didn't get it back until Wycliff. I think that means something."

"A man did it, Mama. Is that your answer? Is it an extra benefit that he's a peer?"

"A respected barrister or baron, both are worthy of you. But I like Wycliff. He made my child remember to live. Whatever you choose, your place is here, if you want it."

I watched Mama sit in her chair. "I need my own. I'll send for Wycliff. I'll tell him everything."

I went to the closet and pulled out stationery, a blotter, and ink. Flopping on the sofa, I curled my feet under me and began writing a short note.

My hands shook, I smeared things terribly, but the words, '*Come. Please come.*,' made it on the page.

I thought about going to him, getting in a carriage. Did I have enough courage for that and to spill my secret? I did. "I'm going to get Jonesy to take me."

"You can do it, Ruth. Do you need me or Ester to come with you?"

I wanted to go by myself, but I couldn't afford to fail. "I'll send this to him. He said he'd come. Thank you, Mama."

I opened the door to the parlor, but Ester was there with her hand poised to knock. "Ruth. This came for you."

It wasn't a ribbon-wrapped note.

I took this one and savored the jasmine scent of the paper. It was from Madame Talease. It was an answer, the proof I needed.

I had to read this, to see if it said what I remembered.

I took my note to Wycliff and handed it to Ester. "Help me get this to a groom. I need this to go to Lord Wycliff as soon as possible."

She took the folded note. "The more I try to stop you, the more it's driving you to Wycliff. I give up. I'll get this to him right away."

"This is a new tactic? The loving little sister indulging her older, daft one?"

"No, this is the loving little sister trying to love you right. Ruth, if you want him, I'm with you."

"And if I am a fool, and this is nothing but something reckless, will you gloat?"

"No. I don't stick my tongue out anymore. I wish you happiness. You deserve that, but I'll be here to wipe your tears. Then we'll plot how to bludgeon the whip-ferrying goat with a poker."

I reached out and hugged Ester, truly hugged her. "I love you, Sis."

"Let me get this to Jonesy. He is the fastest in getting notes delivered to Bex."

Ester dashed away.

A little spent, I decided to go upstairs with my letter. I needed my wits for when Wycliff came.

Halfway up the stairs, I heard Clancy open the door.

Mrs. Johnson slid inside. She wore mourning black, head to toe, with a veil.

She ran and clasped the newel post of the stairs. "Ruth, I

need to see you. I haven't been a good friend."

I glared at this woman. "No friend at all. You need to go."

"I have to see you now. It is of the upmost urgency."

"There's nothing to hear."

I came back downstairs, went to the door, and opened it. "Please leave."

"It's Madame Talease. She's ill. She's dying."

I stopped and grasped the thick paper in my pocket. My heart hurt. Madame Talease was my friend. "To the study. We can talk in private."

Madame Talease had been good to me. I hoped Mrs. Johnson was wrong, dead wrong.

Chapter Twenty-Six

PROPOSING TO MY WIFE

Wycliff's carriage couldn't arrive at Nineteen Fournier fast enough. Ruth had sent for him. He had the ring in his pocket and a marriage license freshly signed by the archbishop.

Ruth's note looked rushed. Had she just come to realize that they were meant to be? To marry her again couldn't undo what she'd suffered, but it was a start. He'd make her happy. He would.

His carriage stopped outside Nineteen Fournier, but his excitement dimmed. Another carriage sat out front.

He had a bad feeling.

Lawden saluted. "Good luck, my lord."

Wycliff nodded and wished luck upon himself. "Be alert. Uncle hasn't been jailed. And Nickie is wounded. That's a lethal combination."

He charged up the steps, anticipating Ruth in his arms... his bed...his life, forever.

Clancy opened the door. "Afternoon, my lord."

Like normal, he took Wycliff's hat and cape.

The fellow had his hands out as if to take his sjambok, but

Wycliff waved him off. "I'll keep it."

The sjambok was an extension of his power, and he was too on edge to lower his guard. Nothing was settled. "Where's Mrs. Wilky?"

"The parlor, my lord. Shall I announce you?"

"No. I'll go to her. Thank you, Clancy." Wycliff straightened the daisy he'd put in his buttonhole. Seizing a big breath, he pushed open the door. "Mrs. Wilky."

She didn't look up. Her arm was about Mrs. Johnson. Both women wept.

The sound of it, throaty, whimpering, reminded him of Cicely the night Mama had died. She'd been so young, but Wycliff had had to comfort her while his father had made arrangements. It had been many hours, too many before he'd been alone to grieve. He'd met Ruth on the docks that night. It was a sign.

"Ladies..."

There was no acknowledgment, but Mrs. Johnson's sobs turned more violent and angry, if tears could be anything but sorrowful.

He closed the door again hard. "Ladies." He went in front of them and stooped to eye level with the seated women. "I'm sorry, Mrs. Johnson, for your loss."

"Are you?" The widow came at him, arms swinging.

He caught her hands and pulled them to her sides. "I'm sorry. Johnson could've reinvented himself with your strength."

She tore away. "I wouldn't have to be in this position if you had helped, if you had eased the credit."

"Johnson had friends, the men who helped him build his stolen empire. He shouldn't have needed an enemy's mercy to survive. Sometimes judgement has to happen."

"Those friends will all be bankrupted. That's my only consolation. For Ruth's sake, I hope you are as clever as you appear. I heard the Wilkinsons. They came to kiss hands and say sorry. I know fakes." She went to the table and picked up a ledger. "They came for this. I brought it to Ruth instead."

"Yes, and she brought a message from Madame Talease, too."

His poor Ruth looked distant and shaken.

Mrs. Johnson handed him the ledger. "If you can use this to bury Soulden Wilkinson like you did my husband, do it."

The widow moved to the door.

"Mrs. Johnson, here is something to help with expenses." He went to his purse and pulled out five guineas. "Again, I am sorry."

Her hand fisted about the coins. "Milly done come up before. Me and this baby, we're going to figure things out."

She walked out with her head high, clutching the coins and her baby bump.

Wycliff had the feeling she would be fine.

He closed the door and went back to Ruth.

Her spectacles were on the table. Was she trying not to see him?

He put the ledger next to them and waited. "You sent for me?"

Cold, isolating quiet. Nothing.

He rubbed at his face. Counted to ten, then twenty, then listened to the clock's *ticktocks*.

"Mrs. Wilky, I take it you haven't forgiven me."

"Where were you?" Her voice was calm as she brushed at her eyes. "Four years is a long time."

"I told you. At sea. Made to work on a frigate, the HMS *Liverpool*. Hard, hard work. Four years of constant labor."

"I wanted to see if the story changed. That's what people do when they don't believe you. They ask you over and over what happened. They pick apart tiny details, looking for something you may have forgotten or blanked from your mind, to be discredited."

"I deserve that. It was cowardly of me not to tell you. But how do you tell someone *I'm your live husband* when she wanted him dead?"

"I never said I wanted you dead. Never."

"But you never wanted Adam back. I, however, clung to a memory of our perfect love."

"It wasn't perfect. I wasn't perfect."

"Well, Ruth, you've told me over and over again how I wasn't, either."

"Could you have sent a note, something while at port? Ships come into port."

"I thought you dead. Graves accept no love letters. I made one missive to my father. That was all."

"How did you live on this frigate?"

"I didn't live. I survived, Ruth. I punished myself with thoughts of you, how I'd allowed you to suffer. Being a sailor, a good one, made the days pass. My nights, those were another matter."

She folded her arms about her, like she was caught in a chilling wind. "You've stayed in love with me all these years? You never thought that we were too young, too stupid?"

"I've never fallen out of love with you. How could I? I was happy when we were together."

"No doubts?"

"None." His horrible voice was loud and strained, but it was his truth. "Ruth, I've only wanted revenge. I've thought of nothing else."

"That's a lot of years to be steeped in hate. Sounds like you were nearly successful with Mr. Johnson's death."

"I didn't kill him, but he deserved death. I know he plotted with my uncle for my ambush. You remembered his voice at Blaren House."

"I remember your cousin's and your uncle's voices. They were at the ambush. They deserve death." She wiped at her eyes. "When do you achieve revenge? When does it all stop?"

"All Uncle's notes have been called. If Soulden does not pay tomorrow, he will be collected by runners and then sent to debtors' prison."

"That leaves your cousin untouched. Will that be enough for you, Adam?"

She said his nickname, the one he'd given her. It didn't sound as well with her voice laced in anger.

"Adoniram is the name my mother gave me. A bit of a mixed bag, an overseer to the king...who was stoned in a revolution." He scooted a little closer. "I now oversee all of my father's wealth, but I did survive my execution. If you are asking if I am the same fellow you knew, the one so full of rage... No. I've learned to be deliberate and methodical."

"If you die before tomorrow, will they inherit the means to pay their debts? Will they win again?"

"I don't intend to die, but my son, my heir, Christopher Wilky will inherit."

"Then you've set the evil on my baby."

He wrapped his hand around her closed fist. "I'm alive. All will be done in a day. I win, unless you make me a loser. Are you going to pretend that what we had, what we *have*, what we rediscovered, isn't enough?"

He took the ring box and presented it to her.

The hinge whined when she opened it, but then she snapped the case closed before the diamond could sparkle in the candlelight.

"Do you trust me, Adori...Wycliff? You've asked me to trust you so often. I need to hear you trust me."

He knelt and took her hand. "Yes, I trust you implicitly. I love you, Ruth. Marry me. Look past your anger at a name and see that I've changed."

"Do you still twist up all the bedclothes and leave the mattress looking crazed?"

He wanted to laugh that she remembered, but Ruth wasn't smiling.

"I'm no longer quick tempered. I'd like to think I'm thoughtful and deliberate. I'm a man who will keep you safe, who will love and cherish you. Be mine again, now and forever."

"Can't we just go one step at a time? Adam…Wycliff?"

"I am Adam, I am Wycliff. I know how precious life is, how things can change in an hour. Let's not wait. Trust that I can make everything right this time."

She held his face close, smoothed her fingers in his beard, then closed her eyes. "I miss your smooth face." She sighed. "If we'd taken things more slowly. We would've had a chance."

He swallowed the lump in his throat. "It's not rushing when we are married, unless…"

It hit him like a cannonball across the bow.

She didn't love him or Adam.

She'd been through too much.

With this last secret, there was nothing left of her for him.

• • •

I felt frozen and empty.

I'd spent the last hour consoling a woman whose husband was truly dead.

Wycliff's face grew darker, more distant.

"I see," he said and stood. "Then tell me how this is to go."

"Well, as you say, we are married."

"Are we, Ruth? Where's your half of the registry? Go get it."

I left him for a moment, went to my room and returned with the trunk. I put it in his hands. "Here."

"Your old trunk." He took it and pulled the registry from the lining. "This is the only thing that proves our marriage exists. Maybe there is a misspelling or something to get you out of this conundrum."

"Now you are being ridiculous. I'm not falling into your arms, so you think I am hysterical. That's not fair."

Wycliff moved closer to the hearth. "It is ridiculous to be in a marriage you don't want."

He turned from me, tugged on his jacket, and bent close to the flames.

"Are you cold? What are you doing?"

"Freeing you."

He lit the edge of the paper. It caught fully, glowing and spitting flames before I reached him. I tried to get it, but it was too late.

Bits of the paper danced as embers on the log. Then it was ash.

It was destroyed. I started to cry. "The proof I needed to prove Chris had a father is gone. That was cruel and unkind. That was my paper. You had no right."

"I just gave up my rights. You can go on with your life. Marry again. I won't stop you. Write back to your ambivalent barrister."

"That was all I had to prove Chris had a father. How could you?"

"Chris doesn't need a claim to the past. He needs someone to love him and shape his future. His cousin Wycliff will do that. I've established my position and your widowhood to all that matter."

"That was my proof."

"I'm the proof. That piece of paper ties you to C. A. Wilkinson, Chatsworth Adoniram Wilkinson. There's nothing to hold us together, just as you wanted."

"I didn't say that."

He started for the door.

I didn't want him to leave, but I didn't know how to make

him stay. I was desperate for him not to walk away.

"Wait. I just need time."

"Four years apart isn't enough?"

I ran to him and put a hand to his shoulder. "You aren't this good. You can't love me this much. It's not possible."

"Everything is possible if you believe. I believed in us." He kissed my hand. "You're free, Ruth. My half is gone. Only you and I know that a young couple committed to loving each other in sickness and in health. In death, I did not part."

I wrapped my arms about his shoulders so he couldn't leave. I was gentle because I knew his neck was so hurt. "You were always so dramatic."

"I've gone to hell and back. It should be allowed. You're free."

"How am I free? You've had weeks to know that I was alive. And you've been deliberate in making me fall for Wycliff. This is your own fault."

He turned his face, holding a gambler's grin, like he'd bet everything and won his nick. "I'm listening."

"You know who your enemies are. I need to prove mine."

"Madame Talease is your villain. She bought you when you sought help. She made you one of her girls."

"No, she didn't. She's dying. That's what Mrs. Johnson came to say. She wants to make amends, clear her ledger entries of all the things unsaid. She sent me a note, telling me good-bye, but she didn't answer my questions."

"She wants to repent from selling flesh, for selling yours?"

I shook my head at him. Wycliff didn't understand. I had to make him. "I need to see her, and you need to take me to her, tonight."

"She's an hour from London."

"Yes."

"No, Ruth. Not now. That road is isolated. We'll be vulnerable. The same people who attacked us before could do so again if they know we leave London. I can't cover that much ground with grooms."

"Then no one will know we are going."

"It's not possible. I'm watched. No, Ruth."

"You have faced your enemies. You've made peace with what was done to you. I need to do the same. Madame Talease knows what was done to me."

"I don't care what you did at Madame Talease's. I don't need to hate any more people."

"But this is *my* story, Wycliff. I want you to hear all the pieces. Then you can tell me what to do. I want my enemies to be in terror like yours."

"If I refuse?"

"You were already out that door. Since you destroyed the registry, you can't stop me from going myself."

He shook his head. "That long stretch of road by yourself is ridiculous. You'll be anxious. You'll not make it."

"If I had my protector with me, I would be fine."

"They're watching here. You could be put in jeopardy again, Ruth. You can't do that."

"The wild child is going to do the wildest thing. I'm going to Madame Talease. I need her statement. I need you to hear it."

He looked down at me, and I felt the anguish rippling through him.

"As much as I want to say no, I know you, Ruth. When your mind is set, you don't stop. It's best I go with you. That way if things go poorly, we might actually die together this time."

He pulled away. "Let me check with Lawden, to see what protections we can put in place. Be ready to go in an hour."

Wycliff left me.

I was terrified, but I was determined. I needed truth. I needed it above everything.

Chapter Twenty-Seven

SECRETS AND SHADOWS

I should've left my spectacles at home, then I wouldn't have had to witness Wycliff's discomfort. The unflappable man seemed so tense. He kept peering out the window, cupping his hands to his eyes, hunting.

The farther his carriage moved from London, the more he shifted.

I put a hand to his knee, and he jerked.

"You are so uneasy."

"Yes. This is foolhardy. We should've waited until next week or the week after."

"Madame Talease is dying. She may not have next week."

He put his head back on the seat. "Yes. Mrs. Johnson, who hates me because her husband has died, convinces you to go out of town tonight. I'm still stupid."

"Madame's letter to me said the same. What is wrong, Adam, Wycliff, Adoniram?"

"No one calls me Adoniram."

"No Adoniram?"

"Go ahead. Tease me. You sound so confident teasing

me. Someone needs to be confident."

I was. The panic that I lived with wasn't there, at least not now, but that wasn't my doing or anything special.

It was Wycliff. He'd taken me out of the house so many times that this felt natural, sitting with him, being in his shadow. He'd helped me spread my wings. It was all him, his support and the strength of his love.

I wondered if his support would remain when he'd heard the truth. I knew pieces, but Madame knew it all. Wycliff and I needed it all.

His head bowed. His hands clasped together with a slap, his fingers forming a steeple. That should have been calming or reassuring, but everything about his form seemed stiff. "I don't like things unplanned, Ruth. I never did."

His raspy voice was rougher, like a washboard, or silk catching on nailhead trim.

"You act like something will happen."

"Isn't something always happening? I just wish to be more prepared."

"You're always confident, always in control. You don't seem so now."

He wrenched at his cravat. "And that is horrible and weak."

"No, human. Makes me think you might actually need someone and not just an ornament to decorate your Blaren House." I eased to his side. "I like you human."

"And that is appealing to you? I've seen my mortality. I've witnessed you die. We have this second chance, and we're taking this risk. You haven't learned anything. I definitely have learned nothing."

"None of this makes you weak."

"Ruth, it makes me an expert in loss. I never planned to lose again."

"Then why did you burn up my half of the registry? That

was an unnecessary loss."

"It gives you what you want. To be free of a marriage that has caused you nothing but pain."

He sat up and did his checks again out each window. "If we make to it Talease's and back, alive, you'll have what you want."

"Must everything be so cut-and-dried?"

"Ruth, this is my world. Then you come in and twist up everything."

"It is a wonder why you loved me all these years."

"Oh, it's no wonder. You're the one for me, Ruth. It's always been that way. Then I let things get ruined."

"Going to Madame Talease ruins things?"

"Ruth, every outing that I've taken you or Christopher on has been thoroughly surveyed by my grooms. I make sure that even the Croomes are protected, because they are associated with me."

"Are you given to conspiracies?"

He looked at me and bit down on his lip. "How much suffering would we have been spared if I'd taken you to Scotland or if I had waited to marry until my affairs were in order?"

Oh, my goodness. He blamed himself as much as he blamed me. "If we had waited, things would be different?"

"Yes, except I'd still be miserable, Ruth. I wouldn't have had you. The best fortnight of my life was eloping with you. The second best was six months of walking with you on the docks by the warehouses. Now you've given me more walks and garden parties. I'm happy."

That was why Wycliff could always get to me. He knew the precise thing to say to make me fall into his arms. He was so sure of us. That had always been the way.

I wished I was as sure. I had been once. Then all the bad had happened. "I'm not going to tell you that you shouldn't be careful."

"Good, because that I will not change, no matter what you ask of me. As soon as this is done, I won't bend again."

His tone held a sense of bitterness.

"You have lied and sweettalked me this whole time to get me to do what you wanted, but you are upset."

"You didn't seem to mind." He mopped at his brow that glistened. "When have you ever listened, Ruth? You get something in your mind, and it's so hard for you to do anything differently."

"No, that's not right. For four years, I did everything everyone else said because I thought my judgement wasn't worthy. I was compliant and muted and chained to act as my family thought I should. Only since you returned have I been coaxed back to me."

"Lucky me."

I clasped his hand. "No, Wycliff, lucky me. I need this. If you can't see this, stop the carriage. Let me out. I'll walk to Talease."

"You're being ridiculous. Do you honestly think I would risk your safety? What if your nerves become problematic being out in the open?"

"I might struggle and freeze, but if I have to crawl to reach the truth, I will."

"Then I will help you get your trouble. If we return unscathed, let me help you get into safer trouble, like dinner with paint fumes."

I didn't like the sarcasm in his voice. This was the wall between us, something dense with only cracks letting light through.

Once we had the truth, all the final pieces, then we'd see if this wall shattered. I'd know if Wycliff and I could be together.

• • •

Wycliff's carriage stopped about a mile from Madame's. I didn't take his arm. We walked in silence, making it to her bawdy house as the sun started to descend.

The setting sun highlighted the gray and pink stones of the wide house.

Then the memories started.

I'd been so sick, so hurt when I'd arrived at Madame's. My ribs had been so bruised I could barely breathe.

One broken arm that had needed to be broken again to be set right.

And so many cuts and bruises.

Hurting in places that should never be seen. Men should die for their terror.

"Ruth." The raspy voice crept up my neck, worse than the burn of a man's coarse shirtsleeve lodged against my throat.

"Let me help you up the stairs."

"Don't touch me." I jerked away, then remembered it was Wycliff behind me. "I mean, I can do it."

He fell back a step or two, and I went forward—climbing, fighting.

The doors to the bawdy house opened. Music and cigar smoke welcomed me. "We're here to see Madame." My voice was low. I had to repeat myself.

A young girl played hostess. "She can't be disturbed. She needs her rest."

"She'll see me. Tell her Ruth Wilky is here."

Another courtesan disappeared, then returned. She pointed us up a set of scarlet carpeted stairs.

I knew those stairs. I remembered being carted up them and discarded like a sack of rotten potatoes.

"Ruth, I'm right behind you."

I heard Wycliff. His voice was a little louder than the

noise in my head.

I nodded and hoped the wild gesture masked my shakes. This place had healed my body, but not my eyes, not the empty space in my chest our attackers had killed.

Somehow, I went that final set of treads and knocked on the door to the main bedchamber.

A weak welcome told us to come in, and we pushed inside.

Lavender walls. Jasmine-scented air.

A big framed walnut bed with mermaids carved in the posts.

Swamped in lace and pillows was my dying friend, Madame Talease.

This lanky woman with titian red–colored hair had proudly proclaimed she wasn't marrying no duke, so she'd use her charms to take their money. Her bawdy houses specialized in the exotic—foreign women, Blackamoors. "Ruth," she said, "Ruthy Wilky, what are you doing here?"

"Milly said you're not long for the world. I had to come."

"Ah, my Spanish señorita, Miss Milly. That's a smart girl with numbers."

I sat on her wide bed and took up her hand. "Do you hurt, ma'am?"

"Of course, silly. Everything does. How's that boy of yours? I heard you had one."

"Big. He's a good boy.

"What did he end up looking like? I'm fascinated by the by-blows. White as a ghost? Dark as your pa?"

"His skin is light, like my mother's, but his eyes are mine."

"Good," Madame said and closed her eyes. "I told you that the baby would have your eyes when you birthed him. No hideous mole, either. I told you."

"No. No mole. My son is perfect."

"Mole?" Wycliff balled his fists. He shifted to the window.

I hoped he didn't punch through the glass.

"Ruth, who's the brooding man?"

"Lord Wycliff," I said, and I looked at him. There was tension and strain in his jaw.

"Wycliff, the whip-swinging man. Thank you for closing down that bawdy house in Mayfield. Peers need to travel for their enjoyment." The woman cackled and coughed. "Ruth, why did you come?"

"I need proof. I need you to say who brought me here. I never asked but I need the answer now."

"You and your possessions were sold to me, but your father paid me back."

I heard Wycliff growl, but I waved at him to quiet. "Who sold me?"

"It's been so long, Ruth. I don't remember so much."

Wycliff came near. "A group of men attacked Ruth and her husband not so far from here. Was it Soulden Wilkinson?"

"It's so hard to remember, young man. Maybe if I had something in my hand.

The woman was dying, yet she was determined to get a coin out of Wycliff.

"What is it you want, Talease?" He was behind me. I could feel the anger radiating.

"Something to help me focus, Lord Wycliff."

"Give her coin. A guinea will make her focus. I remember that."

He pulled a shiny coin from his purse and placed it in her fingers.

Her palm wrapped about it. Her smile became bright. "I remember now. Ruth, it was early in the morning. The sun hadn't risen. A group of men had you. They sold you."

"Was one Soulden Wilkinson?" Wycliff asked. His raspy voice sounded more strained.

"No. But his boy Nicholas was one. Ruth was all bloody

and beaten. We had to clean her. Disinfect her from their abuse. Men can be so horrible to a woman. They'd had at her and beat her bad.

Wycliff started to pace. "Had at her?"

"Yes, I bought Ruth from them. They would've killed her or left her to the elements to die, if I hadn't. My girls must choose to work for me. Ruth had been hurt so bad, she'd never work for me."

I held my friend's hand tight. "I wasn't strong when I left, but I'm stronger now. And my Chris is just mine. He's nothing of the nightmare."

"They came looking for you more than a month ago. I told them you had died from their abuse. Then I sent that trunk."

"You sent it." I looked at Wycliff, then back at Madame. "Milly said she did."

"Milly is an opportunist. I sent it so you'd be warned."

"Nicholas Wilkinson sold you, he used you, and came back to get you, my Ruth?" Wycliff's hands shook.

"Never forget that mole on his lip." Madame coughed.

I couldn't breathe. My head felt light. Images of that day, each of the thieves, took over my reason.

Wycliff put an arm about my waist. We trembled together.

"I'll fix this, Ruth. You could've told me. We didn't need to come."

"Now you have proof. Proof that your cousin was horrible, that all those men were horrible. This is why my love for Adam died. He left me no proof that my Chris was his. Adam's secrets made it seem as if Chris belonged to them. He's too good to be theirs."

The sound of a carriage arriving drew his attention to the window. "We have to go. There's some company I'm not prepared to see downstairs."

I held Wycliff in place, my hand on his. "Madame have

you seen Cicely Wilkinson? She's my sister-in-law. Young girl, mulatto."

"No one by that name. I'd know."

"Ruth, we have to go." Wycliff picked me up and brought me to the window.

I saw a black carriage and three men looking around.

"No wonder you had Lawden park away from here. And pointed the carriage in the right direction for escape."

Wycliff winced. His fists balled, but that arm stayed about me. "They watched me, until I made a mistake."

"Listening to me was a mistake?"

He didn't answer. "Madame, I didn't mean to bring trouble here. Is there another way out?"

"My closet. There's a hidden staircase for my important guests to leave."

I ran and kissed Madame's cheek. "I'm sorry."

"Sometimes trouble comes for you. There's a peace I'm holding to. You're younger, you have more time to find it. When you do, don't let go."

Wycliff's arm wrapped about me again.

Knocking sounded.

"Let me put something on," Madame called out. "Let me get decent."

"Out through the closet with you two."

Wycliff opened the door and shoved me inside.

"Baron, you want your coin back?"

"No, ma'am. You've shown us a good time."

Wycliff closed the door and led me through the gowns, shelves, and strong-smelling floral tonics to the back stairs.

We made it out of the house.

It was dark now.

Guided by stars, we walked quickly through the woods to where his carriage was.

Then I saw it.

A man had a gun on Mr. Lawden.

"Ruth, stay here."

He pulled out his sjambok. "Stay."

I watched Wycliff go to his man's defense.

My ears perked up. Something moving nearby. It wasn't the wind, nor was it imagined. Footsteps crunching twigs.

That feeling like this was all happening again swept over me. This was my fault.

I'd made Wycliff come here.

But this was worse than the past.

At least Adam had known that I loved him. Before he had died, he'd known all my love. Wycliff knew nothing of my heart.

With these glasses, I couldn't make out what it was.

I didn't trust them. I trusted me.

I felt around and found rocks. I gathered a few.

I heard the noise again, soft and low, crouching.

No closing my eyes.

No sitting back.

No taking it and hoping.

This time I'd face the danger and we, my Wycliff and I, would win.

• • •

With his sjambok at the ready, Wycliff started toward the clearing.

He should be hesitant.

Caution should be his guide.

None of that was in his head.

It was black, full of rage.

Killing a man wouldn't be enough. His soul needed an army to die. Everything needed to die for the abomination Ruth had suffered.

Lawden stretched. The signal that he saw Wycliff.

He'd be ready.

Wycliff lifted his sjambok.

He swung.

The leather snapped and crackled. Then the impact, the sjambok slashed the assailant's arm.

The fool yelled. The gun dropped to the ground. It didn't discharge, and Lawden had it in hand the next instant.

But one hit wasn't enough. For Ruth, Wycliff struck the fiend again and again, a lashing times three for every face he remembered at the attack.

One final strike. "That's for harassing Lawden. Lord knows I ask too much of him."

"Have mercy!" the man kept screaming.

No mercy. The sjambok had a life of its own. *Lash. Lash. Lash.*

Then the screaming stopped. He'd beaten the man unconscious.

"My lord." Lawden grabbed his hand. "He's disarmed. Relent."

A bullet whizzed by.

Thwack.

A man screamed then fell forward.

Ruth came from that direction with rocks in her hand. "A shooter was over there. I hit him. I struck him good."

She was resplendent. Coming through the brush, her hair spilling onto her deep-pink dress.

Goodness, he loved her. She looked strong coming to him after hearing Madame's words. But Ruth didn't possess his shock. She'd buried these truths inside her for four years.

Lawden ran up and took the man's weapon. He might've kicked him. "Lord Wycliff, let's be going."

"Yes." He took Ruth's hand and lifted her into the carriage. "Back to Blaren House as soon as possible."

Wycliff couldn't say any more. He didn't have words to express anything, just kept an arm about Ruth's waist. He needed to get them back to safety as soon as possible.

Cousin Nicholas didn't merely have to pay for touching Ruth. He had to die.

Chapter Twenty-Eight

BE MY GUEST

When Wycliff said Blaren House, I was stunned.

He looked at me, that way he often did, as if he'd read my mind. "I'm not taking you back to the Croome household tonight. They may be watching Nineteen Fournier. My grooms are there observing."

I was afraid for my family, my boy, but I knew what Wycliff said was right. I nodded.

"Good. We won't provoke the fight tonight. I'll not bring trouble on your family. I have to be smart. *We* have to be."

His words reached through the fog that had begun to fill my mind. I'd hit someone. I'd defended Wycliff with my own hands.

I'd been strong for him, and that made my soul rejoice.

But the look on Wycliff's face seared my conscience. It was as if these spectacles had collected strong sunlight and burned me.

He was in agony.

I felt the heat of his reddening face. The man was enraged. The nightmare I had lived these four years was new and fresh to him.

"You didn't need to come out here, you know. I would've believed you if you'd explained."

"I couldn't talk about it. I wanted to pretend it wasn't my story. I needed you to hear Madame's testimony. I needed to make sure that I hadn't jumbled things. She's my proof."

He rubbed at his skull, like he'd rubbed my temples.

I felt the pressure of his fingers, as if he'd touched me. I missed that. It had only been two days since the theater, and I missed him.

"You knew they were watching. I understand better your precautions. I guess you're not crazed."

"No, I'm not. I wish I'd been crazed sooner. Then you would have never suffered."

I felt the weight of what he'd put upon his shoulders. I shuddered. How could he survive this every day?

He moved from me to the other side of the carriage.

I stretched and touched his knee, but he didn't look at me. I wondered if he still could. Was I too damaged to him now?

Small talk.

We'd always been good at that. "Lord Wycliff, did Mrs. Johnson set this attack in motion? She came to Nineteen Fournier."

In the lantern light, I watched him untie his cravat that now had dirt stains and sweat. "I don't know. I think she's easily manipulated. She's grieving. She has a baby to come and her husband committed suicide in debtors' prison."

"But she stole the book."

"She knew the trunk from taking this ledger book. She sought an advantage. Crafty but not malicious."

He swallowed like his throat was raw. "I think she'd use anything for an advantage but not plot for a murder, and definitely not yours."

Wycliff stretched out, but the sjambok was by his boot. He looked like a frustrated warrior.

The knowledge we'd just escaped didn't make me feel any better. These acts of revenge weren't done. Soulden and Nicholas Wilkinson would try to hurt us again.

I wanted to be told that everything would be all right now, but Wycliff was quiet.

Another hour went by. It was pitch-black outside, but the blurry trees highlighted by the stars were gone.

Wycliff shifted between folding his arms, clutching the seat, and checking the windows. It was an odd dance, but I understood. I understood him.

The outlines of the city could now be seen.

We were in London proper.

We passed the streets that led toward Cheapside. Then I remembered we were going to Blaren House.

"Thank you for asking about Cicely."

It was the first thing he'd said in a while.

I tried to smile, but I was tired. My head ached, and I was sitting in darkness across from my husband.

"She's my sister-in-law, and Madame would know about lost mulatto girls. She knows about everything."

"You know everything, too, Ruth. No wonder you and Madame are friends."

The tension in his graveled voice felt heavy, like the stones I'd thrown.

"What does that mean?"

"You had to make me take you. You discounted what I said, what I knew to be true. Why is it so hard for you to trust me?"

"Wycliff, I didn't know we'd be attacked."

"But I did. Is this enough for you to believe in my precautions?"

"I have to prove myself and my word to everyone. Why

are you special?"

He rubbed at his face. It was very red, scarlet.

"Are you mad at me for what just happened or for what happened four years ago?"

"Not mad at you at all. I am mad at me, Ruth. I didn't think of this as a possibility, that Nickie would be this cruel. This is my fault. I misjudged things badly. When we married, you suffered. You suffered four years. You suffer now."

I wanted to put my hand on his shoulder, but I didn't know what to say other than it wasn't his fault, but I'd punished myself, too. I'd even taken it out on him. I touched his knee again to feel a part of him.

He took my fingers held them a second then released them as if he held fire.

"Now that you know I was brutalized, Wycliff, I'm damaged goods to you? That truth changes everything? It's why I never wanted to say. Either I wouldn't be believed or you'd hate me for their crimes."

"It changes nothing about you but increases my need for revenge. If you'd trusted me, I would've been sweet to you. Much more patient. You could've told me in a carriage ride like this, just the two of us, talking. I didn't need Madame's testimony or the added excitement of running for our lives."

"You've been sweet to me. You made me feel desired and beautiful. There's no apology for that. But don't confuse my reticence about what happened with you lying to me every day."

"Ruth, I'm a cad if you think taking the opportunity to figure out how to get our love right was wrong."

"What?"

"I didn't get things right the first time. This was to be different. I wanted you to crave me, to feel me in your chest, your thoughts, I wanted you reaching for me always."

He stretched as if he'd take me in his arms, but he drew

his hands to the seat. "The more I suspected that you'd… that you'd been hurt worse than anything I could ever conceive, I needed to be more perfect so that you'd trust my affections."

He had become perfect, and I did love Wycliff more than Adam. Yet, they were the same.

The carriage stopped.

"Ruth, I'm going to rush you inside. I need you protected."

He took his sjambok and flexed it in his hand.

Once on the pavement, he reached inside and helped me down. Then he pulled me close to his shoulder. His cologne, his tangy Bay Rum, settled my nerves.

Swinging his whip, he kept me close. We went up the stairs and barreled into Blaren House. He rested on the other side of the door as a servant took his coat and hat.

I kept my wrap. I wasn't sure I wanted to stay or if Wycliff wanted me here. Too much was happening.

"There are bedrooms upstairs. Go make yourself comfortable. You're safe here."

He left me standing in the wide hall.

I didn't want to be sent away, so I followed him to his study.

Sitting on the edge of his desk, he put his sjambok down. "You should be resting. There's a modest staff of loyal individuals here to assist you."

"We need to determine what we are to do."

"About what, Ruth? Staying alive through the night? Please go rest."

I felt as if I was losing something, and I didn't know why. I came closer. I had to see his face. "You don't love me because of what Madame said?"

He stood up and came to me and placed a palm under my chin. "I'm in love with you as much as ever, but I need a partner. I want to be a father to my son. I don't know how our marriage can work."

"You burned the proof."

"It was half a marriage certificate, like half a marriage, where there's not enough trust. Nothing more links you to Chatsworth Adoniram Wilkinson. You're still the widow of the mythical and flawed Adam Wilky. And I'm Christopher's big cousin. I still get to have a piece of him."

Wycliff giving up? No. To hold on to him, I put my hands on his wrists. "What are you saying?"

"That this is all my fault. My mistakes made you vulnerable, made us take unnecessary risks. I must've made you believe you had to. You don't know me. But that's my fault, too. I've given you Adam and now Wycliff. None of them are for you."

"Don't discount my need for the truth because you think me fragile. I am fragile, but I'm strong, too. I had to hear the truth. You had to hear it from Talease."

He put his fingers to my temples. Then traced lines to my mouth. "The truth was in here. Just say it aloud. I would've believed you, instantly. And why should I not? You're a truthsayer. I trust the truth in you."

"Then why are you pushing me away?"

"Ruth, I'm not a truthsayer, not like you. I'm a protector. I'll do what I must to save you and to avenge threats to my interests." He moved back to his desk. "You're my guest in Blaren House. Let me have you escorted upstairs. The best room in the house is yours."

"Wycliff, no. We should—"

"Let's survive the night.

He clapped his hands and ordered Lawden to bring me upstairs.

My truth didn't break my Wycliff. *I'd* broken him, and I didn't know how to fix him.

I let him push me away.

Chapter Twenty-Nine

CANDLELIGHT

It would be easier to find Nickie and beat him to death with the sjambok. It would be wonderful and liberating for a moment, but Wycliff would never survive the inquest. Everything would point back to him. A barrister like Mr. Marks would make sure of a conviction.

No. The way to get Nickie was the same way all Wycliff's enemies had been conquered, the financial transactions.

He stretched in his father's chair and pored through the second ledger. The rhyme or rhythm of the accounts made no sense. This ledger made it appear as if Wycliff's father had authorized Johnson's illicit transfers. Algernon Nathaniel Wilkinson, ANW, was initialed page after page.

He drummed the desk, tapped the imitation bride sculpture. Wycliff hated the piece again. The romantic tale of men claiming their women was rubbish, horse leavings. Women shouldn't be forced to do anything, not to become a bride, or a lover, or anything.

They shouldn't have the truth hidden, either, even if it was for the best.

Blinking his tired eyes, he flipped another page. There had to be an answer between the two books—one that could end with Nickie jailed like Uncle Soulden would be tomorrow.

"Father, I wish I'd never promised you not to kill." He lifted his glass of brandy, as if he toasted the air.

Lawden came into his study. "Everything is normal at Nineteen Fournier. All the Croomes are safe and accounted for, my lord. Get some sleep."

"I can't. I need to figure out how to end this."

"Seems to me you need to think about beginnings. Mrs. Wilky would like to see you. She's been asking for you."

"This all must be very upsetting to her."

"She's pretty strong." Lawden flipped through the other ledger. "Mrs. Wilky, she saved us. That bullet was marked for one of us."

"I know, but she shouldn't have been there. *We* shouldn't have been there."

Lawden shrugged. "The things you do for love. Don't stay up too long. You know how you hate mornings. Tomorrow is a busy day."

His man left.

Wycliff sat back in the well-worn chair. There was only one time in his life when he'd liked mornings. It had lasted a fortnight, four years ago.

He closed up the ledgers, tucked them under his arms with his sjambok, and headed to the second floor.

Everything was quiet.

From the window overlooking the grounds, he could see his grooms on alert.

Heading to one of his guest rooms, he noticed light streaming from his bedchamber. Ruth was in there. She was up. Maybe he should see her so she could sleep.

He knocked on the door and waited.

"Come in."

Her voice made his heart dance. Pressing open the door, he found her dress was folded in a chair, laid out so it would not wrinkle.

Wearing one of his nightshirts, Ruth sat in the middle of his nicely-made bed, knees up, bare feet showing.

After putting the books and sjambok on his walnut chest, he opened a drawer and pulled out another nightshirt.

Unbuttoning his wrinkled waistcoat, his soiled shirt, he pulled them both off in one floundering motion. He shouldn't rush. He probably looked ridiculous.

A gasp, not a laugh, came from behind.

Ruth must've seen the depth of his scars.

"Do those on your neck hurt?" Her voice was low, a little skittish.

"Yes."

"My arm does sometimes, and you know my headaches."

They were veterans of the same war. He'd never forget that or forgive himself. He finished dressing, pulling on the nightshirt and his onyx robe.

He turned to leave, but Ruth stood at the door.

"You say *my* footfalls are quiet. Yours are pretty quiet."

"Well, you weren't looking for me. I look for you. I like having you near, walking with you. Talking with you, too."

Why did she have to look so lovely in his nightshirt and bare feet?

"Do you need something, Ruth?"

"I want you to talk to me. I don't want to be by myself. I've never been an overnight guest in Blaren House or anywhere. I missed putting my son to bed."

"I'll have you back safe and sound tomorrow."

She brushed at her temples, thick curls dropping to her neck. "What are we going to do?"

He tied his belt robe. "What do you mean?"

"I want to know what you want. I want to hear your

opinion of how we go forward, Adoniram."

He folded his arms. "Well, one, we never use that name."

"Chatsworth? Is that better."

"Definitely not better."

"I need to know what to call my husband. A woman should know that."

"You want this husband, Ruth? After everything I and my relations have done?"

"Yes. I almost lost you again. I don't want that. I don't care about your name anymore, and I don't want to be alone in your house, in your room, in a bed that smells of Bay Rum, when you are here and alive. Do you know how often I sleep on your cape?"

"Ruth, you tell me how we fix this."

She took his hands and put them to her temples. "These lenses have given me a terrible headache."

"Well, we can't have that."

With his fingertips, he stroked her skin. Then he put his thumbs to the nape of her creamy neck.

Her eyes were shut. Her lips were close and kissable.

"I didn't get a chance to thank you for saving me and Lawden."

"You'd do the same if you had good aim."

He chuckled. The laughter felt cleansing. "Heaven help me, I can't even stay mad at you."

"Perfect. What good is it to have a husband if I can't have him near? I definitely can't have him sleeping in his study while I'm comfortable in his bed. Stay with me."

He hesitated a moment then he picked her up in his arms, carrying her like delicate crystal to his grand mattress.

The bed was still red and gaudy, but the ivory sheets were sleek and smooth.

He laid Ruth down and followed her beneath the bedclothes. One moment, they were a foot apart. The next, he snuggled her close. "What's the use of having a husband if you can't share his pillow?"

"My sentiments exactly."

She kissed him and put his palm to her face.

He drew her hand away. "There's nothing to prove. We can take our time, Ruth, learning how we fit together."

"That would only work if you loved me."

"You know I do. Old habits are hard to break."

"I love you, Adoniram. You are the best of Wycliff and Adam."

He kissed her brow. "Just tell no one of that name."

"Are you the only one with such a horrible name?"

"Well, let's see. My father is Algernon Nathaniel Wilkinson."

She laughed a little. "That's not so bad."

And Nickie was Aylmer Nicholas Wilkinson…*ANW*. He wouldn't say the scourge's name aloud, but that was the answer.

ANW. That was why the accounts had never changed. Nickie had been the embezzler for Johnson.

He kissed her temples. "You're brilliant."

"Why, because I ordered you to bed with me?"

"Well, that is genius, but I think you solved the problem. I know how to make the last culprit pay."

"I don't want to talk about him. And not while I'm in your bed."

He closed his eyes for a moment and held her tight. "Yes, ma'am."

Her smile returned. "We need to discuss marrying. You need to make me your wife again. I want that. This is pretty scandalous, the Baron of Wycliff and his bed wench."

"What if I told you that I didn't exactly burn your half of the registry? That it may have been a sleight of hand and your mother's *Morning Post* was destroyed instead."

"Adoniram? You manipulative thing."

"Ruth, my only defense is that I'm too much in love with you to ever let you go. I love you, sweetheart, even when I am mad at the world."

"I'm glad we're married. I'm not the kind of woman to stay with a bachelor, and definitely not in his arms."

"You rest and get used to these arms again. But cousin Wycliff needs to marry Mrs. Wilky in a public event. No more hiding for us."

She stroked his beard, her fingers stopping upon his mouth. "I know you are plotting. I want to be there, Wycliff. I want to see the fear in my enemy's eyes when he's caught."

"Ruth, I don't know. Your eyesight is pretty poor. I don't want him that close to you, definitely not in your face."

"I need to see it."

She did need to see it, needed to witness Nickie punished for his violence. "I should've taught you how to use the sjambok so you could whip the fool. Keep your folding knife on you. That cute little weapon could offer a bit of protection."

"It's my father's. It's purposely discreet." She rubbed his beard, where it curled about his jaw. "I need to see him brought to justice."

"I'll try, but if you can't... If you feel drained or tired, you must leave my study. You come back up here, snuggle under these bedsheets, and wait for me."

She put her arms about his chest and held him tight. "I will. Thank you for trusting me to know my own mind."

He did, and he knew she had to see Nickie's downfall. Wycliff tucked her onto his shoulder and tried to relax. Tomorrow, he'd begin sending for people, making the right offers.

Judgement would come for Uncle Soulden and Nicholas. It would, if everything finally went according to his plan.

It had to be well past midnight. Wycliff blinked and adjusted to the darkness of his bedchamber. The candle had died. He should stretch and light it again, but Ruth remained snuggled in his arms. She breathed warm air onto his scars.

He'd closed his eyes several times but jolted awake every few minutes to check on her—to see if she was truly here, to see if she was frightened, to see if this was all a cruel dream and he was still captive on the HMS *Liverpool.*

It wasn't possible to push out of his head the horror she'd lived through. Leaning a little, pulling free a little, he scooped up a match and struck it. The sulfur smell chased away the scent of roses coming from her hair.

Then she angled her face deeper into his chest, hiding from the light. The rose scent returned.

"You're not sleeping. You're thinking too much." Her voice was crisp, no yawn, not sounding tired.

He adjusted the pillow under his head. "Well, I must be changing. Suddenly I don't want to be a lazybones and lounge in bed. I should be up, getting notes ready for the traps I've planned."

Her pinkie dragged upon his chest, forming a slow heart. "You still hate mornings? That I remember. Me, too. But I can't sleep, either."

"Then we should not fight this. We should get up and start the day. Good plan, Lady Wycliff."

"You sure that's the right name?"

"Quite sure. Neither of us has eaten. Maybe we should go downstairs and see what is in the kitchen? I remember you having a healthy appetite."

Ruth sat up, drew her knees to her, but stayed close. "No, I don't want to leave this room and traipse in the darkness and shadows of Blaren House."

There was a look in her soulful brown eyes that made his heart beat fast. It could be the entire percussion section for the theater pit. "No oysters? Or beefsteak? Teacakes?"

"Just you."

She leaned down and kissed him, boldly, forcing him to confront his hunger for her.

The press of her body against his was undeniable.

She was perfect and beautiful.

Sleep would soon be an excruciating thing.

"You're my weakness, Ruth, but you need to slow down."

He put his hands upon her shoulders. "Platonic marriage. Taking time. Me becoming a eunuch. I thought we discussed that."

"I think that applies to new marriages. We're an old married couple of four years. And you knew me before. And I am with you in my head between the nightmares. I need you, always."

Her grin was different, her mouth ever delicious. The taste for her on his tongue was fresh. "Ruthy, no beefsteak? I know there's some in the larder. I've never lost my hunger…"

The way she looked at him. That stole all the words from his sore throat.

The feel of her lips on his scars—heaven. "You are making this hard, Ruth."

"Then surrender. Take me in love as far as we can go. I want you in my head. I need your love to be louder than the darkness. Don't turn me away."

The hardest thing to do was to say no, to deny how he longed for her.

Ruth, his wife, his weakness.

To deny her was to deny his life.

He stopped fighting the logic of waiting—waiting until *he* knew she was ready, waiting until *his* enemies were vanquished, waiting for everything to be perfect. Heaven and hell could be an hour apart.

His wife knew her mind. She wanted love to vanquish her enemy, and he trusted her.

"I want my husband to know me as I am supposed to be. Tend to me with gentleness and care."

"And with love, Ruthy, always love."

She took his hands and put them to her shoulders.

Wycliff's fingers tangled in her loosed curls. He angled his face up to hers.

The candlelight sparkled like diamonds in her eyes, and it cast shadows upon her nightshirt down her exposed shoulder, and more.

Breathtaking. Then he spied her arm. It was swollen below her elbow, the evidence of a bad set. It had been broken by Nickie and the others.

Gutted, broken, hurting for her, he gathered her up like fragile china and tucked her to his chest. "I need this slow, Ruthy. I need slow."

She pulled away. With her eyes closed tight, she undid the laces of her nightshirt. It was big on her, so it slid all the way down to her waist.

A work of art, she was. The shadows, the lightness, a canvas of curves, a sculpture to shape and mold in his hands.

This was better than the nude bride statuette on his desk.

His bride wasn't porcelain. Ruth wasn't fragile. She was strong. She'd been tested. She was fire. Wycliff vowed to protect and worship this treasure forever. "You've walked through the ashes. You're beautiful."

"Then love me. Wycliff, let it only be you in my head."

He took her into his arms. "Good plan."

Ruth slipped her palms about his neck. She was gentle, taking care with his scars.

Tomorrow wasn't promised, but tonight, he'd be everything she wanted.

And he gave himself up to this slow, perfect union.

• • •

I kissed my husband with my eyes closed.

That wasn't unusual.

I'd kissed him several times like this but only in my dreams.

But then he was dead, and this part of me, this broken, stolen part of me, I thought dead, too.

It wasn't.

It had been hidden inside the space where my heart had died. The space where it had been reborn.

My chest was full again, and I felt new.

"Open your eyes, my love, my Ruthy."

Wycliff 's raspy voice singed my throat, and I offered it to him.

I was new. We were new.

I held Wycliff, traced his scars from his neck to his chest, to me.

I was burned and spent but wanted more of his kiss, more of his mouth on mine.

The craving to be cared for, to be nurtured, coiled about me, linking me more and more to him.

I blinked a few times.

My lashes were damp and sticky, but I saw the face of a man who loved me more than himself.

My Adam, my Wycliff, my Adoniram was alive.

This feeling—the closeness, the not knowing where I began and he ended—I'd thought it gone. It was resurrected in his love. Nothing separated us—no nightshirts, no bedsheets, no secrets.

I wanted his closeness. My passion lived again. Our marriage was whole.

His finger wiped the corner of my eye.

My face leaked.

Tears of joy and pain anointed our lovemaking.

I touched his cheek, and it was wet, too.

His face was so near. I saw him whisper my name.

He asked me questions, like I could answer.

It was him caring for me, making sure I knew I was valued and protected and pleased.

My husband wanted me here with him, nowhere else.

And I am.

Wycliff was my new beating heart, and I was the only one he saw.

And that vision was clean and whole and light.

This was how things were supposed to be.

Me being his breath, him being mine.

We stayed like this, close to each other, until the sun crawled inside Blaren House. It peeked at us through the curtains.

I was tired and spent, but my Wycliff, restless Wycliff, rose from our bed.

After saying his blessings for me, for our Chris, for himself, he headed from the room with the ledgers and his sjambok.

His countenance was strong, battle hardened. He looked ready to fight dragons.

The dragons I knew were mean.

They breathed fire. They didn't fight fair.

Yet, I was no longer afraid.

I was grateful for Wycliff, for my family, for peace, and for war.

I scooted to dress and fight at his side. Dragons and darkness wouldn't win.

Chapter Thirty

FINISH THE GAME

Wycliff stood on the grand staircase of Blaren House's hall. He looked out at the sea of marble. It was quiet, and he was calm, truly calm, inside and out. Ruth loved him again. All the loose tendrils needed to be wrapped up, like a glorious chignon.

Lawden marched to the bottom of the steps, coming from the hall. "All your guests have accepted and will be here be at Blaren House shortly.

"Good. This is almost over."

Wycliff pondered going back upstairs and convincing Ruth to reconsider witnessing Nicholas's downfall. If everything played out according to his plans, the man would be jailed, never to trouble them again.

Oh, Ruthy.

No matter how much he wanted to protect her, she had to do things her way. Wycliff loved that woman so much it was hard to think, but he had to trust her judgement, he needed to prove to her he trusted her. Today was her proof.

"You all right, my lord? You look a little giddy."

"I can say yes. Most definitely."

A knock sounded upon the outer door. Like clockwork, the games were afoot. That sealed his decision to let Ruth go about her plans.

Sjambok in hand, he signaled for Lawden to open the door.

Nicholas stomped inside, his boots tracking mud across the white floor. "Sorry I'm late. I had to watch the runners cart off my father."

Wycliff couldn't help smiling. The man would be in irons before nightfall. A much kinder judgement than he deserved.

"I'm glad, Nicholas, that you've taken my offer. With both our fathers gone, we can strike up a peace."

"Your note talked of financing this peace. That's why I've come. It's the only reason."

Wycliff met him in the middle of the hall. "But you can trust me, Nickie. Not like you would be waylaid along the way."

Nicholas grunted and laughed. "No, not here in the crowded city."

This man was as evil as Uncle Soulden. Actually worse, for he pretended to be a friend.

Wycliff opened the door to his study and showed his cousin inside.

Mr. Marks rose from his chair. Wrinkled hair, wrinkled coat, but bright eyed and ready to exact justice.

"I thought we were going to be alone, Wycliff?"

"No, that can prove deadly with Wilkinsons. Besides, Mr. Marks can do the legal paperwork on the transaction. I want every jot in place. No misunderstandings between us."

Nickie slammed into the empty chair. He put his hand on the bride sculpture. "Misunderstandings have been the capstone of our relationship."

Rage churned in Wycliff as he glanced at Nicholas's hands

on that bride, but the composure he'd developed serving on the HMS *Liverpool* steadied him.

"I was surprised, Cousin, by your generous offer," Nickie said. "You have my father rotting in debtors' prison. Do you know how humiliating it was to see him carted off like that?"

"No, but feel free to describe it in every way. Make me feel like I was there watching."

"Wycliff. Must you be crude?"

"Yes. I should, and I should be mad at you for sending fools to attack me whilst I was out of town."

"Well, you are here. Must not have been good fools. This is nothing to me."

"You never had the stomach for the dirty work. You were the obedient bookkeeper."

"I should've told them to kill you, you know. Father was right about that."

"But he was right about you not measuring up. You didn't have the stomach for that or for fair fights. Even picking on girls, I hear. That's what Madame Talease says."

Nickie grunted. "I was pushed. The fellows my father hired taunted me. You really don't think I wanted something you'd had. Your companion is dead now, anyway. Replaceable, remember?"

That gutted.

Wycliff could swing his sjambok and slay the man for that comment, but it was meant to goad and throw him off his game. "Though doth protest too much. But let's talk about the money. Did you bring the original ledgers?"

"Yes. You have the ten thousand pounds?"

"Of course, but you must prove to Mr. Marks that these markings are legitimate. They could be forgeries or copies like I had, but Uncle Soulden and Mr. Johnson may not have included you in their dealings. You may just be the lapdog."

Nicholas tossed the books to the desk. He stood and

flipped to a page. "See the markings. The authorizations for the transfers from account to account. There's my father's mark, *SAW*, Soulden Arthur Wilkinson. This is Loftus Johnson's, *LJ*. And this one, *ANW*."

"That was to indict my father, Algernon Nathaniel Wilkinson."

"No, you dolt. Those were my transfers, Aylmer Nicholas Wilkinson. I became so good at them, they let me take over. Built up quite a nest, until a little birdie moved the funds."

Marks stood and examined the books. "Wilkinson, you authorized these transfers? *ANW* is your mark, you did this embezzlement?"

"I did the bulk of these, and my father and Johnson lived off the fat, but with his scheming, Wycliff has put them in jail. There's some poetry in that."

Marks rubbed his chin. "It's a crime to embezzle. Isn't it, Lord Mayor?"

The door opened, and there stood Lord Thorpe, the magistrate. The older man, with silver streaks in his hair, came into the room. "It is a crime. And these books are the proof. Do you know what you've done, Wilkinson?"

Nicholas backed up to the door. "I was bragging. It's not true. You set me up. You'll pay."

He grasped the door and opened it.

He stopped and stepped back.

Ruth was there with Nicholas's son in her arms.

Wilkinson cursed and pointed. "You? You have my son."

"Yes. Miss Smith, this boy's mother, is my guest in my husband's parlor."

Wycliff jerked Nicholas backward. "Yes, my wife is such a good hostess. Smart girl, too. She figured out the initials. She knows guilt when she sees it."

Ruth stared at Nicholas, tweaked her lenses. "I needed to see you pay for your embezzlement. It's a pity you can't pay for all that you've done."

She stood, resplendent and courageous, facing her attacker.

Sweat broke upon Nicholas's brow.

Wycliff twisted Nickie's arm a little more. For what he'd done to Ruth, his cousin needed to fear what Wycliff would do to him.

Mr. Marks pulled a ribbon-wrapped document from his pocket. "So, are you taking back your confession, Mr. Wilkinson, and staying here with your cousin, or are you going to sign this confession and take your risk in court?"

Wycliff handed him the paper. "In my travels, I learned a great deal about torture and the ways other civilizations dealt with infidels."

Nickie took the paper. "Yes, just as I told Marks. I did it." He bent at the desk and signed the confession.

Marks took it and the ledgers and handed them to the Lord Mayor.

The Lord Mayor headed to the door. "Go with Marks, Wilkinson. It will look better for you. Or I'll send the runners for you. Marks, let me know."

Ruth followed behind the man, and Wycliff took pride in how well she withstood.

"Cousin, have mercy on my son. You don't need the runners. I'll go with Marks."

Marks pulled out a knife much bigger than Ruth had. "My grooms outside have guns. I can deliver him to the magistrate."

He led Nicholas from the room.

It was over.

Wycliff needed to get to Ruth.

He went to the parlor, borrowed her from Miss Smith and her son, and led Ruth back to his study.

Wycliff spun her around then embraced her. "It's over.

You were—"

The door burst open.

Nicholas charged at Wycliff with a knife in his hand. "You can't win, not like this."

Wycliff's sjambok was on the desk.

He and Nicholas fought hand-to-hand. He elbowed him, and the knife flew to the floor.

They wrestled for control. Both stretched and claimed the knife's handle at the same time.

Nickie elbowed him in the throat.

Wycliff couldn't breathe.

Ruth tossed books. Each hit Nicholas on the head.

The distraction wasn't enough. Nicholas was wild. He was crazed.

He made the blade slash Wycliff's cravat. "I need to finish off that gloating voice."

Wham.

Ruth broke the bride sculpture over Nicholas's head. It split in two.

Nicholas fell back. "You witch."

That was enough for Wycliff to catch a full breath. He overpowered his cousin and drove the knife deep into Nicholas's gut.

He twisted it for good measure. "That's for Ruth."

Lawden came running. "My lord, is all well? Wilkinson stabbed Marks."

"A little late, Lawden, but my wife, my dear wife, was on time.

Lawden helped him up. "I have Marks. The bleeding is under control."

Ruth was silent and pale, but her spectacles were on her face. She'd seen it all.

Wycliff took off his tailcoat and dropped it onto Nickie. "Ruth, it is truly over."

She clasped Wycliff's hand. "I'm going to check on my guests for tea. I'll keep them occupied until Blaren House is clean."

Mr. Marks came back inside. "Ruth. I'm sorry. I'm sorry for so much."

She nodded, glanced down one more time, then left.

The barrister dropped into a chair. "Lord Wycliff, I'm sorry, too. He grabbed my knife."

"Lawden's good at patching things up, but we'll send for a physician."

"And I'll stay for the coroner's inquest. It's the least I can do for you, clearing up these crimes. Consider it a wedding present for Mrs. Wilky."

Wycliff nodded and sat on top of his desk. He put his boot on the broken statue. "Thank you. You need a brandy, Marks?"

"No, but I wish you and Ruth every happiness. She's a special woman."

The barrister kicked out his feet while holding the bandage on his arm. "Go to her. Your man and I will finish up here."

"No. I will wait until everything is done. Mr. Marks, I hope you find what you are chasing, so you can settle down with a woman who makes you dream."

"If there is such a woman, my lord."

There was such a woman for Chatsworth Adoniram Wilkinson, the Baron of Wycliff, and he was blessed every day for having found her—both times.

• • •

I sat in the front parlor of Blaren House. I'd never been in here. The walls were freshly painted white. Every outer wall had large, wide windows. The furnishings were almost identical to Nineteen Fournier. My husband's joke, but it would make it possible for me to have my own Knitting Tuesdays.

Miss Smith, Nicholas's mistress, sat quietly drinking the tea I'd served her. The brunette was stoic, but the boy, his father's death hurt him deeply. He sobbed a long time.

I closed the parlor curtains when I knew my attacker's body would be carted away.

It was over.

The ones I knew that had touched me were dead. The ones I didn't, they were dead to me. I had survived their worst, and I was whole. I was gold, the best kind, the kind that held diamonds.

"Lady Wycliff, thank you for your hospitality," Miss Smith said as she held her son. "Mr. Wilkinson, we hadn't seen him in months. He stopped sending money. It's been desperate. Now we know he wasn't himself. He was ill."

I didn't know what to say, and with Nicholas dead, I didn't feel I needed to tell my truth. For a moment, I thought I saw something in her eyes that told me Miss Smith would believe me. But she needed hope, especially with her son listening. "My husband will help. He'll make sure you two are provided for."

The poor boy was four or five, not much different from my Chris and definitely not old enough to understand all the evil his father had done.

I was sad for boys with no papa.

I had a good papa. I hoped that somehow Miss Smith would raise her son to be good. I'd make sure the boy wasn't forgotten.

I walked them to the door. Mr. Marks and the coroner passed us.

"Lady Wycliff." The barrister tipped his hat.

I didn't know if he had ever read my letter, but he seemed unbothered. I waved at him and wished him happiness. I knew his career would give him all that he needed.

Blurs that looked like my Wycliff and Lawden were at the cart.

I assumed they were talking with the coroner.

My blur turned and headed to me. I watched him walk. I loved his swagger.

Wycliff swept me into the grand hall.

"My heart, are you facing charges for Nicholas's death?"

"No. My cousin's admission in front of Thorpe and his attack of Mr. Marks, one of the Crown's top barristers, made the inquest quite simple. This is over."

Lawden disappeared down the hall.

It was just us.

This was over, truly over.

And my husband lived. And I lived.

"You don't look happy, Wycliff."

"I promised my father that I'd not use my hand directly."

I put my palms about his waist, snuggled in his Bay Rum, and tried not to notice the ferrous scent on his sleeve. "It was you or him. You did what you had to do. Your father never begrudged you anything. He definitely wanted you to live."

"I did want Nickie dead for what he'd done to you, but everyone who hurt you—"

I kissed him. I didn't want Wycliff to say more. No more power to the nightmares. "It's done. No one is going to hurt us anymore. That's my revenge—to live with love, your love and mine."

He led me to the grand stairs. We flopped down, shoulder to shoulder, on the bottom step. "We need furniture, my dear."

I leaned into him more, and we sat there perfectly in tune, he with me, me with him. "I like it simple. Less things to bump into. More places for Chris to run."

Taking both my hands in his, he wove our fingers together.

"I'm grateful, Ruth. I'm so grateful you're strong."

He tried to kiss my cheek, but I didn't want a furry dimple. I kissed him on the lips.

Our love made us strong. For this, I was forever grateful.

He tugged me into a tighter embrace. "We need to go retrieve my son from Fournier, Lady Wycliff."

"Not before a proper wedding. Everyone thinks I'm married to a dead man. You must make me a proper wife again."

"Well, I have a proper license. I will find a proper minister. How soon do you think your mother will have a proper cake made?"

"Since I didn't come home last night, I'm sure it's baking right now. Tomorrow morning for sure. I'll send a note."

"You do that, Ruth."

Wycliff knelt before me and took from his pocket a ring. It was entwined in gold, not silver like our first. This had a shiny diamond, the strongest gem. "Ruth Croome Wilky, marry me again. Love me as I have always loved you. You make my heart warm with comfort, red with desire. I'm made perfect in your love."

"I love you, too, Adoniram, my Lord Wycliff. I like your name."

"Someone should. Might as well be you."

I kissed him before he kissed me, warming to the silk of his face. My arms wrapped about him, and we sank against the steps.

"Ruth, I need a nap. I didn't get much sleep last night. A real nap with my best pillow." His grin was wicked, my wicked Wycliff.

Before I could blink, I was up in his arms. I caught my spectacles before they fell. I laughed hard and yawned and then placed my hands gently about his neck.

The front entry doors flew open.

My heart stopped.

But the blur was small and had a trail of portmanteaus.

"Brother…I'm home."

"Cicely?" With a groan, Wycliff lowered me to my feet. He ran and embraced the young woman. "You scamp."

As I came to his side, Wycliff spun the lithe young woman.

He set her down. "Sister, where have you been? How could you make me so crazed?"

"France, silly. I was with a large party of friends. We traveled for a wedding. It was so exciting. Brother, why are you looking at me like this? You are angry? Did I forget to leave you a note?"

She put her hands to her golden rosy cheeks. "I hope I haven't made you fret?"

Wycliff rubbed his brow. "Just a little, Cicely."

"I needed to be away. I was grieving Papa hard, and I needed some adventure like Mama's poems or your Odyssey."

"Go settle into a room upstairs. Don't come down until my wedding tomorrow. This is Ruth. She's my wife, and I'm marrying her again."

His sister pointed at me. "Wait. You look like."

"I am." I was proud to be the woman Wycliff had first loved and would love forever.

She hugged me. "Ruth, Adam, there have been miracles while I've been gone. It's good to know love doesn't die."

Cicely tossed her head and danced up the grand stairs. "Well, now you know, Brother, what it feels like keeping secrets. Being dead for four years should equal my two months away."

She hummed all the way to the top landing.

Lawden came from the long hall, shaking his redheaded bob. He gathered up her trunks and followed behind Cicely. "You will be hiring more staff, Lord Wycliff, posthaste."

Wycliff put his hands to his head. "Headache. I have a

headache. She needs to be chastised, Ruth, for making this trouble."

I put my arms about him to comfort him. I had more expertise in dealing with little sisters. "No. You need to be grateful that she has returned unharmed."

He led me up the stairs. "Come, my dear. Help me find something."

"What are you missing now?"

"Another moment alone with you. I'm spent."

I leaped into his embrace, and he carried me up the stairs to heaven.

Epilogue

My morning wedding was beautiful, bright and early with all the windows of Blaren House open for the sun to come inside.

Ester, Mama, Clancy, and Mrs. Fitterwall made everything perfect.

White tablecloths on tables of treats.

Beeswax candles edging the grand staircase.

Mama's three-tiered fruited cake with white bliss icing on the pedestal in the center of the hall.

Lady Hartwell and Mrs. Fitzwilliam-Cecil and their husbands brought silver and white bows to hang everywhere.

Cicely stood near Mama, and even with my poor vision, I saw how their faces radiated joy.

My sister was lovely in pink, and she was smiling at me and Wycliff. Then she turned to her tall husband, Bexeley.

Papa sat with baby Josiah. Chris was at his feet, playing with his toy frogs. Sweet Jonesy stood like Lawden, hovering in the rear, ready to help my father.

Wycliff, my Wycliff, trimmed his beard to just a shadow.

He looked young, so handsome in formal dress—black pantaloons, a high ivory collar and swirly ebony-and-purple waistcoat.

I wore the brightest, boldest color gown that my closet held, deep violet with short sleeves and a lilac ribbon about the bosom. There were daisies in the lace collar about my neck. I felt like a queen, Wycliff's queen.

He took my hand and kissed me when he I descended the stairs.

We said our vows again.

But this time it truly was forever.

When the ceremony ended, everyone went into the smallish back garden of Blaren House, but I watched them enjoy Mama's hearty fare of beefsteaks and fowl from the threshold.

Chris ran around the small enclosed yard with Cicely chasing him.

The girl had had an adventure. There was something she wasn't saying to her brother. Perhaps she'd tell me in time.

Nothing mattered. She'd returned to be with her family. This mesh of Wilkinsons and Croomes was strong.

Wycliff came to me and held my hand. He didn't ask me to go beyond the threshold. He looked down at me with all the love in his heart. "My old trunks have arrived from my father's country house. If my half of the registry is to be found, it would be in one of those."

"Have them set in the attic, my lord. I must finish getting Blaren House in order before I dig into the past. Besides, our special license is in one piece."

"As you command, Lady Wycliff."

He started to head in, but I held him in place.

Wycliff understood. He stepped closer and hung an arm about my waist.

My chest felt full, full of love for him and me.

My heart beat strong and wild.

Though I had been scared, I wasn't afraid.

Though my vision was bad, I wasn't without sight.

Though I once had been a victim, I wasn't one anymore.

I was a wife and a mother, a woman who was believed and loved beyond measure.

The proof was visible to all, my fingers entwined with Wycliff's.

Author's Notes

I hope you enjoyed Wycliff's and Ruth's story. This was intense for me to write, and I felt Ruth's hurt and fire throughout the crafting of it. It is my hope not to shock or glorify the bad but to show hope in dire situations. I've taken great care with the themes of passing and a woman's need to be heard and believed.

Every woman may not be afforded legal justice, but she needs to be empowered to tell her truth and to be valued for her journey. I hope Ruth's brings comfort and encouragement. *No matter the testing in your life, know that you are gold, too.* (Job 23:10)

· · ·

Mulattoes and Blackamoors During the Regency

Mulattoes and Blackamoors numbered between 10,000-20,000 in London and throughout England during the time of Jane Austen. Wealthy British with children born to native West Indies women brought them to London for schooling.

Jane Austen, in her novel *Sanditon,* writes of Miss Lambe, a mulatto, the wealthiest woman. Her wealth made her desirable to the *ton*.

Mulatto and Blackamoor children were often told to pass to achieve elevated positions within Society. Letters of Dorothea Thomas, one of the wealthiest mulatto women from the island of Demerara, guided me, offering in detail her desire for her children to pass to further their education and careers.

• • •

Regency Attitudes on Ravishment

Ravishment (rape) was a punishable crime if a person was convicted. However, convictions were rare. Evidence, such as respectable eyewitnesses, was needed as proof of the crime. Women, because of the shame they endured by the violation, the shame they believed was brought to their families, and the expense of paying for prosecution, often did not seek justice. The conviction of William Hodgson in 1811 was one of the first of its kind because the judge did not allow the defense to ask about the victim's previous acts of sexuality or her work history. Harriet Halliday's clear evidence came from multiple witnesses who'd heard her scream. A local surgeon who rescued Halliday financed the prosecution.

• • •

Debtors' Prison

Debtors' prison was a form of punishment for men and women who could not pay their debts. Owing as little as £100 could have one thrown into one of the London prisons: Fleet (closed 1842), Faringdon (closed 1846), King's Bench (closed 1880),

Whitecross Street (closed 1870), and Marshalsea (closed 1842). Insolvent debtors could be imprisoned indefinitely until all debts were paid.

Debtors' families were expected to pay to get them released, but Wycliff being the only solvent relation was not going to pay. Marshalsea was the worst of the debtors' prisons with the foulest conditions.

. . .

Fournier Street

Fournier Street is part of Spitalfields, London, developed by the French Huguenot immigrants dating from around 1720. The townhouses here were large but fell into disrepair and out of favor. I imagine by the 1800s, they could have been accessible to lease or purchase by parts of the Blackamoor and mulatto communities of London, which had grown in wealth but could not purchase in areas like Cheapside or Mayfair.

For more notes and historical information, visit VanessaRiley.com.

About the Author

Award-winning, Amazon-bestselling author Vanessa Riley writes historical romances set in England in the 1800s, giving voice to the voiceless ten thousand people of color who loved, laughed, and lived full lives, even as the sands of time buried their stories. Her novels focus on the ten-thousand-person Blackamoor and mulatto population inhabiting London during the time of Jane Austen. These people were free, and as some gained wealth, some intermarried, but all mingled in Society.

The author of *The Bittersweet Bride*, *The Bashful Bride*, *The Butterfly Bride*, *Madeline's Protector*, *Swept Away*, *Unmasked Heart*, *The Bargain*, and *Unveiling Love*, she has won the Beacon Award, the Colorado Award of Excellence, and placed in the International Digital Awards with her Regency romances. She lives in Atlanta with her career-military husband and precocious child. You can catch her writing from the comfort of her southern porch with a cup of Earl Grey tea. Stop by her website, www.vanessariley.com, and join her mailing list to keep in touch.

Don't miss the Advertisements for Love series…

THE BITTERSWEET BRIDE

THE BASHFUL BRIDE

THE BUTTERFLY BRIDE

Discover more Amara titles…

The Wicked Viscount
a *Campbells* novel by Heather McCollum

Cat Campbell knows all about Nathaniel Worthington, fifth Viscount of Lincolnshire. The determined Englishman is never far from Finlarig Castle, where his sisters train women to do more than read and write. And thanks to the fiery kiss they shared nearly a year ago he is never far from her thoughts. When an urgent letter from Queen Catherine calls Cat to London, Nathaniel can't resist volunteering to escort her. The tension between the two has simmered for months, but the long journey in close quarters creates a raging wildfire that could burn them both.

What a Scot Wants
a novel by Amalie Howard and Angie Morgan

Highlander Ronan Maclaren is in no hurry to marry. And he hasn't found the right woman. Lady Imogen has avoided wedlock for years. Determined to remain independent, she makes herself unattractive to all suitors. When a betrothal contract is signed—unbeknownst to Ronan or Imogen—it's loathing at first sight. They each vow to make the other cry off—by any means necessary. But what starts out as a battle of wits... quickly dissolves into a battle of wills.

THE MARQUESS AND THE MAIDEN
a *Lords of Vice* novel by Robyn DeHart

Harriet Wheatley is the mastermind behind the Ladies of Virtue's quest to rehabilitate the gentlemen of the *ton*. When it comes to selecting her own target, she chooses Oliver Weeks, Marquess of Davenport, the most extravagant wastrel in all of London. She says she'll help him find a bride, but he knows it's only because it gives her the excuse to chastise his indulgent ways. Oliver has good reason for his flagrant overspending, but Harriet will hear nothing of it. So he has no choice but to teach the lady a lesson, even if it means risking his heart to the hard-headed and fiery woman.

HOW TO TRAIN YOUR BARON
a *What Happens in the Ballroom* novel by Diana Lloyd

When Elsinore Cosgrove escapes a ballroom in search of adventure, she has no idea it will lead to a hasty marriage. Now she's engaged to an infuriating, handsome Scottish baron who doesn't even know her *name*! But Elsinore is determined to mold her baron into the husband she wants. Quin Graham is a man with many secrets. If another scandal can be avoided with a sham marriage, so be it. Only his fiancée isn't at all what he's expecting. For reasons he's unwilling to explain, the last thing Quin needs is to fall for his wife.

Printed in Great Britain
by Amazon